Praise for beloved romance author Betty Neels

"Neels is especially good at painting her scenes with choice words, and this adds to the charm of the story."
—*USATODAY.com's Happy Ever After* blog on *Tulips for Augusta*

"Betty Neels surpasses herself with an excellent storyline, a hearty conflict and pleasing characters."
—*RT Book Reviews* on *The Right Kind of Girl*

"Once again Betty Neels delights readers with a sweet tale in which love conquers all."
—*RT Book Reviews* on *Fate Takes a Hand*

"One of the first Harlequin authors I remember reading. I was completely enthralled by the exotic locales… Her books will always be some of my favorites to re-read."
—*Goodreads* on *A Valentine for Daisy*

"I just love Betty Neels!… If you like a good old-fashioned romance…you can't go wrong with this author."
—*Goodreads* on *Caroline's Waterloo*

Romance readers around the world were sad to note the passing of **Betty Neels** in June 2001. Her career spanned thirty years, and she continued to write into her ninetieth year. To her millions of fans, Betty epitomized the romance writer, and yet she began writing almost by accident. She had retired from nursing, but her inquiring mind still sought stimulation. Her new career was born when she heard a lady in her local library bemoaning the lack of good romance novels. Betty's first book, *Sister Peters in Amsterdam*, was published in 1969, and she eventually completed 134 books. Her novels offer a reassuring warmth that was very much a part of her own personality. She was a wonderful writer, and she is greatly missed. Her spirit and genuine talent live on in all her stories.

BETTY NEELS

Three for a Wedding & Judith

◆ **HARLEQUIN**® SPECIAL RELEASE

ISBN-13: 978-1-335-04512-6

Three for a Wedding & Judith

Copyright © 2019 by Harlequin Books S.A.

The publisher acknowledges the copyright holder of the individual works as follows:

Three for a Wedding
Copyright © 1973 by Betty Neels

Judith
Copyright © 1982 by Betty Neels

Recycling programs for this product may not exist in your area.

Printed in U.S.A.

www.Harlequin.com

CONTENTS

THREE FOR A WEDDING

Chapter 1

Phoebe Brook, Night Sister on the medical block of St Gideon's hospital in one of the less salubrious quarters of London, raised a nicely kept hand to her cap, twitched it to a correct uprightness, and very quietly opened the swing doors into the women's medical ward. Her stealthy approach to the night nurse's desk might at first glance have seemed to be a desire to catch that young lady doing something she ought not; it was in actual fact, due to a heartfelt desire not to waken any of the patients. She had herself, when a student nurse, done her nights on the ward, and again when she was a staff nurse; she knew only too well that Women's Medical, once roused during the night hours, could become a hive of activity—cups of Horlicks, bedpans, pillows rearranged, even a whispered chat about Johnny failing his eleven-plus, and what would

Sister do if she were his mum—so it wasn't surprising that the nurse sitting at the desk put down her knitting and got to her feet with equal stealth, at the same time casting a reproachful look at the clock. She was supposed to go to her dinner at midnight, and it was already half past, and that added on to the fact that she had been alone for the last hour, all of which thoughts Sister Brook read with ease and a good deal of sympathy, even though she had small chance of getting a meal herself. She whispered:

'Sorry, Nurse, I got held up on Men's Medical—a coronary. Come back in an hour.'

The nurse nodded, instantly sympathetic, thinking at the same time that nothing on earth would induce her to take a Night Sister's post once she had taken her finals, and why Sister Brook, with a face like hers, hadn't gone out and got herself a millionaire was beyond her understanding.

She crept to the door, leaving the subject of her thoughts to hang her cape on the chair and lay the pile of papers she had brought with her on the desk—the bed state, the off-duty rota, the bare bones of the report she would have to hand over to the Night Superintendent in the morning—she looked at them longingly, for it would be nice to get the tiresome things done before she left the ward, then she might have time to snatch a cup of tea and a sandwich. But first she must do a round. She went, soft-footed, past the first three beds, their occupants, recovering from their several ailments, snoring in the most satisfactory manner, but the occupant of the fourth bed was awake. Mrs Tripp was elderly and extremely tiresome at times, but the nursing staff bore with her because, having bullied the doctor into telling her just what was wrong with her, she was fighting the inevitable with so much gusto that Sir John South, the consultant in charge of her case, confided to his registrar that he wouldn't be at all surprised if she didn't outlive the lot of them out of sheer determination. Nonsense, of course; Mrs Tripp would never go home again to her ugly little red brick house in a back street near the hospital—she knew it and so did everyone else. The nursing staff indulged her every whim and took no notice when she showed no gratitude, which was why Sister Brook paused now and whispered: 'Hullo, Mrs Tripp—have you been awake long?'

'All night,' said Mrs Tripp mendaciously and in far too loud a voice so that Sister Brook was forced to shush her. 'And now I'm wide awake, ducky, I'll have a…'

Sister Brook was already taking off her cuffs, musing as she did so that on the few occasions when she had to relieve a nurse on a ward, she invariably found herself hard at work within a few minutes of taking over. She stole out to the sluice, collecting two more requests on the way, and as all three ladies fancied a hot milk drink to settle them again, it was the best part of twenty minutes before she was able to sit down at the desk.

She had just begun the bed state, which didn't tally as usual, when the doors were opened once more, this time by a young man in a white hospital coat, his stethoscope crammed in its pocket. He looked tired and rather untidy, but neither of these things could dim his slightly arrogant good looks. He took a seat on the edge of the desk, right on top of the bed state, and said:

'Hullo, Phoebe—good lord, haven't you got any nurses about tonight? I've been hunting you all over. That coronary, he's gone up to Intensive Care, so that lightens your burden a bit, doesn't it?'

She smiled at him; she was a beautiful girl, and when she smiled she was quite dazzling. Before he had met her, he had always scoffed at descriptions of girls with sapphires in their eyes and corn-coloured hair, but he had been forced to admit that he was wrong, because Phoebe had both, with the added bonus of a small straight nose and a mouth which curved sweetly, and although she wasn't above middle height, her figure was good if a little on the plump side. She was, he had to own, quite perfect; the one small fact that she was twenty-seven, three years older than himself, he did his best to ignore; he would have preferred it otherwise, but one couldn't have everything... As soon as he had taken a couple more exams he would ask her to marry him. He hadn't intended to marry before he was thirty at least, with a fellowship and well up the ladder of success, but if he waited until then she would be thirty herself—a little old, although she would make a splendid wife for an ambitious young doctor, and looking at her now, she didn't look a day over twenty.

'Any chance of a cup of tea?' he wanted to know.

She didn't bother to tell him that she had missed her own midnight meal; that she would get a sketchy tea into the bargain. 'Yes—but you must be very quiet, I've only just got them all quiet again.' She got up. 'Keep an eye on the ward,' she begged, and slipped away to the kitchen.

She came back presently with two mugs, a thick

slice of bread and butter atop each of them, and handed him his with a murmured: 'I haven't had my meal.'

'Poor old girl—I'll take you out for a good nosh on your nights off.'

'I can't, Jack, I'm going home. Sybil's got a week's holiday, and I haven't seen her for ages.'

Sybil was her younger sister, twenty-three and so like her that people who didn't know them well occasionally confused their identities, which was partly why Sybil, when she decided to be a nurse too, had gone to another training school—a London hospital and not very far away from St Gideon's—but what with studying for her finals and Phoebe being on night duty, they saw very little of each other. Soon it would be easier, Phoebe thought, taking a great bite out of her bread and butter, for Sybil had sat her hospital finals and the last of the State exams had been that morning. When she had qualified, as she would, for she was a clever girl, they would put their heads together and decide what they would do. The world, as the Principal Nursing Officer had told Phoebe when she had offered her the post of Night Sister, was her oyster. That had been three years ago and she still hadn't opened her particular oyster—there were jobs enough, but she had wanted to stay near Sybil until she was qualified. Now perhaps they would go abroad together.

Her train of thought was interrupted by her companion, who put down his mug, squeezed her hand and went out of the ward. Phoebe watched him go, the smile she had given him replaced by a tiny frown. He was going to ask her to marry him—she was aware of that and she didn't know what to do about it. She liked him very much, they got on well together—too well, she thought shrewdly—they had similar tastes and ideals, but surely, she asked herself for the hundredth time, there was more to it than that? And shouldn't she know if she loved him? Was this all that love was, a mild pleasure in someone's company, a sharing of tastes, a gentle acceptance of being a doctor's wife for the rest of her days—for Jack, she felt sure, would expect her to be just that and nothing more, she would never be allowed to steal the scene. Would her heart break if she never saw him again, or if, for that matter, he were to start taking some other girl out for a change? She was older than he; she had pointed this out to him on several occasions, and more than that, being a softhearted girl she had never allowed the thought that she found him very young upon occasion take root in her mind.

The hour ticked away. She solved the bed state, puzzled out the off duty for another two weeks, and was dealing with old Mrs Grey, who was a diabetic and showing all the signs and symptoms of a hyperglycaemic coma, when Nurse Small came back. They dealt with it together, then Phoebe, gathering up her papers and whispering instructions as to where she would be if she was wanted again, went silently from the ward, down the long corridor, chilly now in the small hours of an April morning, and into the office which was hers during the night when she had the time to sit in it. She had barely sat down when her bleep started up—Children's this time, and could she go at once because Baby Crocker had started a nasty laryngeal stridor. She had to get Jack up after a while; he came to the ward in slacks and a sweater over his pyjamas, and they worked on the child together, and when he finally went, half an hour later, she walked down the corridor with him, starting on her overdue rounds once more. At the end of the corridor, where he went through the door leading to the resident's quarters, he gave her a quick kiss, said 'See you' and disappeared, leaving her to make her way to Men's Medical on the ground floor, musing, as she went, on the fact that although his kiss had been pleasant, it hadn't thrilled her at all, and surely it should?

The early morning scurry gave her little time to think about herself. Fortified by a pot of strong tea, she did her morning rounds, giving a hand where it was wanted and then retiring to her office to write the report and presently to take it along to her daytime colleague before paying her final visit to the Night Super. A night like any other, she thought, yawning her way to breakfast, where Sadie Thorne, Night Sister on the Surgical side, was already waiting for her. Night Super was there too, a kindly, middle-aged woman, whose nights were filled with paper work and an occasional sortie into which ward was in difficulties. She was good at her job and well liked, for she never failed to find help for a ward when it was needed and had been known to roll up her own sleeves and make beds when there was no one else available. But normally, unless there was dire emergency in some part of the hospital, or a flu epidemic among the nurses, she did her work unseen, supported by Phoebe and Sadie and Joan Dawson, the Night Theatre Sister. She looked up from her post now as Phoebe sat down, wished her good morning just as though they hadn't seen each other less than an hour since, and went back to her letters, while Phoebe made inroads on her breakfast, thinking contentedly that in another twenty-four hours' time she would be going home. She caught Sadie's eye now and grinned at her.

'One more night,' she declared.

'Lucky you. Going home?'

Phoebe nodded. 'With Sybil—she's got a week off and goes back to night duty.'

Night Super looked up briefly. 'I hear she did very well in her hospitals.'

'Yes, Miss Dean. I don't know how well, but I hope she's in the running for one of the prizes.'

'Like her sister,' murmured the Night Super, and Phoebe, who had gained the gold medal of her year, went a becoming pink.

She packed her overnight bag before she went to bed, because on the following morning there would be barely time for her to tear into her clothes and catch the train. Then she washed her hair, and overcome by sleep, got into bed with it hanging like a damp golden curtain round her shoulders.

The night was fairly easy—the usual mild scares, the usual emergency admission, and hubbub on the children's ward, because one of its small inmates was discovered to be covered in spots. Phoebe, called on the telephone by an urgent voice, made her way there as quickly as she could, sighing. It was early in the night, she still had her rounds to make.

The child was a new patient, admitted just as the day staff were handing over thankfully to their night colleagues, and not particularly ill. She was popped into a cot while the more urgent cases were attended to, presently she would be bathed, her hair washed, and tucked up for the night.

Phoebe, looking quite breathtakingly beautiful in her dark blue uniform, trod quietly down the ward with a nod to the nurses to get on with what they were doing and not mind her. The child was sitting on a blanket in its cot, eating a biscuit. It looked pale and undernourished and was, like so many of the children who were admitted, too small, too thin and with lacklustre eyes— not through lack of money, Phoebe knew, but through the parents' neglect; good-natured and unthinking, but still neglect. She smiled at the elderly little face, said brightly, 'Hullo, chick, what's your name?' and at the same time peered with an expert eye at the spots.

There were a great many of them, and when she peeped beneath the little flannel nightshirt there were a great many more. She straightened up and spoke to the nurse who had joined her. 'Fleas,' she said softly, so that no one would hear save her companion. 'Infected too. A mild Savlon bath, Nurse, usual hair treatment and keep a sharp eye open. Give her a milk drink and let me know if she doesn't settle. She's a bronchitis, isn't she? She'll be seen in the morning, but if you're worried let me know.' She turned away and then came back to say in a low voice: 'And wear a gown.' Her lovely eyes twinkled at the nurse, who smiled back. 'And I might as well do a round now I'm here, mightn't I?'

The night went smoothly after that. She was accustomed to, and indeed expected, the diabetic comas, coronaries and relapses which occurred during the course of it. She dealt with them as they arose with a calm patience and a sense of humour which endeared her to the rest of the night staff. She even had time for a quick cup of tea before she went to give her report.

She arrived at Waterloo with a couple of minutes to spare. There was no sign of Sybil—she would be on the train, a long train, and only its front carriages went to Salisbury; she jumped into the nearest door and started walking along the corridor. Her sister was in the front coach, sitting in an empty compartment with her feet comfortably on the seat opposite her, reading a glossy magazine. She was very like Phoebe, but her good looks were a little more vivid, her eyes a shade paler and her voice, when she spoke, just a tone higher.

'Hullo, Phoebe darling, here by the skin of your teeth, I see. How are you—it's ages since we saw each other.' She was putting Phoebe's bag on the rack as she spoke, now she pushed her gently into a window seat. 'Here, put your feet up and have a nap. We can talk later. I'll wake you in good time.'

And Phoebe, now that she had caught her train and greeted her sister, did just as Sybil suggested; in two minutes she was asleep. She wakened, much refreshed, at the touch on her arm and sat up, did her face, tidied her hair and drank the coffee Sybil had got for her, then said contritely: 'What a wretch I am—I quite forgot. How about the hospitals?'

Sybil grinned engagingly. 'The Gold Medal, ducky! I couldn't let you be the only one in the family with one, could I? I don't get the State results for six weeks, but I don't care whether I pass or not.' She looked secretive and mischievous at the same time, but when Phoebe said: 'Do tell—something exciting?' all she would say was: 'I'll tell you later, when there's no hurry. Look!'

The carriage door was flung open and a horde of people surged in, making conversation impossible. The train shuddered, gave a sigh as though it disliked the idea of leaving the station, and continued on its way. At Shaftesbury, they got out; they lived in a small village close to Sturminster Newton, but Aunt Martha, who had moved in to look after them when their mother had died, and stayed on when their father died a few years later, liked to come and fetch them in the second-hand Austin which they had all three bought between them. She was on the platform now, in her tweed skirt and her twin-set, a felt hat of impeccable origin wedged on her almost black hair, only lightly streaked with grey despite her fifty-odd years. It framed her austere good looks and gave colour to her pale face, which broke into a smile as she saw them. She greeted them both with equal affection and walked them briskly to where the car was parked, telling Sybil to sit in front with her so that Phoebe, if she felt so inclined, could continue her nap undisturbed in the back.

Which she did without loss of time, waking after a blissful fifteen minutes to find that they were already going through East Orchard; at the next village, named, inevitably, West Orchard, they would turn off on to a side road which would bring them to Magdalen Provost, where they lived—a very small village indeed, which Phoebe had declared on several occasions to have more letters to its name than it had houses. It was a charming place, only a mile or so from the main road, and yet it had remained peacefully behind the times;

even motor cars and the twice daily bus had failed to bring it up to date, and by some miracle it had remained undiscovered by weekend househunters looking for a holiday cottage, probably because it was so well hidden, awkward to get at, and in winter, impossible to get out of or into by car or bus because it lay snug between two hills rising steeply on either side, carrying a road whose gradient was more than enough for a would-be commuter.

Aunt Martha rattled down the hill and stopped in the centre of the village where the church, surrounded by a sprinkling of houses, the pub and the post office and village stores which were actually housed in old Mrs Deed's front room, stood. Phoebe's home stood a little apart from the rest, surrounded by a stone wall which enclosed a fair-sized, rather unkempt garden. The house itself wasn't large, but roomy enough, and she loved it dearly; she and Sybil had spent a happy childhood here with their parents, their father, a scientist of some repute, pursuing his engrossing occupation while their mother gardened and kept house and rode round the countryside on the rather fiery horse her husband had given her. Both girls rode too, but neither of them were with their mother when she was thrown and killed while they were still at school, and their father, considerably older than his wife, had died a few years later.

Aunt Martha drew up with a flourish before the door and they all went inside. It was a little shabby but not poorly so; the furniture was old and well cared for and even if the curtains and carpets were rather faded, there was some nice Georgian silver on the sideboard in the dining room. Phoebe, now wide awake, helped bring in the cases and then went upstairs to change into slacks and shirt before joining Aunt Martha in the kitchen for coffee, regaling that lady with the latest hospital news as they drank it, but when Sybil joined them, the talk, naturally enough, centred around her and her success. It wasn't for a few minutes that Phoebe came to the conclusion that it was she and their aunt who were excited about the results and not Sybil herself. She wondered uneasily why this was and whether it had something to do with whatever it was Sybil was going to tell her. Prompted by this thought, she asked:

'Shall we go for a walk after lunch, Syb?' and the uneasiness grew at the almost guilty look her sister gave her as she agreed.

They went to their favourite haunt—a copse well away from the road, with a clearing near its edge where a fallen tree caught the spring sun. They squatted comfortably on it and Phoebe said: 'Now, Sybil, let's have it. Is it something to do with St Elmer's or about your exams?'

Her sister didn't look at her. 'No—no, of course not—at least… Phoebe, I'm giving in my notice at the end of the week.'

Phoebe felt the uneasiness she had been trying to ignore stir, but all she said was: 'Why, love?'

'I'm going to get married.'

The uneasiness exploded like a bomb inside her. 'Yes, dear? Who to?'

'Nick Trent, he's the Medical Registrar. He's landed a marvellous job at that new hospital in Southampton. We're going to marry in two months' time—he gets a flat with the job and there's no reason for us to wait.'

'No, of course not, darling. What a wonderful surprise—I'm still getting over it.' Phoebe's voice was warm but bewildered. They had discussed the future quite often during the past six months or so and Sybil had never so much as hinted... They both went out a good deal, she had even mentioned Jack in a vague way, but she had always taken it for granted that the two of them would share a year together, perhaps in some post abroad. Sybil had known that, just as she had known that Phoebe had stayed at St Gideon's, waiting for her to finish her training. She asked in a voice which betrayed none of these thoughts: 'What's he like, your Nick?'

'I knew you'd be on my side, darling Phoebe.' Sybil told her at some length about Nick and added: 'He wanted to meet you and Aunt Martha. I thought we might fix a weekend—your next nights off, perhaps.'

'Yes, of course.'

'He's got a car—we could all come down together.'

Phoebe smiled. 'Nice—I shall be able to snore on the back seat,' and then, quietly: 'There's something else, isn't there, Syb?'

'Oh, Phoebe darling, yes, and I don't know what to do unless you'll help me. You see, a few weeks ago I was chosen to take a job in Holland...'

Phoebe had her head bowed over the tree-trunk, watching a spider at work. She said placidly: 'Yes, dear—go on.'

'Well, it's some scheme or other cooked up between St Elmer's and some hospital or other in Delft—there's a professor type who specialises in fibrocystitis— he's over here doing some research with old Profes-

sor Forbes, and the scheme is for a nurse from Delft
to come over here and me to go there for two months.
But first I'm supposed to go to the hospital where he's
working—you know that children's hospital where
they've got a special wing—the idea being that I shall
be so used to his ways that it won't matter where I
work. I thought it would be fun and I said I would, and
then Nick…we want to get married.'

'Of course, but you could get married afterwards,
dear. It would only be a few months—not long.'

Her young sister gave her a smouldering glance.
'Yes, it is,' she declared. 'I won't!'

'Well, tell your people at hospital that it's all off.'

'I can't—all the papers and things are signed and
the hospital in Delft has made all the arrangements.
Phoebe, will you go instead of me?'

'Will I *what*?' uttered Phoebe in a shocked voice.

'Go instead of me.'

'How can I possibly? It couldn't be done—it's
absurd—they'd find out.'

'You know you're dying to leave and get off night
duty and try something else for a change. Well, here's
your chance.'

'But I'm not you.'

'Near enough, no one need know. No one's ever seen
us at the children's hospital, nor in Delft, have they?
Even if they had, we're so alike.'

'I thought you said the Dutch doctor had seen you?'

'Pooh, him—he looked half asleep; I don't think
he even looked at me, and we were only together for a
couple of minutes, and I hardly spoke.' She added persuasively: 'Do, darling Phoebe! It sounds mad, doesn't

it? but no one's being harmed and it's not really so silly. And don't worry about the man, I doubt if he even noticed that I was a girl.' She sounded scornful.

'He sounds ghastly—I suppose he speaks English?'

'So well that you know he's not,' explained her sister, 'and he's got those vague good manners…'

'I'll not do it,' said Phoebe, and was horrified when Sybil burst into tears.

'Oh, dear,' she wailed through her sobs, 'now I don't know what I'll do at least, I do. I shall run away and hide until Nick goes to Southampton and we'll get married in one of those pokey register offices and n-no one will come to the w-wedding!'

Phoebe sat watching her sister's lovely face. Even while she cried she was beautiful and very appealing and she loved her dearly besides, she had promised her father that she would look after her. She said now: 'Don't cry, love—I'll do it. I think it's crazy and I'm not sure that if I'm caught I shan't get sent to prison, but it's only for a couple of months and if you don't go someone else will, so it might as well be me. Only promise me that you'll have a proper wedding, the sort Mother and Father would have liked you to have. And are you sure about Nick? I mean really sure—it's for the rest of your life.'

Sybil smiled at her through her tears. 'Oh, Phoebe, I'm sure—I can't explain, but when you love someone like I love Nick, you'll know. You're a darling! We'll fix it all up while we're here, shall we? Just you and me—Nick doesn't know, I was so excited and happy I forgot to tell him and when I thought about it later I couldn't. And Aunt Martha…'

'We won't tell anyone at all,' said Phoebe. Now that she was resigned to the madcap scheme she found herself positively enjoying the prospect of a change of scene. 'I'm quite mad to do it, of course. Now begin at the beginning and tell me exactly what it's all about. Are you sure this doctor didn't get a good look at you?'

'Him? Lord, no, Phoebe. I told you, he's the sleepy kind, eyes half shut—I should think that half the time he forgets where he is. You'll be able to twist him round your little finger.'

'What's his name?'

Sybil looked vague. 'I can't remember. I'll find out for you, and the name of the hospital and where he lives and anything else I'm supposed to know.'

'Which reminds me—I don't know an awful lot about fibrocystic disease—hasn't it got another name?'

'Mucoviscidosis, and you can forget it. The treatment hasn't changed much in the last year or so and you know quite enough about it—I remember telling me about several cases you had on the Children's Unit…'

'Three years ago,' murmured Phoebe.

'Yes, well… I'll bring you up to date, and what does it matter anyway, for the whole idea is that I—you should be seconded to this hospital so that you can learn all about this man's new ideas.'

'And afterwards? Am I supposed to go back to St Elmer's and spread the good news around?—then we are in the apple cart.'

'No, nothing like that. I'm free to do what I like when I come back from Holland. As far as St Elmer's goes, they think I'm giving in my notice so's I can get a job somewhere else when I get back to England.'

'My passport,' hazarded Phoebe suddenly. 'Supposing this man sees it? Or don't we travel together when we go?'

'Oh, yes, that's all been arranged, but remember the British and the non-British split up when they get to the Customs. Anyway, he's hardly likely to breathe over your shoulder, he's not that sort.'

'He sounds a dead bore,' Phoebe said slowly. 'I'm not sure...'

'You promised—besides, there are bound to be other people around—housemen and so forth.' She paused. 'I say, there's nothing serious between you and Jack, is there?'

Phoebe shook her head and said thoughtfully: 'And if there was, this is just what's needed to speed things up—I can't quite make up my mind...'

'Then don't,' said Sybil swiftly. 'Phoebe love, if it were the real thing, you wouldn't even stop to think—you'd know.' She grinned and got up. 'You see, this is just what you need, away from it all you'll have time to decide.'

Phoebe got to her feet. 'Perhaps you're right, love. Now tell me, you and your Nick, when do you want to get married?'

They spent the rest of their walk happily discussing wedding plans and clothes. Phoebe had a little money saved, but Sybil none at all.

'Well, that doesn't matter,' declared Phoebe. 'There's enough to buy you some decent clothes and pay for the wedding,' and when Sybil protested: 'I'm not likely to marry first, am I?' she wanted to know soberly, and then broke off to exclaim: 'Look—three magpies, they must have been eavesdropping. What is it now? One for anger, two for mirth, three for a wedding...'

They giggled happily and walked home arm-in-arm.

By the time Phoebe returned to St Gideon's from her nights off, she and Sybil had their plans laid, the first step of which was for her to resign immediately. It would work out very well, they had discovered; she would be due nights off before she left, time to go home, explain to Aunt Martha that she had taken a job with this Dutch doctor and would be going to Holland, collect the uniform Sybil's hospital were allowing her to keep until she returned to England, and make her way to the children's hospital, where, according to Sybil, she was expected. The one important point to remember was that for the time being, she was Sybil and not Phoebe.

She went to the office to resign on the morning after her return, to the utter amazement of the Chief Nursing Officer. She was a nice woman, interested in her staff and anxious to know what Phoebe intended to do— something, of course, which Phoebe was unable to tell her, for most of the big hospitals knew each other's business and probably the exchange scheme at St Elmer's was already common property. Miss Bates would hear sooner or later via the hospital grapevine, that Sybil had left to get married, probably she already knew that she had been seconded for the scheme, she wasn't above putting two and two together and making five.

'I haven't quite decided,' Phoebe told her, playing safe. 'I think I shall have a month or two's holiday at home.'

If Miss Bates considered this a curious statement from a member of her staff whom she knew for a fact depended upon her job for her bread and butter, she forbore from saying so. She thought Phoebe a nice girl, clever and remarkably beautiful. She hoped that she would marry, because she deserved something better than living out her life between hospital walls. Miss Bates was aware, just as the rest of the hospital, that the Medical Registrar fancied Night Sister Brook, but she was an astute woman, she thought that the affair was lukewarm and Sister Brook, despite her calm disposition, was not a lukewarm person. She sighed to herself, assured Phoebe that she would always be glad to see her back on the staff should she change her mind, and hoped that she would enjoy her holiday.

Phoebe didn't see Jack during her first night's duty; he had gone on a few days' leave and wouldn't be back for two more days—something for which she was thankful, for it seemed a good idea to let the hospital know that she was leaving first. The news would filter through to him when he got back and he would have time to get used to the idea before they encountered each other, as they were bound to do.

They met over the bed of a young girl three nights later—an overdose and ill; there was no time to say anything to each other, for the patient took all their attention, and when he left, almost an hour later, he gave her some instructions to pass on to the nurses, and walked away. Ten minutes later Phoebe left the ward herself. She had done her first round, thank heaven, so she could spare ten minutes for a cup of coffee. She opened the door of her office at the same time as the junior nurse on the ward arrived with the tray and she took it from her with a word of thanks, noting with a sinking heart that there were two cups on it—presumably Jack intended to have a cup with her. She pushed the door open and found him inside, standing by the desk, glowering.

He said at once; 'I'm told you're leaving. Rather sudden, isn't it?'

Phoebe sat down, poured coffee for them both and opened the biscuit tin before she answered him. 'Yes, Jack. I—I made up my mind while I was on nights off. Sybil's leaving too.'

He looked slightly mollified. 'Oh—you're off together somewhere, I suppose. For how long?'

'No—I've decided to have a little holiday, staying with relatives.' The idea had just that minute popped into her head and she hated lying to him, but after all, it wasn't his business. 'I feel unsettled.'

He stirred his coffee endlessly, looking at it intently. 'Yes, well, I suppose if you feel you must—I shall miss you, Phoebe, but I daresay you'll be ready to come back by the time I decide to marry. I shall ask you then.' He glanced up briefly. 'Everything has to be just as I want it first.'

That jarred. Was she not important enough to him—more important—than the set pattern he had laid out for them both, and without first finding out if she wanted it that way? She could see it all—the engagement when he was suitably qualified and had his feet on the first rung of the consultant's ladder, the wedding, the suitable home, suitably furnished, all the

things that any girl would want, so why did she feel
so rebellious?

It was all too tepid, she decided. It would be nice
to be swept off her feet, to be so madly loved that the
more mundane things of life didn't matter, to rush off
to the nearest church without thought of the right sort
of wedding. She passed him the sugar and sipped her
coffee. If Nick could marry Sybil on his registrar's
pay and find it wonderful, why couldn't Jack feel the
same way? She began to understand a little of what
Sybil had meant about loving someone, and she knew
at that moment that she would never love Jack—like
him, yes, even be fond of him, but that wasn't at all
the same thing.

She said quietly: 'Jack, I can't stop you doing that,
but I don't think it's going to be any use.' She stared at
him over the rim of her mug, her lovely eyes troubled.

'I'll be the best judge of that,' he told her a shade
pompously, 'and until then I prefer not to discuss it.'

He was as good as his word; they discussed the patient they had just left until, with a huffy good night,
he went away.

She should mind, Phoebe told herself when she
was alone. She had closed the door on a settled future,
and just for a moment she was a little scared; she was
twenty-seven, not very young any more, and although
she could have married half a dozen times in the last
few years, that was of no consolation to her now. She
sighed and pulled the bed state towards her. It seemed
likely that she was going to be an old maid.

Chapter 2

A month later, on her way to Magdalen Provost, St Gideon's behind her, the doubtful future before her, Phoebe reflected that everything had gone very well—there had been no snags, no one had wanted to know anything, no awkward questions had been asked. Sybil had already left and was at home making plans for her wedding to Nick, whom Phoebe considered to be all that could be desired as a brother-in-law. Sybil was going to be happy; now that she had met him Phoebe had to admit that in Sybil's place, she would have done exactly as she had done. Even Aunt Martha had accepted everything calmly—she had liked Nick too, had been generous in her offers of help to the bride, and was entering into the pleasurable excitement of a wedding in the family with a great deal more zest than Phoebe had supposed she would. And as for her own

future, when she had told her aunt what she intended
doing, without bringing Sybil's part into it at all, the
older lady had wholly endorsed her plans.

'It's high time you had a change,' she stated approv-
ingly, 'it sounds a most interesting scheme and you'll
enjoy a change of scene. What did Jack have to say?'

Phoebe had told her rather worriedly and added: 'I
feel guilty, Aunt, but honestly, I didn't let him think
that I… I don't think I encouraged him at all; we just
sort of liked being together.'

'Well, my dear,' her aunt had said briskly, 'there's a
good deal more to being in love than liking each other's company, and I'm sure you know that. Have you
been able to convince him, or does he still think you
might change your mind?'

'I told him I wouldn't do that.'

She remembered the conversation now, sitting in
the train, and wondered what would happen if she suddenly discovered that she had made a mistake and was
in love with Jack after all, and then dismissed the idea
because they had known each other for a year or more
and surely by now she would have some other feeling
for him other than one of friendship. She decided not
to think about it any more—not, in fact, to think of
anything very deeply, but to take each day as it came,
at least until she returned to England.

It was Nick and Sybil who met her at Shaftesbury,
for Nick was spending a day or so at Magdalen Provost
before taking Sybil to meet his parents. They discussed
the wedding as he drove his car, a Saab, rather too fast
but very skilfully, in the direction of the village, but
presently he interrupted to ask: 'Phoebe, what's the

name of this man you're going to work for? I've an idea I know something about him.'

'Oh, good,' said Phoebe lightly, 'because I don't—his name's van Someren.'

Nick tore past an articulated wagon at a speed which made her wince. 'I knew his name rang a bell,' her future relative told her cheerfully. 'Old van Someren—met him at one of those get-togethers…'

'Then you can tell me something about him,' said Phoebe firmly.

'Don't know anything—surely your people have given you all the gen?'

'Oh, I don't mean that. How old is he, and is he nice, and is he married?'

They were going down the hill into the village at a speed which could if necessary, take them through it and up the other side. 'Good lord, I don't know—thirty, forty, I suppose—and what do you mean by nice? To look at, his morals, his work?'

'Just…oh, never mind, you tiresome thing. You're not much help. There's ten years between thirty and forty, but perhaps you haven't noticed,'

Nick laughed and brought the car to a sudden halt outside the house. 'Poor Phoebe—I'd have taken a photo of him if I'd known. Tell you one thing, though, I'm sure someone told me that he's got a boy, so he must be married.' He turned in his seat to look at her. 'When do you go, tomorrow?'

'On an afternoon train. I said I'd arrive at the hospital in the evening.'

'We'll take you in to Shaftesbury—we'd go the whole way, but we've still got to see the parson about this and that.' They were all out of the car by now, loitering towards the door. 'You'll be at the wedding, won't you?'

It was Sybil who answered for her. 'Of course she will. I know I'm not having any bridesmaids, but Phoebe's going to be there,' she turned to her sister, 'and you'd better be in something eye-catching, darling.'

'It's your day, Syb. I thought of wearing dove grey—that's if Doctor van Someren allows me to come.'

'You'll have days off—all you have to do is save them up and tell him you have to attend a wedding. Anyway, didn't I read somewhere that the Dutch set great store on family gatherings? Of course you'll be able to come.'

She sounded so worried that Phoebe said reassuringly: 'Don't you worry, I wouldn't miss it for the world.'

They went indoors then, to Aunt Martha, busy in a kitchen which smelled deliciously of something roasting in the oven, and no one mentioned the Dutch doctor again.

Twenty-four hours never went so quickly. Phoebe, joining the queue at Waterloo station for a taxi, felt as though she hadn't been home at all. She would miss going down to Magdalen Provost and she doubted very much if she would get another opportunity of a weekend before she left England. She had quite forgotten to ask Sybil the arrangements for her off-duty, but surely she would manage a day or two before she left the children's hospital. She got out of the taxi, paid the man and rang the visitors bell of the Nurses' Home. If anyone wanted to see her so late in the day, the warden would doubtless give her the message. But there was only a request that she should present herself at the Principal Officer's office at nine o'clock the next morning, and when she stated simply that she was Nurse Brook, the warden hadn't wanted to know any more than that, but took her up to a rather pleasant little room, offered her a warm drink and wished her good night. So far, so good, Phoebe told her reflection in the mirror, and went to bed and slept soundly.

The Principal Nursing Officer was brisk and busy. As Phoebe went into the room she said: 'Ah, yes, Nurse Brook. Splendid. Will you go along to the Children's Unit and they'll put you in the picture—I'm sure it has already been made clear to you that this scheme is housed here temporarily, and it's run quite separately from the hospital itself. Anything you want to know, there will be someone you can ask there.'

She smiled quite kindly in dismissal and pulled a pile of papers towards her, and Phoebe, murmuring suitably, got herself out of the office, sighing with relief that it had all been so easy, aware at the same time that she should be feeling guilty and failing to do so because she remembered Sybil's happy face.

The Children's Unit was across the yard. Supposedly there was another way to it under cover, but she couldn't see it and it was a lovely sunny day and she welcomed the chance to be out of doors, if only for a minute or two. The door stood open on to the usual tiled, austere entrance, a staircase ascending from it on one side, a row of doors lining its other wall. On the one marked 'Doctor van Someren' she knocked, for it seemed good sense to get to the heart of the mat-

ter at once. No one answered, so she opened the door
and went inside. It was a small room and rather dreary,
with a large desk with its swivel chair, shelves full of
books and papers and two more chairs, hard and uncomfortable, ranged against one wall. Phoebe, who
had seen many such offices, wasn't unduly depressed
at this unwelcoming scene, however. Hospitals, she had
learned over the years, were not run for the comfort of
their staff. There was an inner door, too. She crossed
the room and tapped on it and a woman's voice said
'Come in.' It was an exact copy of the room she had just
left, only smaller, and had the additions of a typewriter
and a woman using it. She wasn't young any more and
rather plain, but she looked nice and when Phoebe said:
'I'm Nurse Brook and I'm not at all sure where I'm supposed to be,' she smiled in a friendly fashion.

'Here,' she answered cheerfully, 'if you like to go
back to the other room, I'll see if Doctor van Someren
is available. I expect you want to start work at once.'

She went back with Phoebe to the doctor's room,
waved a hand at one of the chairs and disappeared.
Phoebe sat for perhaps ten seconds, but it was far too
splendid a day not to go to the window and look out. It
was too high for her to see much; obviously whoever
had built the place had considered it unnecessary for
the occupants to refresh themselves with a glimpse of
the outside world. But by standing on tiptoe she was
able to see quite a pretty garden, so unexpected that
she opened the bottom sash in order to examine it with
greater ease.

She didn't hear the door open. When she turned
round at last, she had no idea how long the man had

been standing there. She frowned a little and went a faint pink because it was hardly the way she would want an interview to begin, with her leaning out of the window, showing a great deal more leg than she considered dignified for a Ward Sister but then she wasn't a Ward Sister she really would have to remember... And he wasn't in the least like the picture Sybil had painted of him. He was a big, broad-shouldered man and very tall, something her sister had forgotten to mention, and she, for that matter, had forgotten to ask. His hair was the colour of straw which she thought could be streaked with grey; it was impossible to tell until she got really close to him. And she was deeply astonished to find him good-looking in a beaky-nosed fashion, with a firm mouth which looked anything but dreamy, and there was nothing vague about the piercing blue gaze bent upon her at the moment.

'Miss Brook,' his voice was deep, 'Miss Sybil Brook?'

She advanced from the window. 'Yes, I'm Miss Brook,' she informed him pleasantly, pleased that she didn't have to tell a downright fib so soon in the conversation. There would be time enough for that; she only hoped that she wouldn't get confused... 'You're Doctor van Someren, I expect. How do you do?' She held out her small capable hand and had it gripped in a gentle vice. For one startled moment she wondered if he could be the same man whom Sybil had seen, and then knew that it was; his face had become placid, his eyelids drooping over eyes which seemed half asleep, his whole manner vague.

'Er—yes, how do you do?' He smiled at her. 'I think it would be best if I were to take you to the ward—you can talk to Sister Jones, and later there will be some notes and so on which I should like you to study.' He went over to the desk and picked up a small notebook and put it in his pocket, saying as he did so: 'I'm sometimes a little absentminded... I shall be doing a ward round in an hour, I should like you to be there, please.'

He sat down at the desk and began to open a pile of letters stacked tidily before him, quite absorbed in the task, so that after a few minutes Phoebe ventured to ask: 'Shall I go to the ward now, sir?'

He looked up and studied her carefully, just as though he had never set eyes on her before. 'Ah—Miss Brook, Miss Sybil Brook,' he reminded himself. 'I really do apologise. We'll go at once.'

Following him out of the room and up the stairs Phoebe could understand why Sybil had described him as vague—all to the good; she saw little reason for him to discover that she wasn't Sybil; she doubted if he had really looked at her, not after that first disconcerting stare.

Sister Jones was expecting her, and to Phoebe's relief turned out to be a girl of about her own age, with a cheerful grin and soft Welsh voice which had a tendency to stammer. She greeted the doctor with a friendly respect and Phoebe was a little surprised to hear him address her as Lottie. She hoped he wasn't in the habit of addressing his nursing staff by their christian names, for not only would she find it difficult to answer to Sybil, she discovered at that moment that she had no wish to tell him a fib. He was too nice—an opinion presently endorsed when he did his ward round; he was kind too and his little patients adored him.

There were ten children in the ward, most of them up and about, full of life and filled, too, with a capacity for enjoyment which fibrocystics seemed to possess as a kind of bonus over and above a child's normal capacity to enjoy itself. They were bright too, with an intelligence beyond their years, as though they were being allowed to crowd as much as possible into a life which would possibly be shortened. The small boy Doctor van Someren was examining at that moment was thin and pale, but he laughed a good deal at the doctor's little jokes, discussed the cricket scores and wanted to know who Phoebe was. The doctor told him briefly and went on: 'And now, how about that tipping and tapping, Peter?'

A question which called forth a good deal of sheepish glances and mutterings on Peter's part. He didn't like hanging over his bed, being thumped by a nurse at six o'clock in the morning, he said so now with considerable vigour, and everyone laughed, but instead of leaving it at that, Phoebe was glad to see the doctor sit down on the side of the bed once more and patiently explain just why it was good for Peter to hang head downwards the minute he woke up each morning. Having made his point Doctor van Someren strolled towards the next bed, murmuring as he went:

'What a sad thing it is that this illness is so difficult to tackle.' He looked at Phoebe as he spoke and seemed to expect an answer, so she said: 'Yes, it is, but I'm afraid I don't know enough about it to pass any opinion.'

'A refreshing observation,' he said surprisingly. 'I find, during the course of my work, that there are a distressing number of people who have a great deal too much opinion and very little sense. I fancy that you have plenty of sense, Nurse Brook.' He nodded at her in a kindly way, sat down on the next bed and became instantly absorbed in its occupant. Phoebe, standing close behind him, found herself wondering how old he was. She had been right, there was quite a lot of grey mixed in with the straw-coloured hair. She guessed forty, but a moment later when he turned his head to speak to Sister Jones, and she could study his face, she decided that he was a good deal younger than that.

She had been a little disturbed to find that she was to go to Delft in ten days' time, for she had imagined that it would be longer than that, as it wasn't very long in which to get to know the doctor and his methods, and now she very much doubted if she would be able to get home again before she went, for Sister Jones had explained at some length that it was hoped that she would take her days off singly because the time was too short for her to miss even two days together; there was so much for her to learn. She had agreed because there was nothing else she could do, and in any case she would be going home for the wedding—she dragged her thoughts away from that interesting topic and applied herself to what the doctor was saying. He had some interesting theories and a compelling way of talking about them which held one's attention; by the end of the day she found herself deeply interested, both in the man and his ideas, and was a little surprised to find that the ward seemed very empty without him, rather like a room without its furniture, and yet he was a quiet man, there was nothing flamboyant about him—indeed, when he wasn't actually engaged in his work, he was positively retiring.

In her room, after a friendly cup of tea with the other staff nurses, Phoebe undressed slowly, thinking about him, and when she was finally ready for bed she didn't go to sleep immediately, but sat up against the pillows, her golden hair cascading round her shoulders, her lovely face, devoid of the small amount of make-up she used, creased in a thoughtful frown. It wasn't turning out a bit as she had expected—she had expected to feel regrets, even guilt, but she didn't feel either, only a faint excitement and a certainty that she was going to enjoy every minute of Sybil's scheme.

Her feelings were strengthened during the next ten days; it seemed strange to be a staff nurse again, but Sister Jones was a dear and the other nurses were pleasant to work with. There was plenty of work on the ward, for Doctor van Someren was a man who expected his orders to be carried out to the letter, and it was sometimes hard and exacting. He had given Phoebe a number of books to read, some of them written by himself, and she couldn't help but be impressed by the string of letters after his name. He was undoubtedly clever, which might account for his moments of vagueness and for his habit of staring at her, which at first she had found a little trying until she decided that he was probably deep in thought and wasn't even aware of her.

She was to spend five nights on duty, because there was a good deal to do at night and he wanted her to be conversant with that as well, and to her surprise

Doctor van Someren had himself suggested that she should have two days off afterwards so that she could go home before returning to London to meet him for the journey. He had offered no information about the trip. She supposed they would travel by train and cross from Harwich, and although she would have liked to know very much, she hadn't liked to ask him because he had appeared so preoccupied when he had told her; he had moved away even as he was speaking, his registrar and housemen circling around him like satellites round their sun.

Phoebe hadn't been best pleased about going on nights, although she didn't care to admit to herself that the main reason for this was because she wouldn't see Doctor van Someren—and she liked seeing him, even though he was a married man and never seemed to see her at all. Apparently he had no eyes for women, however lovely—unlike his Registrar and George the houseman, both of whom found her company very much to their liking. She sighed and wondered, not for the first time, what his wife was like, then pushed the ward doors open, ready to take the day report from Sister Jones on her first night on. Life seemed strangely-dissatisfying.

The children took a lot of settling; she and Rawlings, the student nurse on with her, were still hard at it when Doctor van Someren came quietly into the ward. Phoebe laid the little girl carefully on to the pillows stacked behind her, conscious that her heart was beating a good deal faster than it should do.

'Any trouble?' he asked quietly, and she shook her

head and smiled at him because it was so nice to see him unexpectedly.

'No, thank you, sir. They're very good, but we've still got two more to see to.' She was apologetic because it was almost nine o'clock, but he made no sign of having heard her, only stood looking down on the child, comfortable and sleepy now, and presently he went away.

He came each night, conveying without words that his visits were simply because he liked the children and not because he had doubts as to his nurses' ability. And in the small hours of the night—her third night on, when Andrew, the ten-year-old in the corner bed, died, he was there again, with his registrar and Night Sister. But Phoebe noticed none of them, doing what she had to do with a heavy heart, and later, when there was no more to be done, going into the kitchen on some excuse or other because if she didn't shed some of the tears her throat would burst. She neither saw nor heard Doctor van Someren; it was his apologetic little cough which caused her to spin round to face him. She said wildly: 'You see, I'll be no good for your scheme—I can't bear it when this happens—he was so little.'

She wiped the back of her hand across her eyes to blot the tears, and despite them, her lovely face was quite undimmed.

The doctor said nothing for a moment, but crossed to the table, ladled tea into the pot, lifted the boiling water from the gas ring and made the tea. 'On the contrary, you will be very good, because you feel deeply about it.' He looked at her and in a voice suddenly harsh, asked: 'And how do you suppose I feel?'

She sniffled, 'Awful. I'm sorry.' She began to gather mugs on to a tray. 'I mean I'm sorry because I'm being a fool, and I'm sorry for you too, because this happens despite all you do.'

He took the tray from her. 'You are kind, Miss Brook, but the boot is on the other foot—soon we shall win our battle, you know.' He kicked open the door. 'And now dry your eyes and have a cup of your English tea—I should warn you that in Holland our tea is not as you make it, but our coffee is genuine coffee, which is more than I can say for the abomination I am offered here.' He smiled at her and she found herself smiling back at him; he really was nice—absentminded, perhaps, a little pedantic and, she fancied, old-fashioned in his views, but definitely nice.

But the sadder side of her work was seldom in the ascendant—there was a good deal of fun with the children too, and the nurses, under Sister Jones' rules, were a happy crowd. And over and above that, Doctor van Someren's enthusiasm spilled itself over the lot of them, so that very soon Phoebe found herself looking forward to going to Holland, where, so Sister Jones told her, his work was having a steady success—no spectacular results, just a slow, sure improvement in his little patients. She found herself wishing that she, in her small way, would be able to help him to attain his goal.

There was a party on the ward—a farewell party for Doctor van Someren—on her last night on duty. She got up an hour or so earlier than usual and went along to help with the peeling of oranges, the dishing out of ice-cream and the wiping of sticky hands. It was noisy and cheerful and it would have been even greater fun if various important people to do with the hospital hadn't been there too, to take up the guest of honour's time and attention. All the same, he found the time to wish each child goodbye and then crossed the ward to thank Phoebe for her help and to hope that the children would settle.

'They will give you a little trouble, perhaps,' he hazarded, 'and strictly speaking it is not good for them, but they must have their fun, don't you agree, Miss Brook?'

She nodded understandingly, aware as he was that during the early part of the night there would be a great deal of chatter and requests for drinks of water, and little tempers as well as tears, but they would sleep eventually and they had loved every minute of it. She looked around her, reflecting how strange it was that a few paper hats and balloons could create a party for a child.

He turned away. 'I shall see you here at seven o'clock in the evening, on the day after tomorrow,' he reminded her, and before she could ask how they were to go to Holland, he had gone, large and quiet, and very quickly.

She spent two busy days at home; there was a great deal she would have liked to discuss with Sybil, but somehow Aunt Martha always seemed to be with them, and beyond a few safe commonplaces about her work, she could say very little. Only when they had gone to bed, Sybil had come along to her room and sat on the bed and demanded to know if everything was all right.

Phoebe nodded. 'I think so—you were quite right, Doctor van Someren is absentminded, but only some-

times. He's a splendid doctor though. I expected him
to be older—he seems older than he really is, I think,
but only when he's worried. I like the work…'

Sybil interrupted her happily. 'There, didn't I say
that it was a good thing when you agreed to go instead
of me? And I bet you're far better at it than I should
ever be. How are you going to Holland?'

'I don't know—I've been told to go to the hospital
tomorrow evening at seven o'clock, that's all. What
clothes shall I take?'

It was well after midnight before this knotty problem
was solved to their entire satisfaction. Phoebe, remembering the doctor's gentle remark that he hoped that
she wouldn't have too much luggage, decided to take
one case, a small overnight bag and her handbag—a
stout leather one capable of holding everything she was
likely to need en route. The overnight bag she stuffed
with night things, and as many undies as she could
cram into it, and the case she packed under Sybil's
critical eye with uncrushable cotton dresses, sandals,
two colourful swimsuits, a sleeveless jersey dress in
a pleasing shade of blue, a very simple dress in straw-
berry pink silk and, as a concession to a kindly fate,
a pastel patterned party dress which could be rolled
into a ball if necessary and still look perfection itself.

This task done, she felt free to wish her sister good
night and go to bed herself. Not that she slept for several hours; her mind was too full of her job, and woven
in and out of her more prosaic thoughts was the ever-
recurring reflection that she was pleased that she would
be seeing a good deal more of Doctor van Someren
during the next few weeks.

The morning was taken up with last-minute chores and a discussion about the wedding, coupled with a strong reminder from Aunt Martha to make very sure that she returned home for it. She was thinking how best to settle this matter when her taxi drew up outside the hospital entrance and she stepped out. There was no one about. Through the glass doors she could see the head porter's back as he trod ponderously in the direction of the covered way at the back of the hall—perhaps she should go after him and find out... She actually had her hand on the door when Doctor van Someren said from behind her:

'Good evening, Miss Brook. You are rested, I hope? If you would come with me?'

It annoyed her that she felt flustered. She wished him a good evening in her turn in a rather cool voice and followed him to the hospital car park.

They stopped beside a claret-coloured Jaguar XJ 12 and she tried to conceal her surprise, but her tongue was too quick for her. 'My goodness,' she exclaimed, 'is this yours?'

He looked faintly surprised. 'Yes—you didn't tell me that you disliked travelling by car. It is the simplest way...'

'Oh, I don't—I love it. Only she's so splendid and she took my breath I didn't expect... And I'm sure it's the simplest way, only I don't know which way that is.'

He put down her case and bag the better to give her his full attention. 'Did I not tell you how we should be travelling?'

She shook her head.

'Dear me—you must forgive me. By car, of course.

We shall load it on to the Harwich boat and drive to
Delft from the Hoek when we land in the morning.
You are a good sailor?'

'Yes—though I've only crossed to Calais twice. We
nearly always went by plane, and I loathed it.'

'We?' he prompted her gently.

'My mother and father and s...' she stopped just in
time, 'me,' she added lamely, and felt her cheeks warm,
but he didn't seem to notice and she drew a relieved
breath. How fortunate it was that he wasn't an obser-
vant man, only with his patients. He picked up her case
and put it in the boot, already packed with books and
cases and boxes—no wonder he had hoped that she
wouldn't bring too much luggage with her.

It was extraordinary how many times during their
journey to Harwich that she had to stop to think before she replied to his casual questions. She hadn't
realised before how often one mentioned one's family during the course of even the most ordinary conversation; she seemed to be continually fobbing him
off with questions of her own about his work, their
journey, details of the hospital where she would be
working—anything, in fact, but her own home life. It
was a relief when he slid the car to a halt in the Customs shed, a relief tempered with regret, though, because he was a most agreeable companion and she had
found herself wishing that she could have told him all
about Sybil and Nick, and her own part in the deception they were playing upon him. When she had con-
sented to take Sybil's place she hadn't thought much
about the other people involved; now she found that it
mattered quite a lot to her.

They had a meal on board and Phoebe talked feverishly about a dozen subjects, taking care not to mention her home or her family, and the doctor made polite
comments upon her sometimes rather wild statements,
and didn't appear to be aware of the fact that she repeated herself upon occasion, but as soon as they had
had their coffee, he observed pleasantly: 'I expect you
would like to go to your cabin, Miss Brook,' and stood
up as he said it, so that there was nothing else for her
to do. Besides, he had a briefcase with him; he was already opening it when she looked back on her way out
of the restaurant.

Possibly, she thought crossly, he had been dying
for her to go for hours past. She undressed slowly and
hung her oatmeal-coloured dress and jacket carefully
away so that they would be creaseless and fresh in the
morning. 'Not that it would matter,' she told herself,
getting crosser. 'If I wore hot pants and a see-through
blouse he wouldn't notice!'

She lay down on her bunk, determined not to go
to sleep so that she would be able to tell him that she
had spent an uncomfortable night—no, not uncomfortable, she corrected herself—it was a delightful
cabin, far more luxurious than she had expected, certainly first class and on the promenade deck. It surprised her that the hospital authorities were willing
to spend so much money on a nurse. She would have
been just as comfortable sharing a cabin with another
girl, although she doubted if she would have had the
cheerful services of the stewardess who promised tea
at six o'clock and begged her to ring her bell should
she require anything further. With difficulty Phoebe

brought her sleepy mind back to Doctor van Someren;
it would be nice if she were to see a great deal of him in
hospital—presumably she would be working on one
of his wards, but perhaps he would leave the actual
instruction to one of the more junior members of his
team. She frowned at the idea and went to sleep.

She slept all night and, much refreshed by her tea,
dressed, did her face and hair with care and went along
to join the doctor for breakfast, looking as though she
had slept the clock round and spent several leisurely
hours over her toilette. His eyes, very bright beneath
the arched colourless brows, swept over her and then
blinked lazily. He wished her a good morning, hoped
she had slept well and begged her to sit down to breakfast, something she was only too glad to do. Coffee and
toast would be delightful, but the ship seemed to be a
hive of activity and they had already docked; perhaps
he hadn't noticed. She mentioned it diffidently, to be
instantly reassured by his easy: 'I have a theory that
it is quicker to be last off the ship.' A remark which,
it turned out, was perfectly true, for by the time they
had finished, the last of the passengers were leaving
the ship and the Jaguar was swinging in mid-air, on
its way to dry land.

There was no delay in the Customs shed but a good
deal of talk in Dutch, which sounded like so much
nonsense in her ears, so that she didn't pay attention
but stood looking about her. She was recalled from
this absorbing pastime by Doctor van Someren's voice
and she turned at once to answer him and in the same
split second was aware that he had called her Phoebe
and she had responded. She felt the colour leave her

face and then flood back, washing her from neck to forehead with a delicate pink. She would have liked to have said something—anything, but her brain, like her tongue, was frozen. It was the doctor who spoke.

'Very interesting. I have been wanting to do that since we met.' His voice was thoughtful, but she could have sworn that he was secretly amused. He turned away to speak to a porter and she followed him to where the car stood waiting in the cobbled yard beyond the station. It was only after she had got into it and he had taken the seat beside her that she asked in a small voice: 'How did you know my name?' and then: 'Are you going to send me back?'

He didn't look at her. 'Your sister mentioned you, and no why should I? You are an admirable nurse, obviously far more experienced than you wished me to believe. I don't know the reason for the deception, but I imagine it was a sufficiently good one.'

'When did you find out?'

He sounded surprised. 'When we met, naturally.'

She faltered a little. 'But Sybil and I are so alike, people can never tell us apart, only when we're together, or—or they look at us properly.'

'And your sister decided that I hadn't studied her for a sufficient length of time to make your substitution risky. You are not in the least like her.'

They were already out of the town, tearing along the highway, but she really hadn't noticed that. She opened her mouth to refute this opinion, but he went on smoothly: 'No, don't argue, Miss Phoebe Brook. I'm not prepared to enlarge upon that at the moment, you will have to take my word for it.'

Phoebe stared out at the flat countryside without seeing any of it.

'I'm very sorry,' she told him stiffly, and thought how inadequate it was to say that. She was sorry and ashamed and furious with herself for playing a trick on him. 'It was a rotten thing to do. At the time, when Sybil—when I arranged to do it, it seemed OK I hadn't met you then,' she added naively, and failed to see his slow smile and the gleam in his eyes.

He gave the Jag her head. 'Do you care to tell me about it? But only if you wish…'

She felt quite sick. 'It's the least I can do.' She stared miserably at a group of black and white cows bunched round a man in the middle of a field as green and flat as a billiard table. 'I'm the one to blame,' she began, faintly aggressive in case he should argue the point, and when he didn't: 'You see, Sybil wants to get married—quite soon…' She was reminded of something. 'I should like to save up my days off and go home for the wedding, though I don't suppose you have anything to do with the nurses' off duty.'

They were in the heavy early morning traffic now and approaching a town. 'Is that Delft?' she wanted to know.

'Yes, it is. I have nothing to do with the nurses' off duty,' he was laughing silently again and she frowned, 'but I imagine I might be able to bring my influence to bear.'

To her surprise he edged the car into the slow lane and then into the lay-by ahead of them, switched off the engine and turned to look at her intently. 'Perhaps if I were to ask you a few questions it would be easier for both of us.' He didn't wait for her to answer him. 'Supposing you tell me where you were working to begin with. You are older than your sister,' he shot her a hooded glance, 'and I think that you have held a more responsible post…'

She choked on pricked vanity—did she look such an old hag, then? Very much on her dignity, she said stiffly: 'I was Night Sister at St Gideon's—the medical block. I'm twenty-seven, since you make such a point of it…' She paused because he had made a sound suspiciously like a chuckle. 'I will explain exactly what happened…'

She did so, concisely and with a brevity which did justice to her years of giving accurate reports without loss of time. When she had finished she stole a look at him, but he was staring ahead, his profile, with its forceful nose and solid chin, looked stern. Perhaps he was going to send her back after all. She conceded that she deserved it. But all he said in a mild voice was: 'Good, that's cleared the air, then,' started the car again and allowed it to purr back into the stream of fast-moving traffic. 'The hospital is in the heart of the city. It's not new—there is a very splendid one, you must go over it while you are here—but the one in which you will work is very old indeed and although we have everything we require, it is dark and awkward. But the children are happy and that is the main thing. You will be on a sixteen-bedded ward of fibrocystics, but all the research work is done at the new hospital—St Jacobus.'

She found her voice. 'What's the hospital called—the one where I shall be?'

'St Bonifacius. You'll find that most of the staff

speak English, and as for the children, I have discovered long ago that they will respond to any language provided it is spoken in the right tone of voice. Besides, there are a number of words which are so similar in both languages that I have no doubt you will get by.'

She hoped it would be as easy as it sounded. They were going slowly now through the compact little city, its winding streets lined with old houses, some of them so narrow that there was only room for a front door and a window, some so broad and solid that they should have been surrounded by parklands of their own. The streets were intersected by canals linked by narrow white bridges. She had the impression that she would be lost immediately when she set foot outside the hospital door.

The silence had lasted a long time. Phoebe asked in a polite voice:

'Is the hospital a medical school? Were you a student here?'

'No—at Leyden, a few miles away, but my home is in Delft—has been for very many years. I took over the practice from my father. Now I devote almost all my time to fibrocystics.'

He turned the car into a narrow cobbled street where there were no pavements and barely room for the car. 'A short cut,' he explained, 'but when you go walking, I advise you to keep to the main streets until you know your way around.'

Nothing was further from her intention than to go roaming off with nothing but a foreign tongue in her head and a poor sense of direction, but there seemed no point in mentioning it to him. She said like an obedient child: 'No, I won't, sir,' and remained silent while he eased the Jaguar through high gates leading to a paved courtyard where several cars were parked and an ambulance was discharging its patient through a heavy door strong enough to have withstood a siege.

Her companion came to a gentle and accurate halt between the ambulance and a large Citroën, and got out. He had her door open before she could reach for it, saying easily: 'Your luggage will be seen to,' and led her briskly through the hospital entrance, where he spoke to the porter before turning to her and saying: 'I hope you will be happy while you are here with us.'

His tone was formal enough, but his smile was so kind that she found herself saying: 'I'm so sorry—the only way I can make you believe that is by working hard, and I promise you I will.'

He took her hand. 'I know you will, and if it is any comfort to you, Phoebe, I am not sorry and I can see no reason for you to be, either.'

She stared up into his face. Such a kind man, she thought confusedly, and perhaps people took advantage of his kindness—she hoped his wife looked after him. He didn't let go of her hand, and when she heard footsteps advancing towards them from the back of the square hall, she was glad of its firm reassuring grip. The footsteps belonged to a rather dumpy little woman in a dark grey uniform with a prim white collar.

The doctor held out his other hand, saying pleasantly in English.

'Directrice, how nice to see you again—here is our English nurse, Miss Brook. I leave her in your capable hands.' He smiled a little vaguely at them, murmured goodbye and went out of the door again, and Phoebe, still feeling his hand on hers, smiled uncertainly at the little lady before her.

Chapter 3

The rest of the day was exciting, tiring and somewhat frustrating; everything was just a little different. She had accompanied the Directrice to her office, drunk coffee and listened to the details of the life she would lead while she was in the hospital, given in a fluent though sometimes quaint English; her salary, her off duty—which the Ward Sister would discuss with her— the length of hours she would work, the advisability of getting herself a dictionary at the first convenient moment… Full of undigested information, she was handed over to the Nurses' Home warden, a white-overalled, elderly woman who walked her through a great many corridors and small passages, an odd staircase or two and through a door in a wall which opened into a modern hallway. That at least, thought Phoebe, was exactly the same as the hall in the Nurses' Home at St Gideon's.

Apparently hospital decorators the world over had the
same unimaginative ideas about dark varnished wood
and pale green walls. But her room, when she reached
it, was pleasant, with a gay bedspread and curtains and
a cheerful rug. Left to herself, she unpacked, changed
into her uniform and mindful of her instructions, found
her way back to the hospital and into Zaal Drie.

Zaal Drie was really three smallish wards, con-
nected to each other by means of archways driven into
the ancient walls of the hospital, the only evidence of
the building's great age, for the beds, furniture and
furnishings were modern and brightly coloured. There
were flowers too and some budgerigars adding their
tiny voices to the cheerful din, for it was already mid-
morning and those children who were up were having lessons at a centre table in the first ward. They
paused in whatever it was they were reciting under the
direction of their young teacher and turned to stare at
Phoebe, who stared back, wondering what she should
do next—a problem solved for her; a small door beside
her opened and the Ward Sister came out.

Doctor van Someren had told her that everyone
would speak English, but she hadn't expected quite
the degree of fluency she was encountering. Zuster
Witsma addressed her in welcoming tones: 'Ah, our
English *Zuster*! We are all glad that you are here, and
we wish you a happy stay. Come, we will have coffee
and then I will show you round. Doctor van Someren
tells me that you are—are *bijdehand*,' she tried again,
'*handig*', and Phoebe said quickly, 'Oh, I think you
must mean handy.'

Zuster Witsma smiled. She had a round, friendly

face and Phoebe guessed her to be about her own age. 'That you can do all things,' she explained happily as she offered Phoebe a mug of coffee across her desk. 'Now I will tell you all—day duty first, and then night duty every four weeks—one week. We work from seven in the morning until three o'clock on one day and on the other day from two o'clock until ten in the evening. The night nurses do duty from nine in the evening until half past seven in the morning. You find the hours strange, yes? But they work very well, you will see,' she nodded her head encouragingly. 'There is always much to do for the children; they depend on us to keep them happy too, and Doctor van Someren will not have that they are treated as sick. Even when they are very ill he does not like that they should know, only then we put them into the last ward—but never until there is nothing more to do, you understand.' Her blue eyes surveyed Phoebe. 'You are very pretty.'

'Thank you,' Phoebe smiled at the other girl, liking her, finding herself looking forward to the weeks of work ahead. 'Where would you like me to start?'

The rest of the morning passed on wings; at midday she went down to the basement, through a labyrinth of passages and odd stairs, with some of the other nurses, and ate her dinner with them in a long dark room with a row of small windows at one end, and listened to the chatter going on around her, wishing she could understand at least some of it, although everyone was very kind. Some of the nurses spoke good English, all had a smattering, and they took care to include her in their conversations when they could. She went back to the ward presently, to do the medicine round with Zuster

Witsma and be shown the mechanism of admitting a
patient, which was exactly the same as in an English
hospital, and then to be initiated into the mysteries of
writing the report, finally to be told kindly that she
might go off duty. 'There will be things you wish to
do,' said Zuster Witsma in a friendly voice, 'and perhaps a little walk, no? Tomorrow at two o'clock you
will come again.'

Phoebe went off duty, conscious of a keen disappointment because she had seen no sign of Doctor van
Someren; there had been a young doctor, who, before
doing his round, had been introduced as Doctor Pontier, the Registrar. There were two other house doctors, he told her gravely, whom she would meet in due
course, and he and they would be glad to help her in
any way they could. He had smiled at her, openly admiring of her good looks, and had said with a flattering
eagerness that he hoped that he would see more of her
soon. She dismissed him from her thoughts as soon as
she reached her room; it was already past three o'clock;
she had intended to write a letter home, now she had
the far better idea of telephoning. She changed out of
her uniform and hurried out of the hospital and was
on the point of opening its front door when a pretty
blonde girl, also on her way out, stopped. 'The English
nurse?' she asked cheerfully. 'You would like that I go
with you and show the way?'

Her name was Petra—Petra Smit. She was, she told
Phoebe rapidly in fluent, ungrammatical English, a
trained nurse working on the surgical ward. 'We all
hear about you,' she informed Phoebe gaily, 'we hope
that you will like us.'

Phoebe assured her that she would and went on to explain that she wanted to telephone. Half way through her explanation she put her hand to her mouth. 'Money!' she exclaimed. 'What a twit I am—I haven't any Dutch money. I never thought to change it before I left and then I didn't think about it...'

'Easy,' said her companion. 'The banks are closed, you understand, but there is a shop—they will take your English money.'

Phoebe got her money, and armed with it and still in the faithful Petra's company, she went to the Post Office where her companion, with pressing business of her own, left her, giving her instructions as to how to get back to the hospital before she did so, instructions which Phoebe immediately forgot in the excitement of speaking to Aunt Martha. But it was a small town, she told herself unworriedly as she strolled along in the warm sunshine, and when she saw a tea-room on the corner of two narrow streets, she went in, took a table in one of its windows, watching the people and bicycles crossing and re-crossing the complexity of canals and bridges while she drank her tea and then applied herself to the street map Petra had thoughtfully bought for her. Refreshed, she set off on a voyage of discovery—the Prinsenhof, she soon discovered, was a useful centre from which to find her way. She had peered into no more than half the shops around it when the city clocks reminded her that it was five o'clock and supper at the hospital was only an hour away. She loitered along, peering down the narrow streets and along the canals, each lined with houses, some built into the water itself. They were narrow and old, their

gabled roofs rising sharply, each with its tiny window
at the very top—she longed to explore one of them.

She played tennis after supper. Somewhere at the
back of the hospital a hard court had been made in the
square of ground around which the greater part of the
building was built. Someone lent her a racquet, the evening was bright and still warm, and they were evenly
matched. The four of them stood, getting their breaths
before they played a final set, and Phoebe peered up at
the windows around them, wondering which belonged
to Zaal Drie. She had given up hope of finding it when
a movement at one of the windows caught her eyes.
Doctor van Someren was standing there, watching
them. She looked away quickly and when they began
the next set, her play, to her vexation, was indifferent,
but at the end of the game, when she stole another look,
he had gone. It was no comfort to her that she played
quite brilliantly during the next game.

She admitted to disappointment when she didn't see
him during the following day either, for he had done a
round, Zuster Witsma told her, that morning, and although the Registrar came during the afternoon, bringing one of the housemen with him, and both young
gentlemen made themselves very pleasant to her, she
went down to her supper quite put out. That this was a
foolish attitude on her part she was the first to admit.
There was no reason why the doctor should make a point
of seeing her; she had come to learn his methods—
just as easily learned from Zuster Witsma and the medical staff—and he was, moreover, an important man
in his own world—he had, to coin a phrase, other fish
to fry.

She went back after supper and set about settling the children for the night. They were tired now, but some of them, despite this, were determined to stay awake as long as possible and tired though they were, couldn't settle. She thumped up pillows, rearranged bedclothes, squeezed oranges and as a last resort with one small boy, Dirk, who had worked himself into quite a state, lifted him out of his bed and sat him on her knee, and because she could think of nothing else to do, began to talk to him in English. That he couldn't understand a word didn't seem to matter; her voice was soothing and gentle, presently he chuckled, tucked his lint-fair head into her shoulder, and forgetting to wail, stared up at her with huge blue eyes. She tucked him a little closer; he was one of the ones who wasn't going to get well, so the Registrar had told her; he had been in hospital for almost a year, on and off, and Doctor van Someren had done wonders but it was a losing battle, although, he had hastened to add, several of the children went home much improved. One day they would cure all the children, he had said determinedly, and Phoebe, recalling Doctor van Someren's absorbed face when he was on his ward round, found herself agreeing, for she imagined him to be a quietly persistent man who didn't take no for an answer.

She winked a gorgeous long-lashed eye at Dirk and looked up to see the man she was thinking about standing beside them. She hadn't heard him come into the ward, probably because she hadn't expected him. She was still deciding what to say when he said 'Hullo, Phoebe,' and added something in his own language, and when she asked in a whisper what it was he had said he shook his head and smiled. 'All alone?' he asked.

'Yes, but only for a short time—Zuster Witsma's gone to supper and the night staff will be here shortly.'

He sat down on the edge of Dirk's bed. 'You think you will like it here?'

She nodded. 'Yes, very much—I felt a bit lost yesterday and today…' There was faint reproach in her voice although she was unaware of it, but he must have heard it, for he said at once: 'I do a good deal of work at Leyden—the Medical School is there, as you know, but I contrive to come here at least once a day, twice if necessary—sometimes more often. I must confess I like working here, although a more out-of-date place would be hard to find.'

'But it's beautifully equipped.'

He nodded a little absently, staring ahead of him and frowning. Presently he asked: 'You're comfortable in the Nurses' Home? I'm afraid you can't qualify for the Sisters' quarters.'

She flushed. 'That's quite all right. I knew I'd be working as a staff nurse. I don't deserve it anyway. My room is very comfortable and everyone is kind to me.'

He got to his feet, took the sleepy Dirk from her and laid him in his bed. His good night was abrupt and she stared after his broad back in surprise, wondering if she had said something to annoy him.

She was on duty at seven o'clock the next morning, and when Zuster Witsma came on at eight, she did the medicine round with her again, studied a case history with an eye to Doctor van Someren's methods, and then listened to the Ward Sister's painstaking explanations of the smallest detail to do with running the ward before going down to the dining room for her coffee. She was half way through the ward door when Zuster Witsma called her back.

'A little talk about your journey home for your sister's wedding,' she said kindly. 'Doctor van Someren has asked me to arrange that you have a sufficiency of free days—for such an important family event it is necessary that you have the maximum.' She led the way into her office, waved Phoebe to a chair and sat down at her desk. 'It is easy,' she went on, refreshing her memory from the odds and ends of forms, notebooks and folders before her. 'You will do the night duty—seven nights, and then you will have five nights in which to make your trip.'

She beamed across at Phoebe and Phoebe beamed back because she had been worrying as to how she should ask for the time off. Apparently Doctor van Someren wasn't so forgetful after all! 'That will be lovely,' she agreed. 'It's in a few weeks' time...'

'Just right; by then you will know the ward routine and you will have learned a little of Dutch, yes?'

Phoebe echoed the yes and hoped she would. It sounded an awful language, but perhaps by then she would have picked up an odd word or two—surely if everyone around her could speak at least a little English, she could do the same with Dutch. She remembered the dictionary in her uniform pocket and promised herself a little steady work with it each day.

She went to coffee then, wondering why Doctor van Someren hadn't seen fit to tell her that she would be able to go home—perhaps he considered it hardly

his business; she was not a very important cog in the
wheel of his scheme, and there was no reason for him
to put himself out.

She was free that afternoon, she went out into the
early June sun, determined to see as much as possible.
Her guide book told her to go to the Markt, with its
fourteenth-century New Church and its Town Hall, but
although she started off in that direction, she quickly
became diverted by a great many other things equally
interesting. Shops for a start, little streets with old
crooked houses which looked half forgotten, canals
lined with trees and behind them, gracious houses with
narrow flat fronts and heaven knows what treasures
behind their solid doors. She strolled along, looking almost fragile in her sugar pink cotton dress, oblivious
of the admiring glances cast at her as she walked. She
had stopped to listen to a street organ when a bunch
of small boys came tearing along, on their way home
from school, she supposed, stepping prudently against
the wall to give them room on the narrow pavement.
But they stopped, pushing and shoving and fighting as
small boys will, hemming her in entirely, so that she
came in for more than her share of kicks and blows.
Phoebe tucked her handbag under her arm for greater
safety and, conscious of sore shins and trodden-on feet,
gave vent to her feelings.

'Oh, move on, do!' she apostrophised them loudly.
'Quarrelsome brats, why don't you kick each other's
shins instead of mine?'

Naturally no one took any notice, at least, none of
them except one small boy of about eight who had
just fetched her an unintentional blow with his school

satchel—its buckle had etched a weal above her wrist. They stared at each other for a long moment and she realised with a shock that he had understood what she had said. He put his tongue out at her, shouted something at his companions, and they all made off together—a good thing, she thought crossly, for her own tongue had itched to retort in kind.

The weal was still very much in evidence when she went on duty the following morning. Zuster Witsma, clucking sympathetically, cleaned it up, but nothing could disguise the nasty bruise around it. She had told everyone that she had bumped into something and left it at that, and when Doctor van Someren, with his registrar and a posse of students entered the ward, she took care to keep her hands behind her back, just in case he might, for no reason at all, want to know how she had come by it, and she had no intention of telling him— she might never see the little boy again, but that was no reason to tell on him.

It was unfortunate that during the round she should be asked to get one of the children ready for examination, for the bruise, although she did her best to conceal it, was very much in evidence; but it wasn't until the round was over, the students bunched at the ward doors, the Registrar standing a little apart and Doctor van Someren standing in the middle of the ward having a few words with Sister, that Phoebe, hanging up charts and tidying beds and buttoning pyjama jackets, saw Zuster Witsma look across the ward in her direction and then walk towards her. She was smiling largely, as though she were the bearer of splendid news. 'Doctor van Someren wishes to speak to you—in the office. Go quickly, Nurse Brook, he is not to be kept waiting.'

Phoebe saw no reason to go quickly; it smacked of being back at school, summoned to the Head because she had been naughty, and as usual, caught at it. The thought put her in mind of the little boy; for some reason his angry face with its thatch of fair hair had stayed in her memory. She pushed open the door, feeling faintly angry herself.

Doctor van Someren was standing by the narrow window, his hands in his pockets, his attention apparently taken by the blank brick wall which was all the view there was, but he turned round as she went in and said without preamble: 'Ah, yes—you have a bruise on your arm. Why?'

And there's a silly question, thought Phoebe pertly. 'Something hit it,' she told him, the pertness in her voice.

He glanced at his watch and frowned. 'Do not waste my time, I beg of you, Miss Phoebe Brook; I am responsible for your person while you are here. I wish to be certain that the—er—something was reasonably clean.' He raised his eyes to her face. 'I am indifferent as to its cause; I have no wish to pry...'

Phoebe could feel her annoyance melting away. She caught at the shreds of it and said a little tartly: 'I'm quite capable of looking after myself, and you have no reason to worry, it was only a school s—the buckle of a bag—someone quite accidentally swung it against my arm. It's as clean as a whistle.'

He was staring at her with a kind of alert thoughtfulness which she found strangely disconcerting; just as though he had remembered something and was putting two and two together.

'Yes? Very well—but please take care; you are not to be replaced.'

She inched to the door. Of course she could be replaced, she knew of half a dozen nurses of her acquaintance who would jump at the chance of her job. She opened her mouth to say something, she wasn't sure what, but it didn't matter because he spoke first.

'Tomorrow you have a day off. I think that you should see the hospital at Leyden—the research department where I do most of my work. I have arranged with Zuster Witsma to bring you there in the afternoon.' He looked suddenly vague. 'Thank you, Nurse.'

She got herself out of the room, hardly knowing whether to be annoyed or laugh. Here he was, arranging her day off for her without a by-your-leave. Presumably she was supposed to be so mad keen on her work that she would welcome its spilling over into her free time. Upon thinking about it she was quite glad to have her day arranged for her; she had hardly had the time to plan any expeditions herself, and to tell the truth she was diffident about going around on her own until she had found out about buses and trains and the easiest way to get about.

Later that day, when she was off duty, she found her way to the VVV, a kind of tourist information centre which supplied leaflets and maps in a great many languages. Here she collected as many as possible about Leyden and went to bed early to study them in peace and quiet, and in the morning, making a leisurely dressing gown breakfast while her uniformed companions gobbled and swallowed against time, she contrived to add to what she had learned by asking a few questions about the hospital at Leyden. She sauntered back upstairs, sorting the facts from some of the more frivolous answers she had been given—the Medical School sounded interesting. She began to look forward to her afternoon, but in the meantime the morning stretched before her in delightful idleness. She dressed and wandered out into the bright morning, intent on finding somewhere pleasant for coffee while she decided how to spend the time before midday dinner.

She went, finally, to Reyndorp's Prinsenhof, where the prices rather took her breath away although the surroundings were worth every penny, and then went to look at Tetar van Elven Museum and afterwards, by way of light relief, window-shopped, a delightful pastime which culminated in the buying of a French silk scarf which she didn't really need but which was just too lovely to pass by.

They were to leave for Leyden directly after lunch, so that Phoebe spent half an hour before then changing her dress and attending to her face and hair. She chose the sugar pink cotton again because it seemed rather an occasion and crowned her bright head with a natural straw hat with a small upturned brim, and got out her nicest sandals and handbag. She was glad that she had done this when she saw Zuster Witsma waiting for her in her Daf. She had dressed for the occasion too—in blue and white; they made rather a nice pair, Phoebe considered as she got in beside her. The drive to Leyden was a short one of only a few miles, but Mies Witsma was a shocking driver so that the

distance seemed twice that length. Phoebe made conversation in a voice which only shook slightly when
they missed a bus by a hairsbreadth and again when
Mies, seeing a dog about to cross the road, shot across
into the path of the oncoming cars, causing a good
deal of horn-blowing and squeaking of brakes. It was
a decided relief when they entered Leyden and slowed
down, and when they entered the Rapenburg, its quiet
waters reflecting the great buildings on either side of
it, Phoebe forgot about her companion's erratic driving
and looked about her, trying to identify them as Zuster
Witsma pointed them out—something which did her
driving no good at all.

They had gone through the gates of the Medical
School and were about to enter its door when Phoebe
said: 'You do look nice I hope you don't mind me saying so...'

The girl beside her turned a beaming face tinged
with shy embarrassment. 'You think? I wish to be chic
today—I hope he will think as you do...'

Phoebe was conscious of a peculiar sensation of
doubt deep inside her—who was this *he*? Surely not
Doctor van Someren? At the idea the feeling, now
tinged with a slight peevishness, became stronger. She
longed to ask and would have done so, but they were in
the entrance hall by now and a young man was bearing down upon them.

He shook hands with Zuster Witsma, uttered a few
words, presumably of welcome, and then turned to
Phoebe, shook her hand too and said: 'Van Loon,' and
she, wishing to be civil, told him: 'I'm Phoebe Brook,'

then remembered that she was Sybil, or didn't that matter any more?

They walked the length of the hall while the young man, in quite beautiful English, explained that he was one of Doctor van Someren's team and had been sent to meet them, and when they fetched up before a massive mahogany door he tapped importantly and threw it open.

Phoebe hadn't known what she expected to see, certainly not Doctor van Someren stretched out in a comfortable chair by one of the long windows, fast asleep. The young man, not in the least put out, stepped forward, tapped him briskly on the shoulder and murmured deferentially, whereupon he opened his eyes and got to his feet and advanced to greet them, his manner imperturbable. Mies Witsma shook hands first, talking animatedly and at some length, and Phoebe watched narrowly, deciding that the doctor was certainly not the *he* her companion had mentioned. This filled her with such pleasure that it showed on her face and her host remarked: 'You look as though you had just made a delightful discovery—nothing to do with me taking a nap, I hope?'

She laughed. 'No, of course not—it seems an awful shame to wake you up, though. I'm sorry.'

He shrugged his great shoulders. 'It is a pleasure to wake and find you—and Zuster Witsma—here.' He looked over his shoulder to where the young man was deep in conversation with her. 'Van Loon,' he said easily, 'be a good chap and let Doctor Lagemaat know that we are ready, will you? And I will see you tomorrow as usual.'

Van Loon said, 'Yes, sir,' and then, 'Good-day, ladies, it has been a pleasure,' and cast a lingering look
at Phoebe as he hurried away, to be replaced in no time
at all by a very tall, very thin man, soberly dressed
in dark grey and a rather dreary tie, but his face was
pleasant and good-looking too in a blunt-featured way,
and Phoebe, watching with quickening interest, saw at
once that this was the one who was to be dazzled by
the blue and white outfit. Zuster Witsma went pink as
he came in and greeted him with the extreme casualness of manner which, to Phoebe at least, was all the
proof she needed. He had smiled nicely at her as he
crossed the room; he smiled nicely at her too as Doctor van Someren introduced him, but he went back immediately to the Dutch girl.

'We will go,' said Doctor van Someren, breaking
into her speculations. 'Arie, you will accompany Mies,
will you not? and I will go with Miss Brook so that she
misses nothing of what is to be seen.'

There was a great deal to be seen, and all very interesting too. Phoebe had never been keen on research,
but she had to admit that it was a fascinating subject.
The path lab engaged her attention too; she spent some
considerable time peering down a microscope while
the doctor patiently explained what she was looking
at. When she finally got to her feet there was no sign
of the others—they were alone at one end of the vast
place and there was no one within earshot.

'Oh, dear,' said Phoebe, 'I've held everything up,
haven't I? I'm sorry—I've kept everyone waiting.'

The doctor's voice sounded amused. 'My dear good
girl, do you really suppose the other two have any idea

as to what we are doing, or where we are? I credited you with an eye sharp enough to see that.'

She smiled at him and a dimple showed itself briefly. 'Oh, yes, I did, but I thought perhaps it was just me. Isn't that nice? She's such a dear and he looks rather a sweetie, only I don't like his tie.'

He let out a great shout of laughter. 'Do your suitors stand or fall by virtue of the ties they choose?' he wanted to know.

'I haven't got any s...' She stopped, remembering Jack.

'What's his name?' enquired her companion with an intentness quite at variance with his usual placid manner, and she found herself answering obediently: 'Jack—only he's not my—my suitor, not really, just persistent.'

They walked out of the path lab and started down a long wide corridor.

'Will he be at the wedding?' her companion wanted to know, and his voice was very soft.

'No—yes, I don't know.' She gave him a bewildered look and encountered his eyes; the gleam in them left her even more bewildered and strangely excited. She turned her head away and said, a little breathless. 'Where are we going now?'

'The small museum attached to the school—some fascinating things there—and we have just time...'

Phoebe peeped at him. He resembled himself again, not the exciting man who had stared at her so strangely a moment ago. She said primly: 'I hope we haven't taken up too much of your time.'

He flung open a door and started down a steep flight

of steps beside her. 'No.' He opened the door at the bottom and ushered her into the museum. Mies Witsma and his colleague Arie were there, staring at an old engraving of some medieval gentleman having his leg amputated and, from the look on his face, taking grave exception to it. Phoebe doubted if either of them saw that, though; they looked up with the slightly bewildered air of people who have been interrupted unnecessarily but are too polite to say so, and her companion must have seen that too, for he made no attempt to join them, merely saying: 'We'll see you both in five minutes in the front hall,' and led her away in the opposite direction.

'I can't possibly see all this in five minutes,' began Phoebe.

'No—but I want my tea. I'll show you the most important exhibits, you shall come again and see the rest.'

She was hurried from one case to the next and whisked through the door again with her impressions nicely muddled and feeling hurt because he seemed in such a hurry to finish their tour. There was a great deal she hadn't seen, she felt sure. What about the wards and theatres and...

'Tea!' boomed Doctor van Someren from somewhere above her, and hurried her along more passages until they emerged in the front hall once more. The other two were there already. 'Coming with us?' he asked them. 'Arie, you take the Daf, I'll take Phoebe with me.' He started down the steps, his hand firmly on her arm.

'I haven't said goodbye,' she protested.

'Quite useless,' he told her cheerfully, 'and unnecessary. You will see them very shortly. Come along.'

'Where to?'

He stopped short. 'Did I not invite you? No, I see that I didn't. You are all coming to tea at my house.'

'At your house?' She was aware that her conversation lacked sparkle, but he was going a little fast for her.

'Yes, of course why not?'

He was crossing the courtyard to where the Jaguar waited sleekly, and she found herself forced to trot in order to keep up with him.

'I'm not sure that I should,' she essayed. 'It's such a great waste of your time, and whatever will your wife think if you bring hordes of people back for tea?'

'Not hordes,' he corrected her, 'three, and I have no wife.'

She got into the car because he had opened its door and obviously expected her to, pity and sympathy swelling inside her—poor man, so he was a widower, or divorced—although she couldn't think how any woman in her right senses would want to let a man like him go once she had him... What a life it must be for him, bringing up a small boy. Someone had told her that children didn't go to boarding school in Holland—perhaps there was a governess. She stifled a pang of disquiet at the thought; someone young and pretty, who might catch her companion unawares and marry him. Her reflections were interrupted by his quiet voice: 'Who told you that I was married?'

'Someone in England—at least, they didn't say that you were married, but that you had a son.' She turned to smile at him and encountered a faintly mocking smile.

'Hardly the same thing,' he murmured, and before she could recover: 'Did you enjoy this afternoon?'

She flushed, sensing his gentle snub. 'Very much,' she told him politely, and went on to enlarge upon the things she had seen until they were back in Delft where Doctor van Someren stopped the car in one of the narrow streets bordering a tree-lined canal, sending her heart into her mouth as they came to a halt, the car's elegant nose poised over the dark water.

'How often do cars get driven into the canals?' Her voice was tart to cover her fright.

He shrugged. 'Daily—we have an excellent rescue service, though.'

Which made her laugh as she got out to inspect the houses crowding on either side of the canal. She had wandered down that very street only that morning; it pleased her mightily that he was leading the way to one of them—a narrow house, five stories high, with a semi-basement and a double step leading to its front door. Inside the hall was cool and quiet and dim but not gloomy, for above their heads she could see a circular window set in the roof, towards which the narrow staircase wound, its carved balustrade forming a narrow spiral at each ascending gallery. The room they entered was cool too, the furniture old and simple and very beautiful, highlighted by the silver in a display cabinet against one wall and the paintings on its white walls. Phoebe halted in the middle of the room and said in a pleased voice:

'That's a Quaker chest, isn't it?' and then bit her

lip because she had sounded rude, but her companion
looked pleased.

'Yes—isn't it delightful? And how nice that you
know it for what it is. You like old things?'

'Very much. I came past these houses this morning
and longed to see inside them, and now I am—I can't
believe my good luck.' She smiled, her sapphire eyes
sparkling, and he said quickly: 'In that case...'

He got no further, for the door opened and Zuster
Witsma and Doctor Lagemaat came in, followed almost immediately by a pleasant-faced woman whom
Phoebe took to be the housekeeper, bearing a tray of
tea things. She had hardly closed the door behind her
when it was opened again and a small boy came in—
the boy who had put his tongue out at her. He shot her
a look of horrified surprise and ran across the room
to Doctor van Someren, who had apparently not seen
the look and said easily in English: 'Hullo, Paul—you
must speak English for a little while, for we have a
guest for tea from England. Come and be introduced.'

Phoebe offered a hand and smiled. Little boys were,
after all, little boys and what was a rude gesture between friends, but although he shook her hand and said
how do you do with perfect good manners, the look he
shot at her for the second time was far from friendly,
rather was it suspicious and wary. She made a few ran-
dom remarks to cover what she felt to be an awkward
pause and was thankful when Paul went to talk to Mies
Witsma and Doctor Lagemaat, with whom, she noted,
he appeared to be on the best of terms. They had tea
then, and everyone talked a great deal save for her host,
who spoke so little she wondered if he were in danger

of falling asleep again; apparently not, for the moment the meal was finished he sent Paul away to get on with his homework and offered to show her the house.

The next hour was a delight, for her host's idea of showing her round was to let her roam at will, merely opening and shutting doors as required, supplying the history of anything she enquired about, and putting into her hands some of his more delicate treasures for her to admire more closely. The size of the house surprised her, for it had great depth, with three rooms, one behind the other on the ground floor and some enchanting passages running haphazardly from the galleries above. There was a walled garden too, sloping down to another, smaller canal at the back of the house; it had a small jetty and a rowing boat, and at Phoebe's questioning look, the doctor said: 'Paul's—it's a safer way of getting around than the streets.'

She nodded, wondering about him and Paul. The boy was devoted to him, she had seen that at once, and the doctor seemed equally fond of Paul, but surely they didn't see much of each other? The doctor was engrossed in his work—ward rounds, teaching rounds, lectures, research work—there was no end to it; there couldn't be much time in which to be with the boy. 'He must have a lot of friends,' she ventured.

They were standing side by side, looking down into the dark water, highlighted here and there by the late afternoon sun. Her companion didn't answer this remark, instead he flung an arm around her shoulders. 'I hope you will be happy here,' he observed thoughtfully, and then to shock her into a gasp: 'You had met before, I gather.'

'Who?'

'Don't prevaricate, you're too sensible for that. You and Paul.' And when she didn't reply: 'Of course, this…' He took his arm away and lifted her hand to look at the still colourful bruise. 'A school satchel—that was what you intended to say, was it not? Very nice of you not to—how do you say—split? Although of course you had no idea who he was.'

'None,' she said faintly.

'But you could have said something just now.'

Phoebe snatched her hand away. 'Who do you take me for?' she asked crossly. 'I'm not in the habit of telling tales, you can't have a very good opinion of me.'

'As to that, it is a subject which, for the moment, I am not prepared to discuss.'

She looked at him then. 'What do you mean? Is it because I pretended to be Sybil?'

He looked amused. 'What an enquiring mind you have! I hope you are satisfied with the arrangements made for your visit to your home?'

A snub which she ignored because she was suddenly stricken. 'Oh, I forgot to thank you—I'm so grateful, it's exactly right, and Zuster Witsma says it won't upset anything at all.' She added a little shyly: 'You must find it very silly of me to wish to go home so soon after I've arrived here, but they wanted to get married before Nick took up this new job…'

'Naturally,' he agreed lazily, 'I think…'

She wasn't to know what he thought; the housekeeper came down the garden and began to speak to him in an urgent voice. He listened without speaking, nodded, said to Phoebe: 'I'm sorry, I have to return to the hospital immediately,' and started to walk back to the house.

'One of ours?' hazarded Phoebe, trying to keep up.

He didn't slacken his pace. 'One of ours, dear girl. You will forgive me?'

She nodded and stopped trying to keep pace with him. 'Thank you for a pleasant afternoon,' she said swiftly, and he turned to smile at her as he went.

Indoors she found the other two sitting close together in the small sitting room which opened into the garden. They had obviously been undisturbed for some time, and when she told them that the doctor had been called away and she would wait in the garden until they were ready to leave, they agreed with such an unflattering readiness that she made haste to go back to the garden. There was someone else there now—Paul, sitting in his boat, doing something or other to one of the oars.

She went and stood close by him and ignoring the scowl on his little face, said coaxingly: 'You understand English very well, don't you, Paul, well enough for you to understand me when I say that I should like to be friends? I don't care a row of buttons about the other afternoon, you know—indeed, I'd forgotten about it. Couldn't we be friends?'

He didn't smile, but at least he seemed interested. He was on the point of speaking when his eyes slid past hers, watching someone coming down the garden. Phoebe turned to see who it was—a girl, tall and dark and magnificently eye-catching. She wasn't hurrying; by the time she reached them Phoebe had the unpleasant feeling that she had been studied from head to toes, assessed, and instantly disliked. Nonetheless, the girl's manners were charming. 'You don't know who I am, so I'll introduce myself—I should have been home for tea, but I was held up by the traffic. I'm Maureen Felman, Paul's governess. You're the English nurse, aren't you? Lucius told me about you.'

'Lucius?' Phoebe forced her voice to friendliness. 'Do you mean Doctor van Someren?'

The girl laughed. 'I forgot—I've been here so long, we've been Lucius and Maureen for years.'

Phoebe let that pass. 'My name's Phoebe Brook. Your English is so good you must be...'

'My mother. I speak both languages fluently.' And Phoebe, already disliking her, disliked her still more for the smugness of her voice. 'Paul and I speak English when we're together—Lucius wants that.'

'Paul's English is very good,' observed Phoebe politely. 'Do you live here?'

'Not yet.' Maureen smiled as she spoke; the smile was smug too and Phoebe's dislike turned to instant hate. 'Lucius is a stickler for the conventions—I live here during the day, though, and while Paul's at school I act as secretary to Lucius and drive him around when he doesn't want to drive himself.'

Phoebe murmured a casual something; it would never do to let this girl think that she was even faintly interested in the doctor. All the same, she found it strange that he liked to be driven. He had struck her as a man who did his own driving, and what secretarial work was there for her to do? There was a secretary at the hospital, who did the ward rounds with him, she had seen that with her own eyes—was this girl hinting that she was something more to him than a secretary-cum-governess? She glanced at Paul and saw that he was watching her in a speculative way which caused her to say airily: 'It sounds a nice job. I hope we meet again before I go back to England.'

'Probably—Delft is small. You must come round one day and Paul shall practise his English on you.' She gave the little boy a malicious glance as she spoke and Phoebe had the uncomfortable feeling that she didn't like him—and she must be on very close terms with the doctor if she could invite people to his house… She said sweetly: 'How nice. I shall look forward to that, and now I must go and find Zuster Witsma.'

That young lady was, in fact, advancing down the garden at that very moment. She spoke coolly to Maureen, with warmth to Paul and swept Phoebe away. 'Doctor Lagemaat has to be back—we'll drop you off at St Jacobius as we go,' she explained.

They paused for a moment before they entered the house and looked back. Paul and his governess were standing watching them, and Maureen was laughing, they could hear the light mocking sound quite clearly.

In the car Mies turned in her seat to say: 'Not nice, that girl, but clever. Doctor van Someren thinks that she is a splendid governess and of such great help to him.' She snorted: 'He is so wrapped up in his work he can see nothing!'

Outside the hospital, when Doctor Lagemaat stopped the car, he turned to say to her: 'We must not bother you with our small differences of opinion, but we are old friends of Doctor van Someren, and I agree with Mies.' He smiled nicely at her. 'May I not call you Phoebe?'

'Oh, please,' said Phoebe instantly, and Mies chimed in: 'And you shall call me Mies—not in the hospital, of course, and him,' she nodded at Doctor Lagemaat, 'you shall call Arie. Thus we shall be friends!'

Phoebe, standing on the pavement, watching them drive away, felt a pleasant warmth. It was nice to make friends; it was nice, too, to know that Lucius van Someren had good friends too. She had a sudden urge to find out as much as possible about him.

Chapter 4

She had her opportunity the very next day, for in the morning, when Doctor van Someren had finished his teaching round, he clove his way through the circle of students to where she was standing behind Mies, and said: 'I have a few hours to spare this afternoon you will be free, I take it? I should like you to visit the Hortus Botanicus behind the university, and should there be time to spare, another visit to the museum might not come amiss.'

Phoebe thanked him quietly, conscious of a pleasurable glow beneath her starched apron, and when he went on: 'At the entrance, then, at half past three,' she had a job not to smile widely with the pleasure she felt; instead she said soberly enough: 'Very well, sir,' and received a little grunt in reply as he wandered away. She watched him go down the ward; at the door he stopped to write in his notebook and she wondered what it could be—a reminder perhaps, about the afternoon's outing.

She was a little late, for it hadn't been possible to get off duty punctually and she had had to change much too quickly, so that she was totally dissatisfied with her appearance as she hurried to the hospital entrance. Nonetheless, she looked cool and fresh in her blue and white striped dress, and because it was unusually hot for the time of year, she had dispensed with stockings and put on a pair of blue sandals which exactly matched her shoulder bag. But if she had hoped for a word of appreciation from her companion she was to be disappointed; he gave her the briefest of greetings and hardly looked at her. They were free of Delft and well on the way to Leyden when he said: 'I'm sorry I had to leave you yesterday afternoon.'

'It didn't matter at all,' she assured him, 'especially as Wil is so much better today—it was for her you went, wasn't it?'

He nodded and she went on, choosing her words: 'I went back to the garden after you left, just for a little while—Paul was there, and then his governess came.'

'Maureen? Ah, yes, she mentioned that she had met you. She organises us—a most efficient girl.'

'And a very striking one,' remarked Phoebe, hoping he would go on talking about the wretched creature if she gave him a little encouragement. But she was frustrated by his: 'You can afford to be generous, Phoebe,' a remark which pinkened her cheeks with annoyance, because what might have been meant as a compliment had been uttered in a tone of voice which verged on mockery. The vague half thoughts she had had of putting a spoke in Maureen's wheel withered away under the sudden sideways glance he directed at her—not in the least absent-minded but very intent, as though he knew what was in her mind. The pink deepened and she looked out of the window and made an observation, stiffly, about the weather. She was sorry she had come, she told herself savagely, and how stupid of her to allow her interest to settle upon a man she was unlikely to see again once she had gone back to England and who was already quite satisfied with his life, and anyway, a small stern voice reminded her, was it quite sporting to try and attract his attention away from the glamorous Maureen? She had no opportunity of solving this interesting problem, because they had arrived at the Medical School once more and her companion was suggesting, in the mildest of voices, that she should get out of the car.

The next hour was a delight to her. They wandered round slowly, and Phoebe, naming each plant as they inspected it, was quite taken aback when Doctor van Someren exclaimed: 'Good heavens, girl, your Latin is excellent—are you a botanist as well as a nurse?'

She denied it, suddenly shy. 'Why, no—my father was, at least it was his hobby. We used to go for walks and he taught me a great deal.'

'Latin or botany?' he asked idly.

'Both, I suppose.'

'What profession had your father?'

She bent to examine a fine specimen of basil. 'He was a scientist.'

They had reached a fine old mulberry tree with a

bench built around it. 'Let us sit,' suggested the doctor. 'The museum can wait until another day—you shall tell me about your father and something of yourself too, and I shall discover even more facets to your character.'

She was taken aback. 'Facets? Whatever for—I didn't know I had any.'

They were sitting side by side and the sunlight dribbled through the leaves on to her bright hair. He answered her quietly: 'Oh, you have a great many—you are intelligent for a start, you have a quick brain, you are kind, impulsive—you like your own way.' He went on, ignoring her gasp: 'I think you may have a nasty temper when you are roused. You are intensely curious...

'What about?' she demanded.

'Me,' he answered simply.

'I'm not,' she began, and he said sharply, 'and do I have to add another facet—a slight twisting of the truth?'

'Well, what if I am?' she snapped crossly. 'It's natural, and at least I haven't turned you into facets like a specimen under your microscope, sir.'

'Ah, yes—something I had forgotten to mention. Would you refrain from addressing me as sir? My name is Lucius; I do not propose that you should address me so in hospital, but surely when we are away from our work we might assume that we are friends. I am not so very much older than you, Phoebe.' And at her look of surprise: 'Thirty-four, and you are twenty-seven.'

'How you do harp on my age,' she protested. 'It's not nice to remind a woman how old she is.'

He lifted colourless eyebrows. 'Indeed? Have I offended you? I'm sorry.' He didn't look in the least sorry; he was laughing at her. After a moment she smiled reluctantly and he said instantly: 'That's better—don't you want to ask me any questions?'

She said without hesitation: 'Yes, of course I do, but it wouldn't be polite.'

His blue eyes twinkled. 'Try me, or shall I answer the first one for you? You wonder about Paul, do you not? He calls me Papa and you have been told that I have a son, and where, you ask yourself, is his wife— dead, divorced, run away with some other man who has no work to fill his days and more money than he knows what to do with?' He paused. 'Yes?'

'Yes,' said Phoebe, thinking how very good-looking he was.

'I have no wife—Paul is my adopted son. His parents—my friends—died in that Italian plane crash four or five years ago—perhaps you remember it? I am his godfather, he has no grandparents; it was right and natural that he should make his home with me.'

The flood of relief she felt quite shocked her. Not stopping to think, she said: 'Oh, I thought—that is, I...'

'I have no doubt you did,' he agreed suavely. 'I should have mentioned it to you before, but it slipped my memory.'

She disagreed quite fiercely. 'Oh, no, why should you? It's none of my business,' and felt irrationally disappointed at the casual shrug he gave in answer. They sat in silence then, the breeze stirring the tree above them, the air full of the varied hum of insects.

'All the live murmur of a summer's day,' uttered the doctor suddenly.

'Matthew Arnold,' Phoebe gave the information automatically and then laughed when he said: 'You are a difficult girl to impress—your knowledge of botany is more than satisfactory, so is your Latin, and now, when I quote an apt phrase, you cap it with its author.'

'Oh, I'm sorry—I didn't mean to—I wasn't trying to impress you or anything.' She added earnestly: 'As a matter of fact, I hardly know any.'

'No? I shall have to try and catch you out.' He gave her a long considering look which so disconcerted her that she suggested that they should finish their tour of the garden.

'You'll come back with me to tea?' he asked her as they got into the car later.

She hadn't expected that and it flustered her. 'Me? Well—I came yesterday.'

He shot the car with heart-stopping precision between a slow-moving lorry and a stationary baker's cart. 'I hadn't forgotten,' he told her mildly. 'I thought it would be pleasant for you to further your acquaintance with Maureen, and it's good for Paul to speak English as much as possible.'

'Why?'

'He wants to go to Oxford. His father and I were there, you see.'

Paul and Maureen were in the garden, sitting on the grass and although the boy ran to greet the doctor and give a hand to Phoebe, his governess made no effort to rise. Only when they had reached her she lifted her head and smiled at them with a casual hello and an offer to fetch the tea into the garden. 'It's so warm,' she explained. 'When Paul came out of school we decided that the garden was the only place to be. I hope you agree, Lucius?' She looked at the doctor, who said vaguely: 'Oh, yes—do whatever is fun for Paul,' and then to the small boy hanging on his arm: 'The rowlock is loose in the boat. Have you seen it? We'll fix it now.'

So Phoebe was left alone to sit on the grass and admire the view and the flowers and watch the two of them absorbed in their work, their lint-fair heads close together. But not for long, for the doctor looked up, said something to Paul and got out of the boat to cast himself down beside her.

'Forgive me, I thought Maureen was here.'

'If you remember she went into the house to fetch the tea tray.'

He looked surprised. 'Did she? Well, why not—it's just the day to have tea out here.'

Phoebe suppressed a smile. 'Don't let me hinder you from mending whatever it is,' she reminded him.

'Paul can manage on his own now, I showed him what to do.' He rolled over to look at her. 'What do you intend to do with your evening?'

She was aware of intense pleasure, although she kept her voice carefully casual. 'Why...' she began, but was interrupted by Maureen, calling gaily for the doctor to go and carry the tray. He got to his feet with no sign of disappointment at not having had an answer, and by the time he had returned and they had settled to their tea, she could see that he had forgotten all about it.

Getting ready for bed that night, she decided that, from her point of view, the tea party had been a failure. Maureen had been charming, she had also been possessive towards the doctor—no, bossy, Phoebe corrected herself as she brushed her hair with unnecessary vigour. She had also managed, with diabolical sweetness, to put Phoebe in the wrong on several minor points during their conversation, and worse, made her out to be a little stupid as well. 'I hate her!' declared Phoebe a trifle wildly, and flung the brush across the room, which did it no good at all, but certainly relieved her pent-up feelings. And Paul had enjoyed her discomfiture too, staring at her with his sharp dark eyes. Only the doctor had been unaware, sitting there, making gentle talk and seeing to their wants. He was an exasperating man!

She went to the mirror and peered at her face without conceit; she was a very pretty girl, accustomed to being looked at at least twice, her voice was quiet and low, she neither giggled or laughed brassily. If she was a little shy, she took care to conceal it. There was nothing, she told her reflection, to which Doctor van Someren could take exception, if indeed he had ever taken the trouble to really look at her.

She got into bed. 'It's a pity nothing ever happens to me,' she told the ceiling, then closed her eyes and went to sleep, and Fate, who had overheard the remark, grinned impishly and went off to make her own arrangements.

It was a glorious morning and Phoebe was free until two o'clock. There was a great deal of the small city she hadn't seen and she took herself off to the Convent of St Agatha, where William the Silent had met his death, and this expedition over, and with time to spare, she decided to wander round one or two of the narrow streets leading away from the prescribed route to the hospital. The houses here were small, their walls uneven with age, their windows small too and filled with flowerpots so that Phoebe was unable to catch a glimpse of their interiors. They were neatly kept, with fresh paint and sparkling windows and here and there a canary bird singing in its cage hung outside an upstairs window. She wandered on, knowing herself to be lost but not worried, because Delft wasn't large enough for her to remain so; she would soon find her way again. She was on the point of doing this when her eye was caught by a cul-de-sac, lined with very small houses indeed, its cobbled centre ornamented by a plane tree. It was very quiet there and although the houses looked well tended, she had the strong impression that the place was empty. She had walked down one side of it and was about to cross over to the other when the door of a house she was passing opened, revealing a very old lady.

Phoebe paused in her walk, smiled, essayed the *'Dag, mevrouw'*, she had learned to say and prepared to move on, but a timid hand was laid on her arm and the old lady started to unburden herself at such length and with so much agitation that there was no use in Phoebe trying to stop her. When she at last came to an end they stood looking at each other in a puzzled way, Phoebe because she had no idea what the old lady wanted, the old lady because she was getting no response.

At length Phoebe said regretfully with a strong English accent: *'Niet verstaan,'* and then with a flash of inspiration asked: 'Help?'

The old lady nodded, muttered, *'Ja, ja, hulp!'*, and

drew Phoebe inside. In the small overfurnished, spot-
lessly clean front room was another old lady, lying on
the floor, her eyes closed. Phoebe lost no time in taking her pulse, which was far too weak for her peace
of mind, just as the pale old face was far too white,
and her breathing was so shallow that there was almost no movement of the old-fashioned black bodice.
She was unconscious, but Phoebe was sure it wasn't
a coronary, not even a black-out, but the old lady was
ill, without a doubt. She selected a beautifully embroidered satin cushion from an assortment on the stiff
settee and placed it beneath the old lady's head, then
mimed the need for a blanket, reflecting that igno-
rance of the Dutch language was putting her at a most
appalling disadvantage. The blanket was fetched, she
tucked her patient up carefully, took her pulse again,
peered under the closed eyelids and then once more
played her desperate charade to convince her companion that she would have to go for help. This, naturally
enough, took time, but once she had made herself understood, Phoebe wasted no time. She shot through the
front door and began to run in the general direction of
the St Bonifacius hospital. Lucius van Someren would
be doing his round, she was quite certain of that, for
whatever else he forgot, he didn't forget his patients.
She could explain to him quickly, far more quickly
than trying to find a policeman, or for that matter, any
passer-by—and there were none at that moment—and
wasting time making herself understood.

   She got there quicker than she had hoped, because
she chanced her luck, taking what looked like a short
cut down a narrow alley and arriving almost in the

hospital yard. She didn't stop to wonder what everyone would think as she belted up the stairs and into the ward. She hardly noticed the surprised faces or the children's quickened interest, only Lucius' calm face and his quiet: 'You want me, Phoebe?'

She nodded, out of breath. 'There's an old lady,' she began, and prayed that he wouldn't waste time asking questions, 'in a little house in the Breegsteeg,' she knew her pronunciation was awful, but she was past caring. 'She's ill—unconscious. I don't think it's a coronary—there wasn't anyone, only another old lady, and I didn't know where to get help, so I came to you.' She looked at his grave, kind face and if she hadn't been so taken up with her errand, might have noticed the expression which passed over it. 'I'm sorry to interrupt the round.'

He asked no questions at all, but said something to Doctor Lagemaat who was with him and then: 'We'd better go and have a look, hadn't we?' and was off down the stairs, with Phoebe, still blown, trying to keep up with him.

In the car she repeated her apology, because to drag a consultant from his ward round—and now she came to think about it, there had been a crowd of students there, so it had been a teaching round—was hardly the thing. She added matter-of-factly: 'I'm sorry if you're annoyed…it's not knowing the language.'

He made a sound which could have been a laugh as he inched the Jaguar through the busy streets with no sign of impatience while she, with something of an effort, held her hands quiet in her lap, thanking heaven that the journey was so short.

The old lady was at the door, looking more bewildered than ever; Doctor van Someren paused briefly to speak to her and went inside, Phoebe close behind him, crowding into the small room. Presently, when he had made his examination, he said: 'You were right, it isn't a coronary—her skin's dry, she's very pale, not grey, just pale, and look at this.' He nodded at the bony arm he was holding. 'Malnutrition, general debility and anaemia, I should suppose, but I'll leave that for the medical side to confirm. Let's get her to hospital.'

Phoebe's lovely eyes asked a silent question.

'Yes, she'll get better—good food, rest, ferri. sulph...'

'And the other lady, what's to happen to her?'

He smiled fleetingly. 'Her younger sister, a mere eighty-two. We'll take her along with us and get the social workers busy.'

'Why are they alone? Where's everyone? Why haven't they enough money to...'

His smile widened. He said patiently: 'Not so fast! They're alone because everyone living in the *steeg* has gone on an outing, but our patient didn't feel up to it, so they stayed behind—presumably she collapsed.' He got to his feet. 'Now, let's get them to St Jacobus.'

They went in the car, Phoebe supporting the unconscious patient on the back seat, her sister, in her respectable, old-fashioned black coat and hat, sitting in front. Phoebe listened to her dry old voice, talking continuously now that relief had loosened her tongue and the doctor's calm tones had quietened her fright. She couldn't understand a word of what was being said, but she was quite confident that he would arrange everything to everyone's satisfaction. He certainly had instant attention at the hospital; with a brief direction that she was to stay in the waiting room with the old lady, he disappeared with the stretcher, a houseman, a couple of porters and a rather fierce-looking Sister. He didn't come back for twenty minutes, and Phoebe, looking up from her efforts to comfort her weeping companion, said, faintly accusing: 'She needs a nice cup of tea…'

'Coffee,' he corrected her. 'We'll all have some, but first I must explain everything to her.' He took a chair and sat down by the old lady and began to talk to her. He sounded reassuring, and presently the old lady wiped her eyes, smiled a little and allowed him to help her to her feet. 'Now we'll go home,' he told Phoebe, 'and have that coffee and then take her back. She's to come and see her sister this afternoon—I've got someone to fetch her and take her back.' He paused. 'I suppose you're dying of curiosity—I'll explain it all to you later.'

She bristled. 'There's no need to put yourself out,' she said haughtily. Really, he was a most irritating man! Why had she ever rushed to him for help and dragged him away from his round and been so sure that he wouldn't be annoyed at the interruption? Vague notions about this floated at the back of her mind, but it was hardly the time to indulge in introspective thoughts. She got into the car with the old lady beside her, and was driven to the doctor's house.

It wasn't yet twelve o'clock. The hateful Maureen had told her that she spent her mornings in typing letters for the doctor, making appointments, filing correspondence and other secretarial duties. She had made it sound very important and Phoebe, despite herself, had been impressed, so that when the doctor opened the door and ushered them inside, she expected to hear the steady tap-tap of a typewriter, or failing that, the utter hush surrounding someone concentrating upon desk work. She heard neither—gales of laughter, the discordant thunder of a lesser-known pop group belting out a number on a record player, and the unmistakable clink of glasses were the sounds which assailed her astonished ears. But if she was astonished, her host was thunderstruck. His mouth thinned ominously, and it struck her suddenly that probably he had a shocking temper which he seldom allowed anyone to see. They weren't to see it now; after the barest pause, he led them to the sitting room, begged them to make themselves comfortable, pulled the bell rope with restrained violence and walked to the window to stare out into the street.

It was the housekeeper who answered it and Phoebe, who rather liked her, felt sorry for the surprise and discomfiture she was obviously experiencing. But her master ignored this, merely asking her to bring coffee, adding something else which Phoebe couldn't understand. Then he went and sat by the old lady and made gentle conversation.

But not for long; the door was opened presently and Maureen, rather pale, stood in the doorway, whereupon he got to his feet, saying in English: 'Ah, yes, Maureen—an explanation is due to me, I fancy— perhaps you will give it to me now.' He looked briefly at Phoebe. 'You will excuse me? And be good enough to pour the coffee when it comes.'

His voice, which he had neither raised nor quickened, was steely. Phoebe, feeling meanly delighted at Maureen's discomfiture, murmured suitably as she watched them leave the room together, then turned her attention to the old lady, who, unaware of any undercurrents, was smiling quite happily and, Phoebe very much feared, was about to embark upon an unintelligible conversation with her.

The coffee came. She attended to her companion's wants, poured herself a cup and listened to the sounds on the other side of the door—subdued voices, feet, a giggle quickly suppressed, and then utter silence. The visitors had gone. Somewhere in the house, behind one of the handsome doors, Doctor van Someren was with Maureen. Phoebe would dearly have loved to have been in a position to peer through the keyhole, or even eavesdrop... She gathered her straying thoughts together, appalled at the depths to which she had sunk. She had been well brought up; such actions were despicable, she reminded herself, and applied herself to the pouring of second cups, then as the doctor came into the room, filled a cup for him too, and because his mouth was set so very grimly and no one spoke, she began a one-sided conversation to which neither of her companions replied. She was aware that she sounded chatty, but they couldn't sit there for ever, saying nothing.

'A lovely day,' she ventured, having exhausted the excellence of the coffee. 'How early summer is this year,' and then losing patience, she snapped: 'It's a pity I can't speak Dutch, for then at least this lady here would understand me and make some sort of a civil answer.'

The doctor smiled then. 'Poor Phoebe! You have my deepest admiration. Here you are, longing, no doubt, to indulge your curiosity and forcing yourself to discuss the weather. It must be agony for you.' His blue eyes studied her reflectively. 'We're going to take Juffrouw Leen here home.'

Having said which he addressed himself to his other guest, who got to her feet, looking quite cheerful, and accompanied him to the door.

Outside Phoebe said stiffly: 'Well, I'll be getting along—thanks for the coffee.'

'You will come with us Phoebe—please.'

She got into the car again, telling herself that she was weak to do so, and when they arrived at the old lady's house, went inside, helped her off with her hat and coat and then waited patiently while Juffrouw Leen, possessing herself of the doctor's hand, began a long and voluble speech—thanking him, she supposed. Presently it was her own turn, but unlike the doctor, who had doubtless said something graceful, she was unable to do anything but smile. But Juffrouw Leen didn't seem to mind. She saw them off at the door, smiling and waving and quite happy again. Phoebe turned in her seat for a final farewell as they turned the corner of the *steeg* and Doctor van Someren said: 'The round will be finished. You're in time for your midday meal before you go on duty?'

'Yes, thank you. If you like to drop me off...'

He took no notice. Perhaps he hadn't heard, for he went on: 'Juffrouw Leen will be all right—a social worker will call each day to make sure she can manage and someone is lined up to take her to and from the hospital.'

'Her sister—will she do?'

'I think so—the right diet, rest, care, and someone to keep an eye on them when she's back home.' He glanced at her and smiled. 'I'm afraid your off duty has been sadly curtailed.'

'It didn't matter—I was only pottering.'

He drew up before St Bonifacius. 'You enjoy that?'

She nodded. 'Very much—in a few days I shall go further afield. I want to see all I can.'

He didn't answer but got out and opened the car door and went inside with her, bade her a brief goodbye and went up the stairs to the ward, and Phoebe, because there was nothing better to do, went down to the dining room and ate her dinner.

She was off duty again the next morning and she went along to see the old lady. There was someone with her—the district nurse, who had a smattering of English so that Phoebe was able to discover that the patient was doing quite well and that Juffrouw Leen was in good hands while her sister was in hospital. She stayed a while and had a cup of coffee with them, bade them a cheerful goodbye and made her way to the shops. She was coming out of Reynders, a piece of genuine blue Delftware tucked under her arm, when she came face to face with Maureen Felman, and before she could make up her mind whether to say a casual hallo and walk on, or stop and say a few polite words, Maureen had stopped, obviously intent on passing the time of day.

'Hullo,' she said coolly. 'I've been hearing all about you and your Nightingale act—I must say you don't look much like a do-gooder. Didn't you find it all a dead bore? Not that you'd be likely to say so.'

Phoebe eyed her thoughtfully. Here, she thought, was the enemy, although she wasn't quite sure why—and declaring war too.

'If I found it a dead bore,' she replied gently, 'I certainly wouldn't say so, but I didn't—I'm sure you would have done the same.'

Maureen smiled brilliantly. 'Not me—there are far too many old souls around as it is. I like life to be gay.' She stared at Phoebe and Phoebe looked back limpidly. 'You guessed that yesterday, I suppose.' Her eyes narrowed. 'Lucius never comes home before twelve o'clock—never—and yesterday, of all days…and you with him, all prunes and prisms! I could have managed him beautifully if you hadn't been there, looking as though butter wouldn't melt in your mouth. I was only having a few friends in for a drink—God knows life's dreary enough in that house.'

'You're rather rude,' Phoebe's voice had a decided edge to it, 'and I hardly know why, and what you choose to do while the doctor's away from home is really no concern of mine.' She smiled with charm. 'I dare say you're still feeling a bit scared—it must have been a nasty shock for you.' She allowed the smile to linger and watched Maureen's face tighten with ill temper. 'I must be going—it was interesting meeting you.'

She nodded and walked away briskly, thinking what a ghastly creature Maureen was and why, on the face of things, did the doctor put up with her. The thought that he might possibly be in love with her crossed her mind as it had done several times already, only now it refused to be dismissed. It remained, well damped down, for the rest of the day, affording her a good deal of disquiet.

It faded a little under the pressure of work during the next few days and even when she saw Doctor van Someren, it was always in the company of Mies Witsma or the other nurses, and their talk was entirely of the patients. It was the evening before her day off before she found herself alone with him; Zuster Witsma had gone to her supper, the ward was in the chaotic state which preceded the children's bedtime. Phoebe, with another nurse, was urging the more active and reluctant of her small patients to start undressing, supervising the washing of faces, the tidying of beds, the comforting of those who were feeling sorry for themselves and engaging, in her own peculiar, sparse Dutch, those who wished to talk in idle conversation. She had, naturally enough, become a little untidy during the carrying out of these tasks—her lovely hair was coming down, her nose shone, her apron was soaked with most of a glass of lemonade which a recalcitrant small boy had flung at her. Her pleasure at seeing him, therefore, was tinged with fears about her appearance, by no means allayed as he sauntered towards her, eyeing her with amusement.

'Fun and games?' he wanted to know gently.

'Bedtime,' she informed him succinctly. 'We don't reckon to look glamorous at this time of day. We're lucky if we get to supper in one piece.' She thrust in a hairpin with an impatient hand. 'Did you want to see someone?'

'You.'

She sternly curbed the tide of pleasure rising beneath her grubby apron. 'Oh? Well, it's not very easy, you can see that, can't you? And there are only two of us. Is it something you could say while I finish getting Piet into his pyjamas?' She was struck by a sudden and unpleasant thought. 'Do you want to tell me off about something?'

His eyes narrowed with laughter. 'I—tell you off? Why should I want to do that? By all means do whatever you need to do to Piet. You have a day off tomorrow, I believe. Paul has a holiday from school; I thought we might all go to the beach and swim—you do swim?'

She nodded, starry-eyed. 'Nothing spectacular, but I can keep myself from drowning. I'd love to come, but will Paul—that is, won't it spoil his day if I'm there?'

He looked surprised. 'I don't imagine so. Besides, you two girls can be company for each other if Paul and I want to go off together.'

'Yes, of course,' said Phoebe faintly. The idea of spending a day in Maureen's company didn't please her at all; on the other hand, she might find out more about her—and the doctor, and besides, this time Paul might be more friendly. She stared ahead of her, her sapphire eyes seeing nothing—her swimsuits were both rather dishy, and there was that nice towelling beach smock she hadn't intended to buy and had.

'You're not listening,' said Doctor van Someren, and Phoebe jumped guiltily.

'I beg your pardon—I was just… What did you say?'

'Ten o'clock, outside the entrance, and mind you're ready.' His voice changed and became businesslike, a little remote. 'And now I should like to take another look at that admission—Johanna—she's in the end ward, I take it.'

There wasn't much of the evening left by the time Phoebe had had supper. She washed her hair and changed her mind half a dozen times over what she should wear in the morning and then, too restless to go to bed, wrote a long letter home, touching lightly on the episode in Juffrouw Leen's house and not mentioning at all that she was to spend the day with Doctor van Someren on the morrow.

Chapter 5

Doctor Van Someren wasted no time in getting to Noordwijk-aan-Zee, and a good thing too, thought Phoebe, for when she had arrived at the hospital entrance at exactly ten o'clock it was to find the doctor at the wheel of the Jaguar with Paul beside him and Maureen, looking a perfect vision in a scarlet and white beach outfit which immediately made Phoebe feel dowdy. Sustaining a polite conversation with her companion on the back seat, even for so short a time, hardly improved her frame of mind. By the time they had arrived, parked the car in the grounds of the Hotel Rembrandt overlooking the sea, and had strolled to the beach, she was beginning to wish that she hadn't come—a wish which weakened under the spell of warm sunlight, a wide blue sky, a wide beach stretching away on either side of her and the inviting sea.

They more than offset the doctor's coolly casual manner, Paul's bright stare and Maureen's sugary manner.

The doctor owned one of the gay little chalets set out where the dunes and the sand met, and the two girls went at once to change in the curtained alcove in its well-furnished interior. They emerged presently, in an atmosphere of artificial bonhomie, Maureen drawing all eyes in her scarlet bikini and white cap. It was some consolation to Phoebe that the doctor merely glanced at Maureen without much interest. He did the same to her, too, which she found disappointing, for while she made no effort to compete with her companion, she was aware that she made a pleasant enough picture in her sky-blue swimsuit. She wandered on down to the water's edge, leaving Maureen to wait for Paul and Lucius; the girl was obviously back in favour after whatever it was that had gone wrong when they had called at his house. Phoebe wandered slowly into the chilly water, wondering just how firmly entrenched the governess was in the doctor's household; she seemed full of confidence and very self-assured; he must like her very much, and although she hated to acknowledge it, probably he fancied her as well. She sighed and started to swim seawards.

She was a competent swimmer, no more. Within a few minutes she was overtaken by the other three, cleaving their various ways out to sea with an ease she frankly envied. The doctor had shouted something to her as he passed, but she hadn't heard what he had said and it didn't really matter. She called back brightly and swallowed so much water that she was forced to tread water while she coughed and spluttered. When she had her breath back she turned prudently for the shore; she had come quite a long way—too far, perhaps. She deliberately made her strokes slow and steady—she wasn't tired, only a little scared. All the same, her relief was very real when Lucius idled up beside her.

'Tired?' he asked.

'No—but I've not been quite as far as this before and I'm not sure how far I can go.'

He headed her off so that she found herself swimming parallel with the shore instead of towards it. 'In that case, we can stay as we are,' he told her, 'tell me if you get tired, I'll give you a hand.'

She applied herself to her swimming, happy that he had sought her company, sorry that it took up so much of her attention that she had little opportunity of doing anything else. All the same when he asked: 'Your plans are made for your trip home?' she was able to say: 'Yes, thank you—after my night duty—you remember?' She spoke cautiously, not quite happy about holding conversations in the North Sea while swimming.

She heard him grunt. 'You will fly?'

'Yes, in the morning—I shall be home during the afternoon.'

'You will meet all your friends?'

It was a question. 'Yes.'

'You have a great many. One in particular?'

She thought of Jack and hesitated. 'Not really. You asked me the other day.'

'I forget,' he said laconically, and then: 'Race you in!' and he allowed her to win.

They were lying on the sand, soaking up the sun, when Maureen and Paul joined them and Lucius asked the boy to go to the chalet and fetch the flask of coffee they had brought with them, but it was Maureen who suggested with an air of great friendliness that Phoebe might like to go with him. 'For he'll never manage the mugs as well,' she said gaily. As Phoebe got to her feet she watched the little smile on Maureen's face. It was amused and faintly contemptuous and she made no effort to hide it because Lucius was lying on his back with his eyes shut, and there was no need.

In the chalet they found the coffee and a tin of biscuits, and when Phoebe asked Paul where she should find the mugs, he shrugged his shoulders and turned his back, making for the door.

'There's no need to be rude,' she told him firmly. 'I asked a civil question and I deserve a civil answer.'

He shrugged his shoulders again and pointed to a wall cupboard. 'They're there.'

She collected four, added spoons and asked: 'Paul, why do you dislike me?'

He stuck out his lower lip. 'I don't know you,' he muttered.

'No—and I don't know you, do I? But that's no reason to dislike a person.'

He gave her a flickering glance from his dark eyes. 'Maureen says you're...' He stopped, and she saw that he wasn't going to say anything more, but at least she had a clue. Heaven knew what the girl had told him. She said quietly: 'Let's go, shall we?'

They lunched at the hotel and later bathed again, but this time Lucius didn't come near her in the water, and yet he had been his usual kindly self at lunch and a very attentive host. She swam around for a little while, then went and lay on the sand waiting for the others, wondering when they would go back—after tea, she supposed, a meal which they took picnic fashion from a tray brought out from the hotel. It was still warm. Phoebe would have liked to have stayed where she was, soaking up the sun and dreaming, but instead she was forced to keep alert, answering Maureen's sly questions and parrying her remarks, sweetly made. 'Such a pity you don't have more time to swim—you poor thing, having to work so hard, you never have a chance to get good at anything, do you?' Her voice dripped kindness.

'No,' said Phoebe, her voice pleasant although she seethed, 'but it wouldn't make any difference. I'm far too cowardly.'

'Oh, never that! Cautious, perhaps some people have no spirit of adventure...'

Phoebe had thought Lucius to be asleep, he had been so quiet, but now he interrupted them. 'A remark which can hardly be applied to Phoebe. I doubt if she would have come to Holland otherwise.' He rolled over and looked at her and smiled lazily. 'You'll come back to dinner, Phoebe? It will be a pleasant end to a pleasant day.'

She thanked him nicely. Only his innate kindness and his beautiful manners had made him invite her, she felt sure, but the invitation gave her a badly needed uplift. 'I've only got my beach clothes with me,' she told him.

His unexpected: 'I like blue, it suits you,' took her quite by surprise and he went on: 'I'm sure none of us mind, and it will give me a good excuse to wear a shirt and slacks.'

He kept his word. When Phoebe went downstairs after making the best of her appearance in one of the beautiful bedrooms at the back of the house, it was to find him as informally dressed as she was so that she forgot the blue and white cotton shift she was wearing— forgot it until Maureen joined them. She, clever girl, had changed into an artlessly simple white dress which showed off her tan to perfection and made her look like some Greek goddess. She had brushed her dark hair until it gleamed and wore plain gold hoops as earrings, and on her bare feet she had gold kid sandals— she was wearing false eyelashes too, and Phoebe drew a thin trickle of comfort from the knowledge that her own, long and curling, were more than their equal. Secure in this knowledge, she was able to compliment Maureen upon her appearance in a serene manner before going to sit by Paul, whom she engaged in uneasy conversation until dinner was ready.

Because Paul was to dine with them, the meal had been put forward half an hour and they ate it in a room at the back of the house, filled with mellow old furniture, the table decked with fine china and silver worn paper-thin with age. The talk was general, and because Paul was with them, of a lighthearted nature. Phoebe, despite the presence of Maureen, enjoyed herself even though the boy avoided speaking to her and his governess, in a dozen subtle ways, allowed her to see just how firmly she was ensconced in the doctor's household. But Lucius at least made it his business to entertain her, so that her chagrin was all the more intense when, after dinner and when Paul had gone to bed, she suggested that she should go back to hospital and

Lucius made no attempt to persuade her to stay, as he might well have done, for it was still early.

'I'll run you back,' he told her, and got to his feet with no sign of regret, and when she protested that she could walk the short distance, he took no notice at all but walked with her to the door while she bade Maureen good night.

They were halted at the door by that young lady's: 'Don't be long, will you, Lucius, and will you take me home? All that fresh air has made me too sleepy to be sociable tonight.'

Lucius had nodded without speaking and Phoebe got into the car beside him wondering what exactly Maureen had meant—was she in the habit of keeping him company in the evenings, or was she merely once more reminding Phoebe that she was firmly entrenched both in the doctor's home and his affections? She mulled it over while they drove to the hospital in silence. It was only when he stopped before its entrance that he spoke.

'I enjoyed our day. Perhaps we may do it again, Phoebe. I hope you enjoyed it too, though perhaps not as much as I.' He turned to look at her. 'I'm indebted to your sister for persuading you to take her place— we might never have met.'

Phoebe sought for a suitable answer to this and could think of none. After a short silence, she came up with: 'I enjoyed myself very much, thank you, Doctor...'

'Lucius.'

'Lucius.' She smiled at him. 'Good night.'

For answer he bent his head to kiss her, a gentle kiss on the corner of her mouth. 'I've been meaning to do that for some time,' he informed her, 'but I've such an

infernal bad memory!' He got out of the car, opened
her door and waited by it until the porter had opened
the wicket in the door. She looked back and waved a
little uncertainly and he raised a hand in casual salute.
All the way over to the Home she was wondering if he
was going to kiss Maureen good night too.

She woke the next morning to the realisation that
she would be going on night duty that evening and
she didn't particularly want to. It would mean that she
wouldn't see anything of Lucius; consultants didn't do
rounds at night, they had their registrars and housemen for that. Only upon very rare occasions or in
some emergency did they appear on the wards, and
that wasn't very often. She would have to resign herself to not seeing him at all and the idea didn't please
her at all. She told herself what fun it had been trying
to capture his attention; that it had been amusing even
if not very successful, but at least he had noticed her a
little and the detestable Maureen hadn't liked it. Presumably the doctor was old and wise enough to know
what he was about, but Phoebe distrusted the governess
as well as disliking her, nor did she think that she had a
good influence upon Paul, despite her air of efficiency.

She wished she knew more about the fracas in his
house, too, although Maureen had got back into his
good graces quickly enough, surely a sign that he
fancied her, for he had been very angry... Phoebe reminded herself that she was very sorry for him. She
frowned at her reflection as she pinned on her cap and
repeated, out loud, that she was sorry for him for all the
world as though she had contradicted herself. He was

wrapped up in his work, unnoticing of the web Maureen was spinning for him—and Paul, would she be good to him? She thought not, for she wasn't the maternal type and the little boy badly needed mothering. She went down to breakfast and consumed her coffee and *boterham*, her head full of gloomy thoughts, not the least of which was that, counting her nights off, it would be a full two weeks before she would see Lucius again.

She was mistaken, for, coming off duty the next morning, yawning her head off and longing for her bed, she found him waiting at the head of the basement stairs.

'Five minutes,' he told her without preamble, and when she looked at him, bewildered. 'You'd better have a cup of coffee, we can breakfast after our swim.'

'Our swim?' she repeated stupidly, her eyes huge for want of sleep. 'Is this something you forgot to tell me, Doctor van Someren?'

He looked thoughtful. 'Possibly—you know what a head I have for remembering things, you must make allowances—anyway, I've told you now, haven't I?'

'I'm tired.'

'So am I,' he assured her. 'I've been up half the night. We need some exercise, so bustle up like a good girl. I'll be in the car.'

It was ridiculous, she told herself, half laughing, half angry, as she tore off her uniform and flung on a cotton dress, pulled the pins out of her hair, brushed it perfunctorily, tied it back anyhow and raced downstairs, her swimsuit under her arm.

'Honestly,' she declared roundly as Lucius opened

the Jaguar's door, 'I've not had time to do anything—I look a sight!'

'For sore eyes. Is that not what you say? You should wear your hair like that more often.'

'In a tangle?' she asked incredulously, 'and with nothing on my face—I feel awful.'

He was going slowly through the still quiet streets of Delft. 'At least you do not have to waste time putting on your eyelashes,' he observed mildly. 'Now shut your eyes and take a nap, I'll wake you when we get to Noordwijk.'

It was difficult to open her eyes; Phoebe felt his hand on her shoulder, but the urge to ignore it was very strong, but the hand was gently persistent, she woke up and found that he had parked the car in the hotel grounds again. 'Come on, lazybones,' he teased her gently as he helped her out of the car, put a key into her hand and said: 'Get undressed while I order breakfast,' and strolled away.

Once she had shaken off sleep she felt better, and by the time she was in her swimsuit she felt almost normal again. It was a lovely morning, cool enough to make her shiver a little as she came out of the chalet to find Lucius waiting for her.

She went to the water's edge, her toes curling under the chilly little waves, poking her hair unceremoniously into her cap, and he joined her there. She had barely tucked the last few stray curls away when he caught her briskly by the hand and ran her into the sea. The water was cold but not unkindly so. Phoebe gasped and laughed and finally swam, feeling her body glow and an energy she didn't know she possessed after a hard night's work.

'This is gorgeous—I could go on for ever!'

He made a wide circle round her, tearing through the water at a great rate before settling alongside her. 'You see? I knew you would feel better for it. We'll do this every morning while you're on night duty.'

He gave her a gentle shove in the direction of the beach.

'But your time?'

'There's always time to do the things one wishes to do, have you not discovered that?' He rolled over on to his back, paddling along slowly to keep pace with her earnest efforts. 'I don't start work until nine or half past, and we shall be back by then.'

'But Paul—won't you miss seeing him off to school?' she spluttered, her mouth full of water. 'And won't he mind!' she managed.

'We go our own ways in the morning—in the winter we breakfast together and during his holidays, of course. When he was quite a little boy we agreed about certain things. He understands that not having a mother he must accept that some things have to be different.'

Something in his voice warned her not to ask any more questions. When they reached the beach she said lightly: 'That was really marvellous—and how lovely it is with almost no one here.'

His eyes swept the empty expanse of sand. 'Just the two of us,' he agreed, and his eyes came to rest on hers. 'Lovely.' And something in his face made Phoebe say hastily, 'I'll go and change, I won't be a minute.'

They ate a gargantuan breakfast, sharing the hotel's

large dining room with only a handful of people, for it was not yet nine o'clock. Phoebe, buttering toast with a lavish hand, observed: 'I could stay up all day, I feel so wide awake,' and had the remark greeted by a derisive chuckle from her companion.

'I'll check on that tomorrow morning,' he promised her, 'and now if you've finished...?'

An hour later, sitting up in bed, she felt so full of energy still that she decided that she wouldn't sleep; she would read for an hour or so and then get up and make a cup of tea. But she didn't open her book at once. She was wondering what Maureen would think, and possibly say, when she discovered that Lucius had taken her swimming and that the exercise was going to be repeated each morning until she went to England. Her satisfaction at the thought of Maureen's annoyance was tinged by regret at having to leave Delft, even for a few days. It would be lovely to see Sybil married, but she wished it could have been at some other time. She closed her eyes on the thought and slept.

She didn't wake until she was called at half past six and when she told Lucius that in the morning they laughed about it together. By the third morning she managed to have a cup of coffee on the ward, so as not to keep him waiting while she went to the dining room, and when they returned from their swim she changed into her cotton dress and sandals, put up her hair and went out to buy another beach outfit. She was coming out of the shop, a woefully expensive but eminently becoming ensemble dangling in its gay carrier bag, when she met Maureen—the last person she wished to see, for she was longing for her bed. The fine energy engendered by her swim was oozing slowly away and she was in no state to parry Maureen's clever thrusts, and she wasn't sure if her temper, now she was tired, would stand up to pinpricks. Maureen had stopped, so Phoebe braced herself.

But there was no need. The governess was pleasant, even friendly—she mentioned the early morning swim and gave her opinion that it was a splendid idea; she sympathised about the lack of time Phoebe had in which to enjoy herself while she was on night duty too. 'But you'll make up for that at your sister's wedding, won't you?' she suggested, laughing.

Phoebe tried to clear her sleep-laden wits. Maureen was behaving quite out of character and she wondered why. Besides, she was sure that she had never mentioned her trip to England to her. 'I didn't know I had told you,' she essayed.

'Oh, you didn't,' her companion agreed, 'but of course Lucius tells me everything—naturally.' Her dark eyes rested upon Phoebe's own blue sleepy ones. 'I know a great deal about you,' she laughed with a merriment which struck a discordant note in Phoebe's ear, 'so I shouldn't confide in Lucius if you want to keep any secrets from me.'

'I haven't any secrets,' said Phoebe flatly, then went a little pink. She certainly didn't want Maureen to know that she had taken Sybil's place, but surely Lucius...

The girl before her broke into her thoughts. 'No? Then you must be a paragon—I've got dozens.' Her glance slid to the package Phoebe was carrying. 'Shopping? It's a waste of time, my dear. Haven't you discovered that he doesn't notice—at least, not unless he's interested in the girl wearing them. Well, I must be off. 'Bye.'

Phoebe, despite her weariness, went over the conversation word by word before she finally went to sleep and decided that Maureen had wanted to make certain that she didn't trespass on her preserve—Lucius van Someren. 'And I wouldn't,' said Phoebe sleepily, 'if I were sure she loved him, but she doesn't.'

There was a message the next morning to say that Lucius wouldn't be able to take her swimming and just for a moment she wondered if it was Maureen's doing, but she didn't think Lucius would allow anyone to dictate to him about what he should do and what he shouldn't. And anyway, there was no sense in brooding over it. She accepted an invitation from two of the nurses to go with them and have coffee in the city and look at the shops, an occupation which filled the morning hours very satisfactorily and made her so tired that she fell asleep the moment her head touched the pillow.

She knew, the moment she opened the ward door that evening, that it was going to be a bad night— Zuster Witsma looked worried for a start, which was so unlike her that there had to be something wrong, and far too many children were wailing and calling out for attention, which was so unlike their usual sleepy high jinks that Phoebe asked at once:

'What's hit us?' and then remembered that Mies might not quite understand, for her English, though fluent, was strictly textbook. 'They're unhappy,' she substituted, and the Dutch girl said worriedly:

'Oh, Phoebe, such a day—and a nurse off sick. An infection, how do you say?'

'Bug,' supplied Phoebe unthinkingly.

'Bug? I thought that a bug was an insect.' Mies frowned because she was a stickler for getting her words right.

'It is, but it's what we call a virus infection—any infection—it's slang.'

'Ah,' Mies smiled faintly, 'now I have a new word. There is a bug of the alimentary tract...'

'D and V,' interposed Phoebe, and explained rapidly what it was.

'Exactly so—so horrid for the children and no rest for any of us all day. I'm afraid you will have a busy night, you and Zuster Pets—you will find gowns to wear in the treatment room and they are all on Mist. Kaolin and some of the worst are on Phenergan. Doctor van Someren thinks that it is not serious—twenty-four hours, perhaps a little longer. It plays havoc with the diets.'

Phoebe put down her cloak and bag, preparatory to taking the report, as Zuster Pets came into the office—a nice girl, large and rather slow but very patient and thorough. Phoebe and she exchanged a friendly hello and Phoebe thought how funny it was that a junior student nurse should be addressed as Zuster while she herself was called Nurse—an interesting point to take up with Lucius when next she saw him. Probably she wouldn't see him—she wrenched her mind away from that possibility and gave her attention to Zuster Witsma, painstakingly reading the report in both Dutch and English for the benefit of both of them.

She had been right about them being busy; it was almost midnight before the majority of the children, worn out and washed out, dropped off to sleep; only a handful of them remained awake, wretchedly ill and disposed to make the most of it. Phoebe went soft-footed up and down the wards, from bed to cot and back to bed again, feeling sorry for their occupants, for they were already fighting one disease, it was too bad that they had to endure this setback as well. Doctor Pontier had been in earlier in the evening, expressed satisfaction as to the small patients' conditions, amended some of the charts, drunk a hasty cup of coffee, invited Phoebe to go out to dinner with him when she returned from England, and went away with the earnest request that she should call him if she found it necessary.

He had barely closed the doors behind him when Night Sister arrived to do her round. She was a short, frankly outsize body, adored by the nurses. She had twinkling blue eyes, several chins, and had buried two husbands, and although she had none of her own she understood and liked children. Walking with a surprising lightness despite her ample proportions, she went from one child to the next, nodded her head in satisfaction and made her silent way from the ward, warning Phoebe to send Zuster Smit to her midnight meal, but on no account to leave the ward herself.

Alone in the ward, and all the children miraculously asleep, Phoebe settled down at the desk—they wouldn't stay quiet all night, but she had a short respite in which to chart temperatures and note the medicines she had given. She had done the first three or four when she became aware of footsteps on the stairs—unhurried and quiet—and she knew whose they were; she looked over her shoulder and Lucius was standing just inside the door.

Phoebe got up with the faintest of rustles from her gown and waited for him to reach the desk. He had been out, for he was in a dinner jacket, her imagination, always lively, pictured Maureen waiting outside in his car, looking glamorous, while she— She glanced down at the voluminous folds of thick white cotton while she schooled her delightful features into a look of calm enquiry.

His voice was very quiet. 'Good evening, Nurse Brook—I'm glad to see that they've settled. They had us all a little worried today—were they very troublesome?'

She spoke calmly, in a voice as soft as his. 'Oh, yes, very, but wouldn't we all be? They're worn out.'

He laughed soundlessly. 'And you?'

She gave him an austere look. 'Not in the least. Besides, I have Zuster Pets on with me, and she's a gem of a nurse.'

He looked interested. 'Is she now? We must keep an eye on her, since you say that.'

'For heaven's sake,' she uttered, 'that's only what I think...sir.'

'But I value your opinion, Phoebe, even when you call me sir in that repressive fashion.'

'I'm on duty,' she reminded him.

'Yes—unfortunately,' and when she gave him a questioning look: 'I'd like to take a look at Wil—and Jantje was a little off colour too.'

He took off his jacket and she tied him into a gown

and went with him as he went to look at the children. When he had finished and was putting on his jacket again, he said very quietly: 'It's peaceful now—but it can't last all night. I don't envy you, even with the redoubtable Pets to be your right hand.' He smiled suddenly. 'Shall I stay and keep you company until she comes back, Phoebe?'

She couldn't see his face clearly in the dimness of the ward. She handed him a chart to initial and said in a steady, practical voice:

'You'll need to go to bed, you must have had a hard day.'

'A polite brush-off!' He sounded as though he were laughing.

'Oh, I didn't mean it to be,' she whispered anxiously. 'I'd love you to…' she stopped herself. 'I have a great deal of work to do,' she informed him sedately.

He nodded. 'A quarter to eight tomorrow morning,' he invited her. 'As it's Saturday, Paul will be coming too.'

'That will be nice, thank you,' and then, because she was unable to prevent herself, 'and Maureen?'

Lucius looked surprised. 'No—she doesn't live with us, you know. I have no idea at what time she gets up, but I imagine early rising isn't one of her strong points. She prefers her amusements to take place in the evening.'

He was standing very close to her; he had bent his head and kissed her and was at the door, his quiet, 'Good night, Phoebe,' a faint echoing whisper, before she moved.

She was a little late off duty in the morning and

tired and faintly ill-tempered with it, but this feeling
melted miraculously away as she got to the hospital
entrance and saw the Jaguar standing waiting. It disappeared completely as Lucius opened the door for
her and squeezed her in beside them, saying: 'You've
had a wretched night, haven't you? Do you want to
talk about it? I promise you I won't be bored, and Paul
won't either.'

She smiled at the boy as the doctor started the car.
'Why, are you going to be a doctor too, Paul?'

He forgot to scowl, his face lighted with interest.
'I'm going to be a vet.'

'Oh, splendid,' said Phoebe with enthusiasm. 'I've
an uncle who's a vet. I used to stay with him when I
was a little girl; he let me help him, though I suppose
I was never much use. Will you go to a veterinary col-
lege in Holland?'

He explained at great length and in great detail, and
by the time they arrived on the beach, Phoebe thought
that he had got over his dislike of her, but somehow, at
some time, something went wrong to make him dislike
her again, for in the middle of a laughing conversation
with Lucius she looked up to find the boy's eyes fixed
upon her with such suspicion and animosity that she
was completely taken aback, lost the thread of what she
was saying, and had to make some excuse for doing
so, and although she continued to laugh and talk as before, the morning, for her at any rate, was spoilt. Her
spirits were hardly improved by the doctor's careless
statement that he would be going to Vienna for several days on the morrow, 'by which time you will be
in England,' he reminded her cheerfully. 'And by the

way, young van Loon will drive you to the airport,' and when she protested, he declared: 'He's been waiting to take you out ever since he met you. This will be the next best thing—he's a nice boy,' and his last remark capped her unsatisfactory morning: 'A little young for you, though.'

Tiredness and some feeling she didn't bother to analyse dissolved into a little spurt of temper. 'In that case, perhaps you'd better warn him not to go with me—there must be some middle-aged taxi-driver whom you might consider more suitable. I had planned to go by train.'

He had either not noticed her pettishness or chose to ignore it.

'Oh, lord, a ghastly journey—that's why I suggested to van Loon that he might take you. Much better go with him, Phoebe. Besides, he'll be so disappointed if you don't—you know what these young men are.'

'Do I?' Her voice was glacial.

He stopped the car outside the hospital and turned to look at her.

'I imagine that you have dealt kindly with dozens of them.' He smiled with such charm that Phoebe found herself smiling back.

'If you're warning me not to gobble him up, I won't,' she assured him, and turned to say goodbye to Paul, sitting in the back of the car, and although he answered politely enough she could see that he disliked her still. She sighed a little, thanked the doctor for her trip, wished him a pleasant stay in Vienna, and got out of the car. She turned to wave before she went into the hospital, but they had already gone.

* * *

She felt lonely during the next few days; she told herself it was because she was tired from her night duty, and even though she went out each morning with one or other of the nurses, the days lagged sadly. It was a relief when she had gone on duty for the last time, packed her case and gone downstairs to meet young Doctor van Loon. At least he was delighted to see her, and made no secret of his admiration. Although she was tired and unaccountably despondent, she found herself enjoying the drive to Schipol; they parted like old friends when her flight was called and she left him vowing that he should take her out for the day when she returned.

The journey passed swiftly, for she had been up all night and slept a good deal, and when she wasn't sleeping, her mind was far too weary to allow her to think coherently, but at Shaftesbury, when she got out of the train and found Sybil and Nick waiting for her, her tiredness evaporated in the spate of news—the wedding, on the day after next, naturally took pride of place, and it wasn't until they were home, sitting round the table eating the belated tea Aunt Martha had prepared, that Sybil asked:

'Well, Phoebe, how's the scheme going? Is it fun? Do you see much of the doctor and has he noticed you yet?' She laughed and Phoebe laughed with her, aware, to her annoyance, that her cheeks had turned a good deal pinker than usual.

'The scheme's fine,' she replied hastily. 'I love working there—the Ward Sister's about my age and we're good friends. Doctor van Someren comes each day, sometimes more often. He's nice.' As she said it she knew what an understatement that was, but for some reason she didn't want to talk about him; but the others did.

'And is he married?' Nick wanted to know, and Sybil chimed in. 'Yes, you said precious little about him in your letters.'

'Well—' began Phoebe, and went on hastily: 'No, he's not, but he's got an adopted son, Paul. He's almost nine and rather a dear, only he doesn't like me.'

'Why ever not?' asked Sybil. 'How funny—but you must have seen quite a lot of him, then.'

Phoebe made quite a business of buttering a scone. 'No, not really. I met him and then I went to the doctor's house with Zuster Witsma after we went to the botanical garden at Leyden...'

'Who took you?'

She evaded her sister's eye. 'It was something I was supposed to see—part of the scheme...'

'Who took you?' Sybil was nothing if not persistent.

'I went with Zuster Witsma—Doctor van Someren took me round.'

'Did he talk?'

'Yes, of course. He's a perfectly ordinary man.' She paused for a moment; he wasn't ordinary in the least, he was someone quite different. Phoebe dragged her attention back to what she was saying. 'We saw the museum too, it was very interesting.'

'What did he talk about?'

'Oh, the garden and plants and the hospital.' She looked down at her plate, remembering all the other things he had said.

'Charming—he sounds a bit dreary.'

'He's not,' said Phoebe sharply. 'He's a...' She stopped, not wanting to put her shadowy thought into words. 'I say, I've brought your wedding present with me, would you like to see it?'—a successful digression which sent everybody up to her room while she unpacked the Delftware coffee set and offered it to the happy pair.

She went to bed early, finding it pleasant to be in her own room again, so quiet and peaceful after the bustle of Delft and the noise from the wards. She went to sleep at once, but not before she had thought about Lucius and wondered where he was and what he was doing. It was too much to hope that he might miss her as she undoubtedly missed him. She slept on that not very happy thought.

There was too much to do the next day for anyone to have time to ask her any more questions. The wedding wasn't to be a large one, but even though they hadn't many relations, they had a great many friends, and Nick's family was a large one. They all drove over to Shaftesbury that evening, where his parents were staying for a couple of days. There were a round dozen for dinner and a very light-hearted meal it was, only broken up by Aunt Martha's firm decision that the bride required her beauty sleep.

Phoebe, waking early the next morning, went at once to her window. The weather had been unbelievably fine for weeks, and if it were to rain it would mean a last-minute rearranging of the buffet lunch which they were to have in the garden behind the house. But she need not have worried. The pale morning sky was clear and the sun, already bright, shone on to flower beds which really looked at their best. The roses were out too; the first buds of the Lady Seton had opened overnight, their pink the exact colour of the dress Phoebe had chosen to wear. She had a wide straw hat to go with it too, laden with matching roses—it was a beautiful hat and she looked nice in it. She found herself wishing that Doctor van Someren were there to see her in it.

She withdrew her head from the window, frowning a little. She was becoming obsessed by the man! She really must try to remember that however interesting she might find him, she wasn't likely to see him once she had left Delft, and that would be soon enough, she remembered with something like a shock as she went downstairs to the kitchen to make the morning tea.

The wedding went off brilliantly and was all that such an event should be. After it was all over and the bride and groom had left, the last of the guests gone and Aunt Martha had retired to her room, happy but worn out, Phoebe went into the garden and sat down in the still bright evening. It had been a wonderful day. Sybil had looked lovely and so very happy and everything had gone without a hitch—besides, it had been fun to meet old friends again, only she hadn't expected to see Jack there. She wondered who had invited him and then dismissed the thought as not worth bothering about. He had greeted her with an assurance which had annoyed her, as though he had only to raise his finger and she would come running.

She moved a little on the bench under the tree, smoothing the silk of her dress with careful fingers; it wasn't until she had come face to face with Jack that she had known that she really didn't care if she never saw him again. There was only one person she wanted to see Lucius van Someren. She supposed, now that she allowed herself to think about it, that she had been in love with him all the time, only she hadn't been prepared to admit it. She sighed and got up and strolled down a garden path and, careless of her fine dress, leaned over the low stone wall at its end. There was Maureen to consider—it was impossible to tell from Lucius' manner what he felt about the girl, and as for herself, he had shown nothing but a pleasant friendliness towards her. And the dice were loaded against her, for Paul hated her and he and Maureen were a formidable barrier between her and the doctor. She felt helpless and hopeless out there in the darkening garden. The only thing which buoyed her up was the fact that she would be seeing him again in a couple of days.

She started walking back to the house, telling herself with a certain amount of force that one never knew what lay around the corner.

Chapter 6

As it happened, it was Doctor Pontier round the corner. He was waiting for Phoebe at Schipol, and she, who had passed the flight in an indulging of impossible daydreams in which Lucius had come to meet her with every sign of delight, had difficulty in schooling her face into an expression of pleased surprise at the sight of his registrar.

He took her case and walked her out to where his car stood waiting.

'The boss asked van Loon to pick you up,' he explained, 'but I tossed him for it.' He laughed and Phoebe, of necessity, laughed with him.

'What about the ward round?' she asked.

'Jan will stand in for me. I told the boss—he said it didn't matter to him who fetched you as long as someone did.'

She was aware of ruffled feelings. It was rather like being a parcel which had to be collected; so much for her half-formed plans and hopes! She had allowed herself to drift from one delightful dream to the next during the last couple of days, and a lot of good they were doing her—a little realism would be a good thing. She turned to her companion and said cheerfully: 'Well, it's jolly nice to see you. I was just a bit worried about getting to Delft, though I'm sure it's easy enough—but this is much nicer. I wonder when I'm expected on duty?'

He got into the car and started the engine. 'I rather think this afternoon—there's a staff nurse off sick, nothing much, but she could be cooking up something. Mies will be glad to see you.'

Nice to be wanted, thought Phoebe, nice to fill a niche, even a humble one. Even nicer if Lucius wanted her back too. She resolutely put him out of her mind and entertained Doctor Pontier with some of the lighter aspects of Sybil's wedding.

She didn't see Lucius until the evening, when after a heavy afternoon's work, he came quietly on to the ward, Mies and Arie with him. She had already seen these two, of course, but there had been little time to say much, only Mies had found time to apologise for asking Phoebe to go straight on duty. She smiled at Phoebe as they came down the ward now, but it was Doctor van Someren who spoke, and his impersonal friendliness chilled the warmth she felt at seeing him again.

'Nurse Brook, we are more than glad to see you back again. I hope you had a pleasant time at your sister's wedding? You were fortunate to have such splendid weather.'

She murmured something unintelligible to this rather prosy remark, but as he wasn't listening she might just as well have said nothing at all. 'Wil,' he went on immediately, 'I'm not too happy about the child. We changed the dosage, didn't we? But the chest infection doesn't respond. We had better try something else.' He turned to Arie Lagemaat and switched to Dutch, and Phoebe, called by one of the children, went to attend to his small wants. When she had finished, Lucius had gone.

She met Paul the next day. The weather had changed with ferocious suddenness to a grey sky, a fine continuous rain and a high wind, but Phoebe, restless and disappointed at Lucius' lack of interest in her return, decided to go out. There was still a great deal of Delft to see; she hadn't visited the Tetar van Elven Museum yet; she dragged on a raincoat and tied a scarf over her hair without bothering overmuch as to her appearance, and started out. She had hours of time, for she had got up early after a night of wakefulness, and she wasn't on until two o'clock.

She lingered in the museum, drinking the coffee she was offered when she had toured its treasures, and then, because there was no sign of the rain abating, started off once more, walking a little aimlessly, until she remembered that she hadn't had more than a hurried peep at the Oude Delft canal; she would walk its length and fill in the time until she was due back on duty. She was halfway along the street bordering it, when the urge to explore one of the narrow lanes branching from it sent her down the nearest, dim and cobbled and on this wet day, dreary. She had reached the right-angled bend near its end when she heard the running feet behind her. They sounded urgent and Phoebe stopped, glancing to the right and left of her, conscious that her heart was beating faster. Probably it was someone taking a short cut in a hurry. But it was Paul, tearing round the corner and stopping short within a foot of her. She managed a calm 'Hullo, Paul,' and waited for him to speak.

When he did, she could hear the excitement in his voice. 'I saw you,' he told her, 'and I wondered if you wanted someone to show you the city.'

She was taken aback. 'That's nice of you, Paul—I've just been to the museum in the Koornmarkt and I've an hour to spare still. I wasn't really going any-where—and shouldn't you be going home?'

He looked away from her. 'No, I—I came out of school early this morning. I could show you some re-ally old houses, near here.' He sounded eager. 'They're mediaeval and not used any more.'

Phoebe hesitated. She had time to spare, it was true, and this was the first occasion upon which Paul had shown any real signs of wanting to be friends. She said quickly: 'All right—where do we go first?'

For a boy of his age, he knew his home city well. They went up one *steeg* and down the next while he pointed out the interesting points of the buildings sur-rounding them. At length Phoebe glanced at her watch.

'Heavens,' she exclaimed, 'a quarter of an hour left! I must go.'

'One more,' he begged. 'There's a warehouse along

here, by the canal.' He led the way through a narrow
alley to a cobbled street, a canal on one side, narrow
houses, grey and anonymous with age, on the other.
They were deserted, forlorn in the rain which pattered
into the dark, sluggish water of the canal.

Phoebe shivered. 'My goodness—this all looks a
bit gloomy! Surely there's nothing…'

But Paul had crossed to one of the warehouses and
pushed its door open. 'It's empty,' he told her. 'I've
been inside lots of times. The room on the top floor is
marvellous—you should just see it.'

Phoebe glanced up at the steep gable above their
heads. It looked a long way away. 'I don't think I want
to,' she said. 'I'll take your word for it.'

She knew she had said the wrong thing the moment
she finished speaking; he gave her a look of scorn and
said: 'Chicken! I didn't know you were frightened.'

'I'm not frightened,' she protested vigorously, 'only
I don't see the point of climbing all those stairs…'

Paul turned away, his shoulders hunched. He said
coldly: 'You keep saying you want us to be friends,
but you don't really.'

'Is that what you want? Just to prove my friendship—to climb some stairs and look at a room?' she
asked robustly. 'OK, five minutes, then.'

He went inside first and although it sounded empty
and hollow, there was nothing unpleasant about the old
house. He led the way rapidly up the creaking stairs to
the first floor and then up successively narrow stair-
cases to the landings above, until on the third landing
there was only a narrow twisting staircase in the wall,
its steps worn and uneven. Paul went first to open the

small door at the top—a heavy door, Phoebe could see, with great bolts top and bottom. She went past the boy into the dimness beyond and found an empty room; it smelled musty and close and because the shutter was barred across the window on the outside, it was darker than it need have been. She rotated slowly, staring round her. 'Why,' she cried, 'there's nothing here…' and turned her head sharply and too late at the sound of the door shutting. Paul had gone; she listened to the bolts being shot with a kind of stunned surprise, but only for a moment. She ran over to the door and rapped on it.

'Paul—I know you're having a joke, but I really haven't time. Will you open the door? I shall have to run all the way to the hospital!'

His young voice sounded thin through the thick wood. 'It's not a joke—Maureen says you're a scheming woman, out to catch Papa—well, you can't now. You didn't think I could be clever, did you? I knew if I waited I'd catch you!'

Before she could draw astonished breath to reply to this speech, he had gone down the stairs. She could hear his feet, echoing hollowly as he went further and further away. When she heard the bang of the street door she gave up calling after him and leaned against the door, trying to think of a way out. The door was fast enough, and far too thick to yield to a hairpin, even if she knew how to use it—besides, there were the bolts, they would surely need a crowbar. The shuttered window wasn't any good either. Phoebe tried shouting through it, but the glass was thick and set in small leaded panes. She peered at her watch and made out that it was already time for her to be on duty and cheered up a little; very soon someone would wonder where she was, but her heart sank when she remembered that she had told no one where she was going. All she could hope for was that Paul would relent and come back for her, or take fright and tell Lucius—or even Maureen—but would Maureen take the trouble to come and let her out? She thought not. It would have to be Paul, and no doubt when he got home and started to think about it, he would return. Having settled this to her satisfaction, she looked round for somewhere to sit. There was nowhere but the floor, so she took off her raincoat, folded it carefully and sat upon that, her head against the wall. Every ten minutes or so she got up and went to the window and shouted, for surely at some time during the day someone would pass along the street below. She told herself vigorously that of course they would and ignored the fact she and Paul hadn't met a soul…

The time passed slowly. Phoebe occupied it by reciting such Dutch words as she had managed to learn, going over the various procedures Lucius favoured for his patients and by writing, in her head, an amusing letter home. Only presently it wasn't amusing; she was hungry and the dry air of the ill-ventilated room had made her thirsty. Besides, the complete stillness of the old house had become something tangible. Supposing it was used by tramps at night, or hippies? After all, Paul had known of it, so others would too…supposing someone came, how was she going to make them understand how she came to be there, locked in? It was a thought she decided not to pursue. She might

as well relax and have a nap, she told herself firmly;
it was broad daylight, and even if no one knew where
to look for her, the police were very good at finding
people, so she had absolutely no reason to panic. Probably at this very moment Paul was telling Lucius what
he had done. She eased herself on the raincoat, her
pretty brow wrinkled. Supposing he didn't—supposing he told Maureen, who appeared to have a strong
influence on him, and she decided that they would do
nothing about it? After all, it was her ill-chosen words
that had put the idea into the boy's head.

Phoebe got up; it was time to shout again. She
would, she promised herself, have a heart-to-heart
talk with Maureen.

A little hoarse, she settled down again, rehearsing
what she would say, and dozed off in the middle of it.

At the hospital, Zuster Witsma had at first been un-
perturbed at Phoebe's absence. She had gone straight
on duty the day before without a word of complaint;
probably she had fallen asleep over a book. But when
half an hour had passed and there was still no sign of
her, she sent over to the Home, only to discover that
Phoebe was not to be found and that the hall porter,
who had seen her go out that morning, was quite sure
she hadn't returned. It seemed a good idea to consult
the Directrice, and that good lady was on the ward,
conferring with Mies, when Lucius walked on to the
ward to collect some papers. The sight of him induced
both ladies to tell him about it and the Directrice concluded: 'I find it strange, Doctor van Someren, that
Nurse Brook should not return—she is not a young,
silly girl even if she is ignorant of our language. I can-

not imagine her allowing that to stand in the way of her telephoning or sending a message.' She added firmly: 'I shall try the other hospitals.'

The doctor had said nothing at all—indeed, he appeared so abstracted in his manner that she wondered if he had heard her, but apparently he had, for after a pause he said: 'Yes, do that, Directrice, but please do nothing more until you hear from me. I have an idea—probably I am wide of the mark, but somehow I think not. You will excuse me.'

For a man of such calm and deliberation, his speed as he drove through the Delft streets to his home was excessive. He wasted no time in entering his house either and strode through it to the sitting room where he found Maureen and Paul. The boy had a free afternoon from school; at lunchtime Maureen had assured the doctor that she would take advantage of it and give Paul a lesson in English reading. However, as he entered Paul was sprawled on the floor, playing half-heartedly with a model car, and his governess was stretched out on one of the sofas, deep in a glossy magazine. The doctor frowned as she started up, but when he spoke it was with abrupt courtesy.

'Maureen, I wish to talk to Paul—you will excuse us,' and as she went out of the room he turned to his adopted son.

Paul had got to his feet. He had gone a little white and he looked decidedly guilty—frightened, even. The doctor sighed. His fantastic idea was likely to prove correct, but he had to be sure. With no sign of anger he said:

'Paul, Phoebe hasn't returned to the hospital, and

she's more than two hours overdue. I have a hunch that you know where she is. You were scared about something at lunch, weren't you? and you ate nothing to speak of, and when I mentioned that she was back at work you looked—er—shall we say guilty?' He strolled across the room and stood looking out of the window, his back to the little boy. 'I'm right, am I not?'

Paul scuffed his sandals, his eyes on the carpet, and muttered something.

'Yes—well, you shall tell me about it later, but now I want to know where she is.'

He had turned round to face Paul, who shot him a quick look. Something in the doctor's calm voice made him answer immediately.

Lucius left his house without a word. Within seconds he was in his car again, taking short cuts to the old warehouses by the canal. He was still driving much too fast and his face was without expression.

Phoebe had awakened from her brief nap unrefreshed and with a feeling that the room had become smaller, stuffier and very hot while she had slept. She also felt frightened, a sensation she quelled as best she could by going to the window and shouting once again through the shutters; at least it was something to do. She had barely seated herself once more before she was on her feet. There was someone in the house, she had heard the door bang below and now the faint sound of footsteps upon the stairs. She opened her mouth to call out, then almost choked herself with the effort to hold her tongue; if it were someone who knew her, they would surely call to her.

Whoever it was, was coming very fast. She faced

the door, scarcely breathing as the bolts were shot back
with some force and Lucius walked in. The breath she
had been holding escaped in a small sound like a whispered scream mixed in with a sigh of relief. The desire to rush at him and fling herself in his arms was
overwhelming, but she suppressed it firmly—and a
good thing too, for he looked quite unworried, leaning
against the door in a casual fashion, as though he were
quite in the habit of releasing those foolish enough to
get themselves locked up in deserted warehouses, and
thought nothing of it. Her relief was swamped by a
splendid rage, so that when he said: 'Hullo, Phoebe—
sorry about this,' in a placid voice, her temper was
exacerbated so that had there been anything handy
to throw at him, she would certainly have thrown it.

Deprived of this method of relieving her pent-up
feelings, she said crossly: 'Pray don't mention it, it
was hardly your fault.' She looked at him with glitter-
ing blue eyes. 'I had a nice sleep,' she informed him,
and burst into tears.

His arms were comforting and his shoulder reassuring. Phoebe muttered into the fine cloth of his jacket:
'You could have called out. I—I thought you were a
t-tramp or a h-hippy!'

A smile, sternly suppressed, trembled on the doctor's lips although his voice was warmly comforting.
'My poor girl, you must have been terrified. What
would you have done?'

'I haven't a clue,' she sobbed.

He spoke softly into her hair. 'I find that hard to believe. You are a woman in a thousand, you would have
handled the situation very well, I have no doubt, and

probably had them showing you the nearest way to the hospital within minutes.'

She laughed then, and presently, her tears dried, she drew away from him. 'How did you know where I was?'

'Paul told me.'

She glanced at him warily and saw that he was watching her closely. It was most unlikely that the little boy would have told him what he had said to her. She said lightly: 'Aren't little boys awful with their pranks? Don't be hard on him, will you? He was joking—I expect he got scared and didn't know what to do.'

Lucius took a long time to answer. 'Possibly, but even a boy as young as Paul would know that he only had to come back here and let you out.'

She didn't meet his eye. 'Yes—well, thank you very much for coming. I'm afraid I've taken up your precious time.'

'There are things more precious.' He had gone to try the shutters and spoke over his shoulder.

'I'll go back to St Bonifacius at once, I'm hours late.'

'You'll come back with me to my house and have a meal. They were managing very well on the ward, they can continue to do so for another hour.'

Phoebe was shaking out her raincoat. 'I'd rather go back—that is, if you don't mind.'

'I do mind. Besides, Paul is at home, he will want to apologise to you.'

She was flustered and furious with herself for being so—she, who had the reputation of keeping her cool at all times. 'Some other time—it surely doesn't matter...'

'Am I to infer that you have some reason for not wishing to meet Paul?' His voice was silky.

'Of course not. Whatever reason should there be?' She put on her raincoat and he crossed the room to help her, turning her round to button it as though she were a little girl.

'A nice cup of tea?' he suggested. 'I know I need one—I had no idea that I could feel so anxious.'

'About me?' The words had popped out before she could stop them.

'About you.' His hands were on her shoulders and he kept them there. 'I'm responsible for you.'

'So you are,' Phoebe said flatly, feeling elation draining from her. How silly of her to have imagined that his anxiety would have been for any other reason. She said brightly: 'I'm ready. Shall we go?'

Paul and his governess were still in the sitting room, he still on the floor with a book on his knees although he wasn't reading it and she still on the sofa, holding a long glass in one hand and still idly turning the pages of the magazine. She put both glass and magazine down hastily and got to her feet. 'Heavens, how quick you were! We didn't expect you… Phoebe, you poor thing! I've been telling Paul what a little horror he is, he should be severely punished.'

Phoebe could sense Lucius' anger, although she wasn't certain against whom it was directed, so before he could speak she said: 'Heavens, why? Didn't you ever play pranks when you were small? I know I did, and what harm's been done? I'm perfectly all right—as a matter of fact, I had a sleep.'

Maureen looked at her narrowly. 'Weren't you the least bit frightened?'

'No,' Phoebe uttered the lie stoutly, 'why should I

be in broad daylight? I was a bit worried about getting back on duty, that was all. What was there to be scared about, anyway?'

She avoided the doctor's eye as she spoke, aware that she was gabbling. It was a relief when he spoke, his voice unhurried. 'Maureen, will you be good enough to go and ask Else to make some sandwiches and a pot of tea—Phoebe has missed her lunch.'

She went reluctantly. It wasn't until she had disappeared from the room that he spoke again. 'Paul, will you come here and apologise to Phoebe.'

The boy came and stood before her, giving her a look of mingled appeal and dislike. When he had apologised she said quickly: 'That's all right, Paul. Actually, I enjoyed our morning together, we must do it again some time.' She turned to Lucius. 'Paul's got a marvellous knowledge of Delft and he's a first-rate guide.' She smiled at him, coaxing him to good humour, and was disappointed when his face remained grave. 'I take it that Paul locked you in for a joke?' he asked her.

She felt her cheeks redden. 'Yes, of course,' she spoke quite sharply, 'and I hope that now he's said he's sorry, we needn't say any more about it.'

'You're generous. Very well, we won't. I don't think he'll do such a thing again, will you, Paul?'

The boy shook his head. His sigh of relief sounded loud in the silence which followed the doctor's remark and which was only broken when Else came in to tell them that she had taken the tea into the small sitting room at the back of the hall.

On the surface at least, tea was a pleasant meal, although Phoebe was the only one to eat anything. She made thankful inroads into the sandwiches and Lucius drank his tea—largely, she felt, to put her at her ease. He talked too, making sure that they all took their share of the conversation, keeping to mundane topics so that any constraint which might still be lurking was stilled. When she got up to go, Phoebe found herself more at ease than she had ever felt before at the house, despite the niggling thought that there must be some reason for Paul's behaviour which she hadn't hit upon.

Lucius, it seemed, had to return to hospital too. They spoke little on the short journey and in the hospital they parted company, he to go to the wards, she to the Home. She thanked Lucius briefly in the hall and was about to turn away when he dropped a hand on her shoulder to hold her still.

'Don't disappear again,' he begged her, 'my nerves won't stand it.'

Phoebe changed with the lightning speed of long practice and while she anchored her cap, pondered his remark. Intended as a joke, she concluded, and indeed, his impersonal friendly manner towards her when she got on the ward seemed to bear this out; not that they exchanged more than a few words, for she was instantly plunged into the ward work after a brief explanation to Mies and a slightly longer one to the Directrice. By the time she had the leisure to look around her, Lucius had gone.

She didn't see him for several days after that—they met on the ward, naturally, but never to speak about anything but ward matters. She had the impression that he was avoiding her, and rendered extra sensitive by her love, she made it easy for him to do so by keeping

out of the way when he did a round and seeing to it that
there was little chance of her being about when he paid
his evening visits. She went out to dinner with Doctor
Pontier, the cinema with Jan, the houseman, and if that
were not sufficient to distract her interest, accepted an
invitation to have supper with Mies.

Mies had the day off, the Dutch staff nurse had
gone off duty at three o'clock, so Phoebe found herself in charge of the ward until ten o'clock—rather a
late hour, she had ventured to point out to Mies, to go
out to supper. But Mies had laughed and told her that
she could sleep it off the next day, as then it would be
her day off, so, while other nurses were getting ready
for bed, Phoebe was wrestling with her hair, changing
her clothes and re-doing her face, rather regretting that
she had agreed to go. But Mies was nice and it would
be fun to see her flat. She snatched up her handbag
and raced downstairs to engage the porter in the difficult task of calling a taxi for her. He shook his head,
however, smiled and gave her some lengthy explanation not one word of which could she understand. She
tried again, getting very muddled, and was cut short
by Lucius' voice behind her.

'Don't struggle with our abominable language any
more, dear girl,' he begged her, half laughing. 'He's
only telling you that you don't need a taxi. I'll take
you—come along.'

Phoebe stayed just where she was. 'Thank you, but
I couldn't possibly give you the trouble. I'm going to
Mies, she told me to take a taxi...'

He looked conscience-stricken. 'Oh, lord, my memory! I quite intended telling someone or other that I should be calling for you; didn't I?'

He looked at her with raised eyebrows.

'No,' said Phoebe, 'you didn't.'

'I'm going to Mies' flat too.' He added, 'For supper,' as if that clinched the matter.

'Oh, well, are you? It's kind of you!' She petered out, so delighted to be with him for the next hour or so that she was hardly aware of what she was saying. She smiled at the porter, cast a quick, shy look at Lucius and allowed herself to be led out to the Jaguar.

Mies lived close by, down one of the narrow streets leading off a busy main street. The house was old, its ground floor taken up by a bakery, the narrow door beside the shop leading directly on to an equally narrow and steep stairs. The flat was on the top floor, three flights up—two attics, cunningly brought up to date, the mod con tucked away where it couldn't spoil the charm of the old low-ceilinged rooms. Mies had furnished it with bits and pieces, but there were flowers everywhere, highlighting the white walls and the polished wood floor.

Phoebe was whisked away to the bedroom, where Mies exclaimed happily:

'I am so glad that you have come—this is a feast, a celebration, you understand. Arie and I are engaged.'

Phoebe kissed the happy excited face, wished the Dutch girl everything suitable to the occasion and followed her out to the sitting room where there was another round of hand-shaking and kissing, first by Mies and Arie and then by Lucius. For a man of such absent-minded habits, he kissed remarkably well, Phoebe thought confusedly.

'There isn't—that is, it's not me you have to con- gratulate,' she managed.

His blue eyes were very bright. 'I never lose a good opportunity,' he told her gravely. 'Besides, I also am to be congratulated.'

She studied his face. 'You're going to be married too?' she asked, and managed, with a fair amount of success, to smile at him.

'You are surprised? At the moment it is strictly a secret.' He let her go and went to open the champagne he had brought with him, and the next half hour or so passed in a good deal of lighthearted nonsense and gay talk. Presently, helping Mies fetch in the supper, Phoebe had a few minutes, away from Lucius, to pull herself together—something she achieved to such good effect that she was able, with the help of the champagne and her resolute common sense, to pass the evening in a very credible manner—a little brittle in her talk, per- haps, and her laugh a little too high-pitched, but that was surely better than bursting into tears.

She awoke late, made a sketchy breakfast and de- cided to go to Amsterdam for the day. It stretched be- fore her, a vista of endless hours until she should see Lucius again. She would have to fill it somehow—just as she would have to fill all the days ahead of her, once she had returned to England. 'The sooner you get him out of your system, my girl,' she told her face as she made it up with care, 'the better.'

She was on her way out of the hospital when she bumped into the youthful van Loon, who said joyfully: 'I say, what luck meeting you like this, Miss Brook. I must bring specimens for Doctor van Someren, but it is also my day off—you will perhaps have coffee with me?'

Any port in a storm. Phoebe gave him a wide smile. 'I'd love to. I was just on my way to catch a train to Amsterdam; I've got a day off too.'

'You're free all day? What luck! May we not go together? I have my car with me. I could show you something of the city.' He grinned widely, 'I would be most happy.'

'What a lovely idea. I'd like that, only we must go Dutch.'

'Go Dutch?' He looked bewildered. 'But I am Dutch.'

Phoebe laughed. 'It's a saying—we use it in English. It means we each pay for ourselves. I won't come otherwise.'

'You do this often in England? This going Dutch?'

'Yes—it's a common practice.' She smiled persuasively. 'No one minds.'

'Then I will not mind also. You will wait here for me?'

He had a Fiat 500, not new; it made the most interesting noises which they occupied themselves in identifying as they drove along. Phoebe, listening to the vague bangings and clangings beneath them, wondered if she would get back safely, but it seemed unsporting to voice her doubts, for her companion was so obviously enjoying himself.

'How long have you had this car?' she wanted to know, and wasn't surprised to hear that he had bought it off another young medic for five hundred guilden, and that this was his first trip of any distance. He added happily that he considered it a lucky coincidence that he should have met her, so that she could enjoy it with him. Phoebe agreed in a hollow voice, her doubts as to whether they would reach Delft again supplanted by the more urgent one as to whether they would reach Amsterdam.

But they did, and what was more, Eddie, as he had begged her to call him, was lucky enough to find a parking place by one of the canals. He stopped the car within inches of the water and oblivious of her shattered nerves, invited her to get out, a request she obeyed with alacrity, to find Lucius watching them from the pavement.

He crossed the road immediately, wished her a good morning, gave the car a considered stare and remarked to van Loon: 'I was told you had bought this car from Muiselaar, but I hardly credited you with driving it.'

Eddie patted its scratched bonnet with pride. 'It goes like a bomb, sir,' he said simply.

'Yes, I was afraid of that.' Doctor van Someren made to move away and Phoebe, longing to ask him where he was going, watched him reach the pavement, only to turn round and come back again. 'I hope you have a pleasant time,' he observed. His eyes flickered over van Loon, whose head was under the boot. 'You will enjoy being with someone nearer your own age. If by any chance this—er—heap should fall apart, be good enough to telephone the hospital and I will arrange for someone to collect you.'

He smiled briefly into her surprised face and once

more regained the pavement, to disappear among the passers-by.

But nothing untoward happened. They spent a cheerful day together and although it was Eddie who decided where they should go, it was Phoebe who kept an eye on the money they spent and an eye on the clock too.

She treated him like a younger brother—a relationship which seemed to suit him very well—and they got on famously. He took her to the Dam Palace where they wandered round the state apartments, which Phoebe declared to be magnificent but dreadfully uncomfortable to live in; she was whisked across the Dam square to look at the War Memorial, treading their way among the hippies to do so, then to drink coffee at a nearby café and then be walked briskly through the city's busy streets to the Rijksmuseum to see the famous Night Watch. She would have liked a chance to do a little window-shopping, but Eddie, determined that she should be stuffed with culture, marched her remorselessly about the streets, in and out of museums, standing her on pavements to crane her pretty neck at the interesting variety of rooftops, taking it for granted that she would leap on and off trams at a word from him. It was fun; the *broodje met ham* which they stopped to eat at a snack bar, the rich cream confections they consumed with their tea during the afternoon, the postcards she bought to send home—she thanked him during the drive back—accomplished despite the bangs and rattles—refused his pressing offer to have dinner with him, and went early to bed, tired out.

She was off duty in the morning, and despite the

drizzling rain, decided to go out. She was at the hospital entrance when the Jaguar drew up beside her and Lucius got out. She wished him a good morning and made to pass him, but he stopped her with: 'Wait a minute, Phoebe,' and joined her.

'I've half an hour to spare,' he told her easily. 'I feel like a walk, if you don't mind?' He gave her a sideways glance. 'You seem determined to stretch my nerves to breaking point.'

She stopped walking the better to look at him. 'I do? How?'

'That—er—car which van Loon drives is hardly safe. Do tell him when next you go out together that he is to borrow the Mini—he has only to ask.'

'But I don't suppose I shall see him again...'

He raised disbelieving eyebrows. 'No? But one day is hardly sufficient in which to see the sights. You had arranged to go with him?'

Phoebe blinked. If she hadn't known the doctor so well she might have deluded herself that he was jealous. 'Of course not! He happened to meet me as I was on my way to catch a train to Amsterdam—he had some specimens of yours to deliver or something of the sort, but he had a day off too—he suggested that I went with him so that he could show me the sights.' She added as an afterthought, 'I didn't know about his car.'

She watched the little smile play around his mouth. 'I was mistaken. It seemed natural that you should spend as much of your free time as possible with someone of your own age.'

'You keep saying that,' she told him, quite put out.

'You know quite well that he's five years younger than I—anyway, I feel old enough to be his mother.'

'Which reminds me—it's Paul's ninth birthday to-morrow, so will you come to tea? You're off in the af-ternoon, are you not?'

She wondered how he knew that. 'I'd love to. Did he really invite me? I must get him a present. What are you giving him?'

'A wrist watch, but I'm still wondering what else to buy for him. Have you any suggestions?'

'Mice?'

He laughed. 'An unusual suggestion from a woman—perhaps you like them.'

'I do not, but little boys do—didn't you keep mice?'

'Yes, but I had a tolerant mother—I'm afraid Mau-reen would never cope with them.'

'But they're not much work, and Paul would look after them. What about a puppy?' she asked, knowing already that it was useless—the governess obviously had the last say in such matters. She fell silent as they walked slowly down a gloomy *steeg*, twisting itself between old houses which had long ago been beauti-ful but were now let out in rooms. She glanced at the door they were passing, noticing its lovely ruined carv-ing, and at that moment it was flung open and a very small puppy was ejected by a heavy boot. Phoebe had scooped the pitiful object up, hammered on the door with an indignant fist and was actually confronting the dour-looking man who opened it before she was reminded that she would be unable to tell him just what she thought of him. She turned to her companion, her eyes ablaze with indignation, and he gave her a smiling shake of the head and began at once to engage the man in conversation. She couldn't understand a word of it, but the man looked annoyed, frightened and then downright cowed, muttering answers to the questions the doctor was putting to him in his calm, commanding manner. It didn't surprise her in the least that the man, after one final mutter, banged the door and Lucius said on a laugh: 'I feel sure that you are about to tell me that this creature is an answer from heaven, although he is hardly the breed I would have chosen. But it really won't do, you know. Maureen refuses to live in the same house as tame mice, so she will most certainly not agree to a dog—and such a dog!'

Phoebe bit back the forceful things she wished to say about Maureen.

'Oh, please,' she entreated softly, 'couldn't you— just him, not the mice—I'm sure he's a dear little dog and Paul would love him. Look how sweet he is!'

A gross exaggeration, she was aware, as she studied the puny, shivering puppy tucked in her arms. He stared back at her hopefully and heaved a sigh which caused his ribs to start through his deplorable coat. She went on urgently: 'We can't let him go back to that awful man.'

'Set your mind at rest, I have rashly acquired him.'

'Oh, Lucius, you dear!' she burst out, and modified this rash remark with rather stiff thanks and an enquiry as to what was to happen to the animal.

The doctor sighed. 'It just so happens that I have a friend living close by,' he sounded amused and resigned at the same time. 'He is a vet—and don't, I beg of you, tell me that he is an answer from heaven too.

I suggest that we take him along now and see what he makes of the little beast.'

They came out of the *steeg* into the Koornmarkt and the vet's house was a bare minute's walk away. He was a man of Lucius' own age and almost as quiet, who listened to Phoebe's earnest explanations, examined the puppy carefully, gave it his opinion that it should do well with proper care and food and bore them both off to drink coffee with his wife while the puppy was taken off to be bathed.

When they left shortly after a brief visit to the now clean animal, Phoebe expressed the view that he was a handsome dog, despite his undernourished frame. She wondered, out loud, what sort of a dog he might be and was indignant when Lucius laughed.

'I shall buy him a collar and a lead,' she declared. 'They will make a birthday present for Paul.' She stopped and turned to look at Lucius. 'You are going to give him to Paul, aren't you?' she asked, suddenly anxious.

He took her arm. 'Of course, but on one condition, that you are at my house by four o'clock tomorrow, for I can see that I shall need all the support I can get when that animal makes his entry.'

Chapter 7

The tea party was in full swing when Phoebe arrived at the doctor's house the following afternoon. She was surprised to find quite a number of people in the sitting room. Two-thirds of them were children, which was to be expected, the remainder were older people—aunts, uncles and a fair sprinkling of guests whom she had already met or seen in or around the hospital—and of course Maureen. One glimpse of her, in a sleeveless green dress, her hair piled in a cluster of curls, silver sandals on her bare feet, was enough to make Phoebe thankful that she had taken extra pains with her own toilette and had put on a blue silk jersey dress which highlighted her eyes in a most satisfactory manner, and added blue kid sandals to match it. Her hair she had done as she always did, rather severely drawn back from her face, and she wore no jewellery at all. She

greeted the doctor sustained by the knowledge that
she looked as nice, if not nicer than the governess; the
thought added a sparkle to her eye and a faint pink to
her cheeks and Lucius, greeting her, paused to take a
second look.

'And what have you been up to?' he wanted to know.
'You look—pleased with yourself.'

She looked at him with innocent eyes. 'Me? Nothing—I've been working all the morning.' She gave
him a smile and crossed the room to wish Paul a happy
birthday. 'And I've something for you, but I'll give it
to you later,' she explained as Arie Lagemaat bore her
off to a corner, where he produced tea and cake for her,
saying: 'Mies told me to look out for you.'

'If I'd known, I would have changed my off duty so
that she could have come—she has far more right to
be here than I have.'

He smiled nicely. 'You're mistaken there. I'm waiting for the great moment.'

'Oh—do you know?'

He nodded and smiled as his eyes met hers. 'I'm to
tell Mies all about it later.'

'Do you think...?' she began, then caught sight of
Mijnheer van Vliet, the vet, standing in the doorway.
A moment later Lucius crossed the room to where Paul
was standing with his own friends. He took the wicker
box hesitantly, his eyes on the doctor's face, and then,
at the small snuffling sound from it, opened it in a
rush. He and the puppy eyed each other for a brief moment and then the boy lifted him out to hold him tight
against his chest. 'Is he really for me, Papa?' he asked
in a strained little voice.

'Yes, for you, Paul—your very own dog.'

Phoebe thought that Paul was going to burst into tears, but instead he said in an excited voice: 'Oh, Papa, thank you! He's so beautiful and so—so noble—I shall call him Rex.'

As he spoke his eyes slid past Lucius to where Maureen was standing. They held pleading and defiance, but she turned her head away as Lucius went on: 'He's been ill, so I'm afraid Oom Domus will have to take him back for a few more days, but you shall go and see him each day and we'll have him home just as soon as he's fit—and as to thanking me, Paul, it is Phoebe whom you should thank for it was she who begged me to have him—you see, someone had just thrown him out and she rescued him.'

Everyone looked at her so that she smiled in lunatic fashion and retreated as far as possible behind Arie, feeling a fool. But when Paul came across to her, the puppy still clutched close, she forgot about the others. 'You really like him, Paul? I thought he had the sweetest face and such soft eyes. He's going to be happy with you; you'll grow up together.' She produced her own present. 'I thought he might wear these just to begin with, until he's learned to obey you, you know.'

She undid the small parcel for him, because he had no intention of letting go of the dog, and watched while he exclaimed over the red collar and lead.

'I don't know much about dogs,' he told her gruffly as he thanked her.

'Something you'll learn very quickly as you go along,' she assured him comfortably, 'and I'm sure Mijnheer van Vliet will give you lots of good advice, and your papa too.' She stroked the puppy's black nose, 'I'm glad he's made you happy, Paul,' she said.

He turned to go back to his friends and then came close to her to whisper so that she had to bend down to hear what he was saying.

'I don't think you're a scheming woman at all—Maureen says I mustn't like you, but I do.'

She said nothing, fearful of breaking the first threads of a friendship which was still too fragile to risk breaking with a careless word. She left soon after that, after a quiet goodbye to Lucius and an exchange of polite words with Maureen, whom, she suspected, was very angry indeed, for as they parted Maureen said with deceptive friendliness: 'You and I must meet some time, Phoebe—I'm sure we have a great deal to say to each other.'

'I'm free on Thursday,' said Phoebe, if she had to grasp the nettle she might as well get it over with, 'can't we meet for tea?'

'My dear, I work, or had you forgotten? But I'll think of something.'

Lucius saw her to the door. On its step he observed blandly: 'I had no idea that you and Maureen were such good friends,' and something in his voice made her look at him sharply, but there was nothing but polite interest in his face.

'We—we know each other very well,' she answered carefully.

He leaned against the heavy door. 'You surprise me. I had quite the reverse impression—which just shows you how unobservant I am.'

She smiled at him. 'Now it's my turn to say I had quite the reverse impression, despite your notebook.'

His hand went to his pocket. 'Good heavens—wait!' He was thumbing through it. 'I know I made a note— yes, here it is. Have I asked you to dine with me this evening? If not, I'm asking you now.'

She laughed. 'No, you didn't, and if I say yes, will you remember that I did?'

He stared down at her. 'Oh, yes, I shall remember. Thank you for making Paul's birthday such a happy one.'

'It wasn't me—you said yourself that it was an answer from heaven.'

He held her two hands in his, staring down at her, and she wondered what he was going to say. When he spoke she was disappointed.

'*Tot ziens*, then. I'll pick you up at the hospital at eight o'clock.'

It was on her way back that she began to wonder why he wasn't taking Maureen out that evening. She might have another engagement, but she was hardly likely to be pleased if he went off with someone else—perhaps he wasn't going to tell her; perhaps their understanding of each other was so complete that it just didn't matter. If she were Maureen, though, she wouldn't share Lucius with anyone, however platonically.

There was one dress in her wardrobe which she hadn't worn yet, a pastel patterned crêpe. She belted it around her slim waist, caught up a coat and went downstairs as the clock struck eight.

She hadn't given much thought as to where Lucius would take her, for she had been far too excited to think sensibly about anything, and the sight of him, standing on the hospital steps, smoking his pipe and exchanging the time of day with the porter on duty, most effectively splintered the cool she had struggled so hard to maintain.

As they got into the car, Lucius said, 'I thought we'd try Schevingenen—everyone goes there. It's a kind of Dutch Brighton, and if you don't pay it at least one visit, no one will believe you've been to Holland.'

They were out of Delft, streaking down the motorway towards den Haag and the coast, before she said diffidently: 'I thought you would be going out with Paul and Maureen—you know, for a birthday treat.'

He sounded as though he was laughing. 'I took Paul to lunch—Reyndorp's Prinsenhof, I expect you've been there? and we spent the evening at van Vliet's, getting acquainted with Rex. Paul has gone to bed a very happy little boy.'

'I'm glad,' said Phoebe, and wished he would mention Maureen, but he didn't. They entered into a light-hearted conversation about dogs which led, somehow, to talking about her home, and by the time he had parked the car outside the Corvette Restaurant, nothing mattered but the delightful fact that they were to spend the evening together.

It was a gay place and crowded and the menu was enormous. She studied it, hoping for some clue from her companion. It was quickly forthcoming. 'I'm famished,' observed Lucius. 'Paul's idea of lunch is consistent with his age group—*pofferjes*, ice-cream and some mammoth sausage rolls—you see, on his birthday, he plays host and orders the food—I merely eat it.'

Phoebe laughed. 'It sounds frightful, but I expect he loved it and thought you did too.' She added helpfully, 'I'm hungry.'

He sighed with exaggerated relief. 'Good—let's have herring balls with our drinks and then oyster soup, duckling stuffed with apples, and finish with Gateau St Honoré?'

It sounded delicious, although she wasn't sure about the oysters; perhaps they would look different in soup, but by the time they had had their drinks and demolished the herring balls, she was prepared to like anything. Over their meal she found herself telling Lucius exactly why she had taken Sybil's place. 'I thought it was an awful thing to do at first,' she explained a little shyly, 'and then Sybil was so determined to leave, and all the arrangements had been made—and I was longing for a change.' Her voice, without her knowing it, was wistful.

'Ah, yes,' his voice was gentle, 'and to get away from someone, perhaps?'

The excellent Burgundy they had been drinking betrayed her. 'Well, yes, that too—though he did turn up at the wedding.'

Lucius lifted a hand to the waiter and sat back comfortably while the plates were changed. 'And does that mean that there will be more wedding bells?' His tone was so casual that she answered almost without thought.

'Heavens, no! It was just that he was put out because I didn't fall into his arms like a ripe plum.' She added ingenuously: 'I've forgotten what he looks like.'

'Yes?' he smiled. 'You're more of a peach than a

plum, you know. One is sorry for the young man.' He speared a portion of duck. 'But you have another admirer, did you know?'

She kept her eyes on her plate. Maureen or not, had she at last made an impression on his vague abstraction?

'Paul,' he went on cheerfully. 'A bit of a slow starter, wasn't he? But now you're female number one in his world. Maureen had better look out.'

And so had I, thought Phoebe, but all she said was: 'How charming of him. I should like to be friends.'

'Nice of you, Phoebe, after that strange episode in the warehouse. I find it hard to imagine that he did it purely for fun—he must have had some reason.' His eyes searched hers across the table, and silently she agreed with him. Aloud she said comfortably: 'Oh, you know what boys are like, always up to something.' She looked around, desperate to get the conversation on to an impersonal level. 'What a delightful place this is. I expect you come here often.'

His eyes twinkled. 'No—why should I? Only when I'm celebrating something.'

'Paul's birthday; it was kind of you to ask me.'

His lips twitched, but he said no more on the subject, but presently asked her how many more weeks she had in Holland.

'Three—less than that.' She forced her voice to sound cheerful, thinking with dismay that the time was indeed short, and a week of it night duty, too. For the first time for some weeks she wondered what she would do when she got back to England. She might have pursued this melancholy train of thought if her companion hadn't said to surprise her: 'The time has gone very slowly, but probably you haven't found it so.'

Phoebe stared at him, her pretty mouth slightly open. 'No—I haven't. It's all fresh for me and everything's strange, but I expect it's different for you—one nurse after the other coming for a few weeks and then going again. I forget I'm one of a number.'

He didn't answer, only turned as the waiter arrived at the table.

'Ah, here is the famous Gateau St Honoré,' he observed. 'I think it deserves a bottle of champagne, don't you?'

She was on the point of begging him to curb his extravagance, but when she caught the gleam in his eyes, she closed her mouth firmly. Only when the waiter had gone and they were drinking it did he ask her:

'And what were you on the point of saying, dear girl? I have the impression that you disapprove of champagne—surely not?'

'Of course I don't.' She hesitated and went rather red. 'I—I just thought it was—well, champagne is rather expensive—you know, it's for special occasions.'

'You don't consider this a special occasion?' He was teasing her now. 'Besides, let me set your mind at rest. I have quite enough money to drink champagne with every meal if I should wish to do anything so foolish.'

The red deepened; the knowledge vexed her. 'I beg your pardon,' she said stiffly, 'I had no intention of prying.'

'You're not prying,' he told her placidly. 'I volunteered the information, didn't I? I'm flattered that you were kind enough to consider my pocket—not many girls would.'

The blush which she had succeeded in quenching to some extent returned. 'That's unusual too,' he went on, 'a girl who blushes. Drink your champagne, we're going for a walk.'

They went first to the southern end of the promenade where the fishing harbour, packed with herring boats, lay under the clear evening sky. There was a great deal to see, at least for Phoebe, who found the fishermen's wives in their voluminous dresses and white caps quite fascinating. They lingered there while Lucius explained the variations of costume to her; he explained about the annual race by the herring boats to bring back the first herrings, too, and showing no sign of impatience, answered her fusillade of questions about one thing and another. And when she had seen enough, he took her arm and walked her back, the boulevard on one side, the firm, fine sand and the sea on the other, until they reached the lighthouse at the other end, pausing to examine the obelisk marking the exact spot where William had landed after the Napoleonic wars, and then walked back again.

It was a fine evening, pleasantly warm and fresh after the rain, and there were a great many people about, strolling along arm in arm, just as they were. Phoebe heaved a sigh of content because for the moment at any rate, she was happy, and although she told herself it was probably the champagne, she knew quite well that it was because she was with Lucius. And make the most of it, my girl, she admonished herself silently.

It was dark by the time they got back to the Kurhaus Hotel; strings of lights festooned the boulevard; the café and restaurants still crowded, were ablaze with lights too, and there was music everywhere. It seemed a fitting end to their evening to sit outside the restaurant, looking at the sea and drinking a final cup of coffee, and surprisingly, still with plenty to say to each other, although thinking about it later, Phoebe was forced to admit that she had done most of the talking.

It was midnight when they reached the hospital and when she began a little speech of thanks as they got out of the car Lucius stopped her with: 'No need of thanks, Phoebe. I haven't enjoyed myself so much for a long time—and I'm coming in—I want to have a look at Wil.'

But that didn't stop her from thanking him just the same, once they were in the hospital. The hall porter had his back to them, there was no one else about. Lucius heard her out, clamped her immovable with his hands on her shoulders and kissed her soundly. 'Go to bed,' he said, 'my delightful Miss Brook.'

She didn't see him at all the next day, and when Doctor Pontier came to do a round on the following morning, she asked with careful casualness where he was.

Her companion gave her a quick look. 'The boss is in den Haag,' he told her. 'Some international meeting or other—it lasts three days, I believe. He's there all day; doesn't get home until the evening and leaves again early each morning.'

She murmured something. Lucius hadn't said anything to her when they had been out together, but then, her common sense told her, why should he? She refused an invitation to the cinema, pleading a headache, and went off to cope with little Wil, who was poorly again.

She had just got off duty that afternoon and was on her way up to her room when the warden called after her that there was a young lady to see her. At least Phoebe, understanding only a few words, guessed that was the message. She turned and went downstairs again; it would be Maureen, her instinct warned her—and it was. Phoebe, seeing her sitting there in the comfortable rather drab little sitting room she shared with the other staff nurses, regretted that she had had no warning of her visitor; she would have re-done her face at least and tidied her hair. She said: 'Hullo, Maureen,' and her visitor smiled from her chair and said slowly: 'Hullo. My dear, how frightfully worthy you look in that uniform, though I must say it's a bit ageing—perhaps you're just tired.'

Phoebe sat down in a small overstuffed chair, smiled her acknowledgement of this remark, and waited for Maureen to begin.

'This business with that damned dog—how clever of you, Phoebe. Did you hope to win Paul over to your side because you knew Lucius is soft about him? If you did, you're more of a fool than I thought. What did you hope to gain, I wonder? Lucius? Oh, I've seen your face when you look at him, so don't pretend that you're not interested. But it's no good, my dear, I've got him where I want him—I only have to whistle and he'll come, he and his home and his cars and his lovely bank balance. You see he thinks Paul adores me and he would do anything for the boy.'

'You'll have Paul too,' Phoebe said flatly.

'I've got him where I want him too, so hands off. I must say you've got a nerve, coming here and making doe's eyes at Lucius. And don't think that you've stolen a march on me with your dinners at Schevingenen and your birthday tea parties and your Florence Nightingale act...'

'How incredibly vulgar you are!' Phoebe spoke in a cool voice which quite hid her rage, bubbling away inside her and threatening to burst out of her at any moment. 'And do you really suppose that I should listen to you? Why, you don't even like me, and that's good enough reason to take no notice of anything you say.' She got to her feet and walked to the door. 'I'm sorry for Lucius—and Paul.'

In her room she took off her uniform, had a bath and then sat on her bed, having a good cry, which, while playing havoc with her face, did her feelings a great deal of good. She had no intention of heeding Maureen, and what could the girl do anyway? She would have to wait for Lucius to ask her to marry him—Phoebe's heart gave a joyful little bound because he hadn't done that yet, and until then, if Lucius asked her to go out with him again, she would most certainly go. He might not be in love with her, but at least he enjoyed her company, even if she could delay Maureen's plans for another week or two. She closed her eyes on the awful vision of Maureen, married to Lucius—but Lucius might not have made up his mind; he was a deliberate man, not given to impulsive action, at least it was a straw to clutch at.

Phoebe dressed and went down to tea and, carried on the high tide of hope, went out and bought a new dress, something suitable for dinner or an evening out—green and silky and extremely becoming. It was a shocking price; she told herself she was a fool throwing money away on a forlorn hope, but she felt a great deal more cheerful as she left the shop.

She saw Paul the next morning, hurrying along the Koornmarkt. It amused her a little to see how cautiously he looked around him before he crossed the road to speak to her. 'I'm going to see Rex,' he told her. 'I suppose you wouldn't like to come with me?'

Phoebe agreed promptly. The vet's house was close by, and she had half an hour to spare. She occupied the short journey with questions about the puppy and listened to the little boy's happy chatter—Rex was to come home in a day or so, he told her; his papa would be back by then to help him decide where the puppy should sleep and what he should eat and when he should go for his walk. There was no doubt about it, Paul was a changed child, and changed towards her too, for at the vet's door he said in an off-hand voice: 'I'm glad I met you. Maureen won't talk about him, you see, and Else hasn't much time, though she says she'll like to have a dog in the house.'

Mijnheer van Vliet was home. He took them through the surgery to his house where Rex was waiting for them, a very different dog from the miserable little creature she had picked up. He flung himself at Paul and watching them together, Phoebe could only hope that Maureen would relent and at least treat the puppy with kindness even if she disliked it. After all, it would be Paul who would be looking after the dog. She met the vet's eyes and smiled. 'They're made for each other, aren't they? I must go I'm on duty in an hour.'

She was at the door when Paul ran up to her and said in a conspirator's voice: 'You won't tell Maureen about us coming here, will you?'

'No, dear, not if you don't want me to anyway, I seldom see her, do I, so it's not very likely I should mention it. But why not, Paul? You're not afraid?'

He wouldn't answer her, but ran back to Rex, leaving her to wonder if Maureen had forbidden him to have anything to do with her, but surely that was a bit high-handed?

The following day was Mies' day off which meant that Phoebe would have charge of the ward from two o'clock until the night nurses came on duty. The ward was quiet when she took over. There was no one very ill, only little Wil, sitting in her cot, her small chest labouring, her face too thin and white. True, she looked no worse than she had done for several days, but Phoebe wasn't happy about her. She confided her opinion to the invaluable Zuster Pets, who, although she didn't know much about it, promised to keep a careful watch on the child.

But it was Phoebe who was there when, just at seven o'clock when the ward was at its busiest, little Wil collapsed. Doctor Pontier had been to see her at teatime and although he shared Phoebe's vague fears, he had been unable to find anything wrong. Phoebe decided that she was being over-anxious—all the same, she

found herself taking a look at Wil at more and more
frequent intervals. And lucky for her that she had, she
muttered as she switched on the oxygen, plugged in the
sucker and rang the emergency bell by the cot. There
was no one in the end ward at that moment. When she
heard someone behind her she said: 'Pets—keep the
other children out and send for Doctor Pontier.'

'Will I do?' Lucius' voice was quiet. She looked
over her shoulder at him, unable to keep the joy out of
her face or her voice.

'Lucius,' she spoke his name instinctively, and then,
remembering where she was, 'Wil has collapsed, sir,
she's been off colour all day. Doctor Pontier came to
see her at teatime, but he couldn't find anything—a
slight temp, but she's had that on and off for a day or
two.' She had put a thermometer under Wil's arm and
she withdrew it now.

'Forty-point-two centigrade,' she told him, 'and a
racing pulse.'

There was no need to tell him the respiration rate,
he could see the small heaving chest for himself. He
was already sitting on the cot, his stethoscope out, his
hands moving quietly over the bony little body. Presently he looked up. 'You know what this is?' he asked.

'Empyema?' she ventured, and glowed at his appreciative nod.

'Good girl, yes—rapid symptoms, I must say, but
I'll stake my reputation on it. Let's try an aspiration.'

Zuster Pets had arrived, solid and dependable. Lucius spoke to her and she went away again and he got
off the cot and took off his jacket. 'I'll just scrub—stay
here, Phoebe, and keep a sharp eye open. We'll need

an X-ray—get someone to warn them. Ah, Pontier, just in time...' He switched over to his own language and Phoebe, passing on the instructions he had given her, went back to her patient.

The X-ray confirmed the diagnosis; Wil would have to go to theatre and have the cavity drained of the pus which had accumulated there. Phoebe was kept busy for the next half hour getting the small creature ready for the small, vital operation, and when she had seen her safely theatrewards, the faithful Pets in attendance, she applied herself to the preparation of the drainage bottles, the making up of the cot and all the small paraphernalia needed for the night.

Wil was back, perched up against her pillows, when Lucius came in. After he had bent over his small patient he turned to Phoebe. 'Fortunately we were able to tackle it at once—I've rarely seen one with such urgent symptoms—in fact,' he grinned at her, 'I've rarely seen one.'

Phoebe folded a small blanket and hung it over the end of the cot.

'I'm so glad!'

'It was thanks to you, Phoebe. No, I know what you're going to say, but you were quick off the mark. Well, I'm off home, I told them I'd be back an hour ago. Pontier will keep an eye on things.'

He nodded and walked rapidly away, but halfway down the ward he came back again. 'I'm almost sure I've forgotten something—I'll telephone if it's anything important.'

It was Sunday the next day and Phoebe's day off again, and although she had no reason to get up early, she did, because lying in bed was too conducive to thought, and she didn't want to think. She made tea and nibbled toast, then sat on her bed, wondering what to do. The beach would be crowded and it wouldn't be much fun on her own, and the idea of a bus trip didn't appeal. She was looking at her guide book when Zuster Pets knocked on the door. 'There's a telephone call for you,' she declared. 'It's Doctor van Someren.'

Phoebe flew to the telephone. It was Wil, of course—something had gone wrong. She snatched up the receiver and said Hullo in a breathless voice.

'Hullo,' said Lucius in her ear. 'You sound terrified—what's the matter?'

'Wil,' she managed.

'Doing well. Tell me, did I invite you to spend the day with us?'

'No.'

'Ah, then that is what I forgot yesterday evening on the ward. Will you?'

'Well…' began Phoebe, disciplining her tongue not to shout an instant yes.

'Good—I'm taking Paul to Noordwijk for a swim, then I thought we might go for a run round for a while. Else has promised us a bumper tea when we get back.'

'Nice! I'd like to, thank you.' Maureen's brilliant image floated before her in the telephone box, but she dismissed it firmly. 'When shall I be ready?'

'Half an hour. We'll pick you up.'

Phoebe dressed like lightning, not bothering with make-up and tying her hair back with a ribbon to match the pink cotton. The half hour was up as she rammed her beach clothes into her shoulder bag.

Paul was sitting in the back with Rex on his knee and there was no sign of Maureen. Phoebe smiled widely at the three of them and got in beside Lucius, who leaned over her to shut the door, remarking: 'Paul was sure you would never be ready—half an hour isn't long.' His gaze swept over her and he smiled nicely. 'But you seem to have made good use of it.'

She flushed faintly and turned to ask Paul about Rex, and the journey to the beach was wholly taken up by a cheerful three-sided conversation about dogs and Rex in particular.

'Is he home for good?' Phoebe wanted to know.

Paul nodded happily. 'Yes, today—we've just fetched him. He'll have all day to get used to being with us before Maureen comes…' He broke off and Lucius said mildly:

'Oh, come now, old chap, Maureen will like him, you see if she doesn't, once he's a member of the family. He only needs to learn his manners—she'll be enchanted with him.'

An opinion to which Phoebe found herself unable to subscribe.

The day was an enormous success; it was still too early for the beach to be crowded. They swam, sunbathed, swam again, and then, after Phoebe had made coffee for them all in the chalet and Rex had renewed his energy with a bowl of milk, they got back into the car. An early lunch, Lucius decreed; they went back inland to Oegsgeest, to de Beukenhof, an inn standing in its own garden and renowned for its cooking. They ate splendidly—Boeuf Stroganoff and strawberries and cream—and Rex, on his best behaviour, sat under Paul's chair.

They went north after that, to Alkmaar and on to den Helder and across the Afsluitdijk, where Lucius, to please Paul, allowed the Jaguar to show a fine burst of speed. But once on the mainland again, he turned off the main road, idling along the dyke roads as far as Lemmer before taking to the main road again, to race across the Noord Oost polder to Kampen and Zwolle and eventually to the motorway to Amsterdam and Delft. Phoebe, trying to see everything at once and failing singularly, found the day passing too quickly. It had been perfect—Paul was friends at last, Maureen wasn't there with her barbed quips and sly jokes, and Lucius—Lucius was the perfect companion; even if she hadn't loved him she would have allowed him that. True, he was not a man to draw attention to himself in any way, but he had a dry humour which she found de-lightful and even in the traffic snarl-ups they encoun-tered from time to time, he remained cool and placid, and when the road was free before then, he drove at speed with the same placid coolness. Phoebe sat be-side him and thought how wonderful it would be to be married to him—an impossible dream. She shook her head free of it and, obedient to Paul's advice, gazed out of the window at a particularly picturesque windmill.

They had a sumptuous tea in the garden, sitting by the water, all of them talking a great deal and doing full justice to the sandwiches and cakes Else had provided. Phoebe was surprised at Lucius' lighthearted mood. Listening to his mild teasing, she wondered how she could ever have found him absent-minded and vague.

Was this his true self, she hazarded, or had he been like this all the time and she hadn't noticed because she had started out expecting him to be exactly as Sybil had described him? She filled the tea cups again, reflecting that it really didn't matter; she loved him whatever he was.

She watched him carry the tea tray back into the house and longed to stay there, in the garden by the water, with the church bells ringing from a dozen churches and Rex snoring on Paul's knee, but she got to her feet as Lucius rejoined them, saying: 'I think I must be getting back—letter to write...'

Such a silly excuse, but it would have to do. She failed to see his smile and found it disconcerting when he said at once: 'I'll drop you off—I want to go to St Bonifacius myself.'

It wasn't until he drew up outside its doors and they were walking up the steps together that he said: 'I'll be here at half past seven—will that suit you? We'll find somewhere quiet to have dinner.'

Phoebe stood on the top step, looking up at him, waiting for her heart to slow and give her the breath to speak. 'I'd like that,' she managed, and went across to the Home on wings, for wasn't there a new dress in the cupboard, waiting to be worn?

Before she went to sleep that night, she tried to recall every second of the evening and couldn't. There was too much to remember; the drive along the motorway to Arnhem, and the village Scherpenzel, such a funny name where in De Witte Hoelvoet, they had eaten their dinner, not one single item of which could she recall. They had lingered over their meal and it had been late when Lucius stopped the Jaguar outside the hospital once more, and despite her protests had walked into the quiet entrance hall with her and in the centre of its utter quiet, had taken her in his arms and kissed her, and this time he hadn't been in the least vague.

She lay in bed, fighting sleep, thinking about it, and when at last she allowed her eyes to close, she dreamed of him.

Chapter 8

Phoebe was due for night duty again at the end of the week, and that meant that in no time at all she would be going home. She began, half-heartedly, to think about the future; perhaps it would be a good idea to go right away—Australia perhaps, or Canada. She had always wanted to travel, but now that urge seemed to have left her and the prospect of doing so daunted her. But there were good nursing jobs to be had in either country, although even the other side of the world, she reflected sadly, wasn't far enough away for her to forget Lucius.

She hadn't seen him for two days now. He was at Leyden, Mies had told her, a member of the Board of Examiners at the Academisch Ziekenhuis, adding diffidently that her Arie hoped to be elected to that august body in a few years' time, which remark naturally led the conversation away from Lucius to the fascinating one of her own future.

'We shall marry quite soon,' Mies confided happily, digressing briefly to explain the laws governing marriage in the Netherlands. 'Arie has a good salary and a splendid job and there will be a flat for us… I shall not work.' She eyed Phoebe speculatively. 'I do not understand how it is arranged, but why should you not take my place as Hoofd Zuster when I leave? You know the work well and you please Lucius, and if you take lessons you will soon learn Dutch—you are a clever girl.'

The prospect appalled Phoebe. It would be an impossibility to stay in Delft, seeing Lucius every day, but only as his Ward Sister, while Maureen… She shuddered delicately. She had done some hard thinking during the last few days; Maureen had told her that she had Lucius just where she wanted him, and although she didn't want to believe it, it was probably true. She was an attractive girl and she knew how to make herself charming, and almost certainly Lucius believed that Paul adored her. Phoebe sighed. How blind could a man be? And he had told her himself that he was going to get married; probably, she thought bitterly, he regarded her as an old friend to whom he could confide his plans.

She ground her excellent teeth and because she didn't want to hurt Mies' feelings, shook her head regretfully.

'It's a lovely idea,' she agreed mendaciously, 'but I don't think it would succeed. For one thing, there must be lots of Dutch nurses with better qualifications than

I, who want the job, and for another I doubt if I could get a work permit for an unlimited period.'

Neither of which reasons were insurmountable, but they sounded authentic, because Mies nodded regretfully. 'That is so—a pity. And now that you are here, we will arrange your free days. I have had such a splendid idea. You have but a week of day duty when you come off nights. I will give you only two nights off, the others you shall add to your day off at the end of your last week, thus you will be able to go home three days earlier than you expect.'

She looked so pleased with herself that Phoebe could not but agree with an enthusiasm she didn't feel. She had no wish to go home three days earlier—three days during which she might see Lucius—she had, in fact, no wish to go home at all.

And not only was time growing short, but everything else seemed against her, for the very evening she went on night duty, the weather changed dramatically to a chilling rain and a fierce wind from the sea which, even if Lucius had suggested it, and he hadn't, would have put their morning swim out of the question. Phoebe's hope that the weather would clear in a day or so proved a forlorn one; if anything it became steadily worse, and her temper with it, largely because she never saw Lucius at all—not until her fourth night on duty, and then he was in Maureen's company.

Phoebe had had a busy night, the third of her week's work. She had gone to bed tired and dispirited and quite unable to sleep. After several hours, during which time her thoughts were of no consolation to her at all, she got up, made herself some tea, wrote a letter home and decided that since it was only six o'clock and she had several hours before she needed to go on duty, she might as well go out and post it. A walk would do her good, she told herself, bundling on her raincoat and knotting a scarf under her chin with no thought for her appearance. She was on her way back, feeling hollow-eyed and pale from lack of sleep, when the Jaguar slid past her with Lucius at the wheel and Maureen beside him.

Maureen had seen her. Before Phoebe could cross the road, Lucius, obedient to his companion's direction, pulled the car into the curb.

It was Maureen who opened the conversation. 'My word,' she said in a voice which dripped a bogus sympathy, 'you do look a wreck! Just look at her, Lucius—the poor thing should be in bed—red-rimmed eyes and no colour!'

Phoebe managed a smile in answer to this perfidious attack. 'Oh, we all look like this after a few nights,' she said in a slightly brittle voice. 'You should try it and see.'

Her smile was as brittle as her voice. Probably it looked grotesque on her pallid face—she didn't care; she included Lucius in it just to let him see how fabulous she felt. But it was a useless effort, for he leaned across Maureen and said: 'Phoebe, you look fagged out. Are you all right?'

Before she could reply Maureen's gay voice cut in: 'You look at least thirty, my dear! I had no idea that a few nights out of bed could play such havoc with a girl's looks. You poor dear, going to a hard night's work just as we're starting out to spend our evening...'

Phoebe suddenly didn't want to hear how they were going to spend their evening; there was a gap in the traffic. With a hasty: 'I must go, or I shall be late,' she fled across the street.

It was after ten o'clock when Lucius came into the ward. She hadn't expected him, naturally enough— indeed, her evening had been made wretched by the thought of him wining and dining Maureen at some fabulous place, drinking champagne and living it up. She and the student nurse had just finished clearing up the mess after one of the smaller children had been sick. She was going down the ward, wrapped in a plastic apron a good deal too large for her, pushing the runabout full of linen to be sluiced. She eyed him uncertainly, decided that to get rid of the runabout was more important than going to meet him and with a murmured: 'I won't be a moment, sir,' she made for the sluice door. He opened it for her and followed her inside, so that she paused in her tracks and exclaimed in a shocked voice: 'Oh, you mustn't come in here, sir!'

'Why not?' he asked lazily. 'Is it sacrosanct?'

Which despite herself, moved her to hushed laughter. 'Don't be ridiculous! It just isn't—isn't suitable for you. Who did you want to see?'

He shrugged wide shoulders. 'My patients—no hurry. Tell me, Phoebe, do you find night duty too much for you? You looked exhausted this evening. Maureen thought…'

It was too much! Phoebe hurled her noisome bundle into the sink and turned on the tap. 'How kind of her to concern herself—I daresay she pointed out my haggard looks with a wealth of detail. I only hope it didn't spoil your evening together.' She turned off the tap with quite unnecessary violence and turned to face him where he lounged against the tiled wall.

He spoke blandly. 'Well, perhaps night duty may not exhaust you, but it certainly sharpens your temper.' He put his hands in his pockets and crossed his legs comfortably. 'As it happens I spent the evening at home—with Paul—and when he had gone to bed, I went to my study and worked, and a good thing I did, it seems, for you appear to grudge me any amusement I may care to arrange for myself.'

There was a wicked gleam in his eye which she ignored. 'I don't!' she declared hotly. 'What about…' She was about to remind him of their evening at Schevingenen and the dinner they had had together, but instead she said with a haughtiness which sat ill on her unglamorous appearance: 'I'm not in the least interested in your private life,' and started to tear off her apron. It was a pity that she hadn't thought to take off her rubber gloves first. After watching her wrestling with an ever-tightening knot Lucius offered mildly: 'If you'll turn round, I'll do it.'

She stood, her back like a ramrod, while he worked away at it, and when he had freed her he said in quite a different voice impersonal, a little cool: 'Good. Now if I might take a quick look at this vomiting infant before I go…'

He went shortly afterwards, wishing her a pleasant good night, whistling softly as he went down the stairs. Phoebe, her pen poised over a chart, listened to his footsteps growing fainter and fainter. They seemed symbolic of the future; she closed her eyes on sudden tears and then opened them resolutely and began to write in her neat hand.

It was two mornings later, as she was on her way out for a morning walk before bed, that she was overtaken in the entrance hall by Mies, running and waving an envelope at her.

She thrust it at Phoebe and said, very out of breath: 'I remembered that you said that you would take a walk. These are reports for Doctor van Someren—they came by mistake to the ward, you understand, and he will not be here today—he is at Leyden, but he goes home, I think, and he can see them there. Please to hand them in at his house.' She smiled in her friendly fashion. 'It is no hardship for you to do this?'

'No hardship,' said Phoebe. He wouldn't be home, anyway, so it made no difference at all. She might encounter Maureen, but her mood was such that she really didn't care. Besides, she might just as well walk past his house as anywhere else.

It was another dreary day, but she hardly noticed the fine rain as she walked briskly through the streets, glad to be out in the fresh air after her hectic night, her mind empty of thought because she was tired. She took the shortest way, deciding to go and have coffee at the Prinsenkelder and then go straight back to bed and, she hoped, to sleep.

She could hear Rex yelping as she raised her hand to the heavy knocker on Lucius' door. She heard Maureen's high-pitched voice, shrill with fury, at the same time, and when no one came she tried the door. It opened under her hand and she went in.

Maureen was in the sitting room with her back to the door so that she didn't see Phoebe. She had the dog lead in her hand and cringing on the floor was the terrified Rex. As Phoebe paused in the doorway, appalled, she raised her arm to bring the lead down once more, but this time Phoebe, galvanised into sudden action, caught her arm from behind, wrenched the lead from her and threw it into the corner of the room.

'You're mad!' she declared incredulously, and turned her attention to the puppy. He was shivering, very frightened, and there was a cut over one of his boot-button eyes. He winced and yelped as she lifted him gently to try to discover if he were injured and was relieved to find that at least all four of his legs seemed normal; she had no idea how long Maureen had been beating him, but undoubtedly he was severely bruised, if nothing worse. She laid a soothing hand on his heaving little body and turned to speak to Maureen.

'You must be mad—whatever possessed you, to illtreat something so small and defenceless—and to hurt Paul? Why did you do it?'

Maureen flung herself into a chair. 'Oh, shut up,' she said roughly. 'Just my filthy luck for Else to go out and leave the door unlocked. Another few minutes and the little brute would have been dead. Take it away, Miss do-gooder, and I'll think up some tale or other about it running away.'

'You'll break Paul's heart—he loves Rex.'

The other girl laughed. 'Don't be such a fool! Do you think I care about that kid's feelings? Do you imagine that I enjoy being a governess? You're so dim. It serves my purpose, that's all—it keeps me near Lucius.'

Phoebe had gone to sit in a chair with Rex on her lap, examining him more carefully; neither of them heard the street door open, and both of them were taken by surprise when Lucius came into the room, but it was Maureen who recovered first. She was out of her chair in a flash, exclaiming: 'Lucius—thank heaven you've come! I'm in such a state! Rex ran out of the door and got knocked down by a car—Else left the door ajar when she went out. Luckily Phoebe came along with some message or other—I've not had the time to ask her—she's looking to see if he's badly hurt.' This remarkable speech had the effect of rendering Phoebe speechless. She gave Maureen an incredulous look and turned to Lucius, but he wasn't looking at either of them; he was bending over the puppy, examining him in his turn. Phoebe, seething with unspoken words, bit them back; a row wouldn't help Rex, for it would waste time. She said quickly: 'I hope he's not badly hurt.'

'It's hard to tell, but I don't think so. Probably the edge of the pavement or a stone cut his eyelid; he must have been tossed clear. Did the car stop?' He glanced briefly at Maureen.

'No—I didn't actually see it happen, only heard the noise—poor little beast.' Her voice was warmly sympathetic as she started to cross the floor towards them. 'I'll take him round to the vet—I can take the Mini…'

Phoebe caught her breath. 'No,' she said more sharply than she intended, 'I'll take him. Mijnheer van Vliet's house is close by—I'll carry Rex.'

There was a short pause until Lucius said deliberately: 'Thank you, but I shall take him myself and I'll pick up Paul from school at midday and take him along to see how Rex is shaping.' He picked up the puppy and started for the door and paused to ask of Phoebe: 'Why did you come?'

'I was asked to deliver some reports. I put them on the table in the hall.'

He nodded: 'Thanks,' and shut the door quietly behind him. There was silence after he had gone. Presently Phoebe left the house too, not speaking at all to Maureen, for she could think of nothing that she could say which might improve matters, and if she uttered the things she wanted to, it would probably make things hard for Paul as well as Rex. Besides, there was the chance that Maureen, after such a narrow shave, might change her ways. Phoebe hurried through the rain, wondering if and how she should tell Lucius about it and would he believe her if she did? Maureen was a clever girl, she would be able to turn a situation, however adverse to herself, to good advantage. Phoebe decided to wait until she was on the point of leaving Holland—only a few days away now. She would tell Lucius then and it would be up to him to sort things out for himself. She had forgotten her coffee. She walked around the streets aimlessly and was on her way back to the hospital when she suddenly decided to go and see Mijnheer van Vliet.

He received her very kindly and led her at once to the room at the back of the surgery where the sick animals were housed. Rex, looking sorry for himself, was in a basket, still shivering, but he opened one eye and looked at her warily and essayed to wag his tail.

'How is he?' asked Phoebe anxiously.

'He'll recover,' the vet smiled at her. 'He's a tough little chap—a few days and he'll be well again.' He added on a puzzled note: 'Only his injuries do not match up with a car accident. I am a little perplexed...'

'Look,' said Phoebe earnestly, wondering why she hadn't thought of telling him in the first place, 'it wasn't a car. I know how it happened, but you mustn't tell anyone—you'll understand why.'

She plunged into her tale, and when she had finished, Mijnheer van Vliet nodded his head. 'So that is the story, and a shocking one, but I must tell you that I am not altogether surprised. For some reason Maureen promised—oh, a couple of years ago, that she would give Paul a puppy. Always there have been reasons why she has not done so it is as if she punishes him by refusing his constant wish to have a dog and now he has Rex, a dog which she has not given him, and she is angry. I do not understand, but I thank you for telling me. I will say nothing, of course, but I promise you that I will keep an eye on him—daily visits perhaps, a check-up each week, something—and until then I will keep him safe here with me.' He eyed her thoughtfully. 'You do not feel that you should tell Lucius?'

She blinked her beautiful eyes in deep thought. 'No—you see Lucius thinks that Maureen is kind and good for Paul and that he's fond of her, and perhaps that is the truth—I don't know. Besides,' she paused, seeking the right words, 'they have known each other a long time, Lucius and Maureen. They're—they're old friends.'

Mijnheer van Vliet growled deeply, coughed hugely

and offered her coffee, making no comment. She refused the coffee, saying that she really would have to get back to the hospital and get some sleep, and after a final look at Rex, she walked back to the Home, too tired by now to think sensibly about anything, and as it turned out, too tired to sleep.

She went on duty looking distinctly haggard and not much caring. The ward was busy, there was a great deal to do, and it was almost one o'clock in the morning when she sat down at her desk in the now quiet ward and a few minutes later Lucius came, looking vast in the dim, shadowed surroundings. Phoebe got to her feet wearily and wished him good evening, and he said softly:

'Hullo, Phoebe—they're all OK, aren't they? I came to see you to tell you that Rex is better. He's to stay with van Vliet for a day or two.'

'And Paul?'

'He was upset, but he feels better now he's seen him.' He leaned over and turned the desk lamp on to her face. 'You've not slept,' he stated baldly, and then, to take her breath: 'What was wrong this morning?'

She faltered a little: 'Wrong? What do you mean?'

His voice was bland. 'You and Maureen. But I see you have no intention of telling me.'

'No.'

He nodded to himself. 'A little tiff, I suppose—you were tired, weren't you, and I daresay, short-tempered, and Maureen is no good with animals. She finds them a nuisance even when she wants to help them. I daresay you arrived just in time to prevent her having hysterics.'

Phoebe eyed him unsmilingly; he had called her short-tempered and somehow put her in the wrong. Well, let him find out for himself. 'You might say that,' she told him.

Lucius turned to go. 'Oh, Paul sent his love. He hopes you will go and see Rex.'

'Of course I will. Please give him my love.'

He lingered. 'You're friends at last. I wonder what stood in the way when you first met?'

She returned his thoughtful stare. 'I have no idea. Good night, sir.'

His lips twitched, he gave her a mocking smile. 'Good night, Nurse Brook.'

She went the following morning to see Rex and this time stayed for coffee with Mijnheer van Vliet and his wife. 'Rex is better,' the vet told her, 'but he's got some brutal weals on his back, poor little beast. He's on penicillin and he eats like a horse. Have you seen Lucius?'

'Yes—on the ward.'

'You didn't tell him?'

'No, and I don't intend to.' She got to her feet. 'Thank you for the coffee. May I come and see Rex again? When is he going home?'

Mijnheer van Vliet laughed. 'Tomorrow or the day after. Paul is longing to look after him and I find it hard to imagine that Maureen will repeat her actions.' He smiled grimly. 'If she does, then whatever you feel, I shall tell Lucius myself and he can find himself another governess.' He walked to the door with her. 'You will be back in England very soon, I understand. I am sorry to hear that; we shall miss you.'

Phoebe sped back to the hospital, wondering if Lucius would miss her too, or if he would forget about her going until she had gone and then wonder where she was.

She hoped that he would visit the ward that night, but this time it was Doctor Pontier. He wrote up a few charts, signed a couple of forms, asked her when she was leaving, hoped for the pleasure of taking her out before she did, and took himself off. He was a nice man, although he had a roving eye. Phoebe thought about him for perhaps ten seconds and then plunged back into her work.

She was late off duty in the morning. Everything had gone wrong—broken thermometers, cross children who refused to be washed, crosser ones who spat out their medicine and the cheerful ones who thought it fun to hide under the bedclothes and have a good romp before being hurried off to clean their teeth and wash their faces. Phoebe, a calm girl when it came to her work, took it all in good part, but by the time she left the ward she was tired enough to go straight to bed.

Breakfast, she promised herself as she went slowly to the dining room, and then a bath and bed. She had done the last night of her duty; she had two days off, so she would sleep until the afternoon, get up, have a walk and go back to bed again. The dining room was almost empty. Phoebe poured coffee, buttered some bread and sat down. She was half way through the coffee when she was told that there was someone to see her and it was urgent. She trailed up the stairs again—the ward had been all right when she left it. It wouldn't be Lucius in this weather; perhaps it was Rex—she hurried her lagging feet as she reached the entrance hall. Paul was there. He looked small and forlorn and wildly angry, and forgetting her tiredness Phoebe hurried to him.

'Paul—what's the matter? Rex?'

He stared at her for a moment and then began to pour out his tale, becoming quite incoherent and mixing Dutch and English together so that she was hard put to understand him. When he had finished she said in a calm voice: 'Let me get this straight, Paul—you stop me if I go wrong. Your father's away in England for how long? Two days. He fetched Rex back last night so that you should have him while he was away and this morning Maureen took him and shut him in the shed at the bottom of the garden, and made you go to school—how did she make you, my dear?'

Tears clogged his voice. 'She said it would be the worse for Rex if I didn't—that Papa had told her to do it, but I don't believe her. She's going to hurt him, I know she is.' He fixed her with a pleading eye. 'You must help me, please, Phoebe!'

'Yes, dear, of course I'll help you.'

His face brightened a little. 'You believe me, then?'

'Yes, of course I do. Where are Else and that girl who comes in the mornings?'

'Maureen told them they could have the day off. She does that when Papa's away—she tells them that he has said so, but he hasn't.'

She could well believe that. 'Any ideas?' she asked.

'Could we rescue Rex and run away, just till Papa comes home?'

She considered the idea. 'Is Maureen in the house?'

'Yes, she has friends in when Papa is away.'

She would! thought Phoebe savagely; there were a

number of questions she was going to ask, but not now. 'So she wouldn't notice if we slipped into the garden?'

He was quick. 'From the canal. Oh, Phoebe, how clever you are! I can borrow Jan Schipper's boat, he lives a little further along—no one will see us, they'll be in the sitting room.'

'Good, though we must be careful. We'll go now, just as soon as I've changed.' She paused, struck by a thought. 'Where can we go to?'

Paul put a hand to his mouth, his eyes huge above it. 'I don't know,' he mumbled. 'Oom Domus—but he's going to den Haag.'

'Think of someone!' Phoebe besought him. 'Aunts, uncles, friends, an old nanny…' He wouldn't know what an old nanny was—but he did.

He said at once: 'Papa's old nanny, Anna, she lives in Amsterdam, I know where. She loves him, she told me so.' He smiled. 'She'll help.'

Phoebe released a held breath. 'Good boy! Sit here and don't move. I'll be ten minutes.'

She was back in seven exactly, not perhaps looking her best, for she had flung on a cotton dress, belted her raincoat over it, concealed her untidy head under a scarf, caught up her shoulder bag, stuffed with a few necessities for the night and all the money she possessed, and raced downstairs again, full of false energy, her sapphire eyes blazing in a washed-out face.

'What about school?' she asked as they raced through the small back streets. When he told her simply that he hadn't been she forbore to say anything. Probably later on she would regret this whole business, but she could think of nothing else and she felt partly to

blame because she hadn't told Lucius about the beating
Rex had had. She thanked heaven silently that she had
nights off and was free to do what she liked.

They came out into the street where Lucius lived,
but at its other end, and Paul led her down a narrow
dark path between two houses, opened the wooden
door at its end and entered a garden. Phoebe hesitated.

'Paul,' she whispered, looking apprehensively over
her shoulder at the house beyond the well-kept lawn,
'isn't this private?'

'It's Jan's home, and he's at school. No one will see
us, and he won't mind.'

They had reached a small jetty, just like the one in
Lucius' garden, and Paul got into the small boat tied
to its side. Phoebe got in too; she wasn't sure about
Dutch law, but she had a nasty feeling that they could
be accused of stealing. 'Undo the rope,' Paul told her.
He had the oars out and was already swinging the boat
outwards. She did as she was bidden, recognising that
he was leading the expedition for the moment, not she.
She crouched opposite him, averting her eyes from
the houses they were passing. Any moment now, she
thought guiltily, some worthy citizen would fling open
a window and cry the Dutch equivalent of 'Stop, thief!'
But no one saw them. Paul shipped an oar and gentled
the boat into the bank. They were there; Lucius' garden, bright with flowers, its beautifully tended lawn
shining wetly in the rain, lay before them, and from
the shed close at hand came a soft, hopeless whimper.

'I'll get him,' said Phoebe. 'Keep the boat close in,
so we can run for it. If anyone comes you're to go on
your own with Rex.' She pulled some notes from her

bag. 'There, I expect this is enough to get you to Amsterdam.' She gave him a cheerful wink and stepped on to the jetty.

The shed door was fastened from the outside but not locked, which was a good thing because she had no idea what she would have done if that had been the case. Rex was tied up inside and whimpered joyfully when he saw her, but she said 'Hush!' in such an urgent voice that he kept quiet while she sawed through the rope with a pair of blunt garden shears. The simple task took an age. With her heart in her mouth Phoebe picked him up and made for the boat, and once there she had to put a hand over the puppy's muzzle to stop his ecstatic greeting of his young master. 'For heaven's sake,' she said, very much on edge, 'row—you can say hullo to each other presently.'

The return journey wasn't as bad as she had expected it would be; perhaps she was becoming inured to crime. She chuckled at the idea and Paul turned round to say: 'You are what Papa calls a good sport, I think, Phoebe.' Well, he wouldn't think that of her now. She handed the puppy to her companion and he asked: 'What do we do now?'

'The station,' she told him, 'and let's keep off the main streets.'

It was still early as they boarded an Amsterdam train, but the morning rush was over. They sat opposite each other, drinking coffee and eating the rolls Phoebe had bought and sharing them with the puppy. Finally, the last of the crumbs tidied away, Phoebe leaned forward.

'Now, Paul,' she said urgently, 'there are some

things I must know.' And when he nodded, she went on: 'Tell me about Maureen, my dear.' She searched his solemn little face. 'There's something…you have always been so careful to be obedient to her and yet I have the idea that you are afraid of her, but if that is so, why didn't you tell your papa?'

He took a deep breath. 'She said that if I did everything she said and—and liked her, she would buy me a puppy; she said it all depended on me whether I had him or not, because she would have to marry Papa before she could get him and if she went away and he had another governess for me she would be old and horrid and I'd never get a puppy of my own; she said,' he gulped, 'that if I said anything to Papa I'd never have anything, not as long as I lived.'

'Is that why you shut me up, Paul?'

He nodded. 'She said that you were a—a menace—that you wanted to marry Papa. Do you?'

Phoebe stared back into his questioning eyes. 'Yes,' she said quietly, 'I do, but you need not worry, your Papa doesn't want to marry me.'

'She said you'd make him.'

She gave a lop-sided smile. 'How, I wonder? Even if I knew, I wouldn't do that, Paul.'

'She said you were a—a—canting hypocrite and a scheming old maid.' He smiled suddenly and endearingly. 'But she's wrong, you're not—I like you. She said I was to hate you, but I don't.' He looked, for a brief moment, forlorn. 'You're a little like my mama.'

She said steadily: 'Am I, dear? I think that's one of the nicest things anyone has ever said to me.' She smiled warmly at him. 'So now we know why Maureen was so angry that you have been given Rex—she has no hold on you any more.'

He didn't quite understand her. 'She said that Rex would die anyway because he was only a street dog, and when he did, she would buy me another, but only if she married Papa.'

'Oh, my dear,' cried Phoebe, 'I often wondered—most people have cats and dogs and a few tame mice or a hamster…'

His eyes sparkled. 'I like kittens too, but Maureen said they're not healthy.'

'Oh, pooh,' said Phoebe roundly. 'We've got cats and dogs and they're a great deal more healthy than some people I know.'

'Have you any mice?'

'Well, no—girls don't like mice, you know, but I can see that they make splendid pets for boys.'

She glanced out of the window and suddenly remembered where they were and what they were doing. 'We're almost in Amsterdam; you take Rex, and I'll get a taxi.'

Anna lived in a long street called Overtoom. It was neither picturesque nor in a particularly good part of the city and in the rain any charm it might possess had been obliterated by the grey-ness of the sky and the dampness of its pavements, but to Phoebe it represented a solution, temporary at any rate, of their most pressing problems. She followed Paul down a flight of stone steps to Anna's front door, just below street level, and waited while he rang the bell.

There was no mistaking Anna when she opened the door, for she was exactly what anyone would imagine an old nanny to be, with bright blue eyes, extremely neat hair parted in the centre and gathered into a bun, and a small round person clothed in a black dress almost completely covered in an old-fashioned print pinny. At the sight of Paul she broke at once into delighted speech and after a minute Paul, remembering his manners, introduced them and said: 'Anna says we're to go inside.'

The rooms were very small and crowded with furniture, all very highly polished, and there was a lovely smell of coffee in the kitchen where Anna bade them sit down at the table. Over their elevenses Paul told his tale, and Phoebe, watching anxiously, was vastly relieved when at the end of it and after a few brisk remarks from Anna, Paul told her:

'Anna says we are to stay here until Papa comes back, and she's glad we came. You're to sleep on the landing, if you don't mind, because there's only one bedroom and I'm to sleep on the floor—I'll like that, and I'll have Rex.'

Phoebe eyed him tiredly. How resilient little boys were! She felt exhausted herself and said a little desperately: 'Will you tell Anna that I'll telephone your papa as soon as he gets back—in the afternoon. You'll be all right once he's home again, and Paul, do you think Anna would mind if I went to sleep for a little while? I can't keep my eyes open.'

'Oh, Phoebe, I forgot, you've been awake all night.' He addressed himself to the old lady, who peered across the table at Phoebe and nodded her head.

'You're to go to bed now,' Paul told her. 'Anna says

you are a sensible girl but that you must have your sleep. You won't be too long?' He sounded wistful.

She shook her head, resolutely ignoring the longing to sleep the clock round. 'An hour or two. Paul, stay indoors, won't you? Is there a yard or something for Rex?'

'A little garden with a high wall,' he told her. She went up three or four steps leading out of the kitchen, guided by Anna, on to a small landing, bare save for a folding bed in one corner and a chair. She smiled sleepily at her kind hostess, tossed her things on to the chair, kicked off her shoes and curled up on the bed. She was asleep within seconds.

It was Paul who wakened her a few hours later, Rex still tucked under his arm. 'It's teatime,' he informed her. 'Didn't you undress? You must have been sleepy.'

Phoebe yawned, feeling heavy-eyed and hollow, fighting a desire to fall back on the bed again and sleep for ever. 'I was. I say, Paul, I want to wash—is there a bathroom?'

He shook his head. 'You use the kitchen sink. We won't look,' he added kindly as he went away. He was whistling cheerfully and a little off key and Phoebe smiled to herself. At least one of them was enjoying himself!

The remainder of the day passed surprisingly quickly. She tried out a little of her Dutch on Anna, and with Paul's help, they had quite a conversation, and even if they didn't understand each other very well, it didn't seem to matter. Anna, Phoebe could tell, was most definitely on their side, and Phoebe, waking in the night because the mattress wasn't all that comfortable, at least had the satisfaction of knowing that Anna approved of what she had done, she only hoped that Lucius would be of the same opinion.

Chapter 9

The rain had eased up in the morning and over their simple breakfast Phoebe discovered that there was a park behind Anna's flat—Vondel Park. It would be a good place to go, she decided as she helped Anna with the washing up. They had to spend the day somewhere until it was time for her to telephone Lucius, and it wasn't fair on Anna to fill her little home to overflowing with a high-spirited small boy and a puppy. They set off presently, with a ball Anna had found from somewhere or other, and strict instructions to be back for their dinner at midday.

The park was pleasant, well laid out and almost empty of people. They walked for a little while, Rex lying snugly in Paul's arms, because, as Phoebe pointed out in her sensible way, they would play ball presently and he would want to join in and he ought not to get too tired.

They had been tossing the ball to and fro for perhaps ten minutes when Paul gave a sudden shout, hurled the ball wildly in the air and started to run towards Phoebe, yelling as he came, his whole face alight with happiness. She spun round, certain who it was she would see—and she was right. Lucius, the ball in his hand, was coming towards them over the grass. He paused to put a hand briefly on Paul's shoulder as they met and then came to a halt before her.

'Don't dare to be angry with him,' she said impulsively, then wished she hadn't spoken, because he was indeed angry, but with her, not Paul. His words bore this out, for when he spoke it was in a silky voice which menaced her far more than a shout.

'I should like to wring your pretty neck,' he gritted. 'How dare you, Phoebe? Such a petty act, it wasn't worthy of you.'

She steadied her shaking mouth. 'But you're back a day too soon…'

His eyes blazed. 'And how fortunate that I am—you had overlooked that possibility.' He smiled, not at all nicely. 'I am at a loss to discover why you should have done this—why should you wish to set Paul against Maureen? She telephoned me in great distress—she imagined that you were friendly towards her, so naturally she feels deeply hurt.'

Phoebe found her voice, keeping it low so that Paul, playing with Rex close by, shouldn't hear. 'Is that what she said?' She was surprised at the mildness of her tone; she felt as though she would blow sky-high with rage.

'Yes. When I returned last night I found a note from her asking me to telephone. She told me then that Paul had disappeared.'

'How did she know that I was with Paul?'

'She had the good sense to telephone the hospital and put two and two together.'

'And how,' went on Phoebe stubbornly, 'did you know where we were?'

'Van Vliet suggested I should try Anna—he remembered that Paul had been talking about her.' He added wearily, 'I tried everywhere else last night.'

'Is Maureen at your house?'

He raised his eyebrows. 'No—why do you ask? She will be there by the time we get back, I imagine. But don't worry, I have no intention of reproving you until we have got to the bottom of this in a rational manner, I'm sure that the three of us can discuss...'

'I won't,' said Phoebe, in far too loud a voice. 'I'll discuss nothing. You can think what you like, what do I care? You're so completely under that woman's thumb...' She stopped, choked and walked away very fast. By the time Lucius, with Paul and Rex, had arrived at Anna's house, she had dried her angry tears, composed her face and was ready with a polite refusal when he offered her a lift back to Delft. And when Paul, aware that something was not right in his little world, began his own muddled explanation, she bade him urgently to be quiet.

'Wait, my dear,' she besought him. 'It won't help now, and it doesn't matter any more, because your Papa is back home, don't you see? Besides, explaining things is so tedious.'

He eyed her. 'You've been crying. I'm sorry I shut you in that house.'

She bent and kissed him. 'I'm going to have a lovely day shopping,' she told him. 'If I see anything for Rex, I shall buy it.'

'The Bijenkorf has some tartan collars with a silver plate on them, for his name, you know they put it on while you wait…'

She smiled at him. 'Then that's what I'll get. Now go back to your father, Paul, he'll be waiting for you.'

He lingered by her. 'You'll come back, won't you? Won't you come with me to the door? You haven't said goodbye to Rex.'

Phoebe couldn't refuse him, so she tickled Rex under his chin, wished Paul a warm farewell and Lucius a glacial one, and went back to the landing, where she sat down on the bed, doing nothing until she heard the door close and knew that they had gone.

She waited a little while, trying to suppress the ridiculous hope that Lucius would come back, and when a half hour had gone by, and she knew that he wasn't going to, she tidied herself, stuffed her bag with her bits and pieces once more and went down to the kitchen to wish Anna goodbye.

The old lady was sitting at the table, knitting, but she got up when she saw Phoebe and without saying a word, drew her through a door into what must have been the parlour, seldom used and so stiffly furnished that it reminded Phoebe of a child's drawing. There was an old-fashioned sideboard against one wall, dominating the room and loaded with photos in heavy frames. Anna picked one up and handed it to Phoebe. It was Lucius as a small boy, leaning against his father's knee, a hand on his mother's arm. There was a baby too, invisible in a lacy shawl, and another small boy, younger than Lucius, sitting on the floor. She looked at Anna, who smiled and nodded and handed her a quite small photograph—Lucius in a student's gown, looking vaguely at the camera as though his thoughts were far away, and the last one, Lucius, older still, standing with a group of earnest-looking men outside the hospital. Phoebe gave that one back too and her companion put them carefully in their places and led her out again. At the door she took Phoebe's hand in her own and patted it, nodding her head in a satisfied way and murmuring to herself with an air of great content. Phoebe, not having the least idea what she was saying, could only nod and smile, and finally wish her goodbye.

The day stretched before her and she would have to fill it somehow. She would stay in Amsterdam until the evening and then go straight back to the Nurses' Home and to bed. She was on duty early the following morning, and in four days she would be able to go back home. She need not see Lucius again—there were ways of avoiding him on the ward. This firm resolution was instantly followed by a variety of reasons requiring her to seek him out. She could explain, she told herself, walking briskly along Ovetoom, and knew she never would. He had believed Maureen—he hadn't even asked her why they had come to Anna's, although to be fair, she hadn't given him much opportunity. She scowled fiercely and a meek-looking man coming towards her sidled past, looking quite appre-

hensive. 'Fool!' she said aloud, meaning herself, and
found that she had arrived at the Leidseplein.

She wandered along, staring into the shops, stopping at a coffee bar, where she had hard work in repel-
ling the advances of a cheerful young man who was
apparently much taken with her looks. He told her so,
in English, after she had informed him coldly that she
couldn't understand Dutch. It took determination to
shake him off. Phoebe plunged into Vroom and Drees-
man, at the bottom of the Kalverstraat, going through
its departments without seeing anything of them. By
now they would be back in Delft. She pictured them
sitting in his lovely house, discussing her; Maureen at
her most charming, cleverly putting spokes in Paul's
small, futile wheel. Well, it wasn't her business any
more, only before she left Delft, she would go and see
Mijnheer van Vliet and make sure that he did something about Rex—perhaps he could tell Lucius once
she had gone—in the nicest possible way, of course.

Phoebe wandered on again and in company with
dozens of other women, lunched in the balcony restaurant of the Bijenkorf. It was a nice store, she decided,
so she would spend an hour or so exploring its departments, have tea, and then catch a train. It wouldn't
matter if she went to bed early; heaven knew she was
tired enough.

She was in the kitchenware department, studying
a colourful display of saucepans, when she became
aware that Lucius was standing beside her, so close
that the sleeve of his jacket brushed her arm. A tide of
feeling rushed over her; it was ridiculous that his presence beside her should have the power to melt all her

carefully built-up resentment, her unhappiness even; to give her an overwhelming desire to cast herself into his arms, whatever he thought of her. Unable to bear it a moment longer, she snatched up a saucepan and studied it with all the interest of a good housewife on the lookout for a bargain. 'Go away!' she said fiercely.

She had lifted the lid and was peering inside when Lucius took it from her with the utmost gentleness and put it down.

'Phoebe, we must talk.' His voice was harsh and urgent.

She wasn't a girl to give in at the drop of a hat. She picked up a small steel object and gave it her full attention. He took that from her too. 'A hard-boiled egg slicer,' he remarked blandly. 'I imagine it to be a useful kitchen tool.'

'Hard-boiled eggs should be sliced by hand,' Phoebe snapped, aware that the conversation, such as it was, was leading them nowhere.

'Indeed? I'm sure you are right.' She thought she detected laughter in his voice now. 'May we talk?'

'No,' said Phoebe coldly. 'I've nothing to say to you.'

'Good, for I have a great deal to say to you.'

'I shan't listen,' she told him defiantly, and shot him a furious glance.

'Yes, you shall listen, my darling heart. I was angry this morning…'

Her mind registered the glorious fact that he had called her his darling heart even while she said in a voice squeaky with indignation: 'Angry? You wanted to wring my neck!'

'Your lovely neck,' he corrected her, 'and now

listen to me so that you will understand why I was angry. When I got home and found Maureen's note and heard what she had to say on the telephone, I lost my temper—I don't often do that, Phoebe, but you see while I had been in England I had dreamed—oh, a great many dreams—of you, of course, and then when Maureen told me that you had made it up with this young doctor in England and pointed out that you were so very English and I was so very Dutch—and wrapped up in my work, and perhaps a little old—it seemed to me that I had dreamed too much.' He turned to look at her. 'It was like coming back to a nightmare—you gone, Paul gone. I could think of nothing else, and then I found you and I remembered the young doctor.'

'And you wanted to wring my neck—well, of all the…' She paused: a saleswoman, a hawk-eyed, bustling woman, was peering at them from the other side of the saucepans, her dark eyes suspicious. She gave Phoebe a sharp glance and spoke to Lucius, who spoke to her in a smooth voice and actually made her laugh. When she had gone, Phoebe demanded:

'What did you say?'

'She suspected us of being shoplifters, I imagine. I told her that as a young wife, setting up house, you needed time to decide upon your purchases.'

Phoebe chuckled, quite forgetting that they were in the middle of a quarrel. 'Oh, Lucius, how could you? Now I'll have to buy something.'

'Buy anything you wish, my darling, only let me have my say. You see, Paul told me everything on the way back to Delft. I never knew, never even guessed—

why didn't you tell me? I can understand why Paul was afraid to tell me, but you—surely you could have said?'

She stared hard at a shelf loaded with frying pans, blinking back sudden tears. 'Maureen said that she was going to marry you and I didn't know if—if you loved her, so I couldn't say anything, could I?' She sniffed and looked at him and away again. 'Maureen said...' she began again.

'My dearest dear, have we not had enough of Maureen? You seem obsessed by her, which I assure you I am not. She was Paul's governess, that was all. I found her good at the job. I thought, heaven help me, that he liked her, that she was kind to him—that was why I allowed her to do much as she wished. It seemed to me that his happiness was more important than the unwelcome visitors she sometimes invited into my house, but once and for all, my darling, I must tell you that never once did I contemplate marrying her.'

He turned her round to face him and said gravely: 'I may be absent-minded and perhaps a little blind to what is going on around me, but there are some things of which I am very sure—my love for you, Phoebe; you are my life and my future. Do you suppose you could surmount the difficulties of marrying a Dutchman and bear with my occasional lapses of memory? Will you marry me, my darling?'

'How do you know I'm not going to marry Jack?'

'Paul told me.'

She leaned back a little against his arm and stared up into his face. 'But he doesn't know anything about him.'

'Naturally not, but you told Paul that you wanted to marry me.'

She drew an indignant breath. 'Well, really—the little horror! Just wait until I see him!'

She felt Lucius shake with silent laughter. 'You won't get a word in edgeways, my dearest. He was so excited when I told him that I was coming back to fetch you. He babbled about kittens and mice, he even offered, once he has a cat or so to keep Rex company, to welcome a brother or sister into the family.'

'Oh, Lucius, darling Lucius, I'll marry you.' His arms tightened around her, his face was very close, but she held him away. 'No—no, just a minute, Lucius, I know we're not going to talk about Maureen any more, but where is she—did you see her—I…'

'Gone. I had a talk with her when we got back, and she left the house for good, my darling. And now don't interrupt me again.'

'You can't—not here—people,' said Phoebe. He kissed her silent, and when presently she had her breath back and began: 'I don't think…' he said comfortably: 'Quite right, my darling, there is no need,' and kissed her again.

In the car on the way to Delft she said shyly: 'I don't know anything about you, Lucius. Anna showed me some photos of you—have you a family?'

'A sister,' he told her, 'married to a Norwegian, a brother living in Canada. My parents are visiting him.'

'Oh—they live here, in Holland?'

'In Friesland—Father is a doctor too. They'll love you, my Phoebe.'

'I hope so. When will they be back?'

'Not for some months. We shall be an old married couple by then.' He drew up before his house and turned to smile at her. 'I told you that I had had dreams while I was in England; they seemed so real that I set about the business of getting a special licence. We can be married very soon, Phoebe.'

She smiled slowly. 'Perhaps that would be a good idea—if we don't get married quickly you might forget.'

They were standing outside the door when she asked: 'Lucius, when we met—you know, in England— you wrote something in your notebook and you looked at me. What was it?'

For answer he took the little leather-bound book from a pocket, leafed through it, found what he sought and handed it to her. The writing was in Dutch, in his neat, rather spidery hand. Phoebe had picked up quite a vocabulary by now, so had little difficulty in reading it.

'A darling English girl,' she read aloud slowly. 'I shall marry her.'

She closed the book gently and looked up into his face, his kind and loving face, his blue eyes very clear and steady. They would be very happy, she was quite sure of that. She said softly: 'Oh, Lucius, I do love you,' and saw the answer in his eyes before he turned away to unlock the door.

* * * * *

JUDITH

Chapter 1

Half past two o'clock in the morning was really not the time at which to receive a proposal of marriage. Judith Golightly swallowed a yawn while her already tired brain, chock-a-block with the night's problems, struggled to formulate a suitable answer. She was going to say no, but how best to wrap it up into a little parcel of kind words? She hated hurting people's feelings, although she was quite sure that the young man sitting in the only chair in her small office had such a highly developed sense of importance that there was little fear of her doing that. Nigel Bloom was good-looking in a selfconscious way, good at his job even though he did tend to climb on other people's shoulders to reach the next rung up the ladder, and an entertaining companion. She had gone out with him on quite a number of occasions by now and she had to admit that, but he had no sense of humour and she had detected small meanesses beneath his apparent open-handedness; she suspected that he spent money where it was likely to bring him the best return or to impress his companions. Would he be mean with the housekeeping, she wondered, or grudge her pretty clothes?

He had singled her out for his attention very soon after he had joined the staff at Beck's Hospital as a surgical registrar, although she hadn't encouraged him; she was by no means desperate to get married even though she was twenty-seven; she had had her first proposal at the age of eighteen and many more besides since, but somehow none of them had been quite right. She had no idea what kind of man she wanted to marry, for she had seldom indulged in daydreaming, but of one thing she was sure—he would have to be tall; she was a big girl, splendidly built, and she had no wish to look down upon a husband, if and when she got one.

She leaned against the desk now, since there was nowhere for her to sit, and remarked with a little spurt of unusual rage, 'Why do you sit down and leave me standing, Nigel? Do you feel so very superior to a woman?'

He gave a tolerant laugh. 'You're tired,' he told her indulgently. 'I've been on the go all day, you know, and you didn't come on duty until eight o'clock last evening—and after all, you don't have the real hard work, do you? Two night Sisters under you and I don't know how many staff nurses and students to do the chores.'

Judith thought briefly of the hours which had passed, an entire round of the Surgical Wing—ninety beds, men, women and children—every patient visited, spoken to, listened to; the reports from each ward read and noted; at least five minutes with each nurse in charge of a ward, going over the instructions for the night, and all this interrupted several times: two admissions, one for theatre without delay, a death, anxious relatives to see and listen to over a cup of tea because that made them feel more relaxed and gave them the impression that time was of no account, a child in sudden convulsions, housemen summoned and accompanied to a variety of bedsides, phone calls from patients' families—it had been never-ending, and there were more than five hours to go.

Her rage died as quickly as it had come; she was too weary to have much feeling about anything, and meanwhile there was Nigel, looking sure of himself and her, waiting for his answer. He must be mad, she told herself silently, asking a girl to marry him in the middle of a busy night.

She looked across at him, a beautiful girl with golden hair, sapphire blue eyes and a gentle mouth. 'Thank you for asking me, Nigel, but I don't love you— and I'm quite sure I never shall.' She rushed on because he was prepared to argue about it: 'Look, I haven't the time... I know it's my meal time, but I wasn't going to stop for it anyway...'

He got up without haste. 'The trouble with you is that you're not prepared to delegate your authority.'

'Who to?' She asked sharply. 'Sister Reed's in theatre, Sister Miles is on nights off, there's a staff nurse off sick and Men's Surgical is up to its eyeballs— you've just been there, but perhaps you didn't notice?'

Nigel lounged to the door. 'Mountains out of molehills,' he said loftily. 'I should have thought it would have sent you over the moon—my asking you to marry me.' He gave her one of his easy charming smiles. 'I'll ask you again when you're in a better temper.'

'I shall still say no.'

His smile deepened. 'You only think you will. See that that man who's just been admitted is ready for theatre by eight o'clock, will you? And keep the drip running at all costs. I'm for bed.'

Judith watched him go, but only for a moment; even though she was supposed to be free for an hour she had no time to do more than write up her books and begin on the report for the morning. She yawned again, then sat down behind the desk and picked up her pen.

A tap on the door made her give an almost inaudible sigh, but she said, 'Come in,' in her usual pleasant unhurried manner, already bracing herself for an urgent summons to one or other of the wards. Her bleep was off, a strict rule for her midnight break, but that had never stopped the nurses bringing urgent messages. It wasn't an urgent message; a tray of tea and a plate of sandwiches, borne by one of the night staff nurses on her way back from her own meal. Judith put down her pen and beamed tiredly at the girl. 'You're an angel, Staff—I wasn't going to stop…'

'We guessed you wouldn't, Sister. Sister Reed's just back with the patient, so you can eat in peace.'

'Bless you,' said Judith. 'Ask her to keep an eye on that new man's drip, will you? I'll be circulating in about twenty minutes.'

The second half of the night was as busy as the first had been. She went off duty at last, yawning her pretty head off, gobbling breakfast, and then, because it was good for her, going for a brisk walk through the dreary streets to the small park with its bright beds of flowers and far too cramped playing corner for the children. She had the Night Superintendent for a companion, a woman considerably older than herself and into whose shoes it was widely rumoured she would step in a few years' time. Judith preferred not to think about that, indeed, when she had the leisure to consider her future, she found herself wondering why she didn't accept the very next proposal of marriage and settle the matter once and for all.

Sister Dawes was speaking and Judith struggled to remember what she had said; something about measles. She turned a blank face to the lady, who laughed and said: 'You're half asleep, Judith. I was telling you there's a measles epidemic on the way—a nasty one, I gather. We must keep our eyes open. I know you're on Surgical, but even measles patients can develop an appendix or perforate an ulcer—for heaven's sake, if you see a rash on anyone, whisk them away. You've had measles, of course?'

'I've no idea,' declared Judith. 'I should think so—everyone has, and besides, I never catch things.'

She remembered that three nights later. Earlier in the evening a young boy had been admitted with a suspected appendicitis; he had been flushed, his eyes and nose were running and his voice hoarse. Judith eyed him narrowly and peered inside his reluctantly opened mouth. Koplik's spots were there all right; she thanked heaven that he had been admitted to a corner bed and that only she and the staff nurse on duty had been anywhere near him. They moved him to a side ward, made him comfortable, and Judith left the nurse with him while she telephoned—the houseman on duty first, Sister Dawes next and finally the Admission Room. The Casualty Officer was new and it was his first post and he might be forgiven for overlooking symptoms which showed no rash at the moment, but the staff nurse should have been more alert. Judith was brief, severe and just as pleasant in her manner as she always was. She gave instructions that everything that had come in contact with the boy should be disinfected and that the nurse should change her uniform. 'I'll send someone down,' she ended, 'but don't let her touch anything until you've dealt with it.'

It took a little organising to find nurses to take over while the surgical staff nurse went away to do the same thing, and then Judith herself went to change, making sure that everything went into a laundry bag with a warning note pinned to it. It took a small slice out of her night and left her, as usual, short of time.

During the next ten days there were three cases of measles—the nurse who had been on duty in the Admission Room, a ward maid and one of the porters. Another four days to go, thought Judith with relief, and they'd all be in the clear.

It was on the very last day of the incubation period that she began to feel ill; a cold, she decided, only to be expected, since although it was late spring, the weather wavered from cold and wet to fine and warm; no two days had been alike, enough to give anyone a cold. She took some aspirin and went to bed when she came off duty instead of taking her usual walk, but she didn't sleep much. Her head ached and so did her eyes and her throat felt sore; she got up and made tea and took more aspirin. She felt better after that, and presently dressed and went down to her meal, to be greeted with several candid opinions as to her poor looks from her friends. It was the Medical Wing Night Sister, a rather prissy type Judith didn't much like, who observed smugly: 'You've got the measles.'

She was right, of course—she was one of those infuriating young women who always are. Judith was examined by the Senior Medical Consultant, who happened to be in the hospital, told to go to bed and stay there, and warned of all the complications which might take over unless she did exactly as she was told.

As she was a sensible young woman, she obeyed him to the letter, and was rewarded by an attack of severe conjunctivitis and, just as that was subsiding, broncho-pneumonia. It took a couple of weeks to get the better of these, but she was a strong girl and disinclined to lie about in bed feeling ill, and in a minimum of time she was on her feet once more, still beautiful but a little on the pale side and a good deal slimmer than she usually was. The tinted glasses she still wore lent her a mysterious air and what with her wan looks she presented a picture to wring any man's heart. At least, Nigel seemed to think so; he had kept away from her until she was free of infection, but once she was back in the Sisters' sitting room, waiting to see what lay in store for her, he came to see her, more tiresomely cocksure than ever, quite certain that the mere sight of him would be enough for her to agree to marry him. She still tired easily; ten minutes of his self-important prosing gave her a headache, and she said rather crossly: 'Look, Nigel, I'm not quite myself yet, but I haven't changed my mind. Do go away and find someone else—there must be dozens of girls longing to marry you.'

He took her seriously. 'Oh, yes, I know that—I could have anyone of them whenever I liked, but I've made up my mind to marry you and I dislike being thwarted.'

'Well, I'm thwarting you,' she declared with something of a snap, and then: 'Nigel, why do you ask me at such unsuitable times? The middle of a busy night— that time I was taking a patient to theatre, and now...'

He had got to his feet huffily. 'I can see you're determined to be irritable. I won't bother you until you've recovered your temper. I've got tickets for that new Burt Reynolds film this evening—I shall take Sister Giles.'

'Have fun,' said Judith, and meant it, although how anyone could have fun with Ruth Giles, a spiteful cat of a girl if ever there was one, was beyond her.

She was given a month's leave the next day. She telephoned her parents, threw a few clothes rather haphazardly into a case, took leave of her friends, got into her Fiat 600, a tight squeeze but all she could ever afford, and set off home through a June morning the brilliance of which made even the streets of London look lovely.

The country looked even lovelier. Judith was making for Lacock in Wiltshire, and once through London and its suburbs and safely on to the M4, she kept going briskly until she turned off at the Hungerford roundabout on to the Marlborough road; it wasn't very far now and the road, although busy, ran through delightful country, and at Calne she turned into a small country lane and so to Lacock.

The village was old and picturesque, a jumble of brick cottages, half-timbered houses and jutting gables. Judith went down the High Street, turned into a narrow road and stopped in front of a row of grey stone houses, roomily built and in apple pie order. The door of the centre house was flung open as she got out of the car, and her father crossed the narrow pavement, followed by an elderly basset hound who pranced ponderously around them both and then led the way back into the house. The hall was long and narrow with a staircase at one side and several doors. Judith's mother came out of the end one as they went in.

'Darling, here you are at last! We've been quite worried about you, although that nice doctor who was looking after you said we had no need to be.' She returned Judith's kiss warmly, a woman as tall as her daughter and still good-looking. 'You're wearing dark glasses—are your eyes bad?'

'They're fine, love—I wear them during the day if the sun's strong and it makes driving easier. It's lovely to be home.' Judith tucked a hand into each of her parents' arms and went into the sitting room with them. 'A whole month,' she said blissfully. 'It was worth having measles!'

After tea she unpacked in the room she had had all her life at the back of the house, overlooking the long walled garden which her father tended so lovingly and already filled with colour. Judith sighed deeply with content and went downstairs, looking in all the rooms as she went. The house was bigger than one would have supposed from the outside: too big just for her parents, she supposed, but they had bought it when they had married years ago and her father had been a partner in a firm of solicitors in Calne, and when he retired two years previously there had been no talk of moving to something smaller and more modern. Her mother had said that it would be nice to have enough room for Judith's children when she married, and meanwhile the extra bedrooms could be kept closed; if she was disappointed that they were still closed, she never mentioned it.

The weather was fine and warm. Judith shopped with her mother, helped her father in the garden and renewed her acquaintance with the large number of friends her parents had. The gentle, undemanding life did her good. Her pallor took on a faint tan and the slight hollows in her cheeks began to fill out. Before the first week was up she assured her mother that she felt fit for work again and played several vigorous games of tennis to prove it.

'You're not bored?' her mother asked anxiously. 'There's nothing to do except take Curtis for his walks and do the shopping and the garden, and you ought to be having fun at your age. We love having you, but what you need is a complete change of scene, darling.'

It was the next morning when the letter came from her father's brother, Uncle Tom. He had known about Judith's measles, naturally he had been told, since he was a doctor as well as her godfather. Now he wrote to ask if she could see her way to going to Hawkshead for a couple of weeks; his housekeeper had had to go home to look after her daughter's children while she was in hospital and he needed someone—perhaps Judith would be glad of an easy little job? keeping her hand in, so to speak. Two weeks would be enough, went on the letter persuasively, she could have the last week at home. There was a girl from the village to do the housework; all he wanted was someone to run the house, answer the telephone and do the shopping. Besides, he would like to see her again.

They read it in turns, and Judith had just got to the end of it when the telephone rang and Uncle Tom added his voice to the written word. Judith found herself agreeing to drive up that very day and stay for two weeks. 'Even if I leave in an hour,' she warned him, 'I shan't be with you much before supper time—I've only got the Fiat 600, you know.' She added: 'It will be more than an hour—I've got to pack and fill up...'

Uncle Tom dismissed this easily enough. 'Two hundred and fifty miles, more or less, even in that ridiculous little car of yours you should be here for high tea.' He chuckled richly. 'Do your best, girl, because I'm counting on you to get here.' He hung up on her.

'Well,' said Mrs Golightly triumphantly, 'isn't that exactly what I said?—that you needed a complete change? We're going to miss you, darling, but you'll be back for your last week, won't you? And Uncle Tom is such a good kind man, and a doctor too.' She added delicately: 'Is there anyone who might telephone or write to you? I mean, someone you'd want to know about?'

'No, Mother. Well, you might send on the letters, but if anyone rings just say I'm on holiday, will you?' She gave her parent a rather absentminded kiss and went upstairs to pack her bag.

Her father had fetched the Fiat from the garage tucked away behind the houses, her mother had cut sandwiches and filled a flask with coffee and they had both asked her if she had sufficient money. She hugged the pair of them; she would really much rather have stayed at home for the whole of the month, but perhaps she would enjoy the last week with them even more for having been away. She started off down the street as the church clock chimed eleven; Uncle Tom would have to wait for his high tea.

She went north from Lacock through Chippenham and then on to the M4 until it reached the M5, when she took the latter to begin the long drive to the Lakes. The motorway was monotonous; if she hadn't been anxious to reach Hawkshead by early evening, she might have chosen a different, more interesting route. At the Birmingham roundabout she switched to the M6 and presently pulled in for petrol and sat in the car, eating her sandwiches and drinking the coffee, glad of a respite, watching with envy the powerful cars tearing along the fast lane. Once more on her way, pushing the little car to its utmost, she thanked her stars that she liked driving even at the sedate pace that was the Fiat's best, otherwise the journey would be an endless one. All the same she heaved a sigh of relief as she left Preston behind her and knew that her long day was almost over. Once past Lancaster and Carnford and she could look forward to turning off the motorway at last.

The turn came finally and at the sight of a small hotel standing by the quiet road, she stopped the car and had tea, a delicious tea with scones and sandwiches and little cakes, all extra good after her long drive.

She was reluctant to leave, but the afternoon was almost over and she still had something under an hour's driving to do. But now the country was wide, almost empty of traffic, the mountains ahead looming over the fields and copses, golden in the sunshine. Judith went slowly through Kendal and out on to the Ambleside road. There was a ferry at Bowness, crossing Lake Windermere and shortening the road to Hawkshead, but she wasn't sure when it ran, so it was safer, if longer, to go round the head of the lake and take the road to Hawkshead. The village lay between Windermere and Coniston Water and had at its southernmost tip yet another lake, but a very small one, Esthwaite Water, and Judith slowed the car, for the country here was beautiful. Grizedale Forest lay ahead, beyond the village, and on either side of the green wooded valley were the mountains. The village lay snugly, a delightful maze of narrow streets and stone cottages. She remembered it with pleasure as she turned into one of its small squares and stopped before a house, larger than its neighbours with a flight of outdoor steps and small latticed windows. As she got out of the car one of these windows was flung open and her uncle's cheerful voice bade her go inside at once.

She had been before, of course; his voice came from the surgery, which meant that he would be unable to welcome her. She went through the half open door and along the stone-flagged passage to the door at the end and opened it. The kitchen, a good-sized low-ceilinged room, was not modern by glossy magazine standards, but fitted with an old-fashioned dresser, a well scrubbed table and Windsor chairs on either

side of the Aga. Judith dumped her case on the floor,
opened up the stove and put the already singing kettle
to boil, for she wanted a cup of tea above everything
else, and then went back down the passage and into the
sitting room. Large, untidy and comfortable—no colour scheme, just a collection of easy chairs, tables, a
fine old cupboard against one wall and rows of books
filling the shelves against another wall. Judith opened
the cupboard doors, collected china and a teapot, found
a tray and took the lot back to the kitchen. She had her
head in the pantry looking for something to eat when
her uncle joined her.

He greeted her heartily and then studied her at leisure. 'Too thin,' he observed at length, 'too pale, too
hollow-cheeked. A couple of weeks of good Cumbrian
air and plenty of wholesome food will make all the
difference.'

'That reminds me—I've put the kettle on. Have you
had tea, Uncle Tom?'

'I was waiting for you, my dear.' His voice was
guileless, his nice elderly craggy face beamed at her.
'And a nice meal after surgery, perhaps?'

'Seven o'clock do?' asked Judith, buttering bread,
spreading jam and piling sandwiches on a plate. 'High
tea, I suppose?'

Her uncle rubbed his hands together. 'Boiled eggs,
and there's a nice ham Mrs Lockyer left in the lar-
der...' He took the tea she offered him and began on
the sandwiches.

'Did you have any lunch?' asked Judith.

'Coffee—or was it tea?—at the Gossards' farm—
the old man has got a septic finger.'

Judith glanced at the clock. 'Surgery in ten minutes. Have another cup of tea while I change—the same room, is it? Then I'll give you a hand if you need one.'

She went upstairs to the room over the surgery, low-ceilinged and very clean with its old-fashioned brass bedstead, solid chest of drawers and dressing table. She opened the window wide and breathed the cool air with delight before opening her case and getting out a denim skirt and a cotton tee-shirt. She had travelled up in a linen suit and silk blouse, both of them quite unsuitable for the life she would be leading for the next week or two, and tied back her long hair with the first bit of ribbon which came to hand. She discarded her expensive high-heeled sandals too and scampered downstairs in a sensible flat-heeled pair which had seen better days.

It was a good thing she wasn't tired now, for what with answering the telephone, laying the table in the rather dark dining room behind the surgery and going to the door a dozen times, she was kept busy until the last patient had gone, but once they had had their meal and she had cleared away and laid the table for breakfast she was more than ready for bed. All the same, she stayed up another half hour talking to her uncle and before long found herself telling him about Nigel. 'He's very persistent,' she finished. 'I sometimes wonder if I should marry him—I'm twenty-seven, you know, Uncle Tom.'

'God bless my soul, are you really? You wear very well, my dear. You're a very pretty girl, you know.'

She went to bed soon afterwards, yawning her head off but looking forward to her visit. Her mother had been right, she had needed a change; her mother had reiterated her opinion when she had telephoned home that evening, sounding triumphant. 'And perhaps you'll meet some interesting people,' she had ended hopefully, meaning of course a young man ready and willing to fall in love with Judith and marry her.

Breakfast over the next morning and her uncle in his surgery, Judith left the girl who came daily to Hoover and polish and went along to the shops. She crossed Red Lion Square, passed the church and turned into one of the narrow streets, making for the butcher's. She didn't hurry, it was a glorious morning and the little cobbled squares glimpsed through low archways looked enchanting; she had forgotten just how lovely they were.

They all knew about her in the shop, of course. Uncle Tom or his housekeeper would have told them and news spread fast in such a small place. Shopping was a leisurely affair carried out in a friendly atmosphere and a good deal of curiosity. It was, the butcher pointed out, a good many years since Judith had been to visit her uncle, but no doubt she was a busy young lady and very successful by all accounts, although London didn't seem to be an ideal place in which to live. Several ladies in the shop added their very decided opinions to this, although two of them at least had never been farther from home than Carlisle. Judith went on her way presently, back in time to make coffee for her uncle before he started on his rounds and to help with the rest of the housework before starting on their midday dinner.

She pottered in the garden during the afternoon and gave a hand with the evening surgery before getting their meal. A busy day, she reflected as she made a salad, but yet there had been time to do everything without hurry, stop and talk, sit in the sun and do nothing...hospital seemed very far away; another world, in fact.

It was on the third morning that Uncle Tom asked her to take some medicine and pills to one of the houses on the edge of the village. 'They're for Mrs Turner,' he told her. 'I could drop them off myself, but I'm not going to that end of the village this morning and she really ought to have them.' And as Judith took off her apron: 'Don't hurry back, my dear, it's a charming walk and such a lovely morning.'

The house stood well back from the lane, a few minutes' walk from the village's heart; grey stone and roomy under a tiled roof covered with moss. Uncle Tom had told her to go in by the back door and she walked round the side of the house, admiring the beautifully kept garden—Mrs Turner must be a splendid gardener—until she came to the kitchen door, a stout one standing a little open. No one answered her knock, so she went in and stood a minute wondering what to do. The kitchen was the best of both worlds: flagstone floor, a beamed ceiling, lattice windows and geraniums on the sills, and cunningly disguised behind solid oak doors and cupboards were all the modern equipages that any woman could want. Judith took an appreciative glance around her. 'Mrs Turner?' She called softly, and then a good deal louder: 'Mrs Turner?' And when no one answered said louder still: 'I've brought your medicine.'

The silence was profound, so she tried again. 'Mrs Turner, are you home?'

A door at the back of the kitchen was flung open with such violence that she jumped visibly, and a furious face, crowned by iron-grey hair, cropped short, appeared round its edge.

The voice belonging to the face was just as furious. 'Young woman, why are you here, disturbing the peace and quiet? Squawking like a hen?'

Judith gave him an icy stare. 'I am not squawking,' she pointed out coldly, 'and even if I were, it's entirely your own fault for not answering me when I first called.'

'It's not my business to answer doors.'

She studied the face—the rest of him was still behind the door. It had heavy-lidded eyes, an arrogant, high-bridged nose and a mouth set like a rat trap. She said coolly, 'I don't know what your business is, Mr Turner, but be good enough to give your wife these medicines when she returns. The instructions are on the labels.' She walked to the door. 'You're a very ill-mannered man, Mr Turner. Good day to you!'

Chapter 2

Uncle Tom was in the surgery, sitting at his desk, searching for some paper or other and making the chaos there even more chaotic. Judith put down her basket and leaned comfortably over the back of a chair.

'I delivered Mrs Turner's bits and pieces,' she said. 'She wasn't home, so I gave them to her husband.'

Her uncle glanced up briefly. 'She's not married, my dear.'

'Then who's the ill-mannered monster who roared at me? He needs a lesson in manners!'

Uncle Tom paused in his quest for whatever it was he wanted. 'Charles Cresswell—an eminent historian, highly esteemed by his colleagues, with a first-class brain—at present writing a book on twelfth century England with special reference to this area. I daresay you disturbed him…'

Judith snorted. 'He was insufferable! He ought to mind his manners!'

Her uncle peered at her over his spectacles. 'These scholarly men, my dear, should be allowed a certain amount of licence.'

'Why?' snapped Judith.

'You may indeed ask,' observed a voice from the window behind her. 'Tom, it's a waste of breath white-washing my black nature—I see I'm damned for ever in this young lady's eyes. We haven't been introduced, by the way.'

He left the window and came in through the door, a very long lean man with wide shoulders.

Uncle Tom chuckled. 'My niece, Judith Golightly—Judith, this is Professor Charles Cresswell, eminent his…'

'You told me,' said Judith, and said, 'How do you do?' in a voice to freeze everything in the room solid.

Professor Cresswell lounged against the wall, his hands in the pockets of his elderly slacks. 'I do very well, Miss Golightly. Of course my ego is badly damaged, but only briefly, I believe.' He spoke with a careless indifference which annoyed her as much as his temper had. 'Tom, if you're visiting up at the Manor would you mind making my excuses for tennis this afternoon? The phone's out of order…better still, I'll ring from here if I may.'

He stretched out a hand and lifted the receiver and sat himself down on the edge of the doctor's desk. He said softly: 'Miss Golightly, you really shouldn't slouch over that chair—you have a beautiful head and a splendid figure, and neither of them show to their best advantage if you will droop in that awkward manner.' He took no notice of her quick breath but dialled a number and started a conversation with somebody at the other end. Judith most regrettably put her tongue out at the back of his head and flounced out of the room. She was seething enough to scorch the floor under her feet.

The Professor finished his conversation and replaced the receiver.

'Married?' he asked casually. 'Engaged? Having a close relationship?—that's what they say these days, don't they? I seem to remember my granny calling it living in sin.'

Uncle Tom chuckled. 'Times change, Charles, and no, Judith is heartwhole and fancy free at the moment. Which is not to say that she hasn't been in and out of love, or fancied that she was, a great many times. She's a handsome girl and she meets young men enough at that hospital of hers.'

'And they fancy her, no doubt—let's hope that some day soon, she'll make one of them happy.' He wandered to the door, then said with some concern:

'She's not here permanently, is she?'

'No, no, two weeks only while Mrs Lockyer's away. And since she's not exactly taken to you, Charles, you needn't worry about meeting her.' The doctor's tone was dry, but his eyes twinkled.

'Thank God for that,' declared the Professor in a relieved voice.

At lunchtime Judith made no mention of the Professor, indeed, she talked animatedly about everyone and everything else, and when her uncle assured her that he had no calls to make that afternoon, and would be home to answer the telephone, she told him that she would take the Fiat and drive over to Coniston and look round the village and visit Ruskin's house there. "'Mountains are the beginning and the end of all natural scenery,'" she quoted rather vaguely. 'I expect he was inspired by the view from his house.'

'And what about Wordsworth—only a step across the street to the school he attended, my dear, as well you know, not to mention the cottage where he lodged.'

'Oh, I haven't forgotten him, Uncle—only I thought a little drive round might be nice.'

'Of course, my dear. Why not go on to Rydal and take a look at Wordsworth's house? Although perhaps you might save that for another day.'

'Yes, I think I will.' For some reason she wanted to be out of the village away from the chance of meeting Professor Cresswell. She hoped most devoutly that he wasn't going to spoil her stay at Hawkshead, but if he really was writing a book perhaps he would stay in his house all day...

She set off after their lunch, going slowly, for it was but two miles to Coniston. Once there, she parked the car and set off for the John Ruskin Museum, then wandered off to inspect his grave in a corner of the churchyard, and then on to Brantwood to make a leisurely inspection of Ruskin's house. And after that she had to decide whether to have a cup of tea or drive on to Tarn Hows. She decided on the latter, and was rewarded by the magnificent views of the mountains when she got there. She stopped the car for ten minutes and sat back, enjoying it all, and then drove on again, past white Cragge Gardens and through Clappergate and so back to Hawkshead, just in nice time to get her uncle his tea.

Next week, she reflected as she boiled the kettle, she would go to Ferry Nab and across Lake Windermere to Bowness, and there was Hill Top, Beatrix Potter's home and Kendal…all easy runs in the Fiat, and if she had the chance, she could go walking—there were paths to the top of the Old Man, towering over Coniston, as well as less strenuous walks through the Grizedale Forest. It was a wonderful place for a holiday; it was a pity that Professor Cresswell's face, so heartily disliked, should interfere with her musings.

Not that she had much time to muse—Uncle Tom, called away to an emergency, left her to keep his evening patients happy until he returned, and by that time, there was little of the evening left.

The gentle routine of her days suited her very well; she was busy enough, but there was always time to stop and chat in the village shops, or spend half an hour with her uncle while he drank his coffee and checked his list of visits. It was several days later when he suggested that Judith might like to go to Kendal directly after breakfast. Mrs Lockyer went once a month, he explained, sometimes more often, and there were several things he wanted—books, a particular tobacco which the village didn't stock, and his whisky was getting low. Nothing loath, Judith agreed happily, made sure that things would go smoothly while she was away, made a neat list of things to be bought, and went to her room to put on something other than the denim skirt and blouse she had been wearing. She hadn't brought many clothes with her; she chose a silk shirtwaister in a pleasing shade of blue, brushed her hair smooth, found her handbag and went round the back to get the Fiat. She was in front of the house, with the engine running, waiting for Uncle Tom to give her some last-minute instructions about the books she was to fetch, when Professor Cresswell put his head through the window beside her.

Judith frowned. She hadn't met him since their first encounter—well, church, of course, but one couldn't count that. He had been in a pew on the other side of the aisle from Uncle Tom and her and she had been careful not to look at him, but all the same she had been very aware of him, for he sang all the hymns in a loud, unselfconscious baritone voice. And after church, by dint of engaging old Mr Osborne the chemist in a long-winded conversation she had been able to avoid him.

'Going into Kendal?' he wanted to know, without a good morning, and at her frosty nod. 'Splendid, you can give me a lift.'

'I'm going shopping—I'm not sure how long I shall be there.'

It was a pity that Uncle Tom should choose that moment to come out of the house, exclaiming cheerfully: 'You'll be back for lunch, won't you, Judith? I want to go out to Lindsays' farm early this afternoon.' He glanced across at the Professor. 'Giving Charles a lift? In that case bring him back for a sandwich.' He beamed across the little car. 'Judith makes a splendid beef sandwich.'

'Thanks, Tom, but Mrs Turner's doing something she calls giving the house a good do and I can't possibly work until she subsides again.' He opened the Fiat's door and inserted himself into the seat beside Judith; the result was overcrowding but there was nothing to be done about that. She waved her uncle goodbye and drove off.

She had intended to go to Sawry and take the ferry to Bowness on the other side of Lake Windermere and then drive the eight or nine miles to Kendal. There would probably be delays on the ferry, although the season was only just beginning, but the alternative was a much longer drive round the head of the lake; besides, she particularly wanted to go that way and she saw no need to tell her unwanted passenger.

They drove in silence until they reached Sawry, and Judith instinctively slowed down, because it was here that Beatrix Potter had lived and she had promised herself a visit to Hill Top Farm before she went back home; if it had been anyone else with her, she would have had something to say about it, but the Professor hadn't uttered a word, which, she told herself was exactly as she wanted it. They drove on to Far Sawry and joined the short queue for the ferry and he still had said nothing at all, and the eight miles on the other side were just as silent. They were actually in Kendal before he spoke.

'Go through Highgate,' he told her. 'Into Strickland-gate—you can park the car there.'

And when she did, pulling up neatly in a half full car park, he opened his door and got out. 'I'll be here at twelve,' he told her, and stalked off, leaving her speechless with rage. 'Just as though I were the hired chauffeur!' she muttered. 'And why hasn't he got a car of his own, for heaven's sake?'

And he could have offered her a cup of coffee at the

very least, not that she would have accepted it, but it would have given her pleasure to refuse him…

The town had changed since she had been there last, many years ago. The M6 had taken all the traffic nowadays, leaving the old town to its past glory. Judith pottered round the shops, carefully ticking off her list as she went, and when she came across a pleasant little café, went in and had coffee, and because she was feeling irritable, a squashy cream cake. She felt better after that and went in search of the books her uncle had ordered, did a little shopping for herself and made her way, deliberately late, to the car.

The Professor was leaning against the car, reading a book, outwardly at least in a good frame of mind. Judith said flippantly: 'Finished your shopping?' and opened the door and threw her parcels on to the back seat.

'I never shop,' he assured her blandly. 'I wanted to visit Holy Trinity Church, there are some Megalithic stones in the vault I wanted to examine.'

Judith had no idea what Megalithic meant. 'Oh, really?' she said in a vague way, and got into the car.

'You have no idea what I'm talking about,' he sighed, 'Not my period, of course, but I felt the need of a little light relief.'

Judith turned a splutter of laughter into a cough. 'What from?' she asked.

'My studies.'

She gave him a sideways look. 'Surely, Professor, you stopped studying some years ago?'

'I'm a scholar, Miss Golightly, not a schoolboy.

What an extraordinary name you have.' He added gently: 'And so unsuitable too.'

Judith clashed the gears. 'Don't ever ask me for a lift again!' she told him through clenched teeth.

They had to wait quite some time for the ferry, and Judith, determined not to let the wretched man annoy her, made polite conversation as they sat there until she was brought to an indignant stop by his impatient: 'Oh, Miss Golightly, do hold your tongue, I have a great deal to think about.'

So they didn't speak again, and when they arrived at her uncle's house she got out of the car and went indoors, leaving him to follow if he pleased.

And if he does, she thought, I'll eat my lunch in the kitchen, and since she found him sitting in the dining room with Uncle Tom, drinking beer and smoking a pipe and listening with every sign of pleasure to his host's opinion of illuminated manuscripts of the twelfth century, that was exactly what she did.

Before he left he poked his head round the kitchen door. 'Your uncle is quite right, you make an excellent sandwich—you must both come to dinner with me one evening and sample Mrs Turner's cooking.'

Judith didn't stop washing up. 'That's very kind of you, Professor Cresswell, but I'm here to enjoy peace and quiet.'

'Oh, we'll make no noise, I promise you—I don't run to a Palm Court Orchestra.' He had gone before she could think up another excuse.

It was the next morning, just as she was back from the butchers with a foot or so of the Cumberland sau-

sage her uncle liked so much, that he wandered into
the kitchen when surgery was over for the moment.

'No cooking for you this evening, my dear—Charles
has asked us to dinner.'

A surge of strong feeling swept over Judith—
annoyance, peevishness at being taken unawares and
perhaps a little excitement as well. She said immediately, 'Oh, Uncle, you'll have to go without me—I've
got a headache.' She was coiling the sausage into a
bowl. 'I'll stay at home and go to bed early.'

'Oh, that won't do at all.' Her uncle was overrid-
ing her gently. 'I've just the thing to cure that—by the
evening you'll be feeling fine again.' He bustled away
and came back with a pill she didn't need or want,
but since he was there watching her, she swallowed it.
'It's a splendid day,' he went on, 'so after lunch I suggest that you get into the hammock in the garden and
have a nap.'

Which, later in the day, she found herself doing,
watched by Uncle Tom, looking complacent. This reluctance to meet Charles he considered a good sign,
just as he was hopeful of Charles' deliberate rude-
ness to her. In all the years he had known him, he had
never seen such an exhibition of ill manners towards a
woman on the Professor's part. He knew all about his
unfortunate love affair, but that was years ago now—
since then he had treated the women who had crossed
his path with a bland politeness and no warmth. But
now this looked more promising, Uncle Tom decided;
his niece, with her lovely face and strong splendid figure, had got under Charles' skin. He pottered off to his
afternoon patients, very pleased with himself.

Much against her inclination, Judith slept, stretched out in the old fashioned hammock slung between the apple trees behind the house. She slept peacefully until the doctor's elderly Austin came to its spluttering halt before the house, and she just had time to run to the kitchen and put the kettle on for a cup of tea before he came into the house.

It would be nice, she thought, if they had a frantically busy surgery that evening, even a dire emergency, which would prevent them from going to the Professor's house, but nothing like that happened. The surgery was shorter than usual; Uncle Tom put the telephone on to the answering service, told the local exchange to put through urgent calls to the Professor's house and indicated that he would be ready to leave within the next hour.

'And wear something pretty, my dear,' he warned her. 'There'll probably be one or two other people there—Charles doesn't entertain much, just once or twice a year—they're something of an event here.' He added by way of an explanation: 'Mrs Turner is an excellent cook.'

She was dressing entirely to please herself, Judith argued, putting on the Laura Ashley blouse, a confection of fine lawn, lace insertions and tiny tucks, and adding a thick silk skirt of swirling colours, her very best silk tights and a pair of wispy sandals which had cost her the earth. For the same reason, presumably, she took great pains with her face and hair, informing Uncle Tom, very tidy for once in a dark blue suit, that she just happened to have the outfit with her.

Which was true enough, although she hadn't expected to wear it.

They travelled in the doctor's car, driving up to the house to find several other cars already there. The house, Judith saw, now that she was at its front, was a good deal larger than she had supposed. It was typical of the Lake District, whitewashed walls under a slate roof, with a wing at the back and a walled garden, full of roses now, encircling it. She went inside with her uncle into a square hall with four doors, all open. There was a good deal of noise coming through one of them; they paused long enough to greet Mrs Turner and were shown into a room on the left.

It was considerably larger than Judith had imagined, running from the front of the house to the back, where doors were open into the garden; it was furnished with a pleasing mixture of old, well cared for pieces and comfortable chintz-covered chairs. It was also quite full of people; women in pretty dresses, men in conventional dark suits. And the Professor, looking utterly different in a collar and tie and a suit of impeccable cut, advancing to meet them.

He clapped Uncle Tom on the shoulder, bade Judith a brisk good evening and introduced them round the room. Uncle Tom knew almost everyone there, of course, and presently, when the Professor had fetched them their drinks, he excused himself and left the doctor to make the introductions himself. Judith, making small talk with a youngish man who said that he was a cousin of the Professor's, took the opportunity to look round her. There were a dozen people, she judged, and only a few of them from Hawkshead itself. And all the women were pretty and smart and, for the most part, young. She thanked heaven silently that she had worn the silk outfit; it might not be as smart as some of the dresses there, but it stood up very nicely to competition. The cousin was joined by an elderly man whom she vaguely remembered she had seen in church; the local vet, he reminded her jovially, and pointed out his wife, talking to the Professor at the other end of the room. 'I've just given her a Border terrier and I daresay they're comparing notes.'

'Oh, has he got one?'

'Lord, yes, and a nice old Black labrador as well. They're in the garden, I expect, but they will roam in presently, I daresay—they have the run of the house.'

'I should have thought that having dogs would have been too much of a distraction for Professor Cresswell—he spends a great deal of time writing, doesn't he?'

'Yes, but he takes them out early in the morning before starting work—I believe they sit with him while he's actually at his desk, so they can't bother him much.' He smiled at her. 'How do you like this part of the country?'

The Professor's cousin had turned aside to speak to a young woman and presently joined them again, this time with his arm round the girl's shoulders. 'You have met?' he wanted to know. 'Eileen Hunt, an old friend of the family.' He laughed. 'One might say, almost, very nearly one of the Cresswell family.'

The girl laughed too, and Judith smiled politely and wondered if they were on the point of getting engaged. She glanced down at the girl's left hand: there was a

wedding ring but nothing else. Eileen caught her eye
and smiled with a hint of malice. 'I'm not going to
marry this wretch—he's got one wife already. You're
not married, Judith?'

The malice was still there. 'No,' said Judith carefully. 'There always seems to be so many other things
to do—I daresay I'll get round to it one day.'

It was a relief when Mrs Turner opened the door
and, accompanied by the two dogs, marched across the
room to where the Professor stood talking to a small
group of people. Dinner, it appeared was ready.

The dining room, on the other side of the hall, was
every bit as pleasant as the sitting room. Judith, sitting
between the vet and a rather prosy elderly man who
had little to say for himself, glanced round the big oval
table. Eileen was sitting beside her host, leaning towards him with a laughing face and what Judith could
only describe as a proprietorial air. Was that what the
cousin had meant? Was the Professor going to take a
wife? Judith felt the vague dislike she had had for the
girl turn to something much stronger, which considering she didn't like Charles Cresswell one little bit
seemed strange.

The prosy man, having delivered himself of a
lengthy speech about local weather, applied himself
to his soup, and Judith did the same. It was excellent,
as was the salmon which followed it and the saddle of
lamb which the Professor carved with precise speed.
The prosy man seemed disinclined for conversation;
she and the vet carried on a comfortable, desultory chat
which took them through the delicious trifle and a glass
of the Muscat which had followed the white Bordeaux

and the claret, before the ladies rose from the table and trooped back into the sitting room.

'Very old-fashioned,' commented the vet's wife, 'but Charles is too old to change his ways, I suppose. Besides, I rather like it, don't you?' She tucked a friendly hand into Judith's arm and strolled to the still open doors. 'Nice, isn't it? Such quiet, and a heavenly view. We only get a chance to come here about twice a year, you know. Most of the time Charles shuts himself up and writes and the rest of the time he's travelling around looking for bits of mediaeval history. Your uncle tells me you're a nurse. That must be interesting.'

'Yes, it is, but I don't think I'll be able to bear London after this.'

'You live there?'

'I work there, my parents live in Lacock—that's in Wiltshire. It's lovely there too.'

Some of the older women joined them then, and the talk became general until the men came in and her uncle came over. 'Enjoying yourself, my dear?' he wanted to know. 'The headache's gone? Do you mind very much if we leave within the next few minutes? I've explained to Charles that I might get a call from the Lindsays later on this evening.'

He turned away to speak to one of the other men and Judith, finding herself with the prosy man again, listened with outward politeness and an inner peevishness to a lengthy diatribe against the local government. She would be glad to leave, she decided silently; she had no interest in Charles Cresswell or his house, or his friends. It crossed her mind at the same time that he hadn't any interest in her either. He hadn't spoken a word to her since his brief greeting; he had invited her out of politeness because Uncle Tom wouldn't have come without her, but he made no attempt to hide his dislike. And she disliked him too—heartily.

'A delightful evening,' she told her host as she and her uncle left a little later, and gave him a smile as insincere as her words. She was greatly put out at his laugh.

'Was it, Judith?' His voice was bland. 'Such a pity that you have to go back to London so soon. You've had very little time to get to know us—you'll forget us, I'm sure.'

She said nothing to this but stood silently while Uncle Tom and his host arranged a date for a day's climbing. She would be gone by then, of course, but she doubted very much if she would have been included in Charles Cresswell's invitation.

They drove the short way back in silence and when she had seen to the small bedtime chores and left a thermos of hot coffee ready in case her uncle was called out during the night, she went up to bed. The evening hadn't been a success—but then, she argued with herself, she hadn't expected it to be. All the same, she was filled with disappointment that she couldn't account for. And she didn't like Eileen; she hoped she wouldn't have to meet her again, although that wasn't very likely. The girl lived in Windermere and she would take great care not to go there.

She went the very next day, much against her will. One of her uncle's patients, an elderly lady of an irascible nature, had driven over from Bowness to consult him. Her car was a vintage Austin and she drove badly. She had reversed into the doctor's stone wall and shaken up the old car's innards so badly that she had been forced to leave it at the village garage and then, considering herself very ill used, had demanded some kind of transport to take her home. It was a pity that Judith should go through the hall while she was making her needs known in no uncertain manner to Uncle Tom who, in what Judith considered to be a cowardly fashion, instantly suggested that his niece would be only too glad…

So Judith had ferried Mrs Grant back home, a pleasant house nearer Windermere than Bowness, and would have made her escape at once, only Mrs Grant remembered an important letter which simply had to go from the main post office in Windermere and would Judith be so kind…

She found the post office, posted the letter and remembered that she hadn't had her coffee, so she left the car parked and went to look for a café. There were any number, and she chose the Hideaway, largely because of its name, and the first person she saw as she went inside was Eileen Hunt.

It was impossible to pretend that she hadn't seen her, and when Eileen beckoned her over to share her table she went over, wishing she'd chosen any café but that one. But Eileen seemed pleased to see her. 'Such a pity you had to go early yesterday,' she observed with apparent friendliness, 'but I daresay you find our little dinner parties rather dull after London.'

'I don't go out a great deal—at least not to dinner parties. I found this one very pleasant.' Judith ordered her coffee and changed the subject. 'What a lovely morning.'

Eileen sipped coffee. 'Yes. I expect you go out a good deal with the doctors in the hospital, don't you?'

'Occasionally,' said Judith coolly.

'How romantic,' said Eileen, and flicked a quick glance at Judith. 'I daresay you'll marry one of them.'

Judith thought very briefly of Nigel. Her mother had forwarded two letters from him and she hadn't answered either of them; she went faintly pink with guilt and Eileen smiled. 'Wouldn't it be thrilling if he came all this way just to see you?'

'Very thrilling,' said Judith, refusing to be drawn. She finished her coffee. 'I must go—I hadn't intended coming out this morning and I've a mass of things to do.' She smiled a polite goodbye, got to her feet and turned round, straight into Professor Cresswell. He sidestepped to avoid her and with a quick good morning, she went past him and out of the café. So much for those learned hours at his desk, brooding over the twelfth century! It rankled that he had found her visit to the house so disturbing—squawking like a hen, she remembered with fury—and yet he could spend the morning with that giggling idiot of an Eileen. Well, he'd got what he deserved, she told herself as she drove back to Hawkshead, and it was no business of hers, anyway. And in three days' time she would be going home.

On her last day, with Mrs Lockyer safely back in the kitchen, Judith took herself off to Coniston. She had promised herself that she would climb the Old Man of Coniston, and although it was well past lunchtime by the time she got there there were several paths which would take her to the top without the need to hurry too much. She parked the car in the village and started off. She enjoyed walking, even uphill, and she was quite her old self again by now, making an easy job of the climb, and once at the top, perched on a giant boulder to admire the enormous view. It was warm now and presently she curled up and closed her eyes. It would be nice to be at home again, she thought sleepily, and there was still a week before going back to hospital— which reminded her of Nigel. She dozed off, frowning.

She slept for half an hour or more and woke with the sun warm on her face. She didn't open her eyes at once, but lay there, frowning again. Nigel was bad enough when she was awake, but to dream of him too was more than enough. She sighed and opened her eyes slowly, and looked straight at Charles Cresswell, sitting on another boulder a foot or two away.

'Why were you frowning?' he wanted to know.

Judith sat up. Denim slacks and a T-shirt did nothing to detract from her beauty, nor did her tousled hair and her shiny face, warm from the sun still. She said crossly: 'How did you get here?'

'I walked.' He whistled softly and the Border terrier and the labrador appeared silently to sit beside him. 'The dogs like it here.'

Judith tugged at her T-shirt with a disarming un-selfconsciousness. 'I must be getting back.' She got to her feet. 'Goodbye, Professor Cresswell.'

'Retreat, Judith?' His voice was smooth.

'Certainly not—I said I'd be back to give a hand at evening surgery.'

'You leave tomorrow?'

'Yes.' She started to walk past him and he put out a hand and caught her gently by the arm.

'There's plenty of time. I should like to know what you think of Hawkshead—of Cumbria—what you've seen of it?'

She tried to free her arm and was quite unable to do so. 'It's very beautiful. This is my third visit here, you know—I'm not a complete stranger to the Lakes...'

'You wouldn't like to live here?'

Just for a moment she forgot that she didn't like him overmuch. 'Oh, but I would,' and then sharply: 'Why do you ask?'

She was annoyed when he didn't answer, instead he observed in a silky voice which annoyed her very much: 'You would find it very tame after London.'

Eileen Hunt had said something very like that too; perhaps they had been discussing her. Judith said sharply: 'No, I wouldn't. And now if you'll let go of my arm, I should like to go.' She added stiffly: 'I shan't see you again, Professor Cresswell; I hope your book will be a success. It's been nice meeting you.' She uttered the lie so unconvincingly that he laughed out loud.

'Of course the book will be a success—my books always are. And meeting you hasn't been nice at all, Judith Golightly.'

She patted the dogs' heads swiftly and went down the path without another word. She would have liked to have run, but that would have looked like retreat. She wasn't doing that, she told herself stoutly; she was getting away as quickly as possible from someone she couldn't stand the sight of.

Chapter 3

Judith left Hawkshead with regret, aware that once she was away from it it would become a dream which would fade before the rush and bustle of hospital life; another world which wouldn't be quite real again until she went back once more. And if she ever did, of course, it would be London which wouldn't be real. Driving back towards the motorway and the south after bidding Uncle Tom a warm goodbye, she thought with irritation of London and her work, suddenly filled with longing to turn the Fiat and go straight back to Hawkshead and its peace and quiet. Even Charles Cresswell, mellowed by distance, seemed bearable. She found herself wondering what he was doing; sitting at his desk, she supposed, miles away in the twelfth century.

She was tooling along, well past Lancaster, when a Ferrari Dino 308 passed her on the fast lane. Charles

Cresswell was driving it—he lifted a hand in greeting as he flashed past, leaving her gawping at its fast disappearing elegance. What was he doing on the M6, going south, she wondered, and in such a car? A rich man's car too—even in these days one could buy a modest house for its price. And not at all the right transport for a professor of Ancient History—it should be something staid; a well polished Rover, perhaps, or one of the bigger Fords. She overtook an enormous bulk carrier with some caution and urged the little Fiat to do its best. There was no point in thinking any more about it, though. She wasn't going to see him again; she dismissed him firmly from her mind and concentrated on getting home.

It was after five o'clock as she drove slowly through Lacock's main street and then turned into the narrow road and pulled up before her parents' house. She got out with a great sigh of relief which changed into a yelp of startled disbelief when she saw the Ferrari parked a few yards ahead of her. It could belong to someone else, of course, but she had the horrid feeling that it didn't, and she was quite right. Her mother had opened the door and Judith, hugging and kissing her quickly, asked sharply: 'Whose car is that? The Ferrari—don't tell me that awful man's here…'

They were already in the little hall and the sitting room door was slightly open. The look on her mother's face was answer enough; there really was no need for Professor Cresswell to show his bland face round the door. He said smoothly: 'Don't worry, Judith, I'm on the point of leaving,' and before she could utter a word, he had taken a warmly polite leave of her mother, given her a brief expressionless nod, and gone. She watched him get into his car and drive away and it was her mother who broke the silence. 'Professor Cresswell kindly came out of his way to deliver a book your Uncle Tom forgot to give you for your father.' She sounded put out and puzzled, and Judith flung an arm round her shoulders.

'I'm sorry, Mother dear, but I was surprised. I had no idea that Professor Cresswell was leaving Hawkshead. I—I don't get on very well with him and it was such a relief to get away from him—and then I get out of the car and there he is!'

'You were rude,' observed Mrs Golightly. 'I thought he was charming.'

'Oh, pooh—if he wants to be, he can be much ruder than I was; we disliked each other on sight.' She frowned a little as she spoke because her words didn't ring quite true in her own ears, but the frown disappeared as Curtis came lumbering out of the sitting room to make much of her.

'Professor Cresswell liked Curtis,' observed Mrs Golightly. 'He has two dogs of his own…'

'Yes, I know—a Border terrier and a labrador. I've met them.'

'So you've been to his house?' Mrs Golightly's question was uttered with deceptive casualness.

'Only because I had to. Where's Father?'

'Playing bowls—he'll be sorry to have missed Professor Cresswell.'

'Well, he's got Uncle Tom's book. I'll get my case…'

'Tea's in the sitting room—I made a cup for the Professor…'

'Cresswell,' finished Judith snappishly, and then allowed her tongue to betray her. 'Where was he going, anyway?'

Her mother gave her a guileless look. 'I didn't ask,' she said, which was true but misleading.

There was a lot to talk about and it all had to be repeated when her father got home. It was surprising how often Charles Cresswell's name kept cropping up; Judith decided that her dislike of him had been so intense that it would take some time to get rid of his image. 'Hateful man!' she muttered as she unpacked. 'Thank heaven I'll never see him again!'

It was nice to be home; to take up the quiet round of unhurried chores, stop and chat in the village with her parents' friends, play tennis at the vicarage and take Curtis for the long ambling walks he loved. The week went too quickly and she found herself packing once more. The prospect of getting back into uniform held no pleasure, indeed she wondered if she really wanted to go back to Beck's. Somehow she felt vaguely dissatisfied with life, and Nigel would be waiting for her, he had told her that in the several letters he had written to her. He hadn't taken her refusal to marry him seriously; it seemed she would have to start all over again, trying to make him understand… Perhaps that was why she was feeling so downcast. She finished her packing and since it was their last evening together, took her parents down to the Red Lion for dinner.

She left at the last possible moment the next day. She would go on duty at eight o'clock the next morning, but a couple of hours would be time enough in which to put her room to rights and get her uniform ready, so that it was already early evening when she drove the Fiat through the wide entrance of the hospital and parked it in the inner courtyard. It was broodingly warm still with the threat of a storm, and as she locked the car and picked up her case she tried not to think of the peace and quiet of Lacock. For some reason she did not allow herself to think about Hawkshead at all.

Beck's loomed all around her, an old hospital being modernised as fast as funds allowed, although nothing could eradicate its Victorian origins. The side door Judith went through still squeaked abominably and the serviceable brown lino on the passage floor was as shiny and slippery as it always was. Her charming nose wrinkled as it met the familiar smells, faint but unmistakable, of disinfectant, supper from the floor above her and the merest whiff of fragrance from the bowl of sweet peas the Warden of the nurses' home, a keen arranger of flowers, had set on a table at the end of the passage, by the door to the home. Judith had never minded the hospital atmosphere before, now suddenly she was assailed by such a longing to be in Charles Cresswell's garden, with its roses trailing over the house walls, scenting the air, that she could easily have burst into tears. She shook her head vigorously, told herself not to be a fool, and went through the door into the hall and began to climb the stairs to her room.

She hadn't finished her unpacking before the first of her friends joined her. Jenny Thorpe was the Accident Room Sister, younger than Judith, small and dainty and fair-haired. She made herself comfortable on Judith's bed and declared: 'How nice to have you back—you'll be on in the morning, I suppose, just to get the hang of things, and then go on duty in the evening? Well, it's busy, ducky. Miles and Reed have managed more or less, but no one replaced you, they made do with an extra staff nurse. Now tell me all about your holiday—you're looking terrific...'

She was interrupted by another girl with a round cheerful face and no looks to speak of. 'You're back,' she observed unnecessarily. 'They want you in the office right away, Judith, and I'll bet my month's salary that Sister Reed's gone off sick; I hear she was complaining all night about her feet.'

She was right. Judith was greeted by the Senior Nursing Officer with the brisk request that she should go on duty that very night. 'I don't know which way to turn,' declared that lady with an emotion she seldom displayed. 'Here's Sister Reed off sick and no one to relieve her and the surgical side so very busy. You will, of course, have an extra night off duty,' she added the ominous words, 'when it's convenient.'

Judith said: 'Yes, Miss Parkes,' in her calm way, well aware that no night was ever convenient. If ever there was a night when she could sit down and put her feet up for an hour, she would eat her very attractive frilled muslin cap!

There was just time to have a cup of tea before changing into uniform, finishing her unpacking and joining the rest of the night staff for breakfast. That she had had one breakfast already that day didn't deter her from eating scrambled eggs and toast and marmalade. She had been on the night staff for some time now and topsy-turvy meals when on duty seemed natural enough.

Ann Miles, the junior Sister, was already at the table when Judith got to the canteen, and uttered a sincere, 'Thank God!' when she saw her. 'I saw one of the surgical nurses as I came here,' she exclaimed. 'There's been an RTA, four injured so far and more in the Accident Room.' She added as an after-thought, 'Did you have a good leave?'

Lacock and Hawkshead seemed a long way away—a different world. 'Very nice, thank you,' said Judith. 'Tell me a bit more about this RTA.'

By midnight she was tired, but there was little chance to sit down even for ten minutes. The injured were all in need of skilled attention and as usual, she hadn't quite enough nurses on duty; she went from one bed to the other and then leaving Ann to cope, went off on her midnight round. She had seen Nigel, of course, but there had been no time to talk, and even if there had been, she was in no mood for personal matters.

She finished her rounds, went back to her office and sat down at last. There was a tray on the desk with a pot of tea and a plate of sandwiches, and she started on her scratch meal as she began on the paper work to be done before morning. Despite her tiredness she wrote quickly and accurately in her neat hand and she was almost finished, a sandwich half eaten, held poised, when the door opened and Nigel came in.

Judith looked up briefly. 'I'm busy,' she said, her mouth full, 'is it about a patient? That man with the shoulder wound…'

'They're all OK until Mr David sees them in the morning. I wanted to talk to you. You didn't answer any of my letters…'

Judith swallowed the last of her sandwiches. 'Not now, Nigel—I'm up to my eyes. I didn't expect to come on duty tonight and I'm tired.'

'Me too,' he yawned. 'What a life! If you married me, of course, you could work a day shift or even do part-time.'

'Or stay at home and be a housewife,' murmured Judith, and drank her tea.

'Well, that would be silly. You're a good nurse and as strong as a horse, and the extra money would be useful. Once I could get a consultant's post you'd have to stop, of course, it would never do to have you working.'

She choked over her tea. 'Nigel, will you go away? I'm busy—I've said that once, and I'm not going to marry you—I've said that several times, and I mean it.'

Suddenly she couldn't bear him sitting there, looking smug and self-satisfied and not minding a bit about her tiredness. He'd be that kind of a husband, she guessed, always expecting her to be at his beck and call, ready to do what he wanted and never mind about her. She got to her feet. 'I'm going to relieve Ann,' she told him, and thought longingly of the tea still in the pot. 'Are you on call for the rest of the night or is Mr Wright?'

Nigel was still sitting looking sulky. 'Oh, Wright's on call if you should need anyone. What are you doing tomorrow?'

'Sleeping,' said Judith, and sailed away.

He hardly spoke to her for the next three nights and then luckily it was nights off for her. Tired though she was after a night which had stretched endlessly, she threw some clothes into an overnight bag, got into the

Fiat, and drove down to Lacock. It took a long time because the summer holidays were in full spate, but to get home to a loving welcome, a hot bath, a delicious meal and finally her own bed was well worth it. She slept dreamlessly with Curtis spread over her feet and was up and dressed and making early morning tea well before eight o'clock.

Her mother, looking at her restored beauty, sighed, 'Darling, would it be a good idea to get a post on day duty somewhere? You looked so weary when you got home…'

Judith bit into toast. 'Well, I was. We've had a trying four nights, I daresay it'll be much easier when I get back—besides, Carole should be back, we've been working one short.'

'It would be nice if you got married,' said Mrs Golightly vaguely.

'First catch your man,' her father chuckled, and Judith laughed with him.

'I will when I find him,' she said.

It was wonderful what two days at home did for her. She went back to Beck's feeling capable of dealing with any number of patients, even coping with Nigel. 'I'll not be home next week,' she told her mother as she said goodbye. 'I thought I'd go and see Granny—she'll put me up for the night. I'm not sure which nights I can take off, so I'll have to telephone in a day or two.' She kissed her mother. 'I'd rather come home, but I daresay Granny wants a bit of a gossip.'

And as it turned out the next few nights held no dramatic upheavals. There were the usual admissions, of course, emergency cases in theatre, youths from rival gangs with broken bottle wounds, broken noses, fractured cheekbones, and besides these tiresome patients, some poor old soul beaten up for the sake of the few shillings they had. A sorry story, thought Judith, filling in her Night Casualty Book each morning, and not just once in a while, either. She was glad to be free at last and pack her bag again and get out the Fiat and make her way to St John's Wood where her grandmother lived in a pleasant little house with Molly, her housekeeper.

Old Mrs Golightly was in her early seventies, and still a spry old lady. She was small and thin, so that Judith towered over her, but although they were very different in appearance, they saw eye to eye about a great many things. She called now from the sitting room as Molly admitted Judith, bidding her to go in at once and have a glass of sherry before lunch.

Judith did so and was greeted by her grandmother, lovingly tart. 'Measles at your age!' she observed. 'How is it you never had them at the proper time? Lost some weight too, I see, though you don't look too bad, I must say. How is your Uncle Tom? It's time he paid me a visit.'

Judith bent to kiss her grandparent. 'He's very well, working much too hard; holidays just don't seem to matter to him.'

'Pour the sherry, child, and sit down—you can go up to your room later. Been up all night, I suppose?'

'Well, yes. But I'm wide awake at the moment, Granny.'

Mrs Golightly shook her head. 'It's not a natural life at all. Time you married, Judith. Surely to goodness you've met someone by now. How old are you? Twenty-seven? High time you settled down and had a family. I never did believe in women working.'

Judith sipped her sherry. There had never been any need for Granny to work. She had married young, slipping naturally enough into the roles of wife and mother, secure from every angle. Even now she lived in comfort with the faithful Molly and sufficient income to allow her the small luxuries of life. Judith sighed soundlessly. It wasn't quite the same nowadays—she would be expected to work, she supposed, at least for a year or so after marriage—everyone did nowadays. A home, she thought wistfully, and a husband who would work his fingers to the bone rather than let her work, even part-time, and children, growing up in a household where Mother was a permanent fixture. She shook the thought from her head. She was getting old-fashioned, the sherry was making her sentimental.

'I had a letter from your Uncle Tom,' her grandmother's brisk voice broke the small silence. 'He enjoyed having you, Judith—said you were a good girl and did a great deal of work. Said he wished he could have taken you out and about more; he seems to have plenty of friends too.'

'Yes, I met some of them.' For the life of her she couldn't stop herself telling her grandmother about the dinner party at Charles Cresswell's house, although she made up for that by saying: 'Of course, I didn't like him—intolerant and rude and arrogant; it's funny how you dislike some people on sight…'

'He disliked you too?'

'Oh, yes,' Judith put down her glass, 'he can't stand the sight of me.'

'How very fortunate that you are unlikely to see him again,' remarked her grandmother drily. 'He seems to have upset you a good deal.'

'Upset me? Of course not, Granny. Nigel's proposed again,' she added.

Old Mrs Golightly knew all about Nigel. 'You refused him, of course?'

'Yes, I—Granny, do you think I'm too fussy? Am I going to end up a dried-up old spinster?'

'No, my dear, you'll marry within the year, I have no doubt.' She nodded her head again. 'And not to that tiresome Nigel.'

Judith gave her an indulgent smile. Old ladies got fancies from time to time, and if it amused her grandmother to make arbitrary statements like that one, it did no harm.

She ate Molly's well cooked lunch with a healthy appetite and then curled up in one of the large shabby chairs in the sitting-room. Her grandmother liked a nap in the afternoons, and there were several books which looked interesting. Judith opened the first of them and was asleep herself within two minutes.

Her two days went quickly although she did nothing much, content to potter in the tiny garden, do a few errands for her grandmother, change the library books and sit and gossip. It was on her last day that she saw an article about Charles Cresswell in a newspaper, lauding him to the skies for his scholarship and brilliant research. The book he was at present writing would be a world-wide success, it was predicted, and once it was published he was to embark upon a research into mediaeval manuscripts. He was, said the article, very modest about his work and disliked being interviewed—almost a recluse, stated the writer. Judith cast the paper from her with a snort of derision; what was so wonderful about twelfth-century England, anyway? And anyone who wanted to could go to the British Museum and look at dozens of manuscripts. The idea entered her head that she might do just that herself. She had an extra night due to her and Sister Read was back on duty. She began to work out the off duty in her head. There was no reason why she shouldn't add the extra day on to her usual nights off; it wasn't take-in week and anyway, each night was as busy as the last, so it would make no difference, for it would be inconvenient whichever she might choose. When she got back to the hospital she added one more night to her three off duty and since no one queried it, arranged to spend a day in London before driving home.

It would have been sensible to have gone to bed for a few hours when she got off duty, but for the moment at any rate she felt wide awake; besides, she would have a night's sleep before she drove home. She showered and changed into a cotton knitted dress and little jacket, made up her tired, beautiful face, piled her bright hair into a careless knot, found sandals and shoulder bag and went to queue for a bus. It was a pleasant change to feel free to do exactly what she liked with her day. Usually, if she went out in the mornings before going to bed, it was for necessary shopping or just for exercise. The bus was exasperatingly slow. She would walk back, she decided, but first of all, when she had spent an hour or two in the British Museum, she would have lunch somewhere.

She got out at last and crossed the courtyard, mounted the steps and went into the cool interior. It was ages since she had been there and she had forgotten how vast it was. She asked an attendant where the mediaeval manuscripts were housed and wandered off in their general direction, wasting a good deal of time on the way, her attention caught by displays of pottery and jewellery, weapons and ancient stone statues. When she finally arrived she saw at a glance that what she had intended to be a casual hour or so glancing at twelfth-century relics was going to turn into an earnest study of several hours in length. She wasn't sure where to begin; the Magna Carta seemed a fair start, except that it wasn't twelfth-century. She hung over the glass case for a long time, trying to understand it, and then passed on to the coins and seals. She was studying the Great Seal of Henry the Second when she felt that she was being watched. On the other side of the glass case was Charles Cresswell, looking at her with a nasty little smile on his handsome face. He said softly:

'Now I wonder why you're here, Judith Golightly? A genuine interest in the mediaeval? Or plain female curiosity about my work?'

She said with instant honesty. 'Curiosity mostly, but now I'm here interest too.'

He looked surprised and the smile disappeared. He said seriously: 'Why, I do believe you mean that.'

'Well, of course I do.' She turned away from him and became engrossed in a Saxon bucket with bronze bands, only to find that he was there beside her, pointing out the relief work on the bands, telling her the possible date where it was made and what it was used for.

'Very interesting,' said Judith, 'but don't let me keep you—I'm only browsing.'

'Then I shall browse with you.' No 'if I may', she thought crossly, and would have made a snappish retort, only he had already begun to lead the way to another section given over entirely to ecclesiastical objects. Indeed he took her arm and forced her to stop before a model of a twelfth-century church and began to point out its characteristics. 'A simple two-cell interior,' he told her, 'with an apse large enough to take the altar, slit windows, of course...' and when Judith asked: 'Why of course?' said impatiently: 'They were troubled times—and two doors in the north and south walls. From this grew the early medieval church. We can learn a great deal from the study of churches up and down the country—it's an absorbing topic...'

He had a pleasant deep voice, which combined with the hushed surroundings and the relics of what must have been another world had a soporific effect upon Judith. His voice took on a dreamlike quality, coming and going in waves, and she was forced to keep her eyes very wide open so that they shouldn't shut tight. She managed that all right, but she couldn't for the life of her stop a yawn; even smothered with a hasty hand it was all too obvious. Professor Cresswell paused in the middle of a fluent description of animal and plant symbols in churches and said in a quite different voice, cold and silky and sneering: 'My apologies Miss Golightly—I bore you.' He turned on his heel and walked away, leaving her shocked into instant wakefulness.

She went and sat down on a hard wooden bench against a wall after that. Her morning was quite spoilt, she longed above all things for a cup of coffee and bed. She closed her eyes and dozed off.

She didn't sleep for long, and when she woke, Charles Cresswell was sitting beside her, reading *The Times*. She sat up with a start and he said without looking up from his newspaper, 'You are a most abominable girl, you should have told me that you had been up all night.'

'Why?'

He ignored that. 'And why the British Museum? Hardly the place to visit with wits addled by lack of sleep!'

'My wits are not addled,' declared Judith, 'and I can see no reason why I should tell you anything.' She rather spoilt it by adding: 'I didn't know you were going to be here.'

'I'm surprised that you knew me—I had the impression at our last meeting that your greatest wish was to forget me as quickly as possible.'

'Well, actually it was, but I was curious about your work.'

He looked as though he was going to laugh. 'You're a very truthful girl, among other things.' He glanced at his watch. 'Shall we have lunch together? in a mutual dislike if you wish.' He smiled so disarmingly that she nodded, aware that she was hungry as well as tired.

'All right,' and then: 'That's twice,' she observed.

He knew what she meant. 'Yes, but the surroundings were pleasanter, were they not?'

'When I think about it it doesn't seem quite true. Are your dogs with you?'

'No—they're happy at Hawkshead and I'm never away for long.' He took her hand and pulled her gently to her feet. 'There's a small place near here, very quiet—no one will mind if you nod off over the soup.'

It was only a few minutes' walk and the fresh air revived her. They had a small table in the window, and without asking her he ordered an iced soft drink, enquired as to whether she disliked anything in particular and ordered for them both—iced melon, grilled sole and a salad and coffee. Judith was grateful that he didn't press her to have a drink. The food had revived her still further and she had better get back while she was feeling wide awake again. They sat over their coffee, talking amicably enough, indeed she found herself telling him all about her home, her pale face wistful so that he asked casually: 'Why do you stay at Beck's? I'm sure you have an excellent job there, but there must be other equally good posts.'

'I'm in a rut,' she told him. 'It needs something to dig me out—you know, something dramatic or urgent, so that I can resign without giving it a second thought.'

He eyed her thoughtfully. 'But preferably with a job to go to.'

'Oh, yes, I have to have a job.'

'Unless you get married?' His voice was casual.

An unwanted picture of Nigel floated before her eyes and she frowned. 'That's unlikely.'

He appeared to lose interest. 'Are you going back to Beck's? I'm going that way myself, I'll drop you off.'

Judith was too tired to refuse. He hailed a taxi and

she got in thankfully and sat silently until it stopped at the hospital gates.

'Thank you for my lunch,' she told him politely. 'I hope your book is a great success,' she added for good measure, 'with rave notices. And please give Uncle Tom my love when you see him.' She sighed very softly. 'The roses in your garden are very lovely—I can't forget them.'

He got out and stood beside her, looking down at her sleepy face with no expression at all on his own. 'Quite lovely,' he said, and took the hand she held out.

'And I'm sorry about the yawn,' said Judith. 'As a matter of fact you were being very interesting. When I've had a good sleep, I expect I'll remember it all.'

'I shall remember too,' he told her gravely, a remark which popped into her head just as she was on the point of sleep and which she couldn't quite understand. She was too tired to bother anyway.

Chapter 4

Judith wasn't sure why she didn't tell her mother that she had had lunch with Charles Cresswell. On her next visit home she described her morning at the British Museum at some length, but left him out, and when Mrs Golightly asked where she had had her lunch, replied with limited truth that she had gone to some little place close to the Museum.

'Rather dull on your own,' observed her mother, who where Judith was concerned had a kind of second sight and felt that she was being put off. Judith agreed readily enough; it would have been very dull on her own. So with this her mother had to be content, though she did drag Professor Cresswell's name into the conversation from time to time in the hope that Judith might let slip some remark about him. She was a firm believer in romance, true love and living hap-

pily ever after, and it seemed to her that Judith and the
Professor, once they had got over their dislike of each
other, might make a delightful pair. Grandchildren,
thought Mrs Golightly happily, coming to visit her for
the school holidays—something to look forward to.
She found an article about the Professor in one of the
loftier magazines and left it lying around, opened at
the right page, and watched to see how Judith would
react. Judith, a loving daughter but very well aware of
her mother's wiles, ignored it.

She drove back to London under a sky heavy with
the threat of a storm, but she was comfortably in her
room, changing to go on duty, by the time it broke. It
was still raging when she went along to take the report of the day's happenings in the Surgical Wing, with
thunder crashing and rumbling and lightning streaking through the window as she sat down to the résumé
left for her. The Ward Sisters would already have given
their reports to the various night nurses on each ward
and presently she would start on her round and read
them all for herself, but now she digested the bones of
the happenings on them, knowing that only the most
serious of the cases would be in her own report. She
had finished reading about the main wards and was beginning on the private patients' corridor when her eye
caught a name. Cresswell—Lady Cresswell. Admitted with suspected leukaemia, aged sixty-one, living
at an upper crust address in Belgravia; nearest rela-
tion: Professor Charles Cresswell. There were two telephone numbers, one a London number, the other, if
her memory served her well, the number she dialled
when she telephoned Uncle Tom. 'Oh, lord,' said Ju-

dith, 'of all the infuriating things to happen!' At least she was on night duty, which meant she would never see Charles Cresswell.

She started on her rounds, dismissing the matter from her mind for the time being. There was enough to attend to in the Men's Surgical ward where there had been four admissions, two of them in poor shape. Half way round, she stopped to have coffee with Sister Reed, compare notes, discuss the patients worrying them, and who was to do what during the night, and then she went on her way again. At least there weren't any theatre cases, which meant that Sister Reed was free to take over her share of the drug checking.

There were ten private rooms beyond the main women's surgical ward, lining one side of a wide corridor overlooking the inner courtyard of Beck's. They were pleasant, as pleasant as a hospital room could look, and had the added advantage of a separate entrance at the other end of the corridor so that visitors could come and go without disturbing the main wards. Judith dismissed the staff nurse who had accompanied her on her round so far; there was enough work to do without her keeping her unnecessarily, and the private patients sometimes took up a good deal of time—not being in the wards they had little idea of the constant round of chores going on, and while Judith found their leisurely attitude towards hospital routine irksome when she was busy, she hardly blamed them for it. After all, they were paying handsomely for their beds and treatment and for the most part they were pleasant, co-operative and grateful.

Of course, there was always the odd man out—and

he was in the first room. She tapped on the door, and went in, sighing inwardly. Mr Forsythe had an ulcer, brought on by his obsession for making money. Even here in his hospital bed, he read the financial papers, spent hours telephoning those he employed to help him amass even more of it, and in between lived on stomach powders and a miserable steamed fish diet. No amount of arguing had made him agree to have an operation, and as far as she could see, they were stuck with him forever. She went over to the bed, wished him a cheerful good evening and listened patiently to his complaints. Most of them were to do with his stocks and shares going down instead of up, and any questions she might have managed to put were impatiently waved aside. His ulcer was a nuisance, but quite secondary to his need to make more money. She coaxed him to take something to make him sleep and went on to the next patient.

Mr King, unlike his neighbour, had no interest in money, for he had very little of it, but he had a loving family who shared the burden of his hospital fees and brought him the cassettes of the classical music he loved so that he could play them incessantly, something he wouldn't have been able to do in the main wards. Judith listened to the last bit of Fauré's Requiem with deep satisfaction, offered necessary pills and went on her way, feeling sad. Mr King was a dear old man and wasn't going to get better. She knew that, so did his family, so did he, and there was very little to be done about it.

The next two rooms were empty, waiting for patients booked for the next day, and in the fifth room the young girl with the appendix was asleep.

The next three rooms were easy, all patients who were on the point of going home, merely wanting a few minutes' chat before settling down for the night, and the ninth was a young woman with a very small baby who had been operated upon for pyloric stenosis. The tenth door was shut, but there was a light over the door still. Judith tapped and went in.

Lady Cresswell was sitting up in bed, reading. Judith hadn't had any idea what she would be like, but she wasn't prepared for the comfortably plump, positively cosy figure leaning back against the pillows, who took off large, owl-like spectacles and beamed cheerfully at her from a round still pretty face, crowned by short white curls.

'Good evening, Sister,' she smiled, and held out a hand. 'I feel such a fraud, lying here, wasting everyone's time. I'm sure all these tests the doctors want to do could have been done at home...'

Judith smiled. 'Well, I suppose so, but it would have been a lot of extra work for them, you know. I see you're only here for a few days—I should enjoy them if you can, bed can be very nice when you're not ill.'

The little lady nodded her head vigorously. 'And I've a pile of books to read.'

Judith glanced at them, a catholic mixture she would dearly have loved to sit down and browse through. 'I'll change places,' she said flippantly because she sensed that Lady Cresswell intended to look on the bright side. She didn't know what her doctors had told her, probably a half truth, paving the way for bad news should the test prove conclusive. She was sure that her patient wasn't a woman to be fobbed off with vague talk, neither did she wish to be drowned in pessimism. They chatted happily enough for five minutes or so, during which time Lady Cresswell made no mention of her son at all. Perhaps they weren't very close, thought Judith, hurrying back to relieve Sister Reed; the bright little lady seemed quite the wrong type of mother for such a cold fish as the Professor.

She forgot all about it during the next hour or so, and when she did her second round, Lady Cresswell was sleeping like a child.

She was awake when Judith did her final early morning round, though; full of cheerful small talk, but Judith learned nothing of her personal life.

'You'll be having your first test this morning,' she told her. 'Nothing to worry about, though. I'll see you this evening.'

She went for a walk in the park before she went to bed; the storm had passed, but it was dull and oppressively warm still. There was really nothing to keep her from her bed and there was another busy night ahead of her. But in bed, she didn't sleep at once; she found herself wondering about Lady Cresswell. If they diagnosed leukaemia, whichever type it was, she had a good chance of being kept alive for a number of years still. Perhaps they would decide not to tell her; she went to sleep pondering the advantages and disadvantages of being told the truth or being fobbed off with a watered-down version of the diagnosis.

The first hour of the night went quickly. Judith was busy, but no more than usual, her rounds went without a hitch, and although Nigel appeared when she was barely half way round the main wards, she snubbed him so severely that he walked off, saying coldly over his shoulder that he wasn't on call anyway, and if she wanted help she should get Mr Wright or Mr Davies. 'I was hoping for a cup of coffee,' he observed frostily.

'Well, I often hope for it too,' said Judith, 'but I don't always get it.' She adjusted a drip to a nicety. 'But I daresay there's some on the stove in the Men's Surgical kitchen if you'd like to help yourself.'

He wouldn't, of course, he was a man who expected to have things handed to him and then cleared away afterwards.

It was earlier than usual by the time Judith tapped on Lady Cresswell's door and went in. Her patient was sitting up in bed looking charming in a pink bed-jacket and discreet make-up, and sitting beside her was Charles Cresswell.

He got to his feet and wished her an unsmiling good evening, then walked over to the window and turned his back on them. Judith flung a glance at his long lean back and then ignored him.

'Well, how did the tests go?' she asked cheerfully. The preliminary results of two of them were already in her report book, but she wanted to feel her way; perhaps Lady Cresswell hadn't been told the result, especially as they weren't conclusive. There was still a test meal to do, to eliminate a simple or pernicious anaemia and a sternal puncture.

'They say they won't know until tomorrow after-noon.' The blue eyes stared up at her as though try-ing to read her thoughts, so she smiled steadily back.

'It takes a bit of time—they weren't too bad, were they?'

'Good gracious, no, my dear. Tomorrow sounds much much worse.'

'Not really. They explained the test meal, I expect? I'll be along very early in the morning to get it started, you'll hardly be aware of it.'

'How comforting you are! But the other thing—I don't much like the sound of that.'

'Over in a jiffy, and done by your consultant's own hand. Nothing to worry about. Have you had your evening drink, Lady Cresswell?'

'Yes, dear. Something very nourishing and milky. And now before you go you must meet my son, Charles.'

He had turned round now, staring at her in a most unamiable manner.

'We've already met, Mother,' he spoke impatiently. 'In Cumbria.'

'Well, fancy that!' His mother looked from one to other of them in a speculative way. 'It is a small world, to be sure.'

Judith smiled in a non-committal fashion. 'Well, I must be going. I'll be along later to make sure you're asleep.'

'Yes, dear. What do you do now?'

'Well, there's still a patient in theatre and we're expecting two admissions as soon as X-ray has finished with them.'

'Good heavens! Don't you have a rest or a meal?'

'Oh, sometimes—it's not as bad as it sounds.' She included them both in her smile. 'Goodnight.'

She left a silence behind her which Lady Cresswell finally broke. 'It's years since I've seen you to be the least bit interested in a girl, Charles.'

He put his hands in his pockets and looked down at his well polished shoes. 'I wasn't aware...' he began in a cool voice.

'No, dear, I daresay not. For a long time now you've treated all females in exactly the same way; pleasant, courteous, very mindful of their comfort and not caring a damn about any of them. But this magnificent creature seems to have got under your skin.' She put her head on one side and added thoughtfully: 'I wonder if she knows that?' And when he didn't answer: 'I was having a little gossip with the Day Sister this afternoon; there's a registrar very keen on this sweet creature—pesters her to marry him. He's a dreadful bore.'

Her son laughed. 'Mother, how uncharitable! He may be a very decent fellow.'

'He's very good-looking, so I'm told, and very conceited—not her type. Charles, before you go—what is her name?' She smiled gently. 'I know the Golightly bit—isn't that sweet—but the rest of it?'

'Judith.' He bent and kissed her. 'I'm going now and you're going to sleep. I'll be along tomorrow, probably in the afternoon.'

'Avoiding each other, are you?'

He shook his head at her. 'Dear Mother, quash your romantic thoughts, will you? I have no plans to marry, or for that matter, fall in love.'

'No, dear.' His mother sounded very meek.

She was asleep when Judith did her midnight round and not a word was said about her son when the test meal was got under way in the morning. Having got it started, Judith left it to the night staff nurse and went to finish her report. Two more nights and she would go home again for her two days off. She tucked the pleasant thought away and bent to her writing.

That evening the report on Lady Cresswell wasn't so good. The red cell count was unsatisfactory and the white cell count was strongly indicative of leukaemia—not, it was thought, an acute type, which meant that with proper care and medication Lady Cresswell might live for a number of years yet. But there was still the sternal puncture result to wait for, and that would clinch the matter. Judith sighed, because she liked the little lady, and then because she had seventy-odd patients to think about as well, dismissed her from her mind for the time being.

Lady Cresswell had been crying, that was apparent to Judith the moment she opened the door of the room. It was equally apparent that her patient wouldn't thank her for remarking upon her puffy eyes and red nose, so she wished her a perfectly normal good evening, remarked on the beauty of an enormous bouquet of choice flowers on the bedside table and waited.

After a moment Lady Cresswell spoke, 'I insisted that they should tell me.' Her voice was small but defiant. 'They weren't going to, you know. They would have called it anaemia or something and advised me not to get too tired and to eat liver. I loathe liver—but now I'm not sure if I want to know after all. Charles says it's a good thing because now I can forget all about it and that I'll probably outlive him, anyway.' She gave a small sniff.

Good for Charles, thought Judith, and said out loud, in a calm matter-of-fact way: 'He's absolutely right, you know.' She sat down on the edge of the bed and took one of Lady Cresswell's delicate little hands in her own capable ones. 'If you were a child or even a young adult, the outlook might not be all that rosy, although they've got these marvellous new drugs nowadays— but the older one gets the longer you're able to resist it—probably you'll live till you're ninety-nine and die of old age! You'll get your ups and downs, of course, but we all get those, don't we? and providing you do what your doctor suggests, you'll be perfectly OK. And I've not made any of that up, either—it's gospel truth.'

Lady Cresswell managed a quite cheerful smile. 'What a nice girl you are, Judith! I think I feel better already. I'm getting used to it, it's that that's so difficult, isn't it?' She paused. 'Tell me something—why am I in a surgical ward? I've only had tests done—they're not going to do anything they haven't told me about?'

'Good gracious, no! Didn't anyone tell you that the medical side was full up when you were admitted? Don't worry, no one's going to do anything. You'll be here for a few days yet while your treatment is worked out, then you'll be able to go home.'

'Charles won't hear of that—I've a flat here in London, you know. I'm most comfortable there and I have a splendid housekeeper, but he insists that I go and stay with him, at least for a month or so.'

'You'll like that. It's so beautiful in the Lakes—I'd live there if I could, and he has a lovely house. But you must have seen it.'

Lady Cresswell had turned her face a little away.

'Yes, dear,' she said vaguely, 'Charles and I spend quite a good bit of time together, that is when he's not writing. He loved it as a small boy and his father left it to him—he doesn't care for London, but of course he has to come here from time to time.' She was silent for a few moments. 'You did mean what you said, didn't you?'

'Yes,' said Judith steadily, 'every word of it.' She got off the bed to check the charts. 'Would you like a mild sleeping pill, do you think? Or would you rather read for a while? I'll…'

The door opened and Charles Cresswell came in. He had a bottle under one arm, and was holding two glasses as well. He nodded to Judith in a careless way and said: 'I've brought my mother a nightcap—champagne. You'll have a glass with us?'

Judith paused half way to the door. 'How kind, but no, thank you.' She wanted to tell him not to stay too long, but one look at Lady Cresswell's face told her that champagne with her son at eleven o'clock at night was going to do more good than the most efficient of sleeping pills. She said merely: 'I'll be back later, Lady Cresswell,' in a tone of voice which implied that she hoped he would be gone by then, added a pleasant goodnight and left them together.

Lady Cresswell sipped her champagne. 'Charles, will you do something for me?'

He said yes without any hesitation at all.

'Will you arrange for Judith to come with me when I come to stay with you?'

'You would like that, my dear?' If she had hoped to surprise him, she hadn't succeeded.

'Very much. She gives me confidence, you see, and I—want that, just for a little while.'

'I understand. Yes, I'll arrange that, but you'll have to persuade her, you know. If I were to ask her she would refuse point blank.'

He spoke pleasantly with no sign of annoyance.

'You won't mind? Judith being in the house? Since you dislike each other, I mean.'

'Why should I? I shall be working for a good deal of the day—I've got the proofs to check, and I hope my manners are sufficiently good to get us through meals.'

His mother peeped at his expressionless face. 'Charles dear, if you hate the idea, I won't ask her...'

He put down his glass. 'Mother, I'm completely indifferent about the matter. It is, in fact, a good idea, because it will leave me free to work without delay and feeling guilty at leaving you on your own.'

His mother eyed him lovingly. He had lived alone far too long, in another few years he would be a dry-as-dust bachelor, sinking into premature middle age. Distinguished, good-looking, well-to-do, much sought after by women on the look-out for a husband, but quite impervious to them. Bother the creature! thought Lady Cresswell wrathfully, remembering the seventeen-year-old girl who had spent a summer charming the heart out of her son's body and then wafting away from him, swathed in white tulle and lace, down the aisle with his best friend. He'd got over it years ago, she was certain of that, although he had never realised it. She doubted very much if he remembered what the girl looked like. It was high time someone broke the spell, and who better than Judith with her lovely face...she

was a thoroughly nice girl too. She said soothingly:
'Yes, of course, dear. Will the hospital let her go?'

'If you can persuade her to come to Hawkshead with
you, I'll see that there are no difficulties.'

And Lady Cresswell nodded happily. Charles had a
way with him when he wanted something. She foresaw
no trouble, and she was so determined to throw them
together. She lightly dismissed the idea that neither
of them might welcome the idea of being thrown—
after all, she concluded inappropriately, love would
find a way.

When her son got up to go presently, she offered a
cheerful face for his kiss, assured him that she was no
longer despairing and promised that she would sleep
soundly. Which she did.

She had decided to say nothing to Judith in the
morning; after a long night's work, she would be in
no mood to be argued with or cajoled. Lady Cresswell possessed her soul in patience, forbore from saying a single word to her son when he came to see her,
presented a bright face to the doctors and nurses and
bided her time.

Judith was earlier than usual that evening. All three
Sisters were on duty, which meant that the work load
could be spread between them. It happened seldom,
they would be back to their usual two on and one off
on the following night, but by then her own nights off
would be due. She worked her way round the wom-
en's surgical ward and started on the private patients'
corridor, feeling a strange reluctance to get to Lady
Cresswell's room. She hadn't expected to see Charles
Cresswell and it had annoyed her so much that she had

slept badly in consequence. But lightning never strikes twice in the same place, she told herself, it was just bad luck that he had come when she was there. All the same, she felt an unaccountable let down feeling when she found her patient alone. A very cheerful patient too.

'I've been waiting all day to talk to you,' observed Lady Cresswell, 'I do hope you can spare me five minutes, Judith.'

'Well, as a matter of fact, I can. So far it's very quiet on the surgical side and I've got two other Sisters with me.' Judith smiled and sat down composedly by the bed. It took no longer to sit down and the patients relaxed more; hovering on one foot by the bed did no good at all.

'I'm going to ask you to do something for me,' began Lady Cresswell. 'You'll say "No" at once, but please, I do beg you, go away and think about it. It's very important to me, but I'm not going to fish for sympathy I have that already, I know that, but I know that I need help, just for a little while. I've remembered all you told me about living to a ripe old age, and I believe you, but I have been given a death sentence, haven't I? I'll accept that as best I can, but it takes a little swallowing. Judith, I want to take you with me to Hawkshead. It's asking a great deal of you—you've a splendid career here, and probably you've a young man here too— you're far too pretty not to have—and I've no right at all to ask you, but would you consider it?'

Judith sat and looked at her hands, lying quietly in her lap. Hawkshead, she thought, and all the glorious country round it. Uncle Tom to visit, the rose garden and last: Charles.

She raised her quiet face. 'I must think about it, Lady Cresswell, but I promise you that I will do just that. May I have a day before I give you my answer?'

Lady Cresswell managed not to grin from ear to ear. 'I understand, of course, dear. I'm to be here for another few days, I believe. I'm not sure how things can be arranged...'

'Or even if they can be arranged. It's rather unusual, you know. In fact I've never heard of it being done.'

Lady Cresswell looked faintly smug. 'Well, we can but try—that is if you agree?' She added: 'They tell me I shall grow no worse for some time, which is a comfort—several years, they mentioned. At my age that's very comforting.'

Judith had read the notes. Five years at the most, more probably two or three. And that with the very best of care and treatment. She said: 'That's splendid news! I may be wrong, but I think you'll find that after you've got over the shock, life will become quite normal again—several years can be anything up to twelve or fifteen.'

'You think so? Then I will too.' The little lady lay down in her bed and allowed herself to be tucked up. 'I shall sleep well, I always do,' she said happily: 'And you won't forget, will you, Judith?'

'No, of course not. Goodnight, Lady Cresswell.'

The rest of the night was quiet too. Judith had time to think, but by morning she had to admit that she had got nowhere at all. Oh, for a sign, she sighed as she started on her morning round. There was none, she had given her report to the Senior Nursing Officer and was making her slow way to breakfast when she came face to face with Charles Cresswell. Hardly the answer to a maiden's prayer but perhaps a way of making a decision.

His 'good morning' was perfunctory and he would have passed her on the stairs. Her weary brain wondered why he was there so early in the morning, but she couldn't be bothered to ask. She fetched up in front of him and said without preamble: 'Your mother has told you that she wants me to go to Hawkshead with her?'

'She has mentioned it.' He spoke carelessly and glanced at his watch, which sent her temper sky high. The effort to keep calm on an empty stomach and with the beginnings of a headache was enormous.

'It's kind of her to ask me, but of course I can't possibly do it…'

'Is the rut too deep, Judith? It's understandable, of course, you're secure and safe in it, aren't you; it leads predictably to steady promotion over the years, and a pension at the end too.' He ignored her angry gasp. 'Or Nigel, of course…'

'How do you know about Nigel?' she asked furiously.

His voice was silky. 'You forget that I spend a good deal of my life upon research work—I'm quite good at it.'

'You have no business to interfere!'

He raised his eyebrows. 'Who's interfering? Let me make it quite clear, Judith, that I am not interfering—I'm not interested enough. But let me also make it clear that I will do everything in my power to make the rest of my mother's life happy. Presumably you've read the reports. Even at their most optimistic, five years is a very short time in the end and in all probability it will be two or three, even less. There's no guarantee. And you did say that you were in a rut. Surely this is a heaven-sent chance to get out of it before you're too old.'

'I'm twenty-seven,' she snapped. Her blue eyes flashed and her pale sleepy face was pink with indignation.

'That's what I mean,' he said infuriatingly. 'I've never thought of you as a timid girl, Judith.' His mouth twitched at the corners and she supposed he was amused. 'You're still young enough to accept a challenge, you're strong and healthy—and with each year the rut's going to get deeper.' He grinned suddenly: 'There's always Nigel, of course.'

'How dare you!' she fumed at him. 'You're insufferable—just because you want your own way...'

'For my mother, Judith.'

She ignored that. 'Anyway, I can't leave at a moment's notice—I have to resign three months ahead.'

He examined the nails of one large, capable hand. 'Yes, I know that. There are exceptions.' He shot her a lightning glance. 'I'm on the Board of Governors, these things can be arranged.' He said in quite a different voice: 'Hawkshead, Judith, early on a summer morning, not a patient in sight, only roses and great sweeps of mountain and calm water—and you would be giving my mother a little longer to live because she trusts you and believes in you and you make her feel normal. Only one patient against eighty, but surely she has as much right to live as any of them?' He added: 'If you

wish, I'll arrange things so that you can return here if
and when my mother no longer needs you.'

He was cutting the ground from under her feet. 'I
won't be rushed,' she said quickly, and he agreed at
once.

'Of course not. Let Mother know this evening, if
you feel you've had enough time to consider it.' Then
he turned abruptly away from her. 'Good morning,
Judith.'

Dismissed lightly like a naughty schoolchild, fumed
Judith, racing down the rest of the stairs and catapult-
ing into the canteen ten minutes late.

'And where have you been?' her friends wanted to
know. 'You look as mad as fire, Judith—was it Nigel?'

'No, it wasn't.' She made an effort to be in good
spirits. 'I've had a messy kind of morning, that's all.'

'Nigel's looking for you,' said someone on the other
side of the table.

'Something wrong? That man in Surgical, the one
with the hernia…?'

'No, silly, not patients. He's got tickets for some
show or other and he wants you to go with him on
your night off. The tickets were given to him,' added
the voice maliciously.

Judith was gobbling cornflakes. 'I'm going home.
You go.'

'He's not my boy-friend.'

'He's not mine either.' She realised as she said it
that he really wasn't, not even in a lukewarm way; she
didn't mind if she didn't see him ever again, she didn't
mind if she never saw Beck's again… I must be mad,

she told herself silently. I'll feel better when I've had a good sleep.

She buttered toast and had a third cup of tea; it was time she had some nights off, she was getting light-headed.

Chapter 5

Judith knew what she was going to do the moment she opened her eyes that evening. She got up and dressed, went along for her breakfast and went on duty, and in due course reached Lady Cresswell's room. Charles Cresswell wasn't there, but she hadn't expected him to be; all the same she felt let down. She wished her patient a good evening, checked the charts, asked how she felt and only then said matter-of-factly: 'I'll come with you, Lady Cresswell, for as long as you should need me. There's one thing, though—Professor Cresswell and I don't get on at all well and I think that must be understood from the beginning. We both know it, of course, and I hope we're adult enough to be sensible about it, and I see no reason why we should have to see much of each other.'

'Charles has said much the same thing to me, Judith.' Lady Cresswell turned a beaming face to her. 'But as you say, you are neither of you childish about it. My dear, I can't begin to tell you how delighted I am! You're sure, aren't you?'

'Yes, I am. I think I've been wanting to get away from hospital life for quite a while, but I needed someone to give me a poke to get me started.'

'And I gave you that poke,' said Lady Cresswell with deep satisfaction. She closed her eyes and looked thoughtful. 'Such a lot of things to think about,' she remarked.

It was a little bewildering how quickly things were arranged. Judith had had no idea that one was able to leave one's employment with so little fuss or delay. True, the Principal Nursing Officer expressed regret at her going, but never once queried it. She had been told that she might go home in three days' time to visit her parents if she wished and then return to the hospital to collect her patient and be driven with her to Hawkshead. There was a chauffeur, it transpired, a steady reliable man called William guaranteed to get them there in comfort and safety. All this was arranged without a sign of Professor Cresswell, let alone anyone consulting her wishes. Once or twice she was sorely tempted to back down and refuse to go, and then the sight of Lady Cresswell's happy face made her change her mind. After all, one could not be so heartless as to cast a damper on what might be the last few months of her life. She bade her friends goodbye and listened to their astonished comments with a detached astonishment as great as their own. She must be mad, she told herself a dozen times as she drove herself home, and was astonished all over again at her mother's pleased acceptance of the situation.

'Nothing could be better,' declared her parent. 'Another year of hospital and you would have become so set in your ways…it would have been a job for life unless you'd married Nigel.'

Judith shuddered; Nigel had been tiresome. If only he had put his foot down and refused to hear of her leaving; declared that he loved her to distraction and married her out of hand—she might even have got to like him in time. He had done none of these things; he had blustered a good deal, but he had plainly been overawed by Professor Cresswell's power to get his own way. Judith had parted from him without regret but with the feeling that she had cut the last link with her past life. Starting again had its attractions, somewhat marred, though, by Professor Cresswell's dislike of her.

She spent two feverish days at home, packing clothes. It was high summer, but it could be chilly in Cumbria. She weeded out her wardrobe until she had slacks, cotton tops, cotton dresses and a thick cardigan, and just in case there should be any social activities, which she very much doubted, a couple of pretty crêpe dresses, a plastic mac, a pair of low-heeled worthy walking shoes, some frivolous sandals and a modicum of undies. She had no idea how long she would be with Lady Cresswell, but she doubted if they would stay there for more than a month, and when they did leave, she would just have to come home again and get warmer clothing.

Driving back to London, she reflected that her parents had been surprisingly calm about the whole business; after all, she was, from a practical point of view, being rather silly—giving up a good job with a certain secure future for something which might last only a few weeks, even months before she would have to find something else. Oh, well, it was too late now to worry about that. She was to be well paid and since there would be small opportunity of her spending any of her salary at Hawkshead she wouldn't be destitute. Besides, she had a small nest egg which she had prudently added to from time to time.

Her spirits lifted. It was very early in the morning and it was going to be a splendid day. The sun was already warm and the sky cloudless and the thought of being free—well, almost free—filled her with sudden pleasure.

She had arranged for one of her friends to borrow her car while she was away, a cunning move to ensure that it was taken care of and parked in comparative safety at the hospital. Lady Cresswell's old-fashioned Daimler was already parked at the entrance and a sturdy middle-aged man, whom she took to be the trustworthy William, was sitting at the wheel. He got out as she approached, took her case and overnight bag from her, greeted her civilly and expressed the hope that Lady Cresswell wasn't going to be too long in coming as the traffic was getting thicker every minute.

Judith took the hint and hurried up to the Surgical Private Wing where she found her patient dressed and almost ready but having second thoughts about which scarf she should wear with her elegant grey silk suit.

'The pink,' said Judith promptly, and to the little nurse who was in attendance, 'If you'll ring for the porter and a chair, Nurse, I'll go along and tell Sister we're ready to leave.'

'Lucky you,' declared that young lady when Judith poked her head round the office door, 'off to heaven knows what fun and games while I'm stuck here for ever.'

'Well, there won't be fun and games,' observed Judith, 'and I daresay I'll be looking for another job in a few weeks' time.'

'Time enough to get our Charles in tow—we're going to miss him.'

'I haven't seen him for I don't know how long,' said Judith not quite truthfully, 'and he'll be buried in his books, I fancy I'm to be seen and not heard and make sure that his mother doesn't distract him.'

'It won't be his mother who distracts him,' her companion looked her over slowly. 'I hate to say it, Judith, but you look uncommonly pretty this morning. He's rather a charmer, you know.'

'Not my cup of tea,' said Judith lightly, not quite sure if she meant that or not. 'Are you coming to see us off the premises?'

She couldn't resist a quick look round her when she reached the entrance. She hadn't expected to see Charles Cresswell, but there was just the chance that he might have come to see them safely on the road to his home.

Lady Cresswell said quickly: 'No, dear, Charles isn't here. He went back last night.'

William, despite his stolid appearance, proved to be a fast driver once they were on the motorway; even so it was a journey of nearly three hundred miles and Ju-

dith wasn't surprised to hear that they were to spend a
night on the way—a piece of news Charles Cresswell
hadn't bothered to tell her, but then he had behaved in
a very high-handed manner throughout the whole business and doubtless would again. There was no point in
getting vexed about it, so she enquired placidly where
they were to put up and was told that he had booked
rooms for them at a hotel in Shifnal, north of Birmingham. They would leave the motorway to reach it, but
it was a small elegant establishment, said Lady Cresswell, and quiet, in its own grounds.

With a stop for lunch, they reached the hotel in the
late afternoon and Judith got her patient into bed without delay. Lady Cresswell was happy and excited, but
she was also tired. Judith stayed with her while she
ate a light dinner, and then went down to the dining
room herself, where the head waiter, quite taken with
her pretty face, gave her one of the best tables and
made sure that she lacked nothing. She ate a delicious
meal, quite unconcerned by the admiring glances cast
upon her from those around her. She was aware that
she was beautiful; she would have been a fool if she
hadn't known that, but she deplored her magnificent
figure, considering herself far too generously built,
even although she was tall with it, so that her vanity
was small. She thanked the waiter nicely as she went,
asked if she might have breakfast early in her room,
and went back to Lady Cresswell, now ready to be settled for the night, but ready too for a cosy chat before
she slept. It was almost an hour later by the time Judith
went to her own room next door and another hour before she got into bed. She had meant to do some think-

ing, but she was asleep before she had even a vague thought in her head.

They reached Hawkshead in the late afternoon and Charles Cresswell, with Mrs Turner hovering behind him, was waiting for them. She had to admire the way in which he had everyone organised with the minimum of fuss and time. William dealt with their luggage, Mrs Turner bore the tea tray into the sitting room and relieved Judith of the impedimenta with which Lady Cresswell found it necessary to travel, and Charles Cresswell installed his mother in a high-backed chair while Judith poured her a cup of tea. Only then did he turn to her and ask formally if they had had a good journey.

'Excellent, thank you.' She handed him a cup of tea and poured one for herself.

'If you wish to telephone your parents, please do so—your uncle too.'

There was no warmth in his voice and she thanked him woodenly before addressing herself to Lady Cresswell's wants.

And after that she hardly spoke to him, let alone saw him for several days. True, he took lunch with them and if his mother stayed up for dinner shared that meal with them too, but if Lady Cresswell had a tray in bed, then Judith dined alone, for it was always on such a night that he was dining out, unable to leave his writing, or setting out on some errand which had to be done just as dinner was announced. Judith pretended to herself that she didn't mind; it was so obvious that he was avoiding her, and she told herself that she couldn't care less. All the same, she felt hurt and puzzled too, for why had he been so insistent about her accompanying his mother if he couldn't bear the sight of her?

The days wove themselves into a gentle pattern. Lady Cresswell didn't like to be roused until half past eight at the earliest, so Judith quickly formed the habit of getting up early, having tea with Mrs Turner in the kitchen and then pottering round the garden for an hour before she had her own breakfast—alone, of course; she had no idea where or when Charles Cresswell had his. She would have liked to have had it in the kitchen with Mrs Turner, but that lady didn't hold with that, so she ate it in lonely state in the dining room before going upstairs to wake Lady Cresswell.

The mornings were pleasant enough, and after the ordered rush of the hospital, very welcome. Lady Cresswell hadn't given in to her illness; her make-up was as faultless as it always had been, every hair was in place, every day time and thought was given as to what she should wear. Judith liked her for that and took pains to see that she looked as well turned out as possible, and on the days when Lady Cresswell wasn't feeling so well, Judith did her hair, helped her dress, and added a little colour to cheeks which were paler than they should have been. They sat in the garden after that, and if it wasn't warm enough, in the drawing room while Lady Cresswell worked at her tapestry and Judith knitted a sweater for her father and sometimes she would read aloud. It was all very peaceful and quiet and it might have been a little dull, but after lunch each day, when she had settled her patient for her nap, she was free for a couple of hours, and then she would go down to see Uncle Tom or walk or climb a little. No one had suggested that she should have a free day and by the end of the second week she decided to ask for one. A trip to Kendal would be nice and there were one or two things she needed. The butcher's son had offered to drive her in on any day she chose to name, and she would take him at his word.

She was on her way to the dining room to eat her dinner that evening when the Professor came out of his study, looking handsome and remote in a dinner jacket. He would have passed her with a murmured greeting, only she stopped in front of him so that he had to come to a standstill.

'I won't keep you a minute,' said Judith pleasantly, 'but I see you so seldom that I must make the most of the opportunity...'

'Tomorrow morning?' he asked impatiently. 'I'm already late.'

'No, because tomorrow morning you won't want to be disturbed, or you'll go out. I don't expect you know it, but I'm entitled to a day off—one a week at least—and I should like one this week. Friday would do nicely if you could arrange to be at home with Lady Cresswell, or perhaps Mrs Turner could be with her?'

It was obvious that he hadn't given the matter a thought. He said stiffly: 'I'm sorry, I should have thought of it and made some arrangements. By all means have your day, and perhaps you'll be good enough to let me know at the beginning of each week which one you want. How long do you wish to be away? Perhaps I should warn the district nurse...'

'No need. I'll go after breakfast and be back by tea time.'

'You will be going with someone?' He spoke carelessly.

Judith thought of the butcher's son. George was a nice young man and there was no need to tell the Professor that she was going with him in the butcher's van. She told him yes, still very pleasant.

He nodded, glanced at his watch and said: 'If there's nothing further, Judith, I'll say goodnight,' and went.

She drank her excellent soup gloomily. It seemed very likely that he was rushing off to a date—that awful Eileen Hunt. There had been no sign of her yet, but Judith had been sent to the study by Lady Cresswell that morning when her son hadn't been there, to retrieve a letter she wanted to answer, and on the large cluttered desk there had been a large photograph of the girl with 'Always Yours' scrawled across one corner. Judith wondered if Lady Cresswell knew about her and if she liked the idea of having her for a daughter-in-law. It had seemed to Judith, studying the pretty, hard little face, that Eileen was the kind of girl who would arrange to have her mother-in-law admitted to a nursing home; it would be done very nicely and so swiftly that no one would notice or quite realise what was happening.

She ate the rest of her dinner with small appetite so that Mrs Turner wanted to know in some alarm if she was sickening for something.

After the first few days it was apparent that Lady Cresswell hadn't taken any harm from her journey, so Judith suggested that the pair of them might take a short drive each day, after tea when Lady Cresswell was rested. There was another car in the garage beside the Ferrari Dino and the Range Rover, a Mini, not often used from the look of her. Judith cast an eye over the little car and went straight to the study, where, undeterred by Charles Cresswell's cold voice bidding her enter, she asked for the use of it. He hadn't answered her for a minute or two, eyeing her thoughtfully, then: 'Quite a good idea, Judith. I've wondered if I should have kept William here so that my mother could be driven round. By all means borrow the Mini—you will, of course, be careful…'

Judith drew a breath. 'You can always send for William,' she suggested sweetly.

'And if I think it advisable, I shall do so.' His voice was silky. 'And now, if you don't mind, I'm working.'

It was a pity, she thought as she shut the door with exaggerated quietness, that they couldn't speak to each other without being thoroughly unpleasant.

She took Lady Cresswell for a short drive that very evening. Someone had cleaned and polished the Mini and the tank was full; she really had to give the Professor full marks for getting things organised, but of course he was a good son, anxious to do everything possible to keep his mother happy.

They drove to Clappersgate, Skelworth Bridge and Coniston and then took the cross-country road back to Hawkshead, a successful little outing which she hoped would be the first of several.

Two days later she went to Kendal with George, sitting beside him in the butcher's van. They parted company in the car park with a mutual promise to meet at half past three and Judith wandered off to look at the shops, buy the odds and ends she needed, and give herself lunch.

George was already there when she got back, and she squeezed in beside him, rubbing shoulders with the Canterbury lamb and half pigs loaded into the back. She was busy removing a muslin-wrapped pig's trotter from the back of her neck when she glanced up and saw Charles Cresswell and Eileen Hunt watching her from the pavement. Eileen was frankly laughing; the Professor was inscrutable.

That evening at dinner, without referring to the butcher's van, he told her that in future she was to have the use of the Mini on her day off. He didn't wait for her thanks but made some remark to his mother, and as soon as the meal was finished he excused himself and shut himself in his study. He came out again as Judith was going to bed some hours later and very much to her surprise expressed the hope that she had enjoyed her free day. Moreover, his voice was kind and he smiled warmly at her.

She got up very early the next morning, prompted by the clear sky and the sunshine. The house was very quiet; she wrapped her dressing gown around her and crept downstairs. Mrs Turner wasn't down yet, and wouldn't be for another hour. Judith put on the kettle, opened the kitchen door and wandered out into the garden, sniffing at the cool breeze and the scent of the roses before going back indoors to make the tea. Too early to take Mrs Turner a cup and far too early to rouse Lady Cresswell. She took a mug from the dresser and carried the steaming brew on to the doorstep. Life was really rather splendid, she thought; Lady Cresswell was looking decidedly better—probably she had entered a period of recession which might last for weeks, if not months—the country around her was heavenly and it was going to be a lovely day, and over and above that, Charles had actually smiled at her! Quite carried away by her feelings, she began to hum softly and presently to sing, not very loudly at first, imagining herself to be Julie Andrews skipping over the mountains. She was a sentimental girl and the music seemed to suit her mood; for some reason she felt happy, although she really didn't know why. She sang a little louder; the bedrooms were on the other side of the house and no one would hear her. 'The hills are alive...' she was carolling happily.

'And if you don't stop that infernal racket this instant you'll be dead!'

Charles Cresswell stood in the kitchen doorway, looking murderous. He was still wearing the suit he had worn the evening before and it looked crumpled. He needed a shave too and his hair was standing up in spikes.

'Your room,' said Judith coldly, 'is on the other side of the house—you can't possibly have heard me.' She studied him for a moment. 'But of course, you've been up all night, living in the twelfth century.'

'The thirteenth,' he snapped, 'and how the hell am I to work? There's no peace in this house with you in it!'

She got to her feet, her splendid bosom heaving with indignation and, although she didn't recognise it as such, unhappiness. 'In that case—' she began haughtily.

'Don't be a fool,' he begged her. 'Wallowing in hurt

pride just because I uttered a mild reproof—and God knows I have good reason—all that sentimental non-sense about the hills being alive!'

She interrupted him fiercely. 'But they are, they are—when you're happy and content and the sun is shining. But how would you know about that? You're not alive, you're buried in the twelfth century,' she corrected herself—'well, the thirteenth, surrounded by dusty old books and papers shouting at people when they disturb your train of thought.' She slammed down her mug. 'Bah!' she said grandly, and swept past him into the hall and up the stairs.

Mrs Turner was coming down the stairs. 'Do I hear you having words with the Professor?' she asked in a soothing, motherly voice as she came abreast of Judith. 'A nasty temper when he's roused, has our Mr Charles. Don't you take any notice, dearie, he'll be sweeter when he's had his breakfast.'

Judith muttered and ran on up to her room. Nothing would sweeten Charles Cresswell, he was sour, rude and quite impossible. Let him eat his breakfast alone, she'd choke if she had to share it with him!

She heard him come upstairs presently and go along to his room. She dressed quickly and crept down to lay a tray for herself under Mrs Turner's sympathetic eye. 'A nice pot of tea, Miss Judith,' coaxed that lady, 'and there's a lovely brown egg just waiting to be boiled, you've plenty of time to eat it before you see to Lady Cresswell. Why not take the tray up the garden? There's that nice quiet corner behind the summerhouse…'

Judith gave her a quick hug, agreed that it was a splendid idea and bore her breakfast along the brick path between the roses, to perch on the small stone seat snugly built into the corner hedge and demolish the brown egg, a large amount of bread and butter and several cups of tea. She was almost finished when the Professor stuck his head round the corner of the summer house. 'Hiding?' he wanted to know, nastily.

'Certainly not. I like to eat breakfast out of doors.'

'And not share it with an ill-tempered historian who's never civil?'

'You said that,' she pointed out sweetly, 'not I,' and glanced at him, to see an expression on his face which puzzled her. Regret? Disappointment? Sad resignation? It might be any of those on anyone else, but certainly not on his handsome features.

He said evenly, 'It will suit me better if I breakfast in my study—it will be less of an interruption to my work.'

He had gone before Judith could reply, and presently she went back to the house to take up Lady Cresswell's breakfast tray and start off on the leisurely business of getting her patient ready to face another day. It was after she had done this and gone off to the village on an errand and to have ten minutes' chat with Uncle Tom that Charles joined his mother under the beech tree in the garden.

'I've been on the phone to Dr Thorpe,' he told her. 'He's very pleased with the latest tests and thinks that this is a period of recession—possibly a lengthy one. That's splendid news, my dear, and I'm wondering if it gives you the confidence to enjoy a change of scene? I don't have to tell you that I enjoy having you here, but

a few weeks' warm sunshine before the colder weather
might do you good…'

'I'm preventing you from working, Charles?'

He smiled at her. 'No, Mother.'

'But Judith is?'

She asked the question quietly and he didn't answer her, staring away over her head. 'Shall I get another nurse?'

He said instantly: 'No. She's a splendid nurse and
companion for you and I trust her.' He smiled again,
rather bitterly. 'I find her—er—disturbing—larger
than life…'

His mother nodded, taking care not to smile. 'A big
girl,' she offered, 'what your father would have called
a fine figure of a woman.' There was a pause until she
went on easily: 'I know where I should like to go. Do
you remember our holidays in the Algarve? Before you
were born we used to go there too, at the foot of those
mountains—the Monchiques. I'd like to go there again,
Charles. Could you find us a villa somewhere between
Silves and Monchique village? For three weeks or a
month?'

'It will still be very warm…'

'You forget we shall be near the mountains and much
cooler. We shall want a swimming pool, of course, and
a housekeeper and a gardener who can drive.'

'You would really like that?'

'Yes, dear. Will you see to everything? I'd like to go
as soon as possible, while I'm feeling so well—shall
we say a month? That should give you time.'

'Time for what, Mother?' He was looking very intently at her.

'Oh, to get your research done, Charles.' Lady Cresswell raised innocent blue eyes to his, and he smiled faintly, this time with amusement.

'I'll see about it right away. Will you tell Judith?'

And when Judith got back she was told—in a vague roundabout fashion and given no chance to say much, because Lady Cresswell launched into a rambling discussion as to ways and means; clothes, passports and whether Judith would like to go home for a day or two before they went? She had no clear answers to any of the questions Judith put to her, it was Charles Cresswell, coming in during a more than long-winded reminiscence of his mother's, who settled everything with a few words. He would be going to London on the following day, he would collect his mother's passport and anything else she might need if she would make out a list. 'And you?' he asked Judith, who was still getting used to the idea. 'Do you need anything?'

'My passport, my clothes—they're at home.' She didn't add any more—let him worry about how she was to get them, since he was the one responsible for the sudden upheaval.

'Give me a letter for your mother and I'll bring what you need back with me. You may like to telephone her.'

She thanked him calmly; there was no point in arguing. It would get her nowhere, nor had she any reason to be grateful for his offer. She had been bustled into the whole thing with no vestige of consideration just because it suited him. When she had a chance she would tell him so.

She had no chance; he left early the next morning, telephoned his mother the following day to say that he

had rented a villa just outside Silves for three weeks,
and told her that he would return late on the following day.

Judith, informed of this by Lady Cresswell, mar-
velled at the speed with which everything was being
arranged. She supposed that knowing the right people
and having the money to get what one wanted must
help, plus his desire to get rid of her as soon as possible, because in the light of their unfriendly encoun-
ters, that must be the strong reason spurring him on.
Indeed, she was so sure of this that she had suggested
to Lady Cresswell that she might like to engage another nurse, only to be met with a tearful demand as
to whether she wasn't happy, or being paid enough
or was bored to death, mewed up all day with an old
woman. She had hastily rescinded her suggestion and
had spent the rest of the evening coaxing her patient
into a happy frame of mind again.

She lay thinking about it after she had gone to bed;
away from the Professor probably she would be much
happier; somehow he cast such a gloom over everything—she supposed that was why she felt vaguely
unhappy. Before she fell asleep she heard the car and
presently his quiet tread in the house. He didn't come
upstairs immediately, and she was asleep long before
he did.

They set out a few days later. Judith had been a little
surprised at her parents' pleasure at her going; it was
obvious to her that Charles Cresswell had presented
them with the charming side of his character when he
had gone to her home to fetch her things and they were
wholehearted in their approbation of him. Her moth-

er's letter had been full of enthusiasm about the whole thing and had taken it for granted that Judith was just as enthusiastic. And so had Uncle Tom.

She had spent a busy day or two packing for both of them, and when the Professor, after half an hour's talk with his mother, had got into his car and driven away on the evening previous to their departure, she hadn't been surprised. He had given her a list of things to do and remember: the local doctor, the local hospital, the bank she should go to when they needed money, the names of the housekeeper and her husband, the gardener/chauffeur, telephone numbers where he himself could be reached if necessary—even the current rate of exchange—there was even a substantial sum of money to cover expenses. But he hadn't wished her goodbye.

William had arrived the night before to drive them to Manchester Airport so that their journey there was effortless. Lady Cresswell was excited and talked incessantly, and once or twice Judith caught a smug expression on her face and wondered why.

She found out soon enough. Charles was waiting for them at the airport and she realised with a mixture of pleasure and annoyance that he was travelling with them; indeed, her tongue betrayed her into asking: 'You're coming too, Professor?' In a voice which sounded far from pleased.

His smile was thin. 'Don't worry, Judith, I shall see you safely into the villa and then return home—a matter of a day or two.'

She went pink under his amused eyes.

They travelled in comfort, first class, of course, and by the time she had settled Lady Cresswell, found the

book she wanted to read, provided her with her handbag and the barely sugar she was sure would overcome any tendency to sickness, they were airborne.
Judith, sitting on the opposite side to mother and son,
peered out of the window, watching houses and fields
and villages getting smaller and smaller until the air
hostess came with their lunch. When she looked again
they were over water and presently crossing northern
France. There was cloud after that as they crossed the
Bay of Biscay, so she sat back quietly, reviewing the
next few weeks, making sure that she understood her
instructions. She had brought a phrase book with her;
she opened it now and struggled with a few everyday
words. Lady Cresswell spoke a little Portuguese, but
she wouldn't always be there. It looked to be a difficult
language, perhaps she would pick it up more quickly
once they were there. She closed her eyes and dozed
until a voice advised her to fasten her seat belt.

They were out of the cloud now and the sea and
coastline lay below. It looked very different from
England, even the earth was a bright terra cotta and
there were a great many trees. They would be passing
over the mountains which separated Algarve from the
neighbouring province, and Lady Cresswell leaned
across to say: 'That's where we're going, Judith—it's
beautiful, and did you ever see such a lovely blue sky?
I can't wait!'

The Professor had his handsome nose buried in a
book, but he lowered it now with an air of resignation as the plane slid smoothly over the coast, circling
over the golden sand below to make it's final run in.
The airport at Faro was a small one and the formali-

ties brief. He ushered them both towards the entrance where a man met them with wide smiles. Judith wondered idly how Charles had contrived to have everything so smoothly arranged in so short a time. Probably he was an old hand at the game; he didn't appear to be the kind of man to travel in even the smallest discomfort, and to give him his due, he would take care that his mother had no delays or discomfort either. Judith smiled at the driver as he ushered them to the car and he smiled even more broadly. She hoped she would be able to sit in front with him; he looked friendly and the Professor looked even more unfriendly than usual.

She was doomed to disappointment. The two men held a brief conversation, then Charles helped his mother into the back seat, invited Judith to join her and got behind the wheel himself.

'I shall have a nap,' declared Lady Cresswell, 'but I want you to wake me when we get to the hill above Silves, dear.'

Which left Judith sitting behind a silent Professor, looking at all the strange sights around her and not daring to ask him about them.

A bad start, but perhaps it would be better when he'd gone back home.

Chapter 6

There was such a lot to see. It was the hottest part of the day and the whitewashed houses with their red-tiled roofs looked brilliant against the vivid blue sky. They had taken the coast road, going west away from Faro, and once clear of the town they saw that it was bordered by orange and lemon trees, fig trees and almond trees and geometrically neat rows of vines, and every few miles a village dominated by a whitewashed church, its small houses shuttered against the sun, dogs lying in the shade and almost no one to be seen. And flowers—flowers everywhere.

The Professor drove fast, seemingly as much at home on the opposite side of the road as the local inhabitants. He had taken his jacket off and was in his shirtsleeves, and for all the notice he took of Judith he might have been alone. She gazed out at the strangeness of it all, longing to ask why the chimneypots looked like miniature minarets, why there were no cows, why the village shops looked like dim caves... Lady Cresswell was asleep, so there was no one to ask. She contained her impatience, watching for signposts and the names of the villages they passed through.

There was a glimpse of the sea from time to time, but presently they took a right-hand fork in the road which was signposted Silves and drove along steadily rising ground, well surfaced but narrow. Indeed, the oncoming traffic passed them with inches to spare, and without slackening its speed. Charles Cresswell didn't slacken his speed either, nor did he seem in the least discomposed. Judith, who had been getting a little tense, allowed herself to relax and turned her attention to the scenery once more.

There were some splendid villas, she noticed, with magnificent grounds and a glimpse of swimming pools, a contrast to the small box-like flat-roofed houses lining the village streets, but although there might be poverty she could see no squalor, and the sunshine and the warmth were kind to even the dullest of them. They reached the crown of a hill and there before them was Silves, lying cradled in the hills, overshadowed by its ruined castle and the white-walled cathedral. Charles Cresswell drew into the side of the road and looked over his shoulder. 'My mother wanted to be wakened,' he reminded Judith.

Lady Cresswell opened her eyes at once and said like a child: 'Oh, it's hardly changed. Don't you find it charming, Judith? And this is the best view of the town.

Charles, I want to stop just for a minute. You can drive
up to the cathedral, can't you, and turn?'

It did look charming, thought Judith, with its white
houses clustered under the blue sky. She asked: 'How
old is the castle?'

'Moorish,' said the Professor at once. 'It had a very
interesting history—the cathedral is built on the foun-
dations of a mosque. It's a little disappointing inside,
but well worth a visit—in any case, I doubt if you'll
find much to engage your interest.'

'Why not?'

'I'm under the impression that you find ancient history boring.' He sounded so bland that she longed to
hit him.

'It rather depends on who's telling me about it,' she
told him. She found his soft laugh very irritating.

They drove on presently, down the hill and then
along the road curving to the town's centre and then up
the hill towards the castle, but Lady Cresswell didn't
get out, only sat looking round her. They went back
down the hill then and out of the sleepy little town, past
a handful of shops and a mixture of tiny square houses
and modern villas, until the last of the houses dwin-
dled away and only the villas, getting more and more
splendid as they climbed, remained. The mountains
were much nearer now and Lady Cresswell observed
excitedly: 'We must be nearly there—you did say it
was before we reached Caldas, didn't you, Charles?'
She turned to Judith. 'Caldas is a spa—a very small
one—just off the main road to Monchique village.
We'll go there one day—one has to drink the waters,

of course, but there is, or there was, a small restaurant there. There's a hospital there too,' she added.

'For the spa patients,' observed Judith briskly. 'I expect the water tastes foul, but it would be fun to go, wouldn't it, and Monchique—is that larger than Silves?'

It was Charles who answered her. 'No, it's fairly high up in the mountains, magnificent scenery and that's about all.'

He had slowed the car and now turned off the road, going up a dirt track through orange trees merging into the forest on the lower slopes of the mountains. The track ended in a pair of gates, standing open, and beyond a short drive leading to an elegant villa, white-walled and red-roofed like every other house, but with a terrace and a verandah and wrought iron balconies. The front door was solid and carved, and was opened as they reached it by a small thin dark woman, dressed entirely in black, who greeted them unsmilingly and stood aside for them to go in. The hall was large and cool and dim with doors on all sides, and an open arch-way leading to a lofty room with windows on two sides, its tiled floors strewn with rugs and comfortable chairs scattered round. There was an open fireplace in one corner, crowned by a great hood, and tapestries on the walls. A rather lovely room, thought Judith, and very different from home.

The Professor spoke to the woman as they went in, and a tiny bit of Judith's mind registered the fact that he spoke Portuguese. Clever Dick, she thought crossly, trust him to be perfect, not for him sign language and speaking English rather more loudly than usual, which was what she'd have to do…

She settled his mother in a chair and as the woman reappeared with a tea tray, drew a small table beside it. 'This is Teresa,' observed Charles Cresswell. 'She and her husband Augusto will be looking after you. A girl will come each day to help with the cleaning and to see to the laundry and so on.' He glanced at Judith. 'You have all the information you're likely to need, if there's anything else, I shall be here for the next two days.'

Judith said blankly: 'Oh, will you?' and he laughed. She looked away, colouring faintly because it was quite clear that he had read her thoughts.

They went upstairs to their rooms after tea, large airy apartments at the front of the villa with a communicating door, and opening out on to a shaded balcony. It gave a splendid view of the garden and surrounding countryside, heavily wooded with cork trees merging into orderly rows of orange trees. The garden was lovely, a riot of roses and summer flowers and close to the house a swimming pool. Judith gave a sigh of pleasure and went to unpack for her patient and settle her down for a nap on the chaise-longue at the open window.

Lady Cresswell was tired but happy.

'How about dinner in bed?' suggested Judith. 'I'll unpack and then get you comfy in bed and bring up a tray of something light. It's been a long day.'

It hadn't occurred to her that there might be difficulties in making Teresa understand about a light supper on a tray. Even with her phrase book and a lot of arm waving and exploring of cupboards, Judith found herself getting nowhere very fast. Teresa was more than willing, but the phrase book wasn't very helpful and there were long delays which she spent thumbing through the pages. Finally Judith went in search of the Professor.

She found him stretched out in a large leather chair drawn up by the open doors in the sitting room. He looked cool and elegant, and she gave him a cross look. She was untidy and warm and vaguely irritable, a feeling strongly increased by the way in which he got to his feet and looked her up and down with faint smile.

'Poor Judith, you look a little...' He left the sentence unfinished in mid-air and she ground her splendid teeth. 'In trouble?' he wanted to know.

'Your mother would like her supper in bed and I think it would be an excellent idea, only I can't find anything in the phrase book that says so—scrambled eggs, too, and creamed potatoes...' She had answered him haughtily to begin with, but the haughtiness had petered out with the potatoes. She put up a hand and pushed back her golden hair from a flushed forehead. Suddenly she longed to sit down with a long cool drink while someone else coped. Charles must have read her thoughts.

'Sit down.' He poured something cold and iced from a glass jug on a side table and put it down on the table beside her chair. 'Tell me what you want Teresa to do and I'll tell her. Augusto understands English and speaks a little; he's not here at present, but you'll find that he'll be most helpful.'

'Scrambled egg on thin toast,' said Judith, 'and a little creamed potato and perhaps a tomato salad—

no bread, but could she manage a caramel custard or something similar? And wine—I thought a glass of white wine might be nice…'

'Vinho Verde—the owner told me that there was some in the cellar.' The Professor sauntered to the door. 'I'll be back presently.'

The drink was delicious, the early evening air cool and scented from the garden. Judith curled up on her chair and closed her eyes.

She woke with an instant feeling of guilt and leapt to her feet, then felt foolish because there was no one there anyway, at least not at that precise moment. Charles Cresswell came through the open door a moment later and remarked in his usual withering tones: 'How guilty you look. I wonder why?'

She ignored this. 'Thank you for organising Lady Cresswell's supper. I'll go and see when she would like it.'

He said nothing, only smiled a little and looked at the ornate clock on the wall behind her. Naturally she looked too, and drew a sharp breath when she saw the time. More than half an hour had elapsed since she had sat down and closed her eyes—but only for a few minutes, surely. Charles had only just returned—the clock was wrong.

'No, it's not,' he told her disconcertingly. 'You've been to sleep; I hadn't the heart to wake you and there was no need, my mother is asleep and you must be tired.' He studied her for a long moment. 'Why not tidy yourself and come down for a drink?'

She was surprised and showed it. 'Well—thank you, but what about Lady Cresswell—if she should wake…'

He raised his eyebrows. 'Surely you can deal with that?' he wanted to know. 'Stop fussing and do as I say.'

Rather to her surprise, Judith went meekly upstairs, showered, changed into a cotton crêpe top and wide skirt, arranged her hair with more than usual attention, slapped make-up on to her pretty face, and went downstairs again. Lady Cresswell was still sleeping and she had no idea at what time they were to dine. She found Charles Cresswell bending over a large street plan and he paused only long enough to give her a drink before asking her to look at it. 'Silves is small,' he told her, 'but you will need to find your way around. I have marked the addresses of the people you are most likely to contact. You will find the doctor most helpful and his English is very good. I should contact him about any problem which may arise—and by that I mean not only my mother.'

'Very well. She mentioned several places she wanted to visit again. They're not too far away?'

He shook his head. 'An hour or so in the car at the most. Don't let her travel during the heat of the day, though. The shops close between noon and three o'clock, so encourage her to do her shopping in the evening.' He folded the street plan and gave it to her. 'You're not afraid of the responsibility?'

'No, and I'll take great care of your mother, Professor Cresswell.'

'I know that, Judith, I should never have allowed her to come here otherwise. I trust you completely.'

But he didn't like her. She felt desolate at the thought. 'I'll go to the kitchen and see how Lady Cresswell's supper is getting on,' she told him, and was at the door, to find him beside her.

'If I were to come too,' he murmured, 'it would be easier.'

He was surprisingly helpful; his Portuguese, he told her, was sketchy, all the same he and Teresa seemed to get on very well, and next time, Judith decided, a breakfast or supper tray in bed would present no hazards. She went away presently to find Lady Cresswell awake and wanting her supper and in the best of tempers.

Judith left her eating with an appetite and went downstairs again. She was hungry herself, but the prospect of a meal with the Professor had taken the edge off her appetite. They would make stilted conversation and he would look down his nose at her and snub her with his cold politeness. But she didn't allow her reluctance to show. She walked into the dining room looking cool and serene and very, very pretty, and took her seat opposite him at the round table laid with crisp white linen, shining silver and elegant glasses. The dining room was a good deal smaller than the sitting room, furnished rather sparsely but with great good taste, and the evening sun shone through the wide doors leading to the patio. It shone on Judith's golden hair, and her companion stared at her for a long moment when she turned to look out into the garden. She was, in fact, not looking at the garden at all but feverishly searching for something to say—a wasted exercise, for the Professor leaned back in his chair and embarked on a gentle monologue calculated to put her at ease within minutes. She ate the small dish of salad put before them by Teresa, the swordfish with its delicious sauce, the chicken cooked in cream and wine and the almond and honey tart, in a kind of dream, unable to believe that her charming companion was really Charles Cresswell, and even two glasses of Vinho Verde didn't help, indeed she found herself regarding him with a positively friendly eye and over coffee, accompanied by something called Brandymel which he gravely assured her was a drink composed of honey and brandy, she allowed her tongue to run away with her.

'You're being very nice,' she told him. 'Usually you ignore me or snub me.'

He smiled a little. 'I must be feeling well disposed to everyone this evening.'

Which wasn't the answer she had wanted to hear.

And it was a little disappointing, after all that charm, to hear him acquiesce quite cheerfully to her suggestion that she should see to her patient and then go to bed herself. She would keep well out of his way, she decided. There would be plenty to occupy her on the following morning and she would go down early and get breakfast for herself before anyone was up.

But Teresa was already in the kitchen when she crept down at seven o'clock and gave her coffee and rolls as light as air, sitting on the patio in the glorious morning sun. And when Teresa came out with the coffee pot Judith ventured: 'Professor Cresswell?' and received a vague wave of the hand towards the mountains in the distance.

Good, he was out of the house, perhaps for hours. She finished her breakfast at leisure, dressed and went to wake Lady Cresswell.

It was mid-morning, and she had helped her patient dress and then escorted her to a cool corner of the patio and was on her way to the kitchen to get a cold drink for her when the Professor came into the hall through the screened door.

There was no 'good morning'. 'There you are,' he declared, for all the world as though she had been hiding from him. 'How long will you be?'

She eyed him coolly. 'Good morning, Professor Cresswell. Doing what?'

'Whatever you are doing. I want to take you into Silves,' and at her look of disbelief, 'Oh, not for pleasure, I assure you; there are people I think that you should meet before I leave!'

Judith smouldered inwardly. 'I'm getting a drink for your mother. She may want me to stay with her.'

'She is on the patio.' He strode past her and she heard a murmur of voices as she poured iced lemonade into a frosted jug.

She had hoped that Lady Cresswell might object to her leaving her alone, but on the contrary, that lady seemed to be delighted at the idea of her going into the town with her son. 'Such a good opportunity,' she observed, 'because Charles returns home tomorrow and you'll be without young company for a few weeks. Take a hat with you, dear, the sun's hot.'

Thus dismissed, Judith had nothing more to do but fetch her purse and go downstairs. She had no hat; she supposed she would have to buy one.

The Professor was already behind the wheel, a perfect study of impatience held in check at all costs. He opened the door for her, slammed it shut, waited just

long enough for her to fasten her seat belt and set off
down the drive. They were half way along the dirt track
before he spoke.

'You'll need a hat.'

'So your mother tells me. I hope there'll be time for
me to buy one this morning.'

'As long as you don't take all day over it. I think a
plain sensible straw is what you need.'

She couldn't stop her chuckle. She said sedately: 'I
expect I can choose a hat for myself.'

They went first to the bank where they were received by the manager, given little cups of black coffee and assured that Miss Golightly could depend upon
help for anything she might need during their stay.
The manager was friendly and impressed by Judith's
good looks; he shook hands warmly when they left and
begged her to remember that he was her friend. She
thanked him prettily, rather more so than she needed
to because Charles Cresswell looked so disapproving.

The visit to the doctor was just as successful. He
was a youngish man, dark and rather thick set, and
made no bones about his admiration for Judith. Since
the professor's handsome features still wore a look of
remote politeness, she did nothing to discourage him.
They arranged a visit to Lady Cresswell for the following day, discussed her illness and her treatment, drank
more coffee and took their departure.

The car had been parked on the cobbled stretch
below the castle, and since the doctor's house was on
the other side of the little town's main road, they had to
walk back through narrow streets crowded with people, children, mule carts and dogs. They were wait-

ing at a crossroads when the Professor observed: 'You make friends easily, Judith.' He said it so silkily that she looked at him and encountered a mocking smile.

'Me?' She chose to ignore the mockery. 'Not specially—I like people.' She added: 'You find that hard to believe, I'm sure, you like books.' And before he could reply: 'You're very clever, aren't you? Uncle Tom told me. I expect you find ordinary folk a bore as well as nuisance.' She went on recklessly: 'I'm both, aren't I?'

He didn't answer but shepherded her across the road and once on the other side, said: 'You wished to buy a hat. There's a shop close to the castle which caters for tourists, you'll find one there.'

Judith walked beside him in silence. Her own fault that she had been snubbed, of course. She should have learnt better by now. She told herself that she didn't mind as they went up to the shop through the cobbled street.

It was cool inside and full of the kind of things people want to buy when they are on holiday. Judith prowled round for a minute or two before discovering a table loaded with hats: white cotton ones, like a very small boy's, highly coloured ones, heavily embroidered, plain straw ones… Mindful of the Professor's preference, she chose a natural straw with a wide brim, paid its modest price and went out into the bright sunshine.

He looked faintly astonished when he saw her. 'You were very quick…'

'Well, you probably want to get back to the villa.

Besides, it was easy to choose—a plain sensible straw, you said.'

He looked at her, the hat was very becoming. 'It suits you,' he said reluctantly, and then: 'Since we have some time in hand, you might like to look round the cathedral and the castle; neither takes long.'

She followed him into the dim vastness. The cathedral had been built in the Spanish style with a white-washed exterior and inside it was empty of chairs or pews. Great columns supported its ceiling and there was a small chapel to one side where Henry the Navigator had been buried. Judith liked its bareness, wandering round, quite forgetful of her companion. She remembered him presently and saw him waiting by the door and hurried over, feeling guilty, but all he said was: 'You like it, so do I—it's simple, isn't it?' He led the way out, dropping some coins in the dish an old woman was holding by the door. 'And now the castle.'

It was a stone's throw away; a path between low-growing shrubs and the orange trees Judith still hadn't got used to led them past a crumbling wall and into the ruins of the castle. There wasn't a great deal to see, although she supposed that to a learned scholar like Charles Cresswell, it was of the greatest interest. She asked him one or two questions, but his answers were brief and uttered in an impatient voice so that she gave up after the first few attempts, admired the view and made for the ruined archway which would lead them back to the path. She was ahead of him with the wall on one side of her when she stopped. The wall was full of cracks and niches and in one of these, rather bigger than most, there was a small thin cat with

two tiny kittens. The cat mewed at her, looking at her
with a resigned hopelessness which brought her to an
abrupt halt.

'Has this cat got a home?' she asked the Professor.

'Most unlikely. Cats and dogs aren't ill-treated
here, neither are they regarded as household pets.' He
looked thoughtfully at the animal. 'She's starving, poor
thing—she can hardly hold up her head. Probably she
hasn't been able to leave the kittens while she looks for
food; they can't be more than a few days old.'

Judith put out a finger and the little cat licked it
tiredly. Its mew was plaintive. 'What are we going to
do?' she asked him fiercely.

He stood looking down at her, half smiling. 'If you'll
take off that highly becoming hat, we could put all
three of them into it. I'm sure Teresa won't object to
them providing you keep them out of her kitchen.'

No sooner said than done. Judith didn't waste time
in thanks, that could come later. Mother and kittens
needed urgent attention if they were to survive. She
carried them carefully, too weak to protest, to where
the car had been parked, and got in carefully, her hat
on her knees. Half way to the villa she asked: 'Do you
think we'll get her well again? She isn't too starved?'

'You'll get her well, Judith, I have no doubt of that.
I shan't be here.'

'Oh—you're leaving tomorrow?'

'This evening.'

She was astonished to find that she didn't want him
to go, but it would be just as well—he was growing on
her; impatience, ill humour, mockery, the lot. She said
'Oh,' again and then: 'Thank you very much for letting

me have this little cat and her kittens. I'm very grateful. Do you think I'm very silly? You don't approve of
sentimental people, do you?'

'I'm not above modifying my opinions,' he told her,
'I dislike mawkishness. And I don't consider you silly,
Judith. I would have done exactly the same.'

She turned to look at him. 'You would?' Her astonishment made him wince.

Lady Cresswell, told about the tiny creatures still
in Judith's hat, was instantly diverted. Teresa was sent
for, a box was requested, a saucer of powdered milk,
suitably warmed, was fetched, and the cat and her kittens gently transferred to their new quarters and the
mother fed. She supped languidly, but she purred too.
Judith said anxiously: 'Do you suppose we've got her
in time? She's all skin and bone.'

'With regular light meals and plenty of water she
stands a very good chance.' Charles Cresswell, standing with his hands in his pockets, moved towards the
door. 'I'll go and talk to Teresa and suggest that you
make yourself responsible for this creature's food and
well being.'

When he had gone Judith asked: 'You don't mind,
Lady Cresswell? We couldn't leave her...'

'Of course I don't mind, child—Charles has been
bringing home lost and sick animals since he was a
very small boy. His dogs were both abandoned—both
past their first youth when he found them too.'

Judith paused in the pouring of a cool drink for
Lady Cresswell. 'I've just thought—what will happen
when we go back...?'

She hadn't seen the Professor standing in the open

door leading to the patio. 'They'll have to go into quarantine, of course,' he observed 'and then presently take
up residence at Hawkshead.'

Judith beamed at him. 'Oh, they'll love it there—
how kind you are!'

His smile mocked her. 'You overwhelm me, Judith.'

She bent her head over the box, feeling the colour
flooding her face. Presently she put the box down,
murmured about fetching more milk and went away
without looking at him.

When she went back, almost half an hour later, he
had gone. She fed the cat again, read the most interesting bits from the English papers they had brought
back with them and then sat idly chatting until Lady
Cresswell dozed off. There was another feed due by
then. Judith went to the kitchen once more, this time
for chicken broth, fed her charge, pleased to see that
she was looking more lively already, and then went to
get writing paper and pen. She had started on a letter
home when the Professor returned.

'If that's to your parents, let me have it and I'll post
it in England. But why not ring them up? The telephone's in the hall and there's another in the small room
behind the dining room they call the study.' He smiled
at her, this time with no mockery. 'Off you go now—I
want to talk to mother when she wakes up anyway.'

Judith allowed herself to be dismissed and went
along to the study where she had a long and satisfying
chat with her mother and then, since no one had asked
for her, went through a side door into the garden, where
she lay on the beautifully tended grass and let the sun
drench her. She should have used her Ambre Solaire

and worn a hat, but she didn't think it mattered. A view not shared by Charles Cresswell, who came strolling towards her a little later. 'You'll have a headache and look like a lobster if you don't move into the shade,' he told her forthrightly. 'I'll allow that you're not a conceited girl, but who wants to look a figure of fun? Besides, it's painful.'

She scrambled to her feet, feeling a fool. 'I never do anything right, do I?' she demanded snappishly, and stalked off indoors, to rush to her room and inspect her face and person for signs of sunburn.

They lunched, the three of them, in the shade of the patio, on a cold fish salad and a light-as-air pudding called Mountain Rose.

Charles Cresswell waved a hand in the direction of the mountains in the distance. 'The Monchiques are covered with them—rather like our own wild rose, but butter-coloured—hence the pudding's name.' He had talked more than usual, perhaps because his mother, although she said very little about it, didn't want him to go. He had teased her into a cheerful frame of mind by the time the meal was over, and Judith, escorting her to her darkened, air-conditioned room for a nap, was pleased to see that. She offered pills and a cool drink, assured Lady Cresswell that she would rouse her in good time for tea, and went along to her own room. She had no particular wish to stay there, but she was reasonably sure that the Professor wouldn't want her company. She had brought the cat and the kittens upstairs before lunch, together with a supply of nourishing food. Now she attended to the little creature's wants, watched it settle down once more with a protecting paw over the kittens, and went out on to the balcony.

It was very hot. She supposed she would have to stay in her room unless Charles went out. She leaned over and carefully inspected the garden and as much of the patio below as she could see. She was about to withdraw her head when he stepped from directly under her balcony and looked up at her.

'Yes, I'm still here. Afraid to come down, Judith?'

She replied with something of a snap, 'Certainly not! I was just looking around...'

'In that case get your bathing things and come and have a swim in the pool.'

She hesitated for a couple of seconds, but the prospect was too inviting. She nodded and went to find her bikini.

The pool was large, the water warm and she swam well. Beyond a brief greeting, the Professor had had nothing to say, but had plunged in from the side and was swimming strongly away from her. Judith pulled on her cap and dived in from the board at one end, passing him halfway going in the opposite direction. They did this several times and she began to wonder if he thought he was alone; he could at least pass the time of day... She hoisted herself out by the board and went and stood on it.

Her bikini was a brilliant blue, beautifully cut and did her figure full justice, but as far as he was concerned, she suspected that an old sack would have done just as well. As he swam towards her, she sprang up and down on the board without actually diving in; she had very little vanity, but just for once she would have liked him to have made some comment—that she could swim well, that he liked the colour of her bikini, that he could see her, even…

'Why are you leaping up and down like a scalded cat?' he wanted to know, and before she could answer that, had turned and begun his powerful journey back to the other end.

He hadn't quite reached it when she nipped off the board, picked up her towel and went back to the house. He was rude, intolerant, pigheaded, and thank heaven he was going back to England within a few hours! She was glad, thrilled to bits, she wouldn't have to put up with his company for three weeks. She stopped dead in her tracks, suddenly aware that three weeks was a lifetime, longer than that. He would be miles away and she wouldn't see him or know what he was doing or who he was with. That beastly Eileen Hunt, probably. When she saw him again, if she ever did, he might be going to marry the girl; at best, he would have forgotten her. Judith stood on the stairs, wrapped in her towel, dripping gently. Charles wasn't going until the evening, he had said, so she would see him again, perhaps she would have a chance to tell him… Tell him what? she thought wildly. That she had just discovered that she was head over heels in love with him? Tiresome, ill-tempered creature that he was. And she could imagine that mocking smile and the blandly spoken answer she'd get to that!

She went on up the stairs to her room, had a shower and dressed, and outwardly looking cool and self-possessed, went down to the patio. Await events, her father had always advised her when she had been uncertain of something, and that was exactly what she intended doing.

It was very quiet. Teresa and Augusto were having their midday rest, the cat and kittens were peacefully sleeping, so was Lady Cresswell—she had peeped in to see. And of Charles Cresswell there was no sign. At four o'clock she went to wake Lady Cresswell, fed the cat and went to the kitchen to ask for the tea tray to be brought to the patio, and over the tea things she learned that Charles had gone to Silves on some business of his own. 'He'll be back shortly,' observed Lady Cresswell. 'He told me he wants to have a little talk before he goes.'

Which was her nice way of warning Judith to keep out of the way. Judith was at the other end of the garden, cutting roses in the early evening cool, when she heard the car start up. She didn't give it a second thought. Charles wouldn't go without saying goodbye, even if they weren't on the best of terms. She cut a few more roses, rehearsing the little speech she was going to make to him; she had thought it out carefully and she hoped that hearing it, he would understand that she would like to be friends in future. Once they were friends, who knew what might happen?

She wandered back to the house and found Lady Cresswell in the sitting room, reading a novel. 'There you are, dear,' she remarked a little too brightly. 'Shall we get out the backgammon board? I always feel a little low when Charles goes.'

'Goes?' asked Judith woodenly.

'Why, yes, dear—about ten minutes ago.' She peeped at Judith's downcast face and allowed herself the faintest of pleased smiles. 'We shall miss him.'

Chapter 7

Judith had never been much good at backgammon, and that evening she was quite hopeless. Lady Cresswell won with no trouble at all, elected to stay downstairs for dinner and then sat for a little while with the tiny cat and her kittens in their box beside her. Judith guessed that she was missing her son more than she would admit and probably faced a bad night. But she went to bed finally after an hour of making plans for the next week or two, and Judith stayed with her for a while, pottering softly around the room, carrying on a murmured conversation until Lady Cresswell finally went to sleep. She went to her own room then, settling her charges on the balcony with the door open. It was a warm night and they would come to no harm. She gave the cat a final small meal, stroked the scraggy little head and went to bed herself, to lie awake and think of Charles. He would be back in England by now. She wondered where he would spend the night and wished she knew more about him; his life was something of which she knew very little. An historian of some repute, living comfortable life with sufficient money to do as he pleased, possessed of a number of friends—beyond that she could only guess. A useless exercise anyway.

Presently she got out of her bed and went to sit on the balcony. There was a moon, almost full, and the garden, dim in its light, smelled delicious. She could make out the mountains not so very far away and lower down the faint lights of Silves. It was quiet too, so that the occasional rustle from the cats' box sounded loud. Judith stayed for some time, trying to sort out her thoughts and getting nowhere. She made no bones about being in love with Charles; she was, and that was an end to it. It was a silly thing to do and she couldn't think why she had done it. He had given her no encouragement at all, and he would make a by no means perfect husband. The thing was to do something sensible about it, like forgetting him. She contemplated this idea briefly and threw it out. Charles wasn't a man one could forget easily, whatever one's feelings towards him were. Getting as far away as possible from him was more sensible, only she couldn't do that just yet. Lady Cresswell had to be considered. Judith had grown fond of the valiant little lady and had no intention of giving her even the smallest worry for the limited time that she had left to her. That might mean months and she wasn't sure what was worse—the prospect of trying to avoid Charles whenever possible, or seeing him every day and pretending that she had no interest in him whatever. She decided that they were as bad as each other, which made the future look gloomy. She had three weeks, of course, before they returned to England, and perhaps Lady Cresswell would decide to stay in her own home in London, which would solve the problem nicely. She doubted if they would spend the winter in Cumbria and perhaps if she didn't see him for weeks on end he would fade... Upon due reflection she came to the conclusion that the Professor wasn't a man to fade. She sighed and went back to bed. She had always prided herself on her good sense, but that didn't stop her having a good cry.

But there was no sign of her sleepless night the next morning. She swam in the pool, drank her morning tea, saw to the cats' wants, dressed and went to see how Lady Cresswell was. Surprisingly cheerful, as it turned out, full of plans for a drive up into the mountains within the next few days, a visit to the spa, a drive down to the coast, and perhaps a picnic there. 'You could have a swim,' she encouraged Judith. 'We'll go to Praia da Rocha, there's a lovely beach there, and perhaps it would be better if we had lunch at the Algarve Hotel. We'll do that tomorrow. Charles said I wasn't to do anything today, so I won't.'

'The doctor's coming to see you,' Judith reminded her. 'He said he'd be here some time after three o'clock.'

Lady Cresswell nodded. 'He can have tea with us. I'm going to lie in the shade this morning and do nothing.' She sat up. 'No, better still, you shall splash around in the pool and I'll watch you.'

So the morning passed pleasantly enough. Judith

swam and dived and lolled around with a watchful eye on her companion and her thoughts miles away. Charles would be on his way home by now, already there, perhaps. They were having lunch on the patio when he telephoned. Judith, who had answered the phone, felt the colour rush to her face when she heard his cool voice. 'Judith, I should like to speak to my mother.'

No 'Hullo', or 'How are you?' She said in a voice equally impersonal: 'I'll fetch her,' and did so, making her comfortable in a chair before going out of the room. There was a great lump in her chest like heavy dough. She wanted to run out of the house, go back to England, to her home, to the hospital, to the time before she had met him. When she heard Lady Cresswell calling to her she went back, half hoping that he wanted to speak to her too, but Lady Cresswell had hung up.

Dr Sebastiao arrived punctually, and because Judith was lonely and unhappy she responded to his quite obvious admiration. He examined his patient with great care and thoroughness, took a sample of blood, stayed to tea, entertaining them with light-hearted talk about Portugal and Algarve in particular, and suggested that they might like to go for a drive one evening, then took himself off.

'He took a fancy to you, Judith,' commented Lady Cresswell as they watched him race away down the drive. 'He's a very nice man; I hope he invites you out for an evening.'

Judith smiled and nodded vaguely. Why was it, she wondered, that a man you had not the least interest in chatted you up whenever you met, and someone you

desperately wanted to like you—even notice you—
behaved as though you were yesterday's cold potatoes?

'How old did you say you were, dear?' asked Lady
Cresswell suddenly.

Judith looked at her in considerable astonishment.
'Twenty-seven—halfway to twenty-eight, actually.'

She was still more astonished at Lady Cresswell's
satisfied: 'Just the right age.'

Judith was dying to ask the obvious question, but
on occasion her patient could be as withdrawn as her
son. She decided to say nothing, and spent the remainder of the day consumed with curiosity.

They went to Praia da Rocha the following morning,
driven by Augusto in the car hired by Charles before
he left. It wasn't too hot as yet and the country was a
feast of colour and the grape harvest was in full swing,
almonds were being gathered, and figs, and there were
flowers everywhere. Even the smallest cottage had its
garden with a vine trailing over the porch, orange and
lemon trees casting a welcome shade in which a mixture of vegetables and flowers grew. 'Isn't it funny,' observed Judith, 'that with so much colour around them,
the women all wear black?' She gazed at a group of
women standing by the road. 'And their black felt hats!'

'To keep off the sun,' explained Lady Cresswell.
'And I expect most of them are widows.' She added:
'Charles would be able to answer all your questions.
Such a pity that he isn't here.'

And Judith silently agreed.

They drove through Portimao before they reached
the sea—a bustling little town, famous for its sardine
fisheries. The harbour was full of fishing boats hung

with nets, each with its eye painted on the prow. Judith would have liked to explore the town, but probably she would have the chance before they went back. They were near the sea by now, the white villas with their red-tiled roofs were scattered thickly and there were several tower blocks to which Lady Cresswell took instant exception. But they were forgotten as they rounded the ancient fort facing out to sea below the harbour and they saw the great sweep of golden sand and the blue sea beyond. There weren't a great many people about, the height of the season had passed and the children were back at school. 'You're going to enjoy this,' declared Lady Cresswell. 'We'll go to the hotel and have coffee and order lunch and I shall sit on the terrace while you swim. You can go from the hotel, of course.'

It would never have entered Judith's head to use the hotel, but when they went in its rather grand entrance, nothing could have been easier. Lady Cresswell was escorted on to a shady terrace overlooking the beach and the pair of them had coffee before Judith went away to change for her swim.

The sea was warm and as smooth as silk; she swam until she was tired and then padded back to the terrace.

'That's a very eye-catching bikini,' remarked Lady Cresswell. 'You've a splendid shape, my dear. I daresay the sea is a great deal nicer than the pool at the villa.'

Judith was lying on a sunbed letting the sun sink into the seawater and Ambre Solaire. 'Much nicer,' she agreed.

'But I daresay you enjoyed your swim with Charles?' persisted Lady Cresswell. She had a high clear voice and sometimes there was a note in it which compelled an answer.

'We quarrelled,' said Judith briefly.

'Dear, dear,' murmured her companion. 'Of course, dear Charles can be most vexing at times.' She took off her sunglasses and polished them carefully. 'All the same, I miss him—he seems such a very long way away.'

Dark glasses were useful things, thought Judith, one could hide behind them. She said carefully: 'Only a little under three hours by plane. I expect he's getting a lot of work done.' Despite herself, there was a note of bitterness in her voice.

'I'm not sure of that,' said his mother, and smiled a little.

Judith hadn't seen the smile. 'I'll go and change,' she said. 'I won't be a minute. Can I do anything for you before I go?'

'No, dear. We'll have a cool drink when you get back and decide what we're going to eat. After lunch I'd like to look round the boutique…'

'Of course, but a rest first, don't you think?' Judith lingered by her chair. 'Would you like to do anything later on?'

'Augusto will drive us through the town after tea, if we see a shop we like the look of we can always get him to stop. We might see some books.'

Judith eyed her carefully; she was standing up well to the days activities and she didn't look tired. 'Yes, let's do that,' she agreed cheerfully.

They lunched in a cool dining room, off iced melon, a fish salad and ice cream, and had coffee on the terrace again, and presently Lady Cresswell dozed off in her shady corner while Judith lay in the sun. It was very hot, she could feel the heat through her thin sleeveless dress, but she had rubbed in more sun lotion and popped her straw hat on to her head. She had a thick creamy skin which didn't burn easily and she wanted to go home with a splendid tan. Presently she slept.

They had tea later and then, as it grew cooler, they went to inspect the boutique in the foyer. Judith bought a handful of cards to send to friends and family, but Lady Cresswell ignored them. She could telephone, she pointed out, so much easier and quicker than all that writing. More expensive too, but she wasn't concerned with that. She turned over the dainty mats and cloths and bought several, as well as some pottery she liked the look of, and finally she bought half a dozen exquisitely embroidered handkerchiefs and gave them to Judith. It all cost a staggeringly large sum of money, but that only whetted Lady Cresswell's appetite to do a little more shopping. Augusto was instructed to drive slowly along the promenade until a bookshop was found, where they spent a considerable time while she chose a dozen paperbacks. 'And get whatever you want for yourself, dear,' she told Judith, who, feeling very much in the mood for that sort of thing, chose Jilly Cooper's *British in Love*.

They went home after that because Lady Cresswell looked tired. Judith whisked her off to bed and bore up a supper tray presently. 'A lovely day,' she observed cheerfully, 'but let's have a lazy day tomorrow. I have got dozens of postcards to write, and Teresa has prom-

ised me she'll show me how to make Mountain Rose
pudding—at least I think that's what she said.'

Lady Cresswell agreed readily enough—perhaps
she had done too much, thought Judith worriedly, but
her pulse and temperature were normal and there was
no sign of purpura. She would see how things were in
the morning and if she still felt uneasy she would get
Dr Sebastiao to call in the morning.

She ate her own dinner, with one ear listening for
her patient's bell and the other for the telephone—just
in case Charles rang up. But he didn't, and in the morning Lady Cresswell was quite recovered. All the same,
Judith kept to the plan and they spent a quiet day reading and talking and listening to the record player, and
at lunchtime Charles did telephone, wasting no time on
her at all, merely asking to speak to his mother. Judith
sat there, peeling an orange, shutting her ears to Lady
Cresswell's voice saying yes and no, willing him to ask
for her. But he didn't, and she was forced to listen to her
companion's vague account of how busy he was with
his book—the research was going well. 'Oh, and he
asked after the little cat, Judith—I said she was doing
very well and so were the kittens. Shouldn't we find a
name for her—for all of them, since they'll be coming
to live with us?' She frowned. 'Something English.'

'Mrs Smith,' suggested Judith without giving it
much thought, 'that's very English—and call the kittens George and Mary.'

'What a good idea—they're so sweet, even Teresa
likes them.' Lady Cresswell sipped her coffee. 'What
shall we do tomorrow, Judith?'

'You'd like to go somewhere?'

'Indeed yes. Shall we go to Caldas and drink the water? I believe it's quite fashionable nowadays, although I can't think why. It's off the main road and only a small village.'

'It's not far from here?'

'No distance at all. Shall we go in the morning and have lunch and come home directly after?'

'That sounds fun…'

Lady Cresswell interrupted her: 'And we must go to Monchique.'

'On another day, perhaps? Didn't you tell me there's an inn there where we can have tea and look at the view?'

Lady Cresswell agreed enthusiastically. 'And we must go to the sea again so that you can swim, and there are several towns—Sagres and Lagos and Albufeira. I do hope that nice Dr Sebastiao takes you out, Judith.'

'Well, you know, I'm happy just to be here and do nothing all day, being bone idle is such a delightful experience—besides, the pool here is quite super.' Judith got up and gave her arm to her companion. 'I shall have a swim while you're taking your nap.'

It was lonely in the pool. She swam up and down and thought about Charles; sitting with his handsome nose buried in some dry-as-dust old tome, she supposed. On the other hand, he might be dallying with Eileen Hunt—the girl had a clear field and time enough to mug up bits about the thirteenth century so that she could look intelligent when he enthused about churches and Magna Carta and feudal Law…

She was suddenly tired of the pool; she got out and

lay in the sun drying and then went indoors to dress.
Lady Cresswell was still asleep and to stay indoors
seemed a great waste of the splendid weather. Judith
found her hat and wandered off down the drive and
along the dirt track towards the road. She turned away
from the direction of Silves and strolled along towards
the mountains, meeting no one, and no houses in sight.
The dog coming towards her was the only thing moving, and he was doing that in a tired way that made
her stand still and look at him. He wore no collar; and
Charles had told her that all dogs in Portugal had to
wear a collar if they were owned, although some of
the owners didn't bother, but this animal looked as if
it wasn't owned. He was a large, loosely put together
animal, not so very young and sorely in need of a bath
and a good brush and, more than these, a good meal.
He advanced towards Judith in a hopeful way and after
a glance at her face, trotted along beside her. And when
she turned for home presently, he turned too.

She was a tender-hearted girl and at times impulsive, so she allowed him to accompany her back to the
villa, where, no one being about, she filled an old plate
with odds and ends of food and took it out to where he
was waiting patiently at the back door. He paused just
long enough to wag his thin pointed tail before wolf-
ing down the lot and then he looked at her so hopefully
that she went back to the kitchen and piled the plate
again. He ate that too and then sat down watching her;
it was obvious that he considered himself her dog. She
led him to a corner of the garden where he wouldn't be
seen immediately, for Teresa would be coming presently to get their tea and Judith wasn't sure if he would

be welcome. 'Be a good quiet boy,' she begged him, and hurried upstairs.

Lady Cresswell was awake and in splendid spirits and it took less than a minute to explain about the dog and ask, a little warily, if there was any chance of keeping him. 'He would be nice to have about the house—and he's gentle enough, only scruffy and tired.'

'Why not?' Agreed Lady Cresswell. 'He'll be company for Mrs Smith and the kittens—it's a splendid idea. Send Teresa to me, dear, and I'll do my best to explain.'

'Oh, thank you, Lady Cresswell—if we could just feed him up a bit…'

'He can come back with us,' declared Lady Cresswell. 'Charles won't mind.'

'But how could we get them back?'

'We can always charter a plane, dear.'

The dog was still there, he didn't appear to have moved an inch. Anxious to make the most of his looks, Judith found a brush and did her best with his appearance. His coat was dull and dusty, but at least she smoothed it to some sort of order and he submitted quietly enough. He cringed a little when Lady Cresswell joined them, but upon Judith begging him not to be a silly boy he wagged a tail and flung out his boney chest so that Teresa, who had followed Lady Cresswell, had to admit that there seemed no harm in him. He wasn't a local dog, of that she was sure; most likely turned loose at some time or other, but provided he behaved himself and didn't go into her kitchen, she gave her grudging approval to his joining the household.

So Judith went in search of Augusto to find a lead

and a collar and a place for the dog to sleep and, since
he still looked hungry, another plate of food. He went
and sat quietly by Lady Cresswell after that, and even
the arrival of Mrs Smith and her kittens, carried out
in their box to take the cooler air after tea, left him
unmoved. It kept Lady Cresswell nicely occupied and
interested until dinner time, and when Charles telephoned soon after that meal, Judith heard her telling
him about the dog, even out on the patio Lady Cresswell's high clear voice carried.

They were to keep the animal, Lady Cresswell told
her triumphantly, and he was to return with them when
they went home. 'I told dear Charles that chartering a
plane to take us all back was a small price to pay for
the pleasure I get from the creatures.' She twinkled at
Judith. 'I think if I asked for the moon, Charles would
climb into the sky and get it for me. He has his faults,
but he is a good son and he'll be a good husband.'

'Oh, is he thinking of getting married?' Judith
hoped her voice sounded unconcerned.

'Oh, definitely, my dear.' Lady Cresswell peeped at
her quickly. 'At least, when I say he's thinking about
it, he doesn't know that he is, if you understand me.
These clever men are sometimes so slow to see something any ordinary person would have discovered in
no time at all. And now I think I'll go to bed; we'll
make an early start in the morning, shall we? And
perhaps we'd better take the dog with us—the quicker
he knows he belongs to us the better. You won't mind
taking him on a lead?' She added: 'Charles does hope
he's house-trained!'

Something Judith hadn't thought of; he was hardly

a dog to grace a home such as Charles's either. Perhaps it would be a good idea if she took him over once they were in England, and there was the question of the cat and kittens too. He had said that they might find a home with him, but if he was going to marry and if his bride was to be the horrible Eileen, the chances were that an outcast dog and a tatty moggy would be shown the door. Not by Charles, of course—she gave him that—he wouldn't be intentionally unkind, but if he was besotted he might not even notice. She put the problem aside and allowed his austere image to fill her mind—something done with such success that she didn't fall asleep until the small hours.

They left for Caldas very shortly after breakfast, for Lady Cresswell professed herself full of energy and anxious to start. Judith spent a busy hour, getting that lady ready for her day's outing, attending to Mrs Smith and the kittens, feeding the dog, brushing him and installing him, to his great surprise, in the car. She prudently laid an old blanket on the seat first and he seemed to know what was wanted of him, because he curled up at once. With a collar on and a few good meals inside him he looked more presentable, although it was obvious that the variety of his ancestry was without number. Studying him, Judith asked: 'Do you suppose the Professor will mind having him? He's—well, he's not exactly handsome.'

Lady Cresswell looked over her shoulder at her. 'Charles will take him. He said so; he never goes back on his word.'

Judith hadn't known what to expect at the spa, a miniature Baden-Baden perhaps as she remembered it on TV, certainly not the quaint little village away from the main road with a cluster of white-walled and stone buildings and a small modern hospital beyond. Augusto parked the car on the cobbled road and they walked the few yards to a square surrounded by buildings and with two lines of trees shading a row of seats down its centre, presumably for the comfort of those desirous of drinking the water. There was a restaurant, a café and two shops, already doing a brisk trade with visitors. But Lady Cresswell ignored these. 'The water first,' she observed, and took a path away from the square to a small glass-roofed building.

'Will they let the dog in?' asked Judith. They both stopped to look at him, not a prepossessing creature but very docile.

'Why not?' asked Lady Cresswell, used to getting her own way.

In fact no one noticed him. There were few people there; they walked in, obediently took their glasses, sipped the sulphur-flavoured water under the eye of the lady behind the counter and went out again.

'A cool drink?' suggested Lady Cresswell. 'I'd forgotten how nauseating spa waters can be. These, by the way, are supposed to make you ten years younger.'

Judith laughed. 'Well, so they should, they taste beastly enough!'

They had their drinks sitting in the little square at one of the tables outside the café. It was pleasantly cool and the dog had subsided thankfully at their feet and was sleeping. Lounging on a wall some distance from them a young man, long-haired and burnt brown by the sun, was playing *Greensleeves*, on a tin whistle.

He played well and the charming little tune tore at Judith's unhappy heart. Not wanting to hear any more of it she asked: 'Shall I get you another drink? It's so pleasant sitting here...'

Lady Cresswell didn't want anything else, she wanted to browse round the two shops. 'Not that I want anything,' she remarked vaguely, 'but we might as well have a look while we're here.'

So they strolled across the square and the young man waved them goodbye and Judith waved back. She tied the dog to a tree before they went inside, and Lady Cresswell said: 'We must give him a name—something suitable...'

'Something typically English, so that he'll feel he's one of us,' suggested Judith. 'How about George or Arthur?'

Lady Cresswell considered. 'Arthur—it suits him.' She patted his head. 'Good boy, Arthur.'

The shop was really only a room in a cottage, but it was full of enticing things to buy. Lady Cresswell spent a long time wandering from embroidered teacloths to pottery, from carved wooden boxes to knitted jackets and shawls, before she decided to buy something of everything. Judith, leaving Arthur to keep Lady Cresswell company, took their parcels back to the car and had to rouse a somnolent Augusto to open the door.

It was getting warmer now and she suggested that they might sit in the shade for half an hour before they had lunch—a light meal of salad, fish and ices. By now Lady Cresswell was tiring and it didn't take much to persuade her to get into the car and be driven back to the villa, where Judith lost no time in making her comfortable on her bed for an afternoon nap. And, that done, she saw to the animals, got into her swimsuit and spent half an hour in the pool before going to lie on the patio. It would have to be a quiet day tomorrow, she decided, and probably the next one as well.

It seemed as though Lady Cresswell was content to idle her days away now that she had had an outing or two, and as the following day was more than usually warm, she was content to sit in a shady corner of the garden, reading and gossiping and amusing herself with the animals, and on the day after that, although she expressed a wish to drive up into the mountains, Judith was able to dissuade her without much trouble. They ate out of doors and played backgammon and talked about clothes, and Judith was relieved to see that her companion was her usual bright self again. There would be days like that, she knew, when Lady Cresswell would be tired and a trifle irritable, and as time went on they would become more frequent, but they could be faced and dealt with; meanwhile, Lady Cresswell was holding her own nicely. 'It's so nice to have you, Judith,' she observed. 'I can talk to you, I don't have to pretend and you always know when I'm frightened, don't you? Not often now, though. I feel so well for most of the time, it's hard to believe…'

'You're holding your own,' Judith told her, 'and that's more important than anything else. Talk about it if you want to; I'll help you all I can, you know that.'

They smiled at each other in mutual understanding.

They played an hilarious game of Racing Demon that second evening and Lady Cresswell went to bed later than usual. Judith came downstairs again into the quiet house. For Augusto and Teresa had gone to bed and only Mrs Smith and her kittens, snug in the kitchen, were waiting for a last drink of milk, and Arthur, sitting watchfully in the hall, waited too, knowing that a last snack before bed would be offered him. Judith saw to Mrs Smith, fetched a handful of biscuits from the kitchen and went into the sitting room with Arthur. It was a lovely night, warm and bright, with a full moon, and she opened the doors on to the patio at the back of the house. It was quiet too, if one ignored the crickets. She leaned her elbows on the patio railing and looked at the moon, and Arthur came crowding up to her to thrust his rough head against her. He had been bathed for the second time and at last he was beginning to look less like a scarecrow. He growled now, low in his throat, and at the same time Judith heard a car coming up the dirt track. She caught its headlights in the glass doors as a reflection, as she went indoors and shut them and crossed the hall. It might be the doctor, but she didn't think so—not at almost eleven o'clock at night. It might be Charles Cresswell—he hadn't phoned for a couple of days, but she thought that unlikely. She waited for the door bell to ring, but although she had distinctly heard the car stop there was no sound. She stood in the hall, staring at the door, just a little scared and glad to have Arthur's company. He growled again and she turned at the faint sound behind her. Charles Cresswell was standing in the sitting room doorway, watching her.

She said in a tight voice, 'Why didn't you ring the bell instead of creeping in like a thief—scaring me to death?'

He put his hands in his pockets. 'I credited you with more sense. Who else would come as late as this, anyway? And thieves don't usually drive up in a car and park outside the front door. I saw the light in the sitting room and thought you were there.' His eyes moved from her face to Arthur. 'Good God, what have you got there?'

'Arthur—the dog your mother told you about. He's a very good dog—he growled. I daresay if I told him to he'd bite you.'

The Professor laughed softly. 'You look as though you'd like to do that yourself. Always so welcoming, Judith.' He took a hand from his pocket and snapped his fingers, and Arthur went to him at once and stood gazing up at him as though he worshipped him. 'At least the dog likes me,' observed the Professor. 'Aren't you going to ask me why I'm here?'

'No, it's none of my business. Do you want a drink or something to eat?'

'The perfect hostess! No, thank you, I'll get myself a drink and go to bed. Is my mother in good spirits?'

'Yes. Dr Sebastiao is quite satisfied with her, she's been resting for the last two days, but only because it's been warmer than usual.'

He nodded. 'Then we'll say goodnight, shall we? Where does Arthur sleep?'

'In the kitchen with the cats.'

'I'll see to him.' He moved from the doorway and came towards her. 'Thank you, Judith, for taking such good care of my mother. I appreciate it.'

He bent his head and kissed her surprised mouth,

presumably to show his appreciation. It left her shaken and trembling so that she hurried away and up the stairs without looking at him.

Chapter 8

Naturally enough, Judith spent a rather sleepless night and got up early. The house was quiet and there was no one about as she went down to the kitchen and put on the kettle for a cup of tea. The animals woke at once, of course, and sat looking at her with hopeful eyes until she produced their food and opened the door to let Mrs Smith and Arthur out into the garden. They were back before she had made the tea, still not quite believing that the door wasn't going to be shut in their faces. She told them briskly that they were a silly pair, gave them second helpings and bore her tea tray upstairs, to have it taken from her when she reached the landing by the Professor, wearing a dressing gown of subdued magnificence.

'Be a good girl and fetch another cup,' he said. 'I'll take this in to my mother.'

'Good morning,' said Judith pointedly. 'Your mother is probably still asleep.'

'Then I'll wake her up.' He stood looking at her. 'That's a pretty thing you're wearing. Shall we have a swim in the pool before breakfast?'

She remembered the last time and went pink. 'No—I've got several things to do. I'll get another cup...'

And when she went back again with it: 'Why only one? Don't you have tea in the morning?'

She was suddenly irritable. 'Yes, of course I do. That's my tray, I was taking it to my room. Your mother doesn't have hers until eight o'clock.'

'*Mea culpa!*' He didn't look in the least sorry.

'And stop showing off your Latin, because I'm not listening.'

She ran downstairs again, furious because he was laughing gently at her, closed the door and put the kettle on again. He was horrid, the most unpleasant man she had ever met, thoughtless and arrogant and making her feel a fool. She was quite mad to love him, and what a frightful waste of time that was—and probably if he ever found out he'd laugh and make some snubbing remark in a silky voice. She drank her tea, still in a rage, and then crept upstairs to her room, changed into a bikini and went down to the pool. She met him, as she hoped she would, as she was going back into the house, and swept past him with as much dignity as she could muster, draped as she was in a large towel and her hair streaming wetly all over the place. She didn't look at him as she went past, or she might have stopped at the look on his face.

When she went along to Lady Cresswell's room, it

was to find that Lady in a state of happy excitement.
'Only imagine, coming late last night! I was so very
pleased to see him this morning—and just think, he's
going to drive us to Monchique this afternoon. I think
I'll get up a little earlier today, dear, I feel so well. If
I have my breakfast now I'll be ready to dress by the
time you've had yours.'

Judith turned a serene face to hers. 'Pills and chores
first,' she said cheerfully, 'then I'll get your breakfast
tray. Are you going to sit in the garden in that nice
shady corner, or would you perhaps prefer the patio?'

'Oh, the garden, I think, we've such a lot to talk
about you can have an hour to yourself, dear.'

'And Arthur can do with a walk. I'll go down the
road and follow that track on the other side where the
orange groves are.'

The Professor joined her for breakfast, maintaining
a polite flow of conversation, all of it trivial. It was the
kind of talk two strangers might have exchanged, sharing a hotel table, and she was heartily relieved when he
said that he had to go into Silves to see the doctor and
left her to drink her last cup of tea alone.

He was back before Lady Cresswell came downstairs, sitting in a cane chair in her usual corner. He
got to his feet as she joined him and helped her to arrange herself just so, while Judith disposed of the variety of articles necessary for a morning in the garden,
and when she had done that she fetched Mrs Smith
and the kittens.

Lady Cresswell examined them narrowly. 'They're
looking well, Judith. We're going to have lunch a little
later, so don't hurry back. You'll take Arthur with you?'

Judith said she would, said goodbye without look-ing at the Professor and went to get Arthur's lead. At any other time she would have been delighted to have had a couple of hours to herself, but she couldn't get rid of the suspicion that they were going to discuss her. If Charles was going to marry Eileen Hunt she wouldn't be wanted, she was sure of that. His would be the task of persuading his mother that other plans for her fu-ture comfort would be just as satisfactory as having Judith. And to a man in love these would be perfectly feasible; he must think that his Eileen was a paragon among women, willing to devote herself to her mother-in-law. His mother had said that he was too clever to see things that the less bright cottoned on to at once, and she should know. 'He needs someone to look after him,' she observed to Arthur, and was comforted by the understanding look that he gave her.

They had crossed the road and were quite a dis-tance from it, going towards the line of cork trees half way up the foothills, when the sky began to fill with cloud. Judith hurried her steps. There was plenty of shelter ahead of them and if it were to rain she could take cover easily enough.

It began before she was half way there, with Arthur trotting along beside her, just as anxious to get out of the wet as she was. It was no light drizzle either, but a downpour that soaked them both within seconds. What was more, there was a rumble of thunder and then lightning zigzagging across the sky.

Under the trees at last, they made shift to shake themselves dry and then sat down on a patch of ground, trying to keep away from the great drops falling be-

tween the branches. 'It won't last,' Judith told Arthur
reassuringly, and peered around for a sign of blue sky.
There was none; the rain was as drenching as ever and
the storm seemed to be almost overhead. It was a fortunate thing that she wasn't particularly nervous of
thunder and lightning, because Arthur was. He had
got as close as he possibly could to her, and shivered
at each flash. But even Judith was scared speechless
as a nearby tree was struck by lightning and some of
its branches came tumbling down. There was no time
to get away. She slung her arms about Arthur's hairy
chest and ducked her head.

Most of the branches fell clear of them, but by some
freak of fate, the last to fall, a solid forked branch, fell
squarely across Judith's ankles, not harming them but
imprisoning them just as surely as iron fetters. She
had let out a frightened shout, but now she sat up and
leaned forward as far as she could to free herself. But
it was no good, she couldn't get a purchase on the
branch. After some futile tugging and pulling, she lay
back again. 'This is silly,' she told Arthur briskly. 'If
you and I had a mutual understanding of each other's
language I could tell you to go home and fetch someone, but that's out, isn't it? We must think of something
else, and on no account must we panic.' She tugged
gently at a bedraggled ear. 'Actually, I'm in a panic
already and I expect you are too.' Despite herself her
voice shook a little. 'Let's have another go.' She tried
to wriggle on to her side, but that didn't help at all; she
wriggled once more, trying to get nearer to her feet so
that she could pull harder on the branches and not suc-
ceeding at all. Presently she gave up and lay back on

her elbows. The storm was rolling away now, rumbling and muttering as it went, but the rain was still pelting down. No one in their senses would be out of doors in such weather—besides, the track she had taken had not the signs of much use about it. 'Oh, what's to be done, Arthur?' she asked her companion, and was surprised when he growled deep in his throat and then began to bark. He hadn't barked since he had attached himself to her, and she was suddenly frightened. Supposing it was someone who wouldn't be prepared to help her? Someone she wouldn't understand anyway. She could be robbed…she had no purse with her, but she was wearing a gold watch and a plain gold chain, not wildly valuable but worth something.

Arthur barked again and cocked an ear, waving his deplorable tail, and now she heard whistling—not a tune, just a whistle any man might use to call his dog, and she'd heard it before—at Hawkshead. She took a deep breath and shouted with all her might.

Charles Cresswell came out of the trees seconds later. 'All right, all right, you don't need to bawl like that,' he spoke testily. 'And why the hell are you lying there?'

The great wave of delight and relief which had warmed her ebbed away and left her cold. She said with dignity and only a very small tremor in her voice, 'Because I'm unable to get up.' The tremor threatened to get out of control. 'I have tried…' It would be best not to go on in case he thought she was crying. She looked away and wiped a tear away. 'I've had Arthur for company, he's been awfully good…'

He stood looking down at her. 'And rather more

sense than I expected—I hoped he'd answer my whistle. Why are you crying?'

'I'm not!' she flared up at once. 'It's raining and I'm wet. I'd be grateful if you would pull that wretched branch off my feet. I'm very wet...'

He had no jacket and his shirt and slacks were sopping, his hair plastered on to his head like a grey helmet. 'So are you,' she added.

He grunted something, bending over her feet and testing the weight of the branch. 'You're not hurt?' he asked. 'You're pinned down as neatly as though you'd been measured for it. Keep very still and don't lift your feet—not so much as an inch.'

He began to pull steadily and in a few moments she was free. 'No, don't move yet!' Judith was surprised at the sharpness of his voice. He picked up each foot in turn and felt it carefully. Only when he had done that did he bend again and lift her on to them, and that surprised her still more, because she was a big girl and no light weight.

Charles made no effort to release her; he stood with his arms round her holding her close, staring down into her wet face, frowning a little.

'Why are you looking at me like that?' she demanded.

'I'm trying to remember why I didn't like you.'

'But you still don't—you told me not to bawl...'

'Ah, that was because I was afraid you'd been hurt— it made me angry, you see.'

'Angry?' She studied his face carefully, the cold inside her rapidly turning to a warm excited glow.

He didn't answer her but bent his head and kissed

her. For a professor of Ancient History whom one would suppose to be indifferent to kissing girls, thought Judith, he was doing rather well, it was a pity that she loved him so much, even if he were beginning to like her just a little, because that wouldn't be enough.

He kissed her again, gently this time. 'I think it would be a splendid idea if we were to be married,' he observed, and smiled at her to set her heart ricocheting round her chest. 'But first we'd better get back to the villa and dry clothes.'

It was difficult to answer him. Judith debated the best way to do it and gave up. Did she say 'What a splendid idea', and would that do for both remarks, or should she answer the one about getting married? If she ignored that and said 'Yes, let's,' he might think she was referring to getting married and not to going back to the villa. She ended by saying 'Well—um…' and slipping out of his arms and starting to walk back along the track with Arthur trotting beside her and Charles beside her.

She reflected that she wasn't over-lucky with her proposals—the middle of the night when she was half dead on her feet, and now in a downpour of rain with the tail end of a storm still rumbling its way to the other side of the sky, and her looking like a half drowned creature, covered in mud and twigs and her hair like nothing on earth. He couldn't have meant it. And this opinion was borne out by his manner as they walked back; beyond curt warnings as to where she should walk, he remained silent. Even at the most difficult bits when he gave her an impatient hand, he had nothing to say.

By the time he had reached the villa the sky had
cleared and the sun poured down once more, warm-
ing her chilled bones but not her bewildered heart.
Lady Cresswell, sitting on the patio still, eyed them
with interest.

'You're both very wet, my dears. Go and change
quickly and tell me all about it when you have; there's
just time before lunch.'

Judith went pink. 'It—it rained,' she said, quite unnecessarily, and whisked herself away without looking at Charles. She told herself fiercely that she was
a fool as she showered and got into clean clothes, but
that didn't stop her from putting on her make-up with
extra care and brushing her hair to a shining perfection
and then at the last minute changing her dress for one
she hadn't worn before; handkerchief lawn in blue—it
matched her eyes exactly.

The Professor and his mother were deep in talk
when she went downstairs and they both turned to look
at her as she joined them. He handed Judith a glass of
sherry and when she had sat down, sat himself. He said
quietly: 'I asked you to marry me just now, Judith, but
you didn't believe me, did you? So I'll ask you again
before a witness.'

Judith put down her glass with such speed that she
spilt the sherry. She tingled with excitement and delight
strongly tempered with resentment that this, another
proposal of marriage, should be a public one. Was she
never to have the romantic occasion so familiar in all
the best romantic novels? She looked at Charles, who
was looking at her pleasantly enough, but quite lack-
ing that same romantic air she would have liked. The

temptation to say yes at once was enormous, but she had no intention of being too eager—he had asked her to marry him, but he hadn't said he loved her...

She glanced at Lady Cresswell and saw that that lady's face was alive with happy anticipation. 'It's the dearest wish of my heart,' Lady Cresswell smiled at her. 'I've been hoping...but of course it's for you to decide, Judith.'

Judith emptied her glass and Charles filled it again without asking. 'Suppose you think about it for a bit?' he suggested. 'Maybe our trip to Monchique will help you to decide.'

And later, sitting beside him as he drove up into the mountains, she changed her mind a dozen times. Perhaps she was expecting too much, perhaps in real life men didn't say and do the things they did in books? She had always prided herself on being modern and matter-of-fact, but she suspected that she was neither. And what about Eileen Hunt? She had forgotten the wretched creature. She stared at the winding uphill road ahead.

'I have always supposed,' she said carefully, 'that you were going to marry Eileen Hunt.'

He showed no surprise at the unexpectedness of her remark. 'I can't recall ever wishing to do so,' he told her, 'I've never wanted to marry until I got to know you, Judith.'

And with that she had to be content. He began to talk about the country they were passing through, pointing out the cork trees lining the road and the great sweep of country below them with the sea in the distance. And when they reached Monchique village he drove slowly, allowing her to see its tiny square and the handful of shops before turning into a steep uphill road; the last stage of their drive.

Lady Cresswell, dozing on the back seat, woke up as they left the village, declaring that the scenery was as beautiful as ever and she longed for a cup of tea.

'Which we will have in a very few minutes now,' her son assured her, and presently pulled into the side of the road overlooking the forest below. The *estalagem* where they were to have tea was built into the mountainside on the opposite side of the road, a charming little inn with a terrace overlooking the road and the view beyond and a friendly proprietor who ushered them to a table and brought tea and little round cakes. They sat for some time in the warm sunshine while Lady Cresswell talked about her previous visits, and presently she insisted on taking Judith into the inn to look around its elegant sitting room and pretty dining room with the small bar beyond. 'I've stayed here—oh, years ago,' she explained. 'The bedrooms are charming and it's so peaceful, although in the summer it's always full, of course. It would be a splendid place for a honeymoon,' she added hopefully.

'I'm not sure that I'm the wife for Charles, Lady Cresswell.'

'But you are, my dear. I knew that the moment I set eyes on you. He's difficult, I know, and wrapped up in his work; he doesn't suffer fools gladly and he hides his feelings. He can be ill-tempered and arrogant too, but I think you could deal with that. He can't bear to be fussed over, and you never fuss.' She smiled gently.

'You mustn't think that because he isn't demonstrative he doesn't care.'

Which was precisely what Judith had been thinking.

They drove on after a while, along the gently winding road, past an occasional villa standing in a sea of flowers, and always orange groves on either side of them and the mountain rose covering everything. There were no villages, though looking down the mountainside it was possible to see a great sweep of country running down to the sea, dotted with houses and an occasional town. And finally at the top, they came out on to a broad stretch of land, strewn with great boulders and housing a radio station. There was a restaurant there too and several houses, built in a rough square, and it all looked rather lonely. Judith, invited to get out and have a look, did so, climbing an outcrop of rock so that she could get a better view. The mountains sloped away to the plains beyond and the late afternoon sun sparkled on the distant sea. Beautiful, but quite unlike England, but then England seemed so far away, as did her life there. She knew now that she could never go back to it, even if she didn't marry Charles, and although she longed to do just that, she still wasn't certain if he loved her.

He came and stood beside her on the rocks and flung an arm around her shoulders. 'Lonely, isn't it?' he observed, 'and beautiful too. When will you marry me, Judith?'

His voice hadn't altered at all, he could have been making some further remark about the view—moreover, wasn't he taking her for granted?

'The future will be bleak without you, my dear.' And

now his voice was warm. To her own surprise Judith heard herself saying: 'As soon as it can be arranged, Charles, and providing your mother keeps well.'

He dropped a light kiss on her cheek. 'I think we'll have to make our plans as and when we can—it does depend on the next report, doesn't it?'

And with that she had once more to be content. If she hadn't loved him so very much she would have resented his matter-of-fact attitude. Perhaps he would get better as time went on—after all, he had spent a good many years with his nose in books and manuscripts, none of them romantic.

But if Charles lacked romantic ideas, his mother made up for it. She was delighted when they told her presently, and the whole of the return journey was taken up with her excited plans for the wedding, although when they reached the villa she declared contritely: 'I'm being a silly interfering old woman, my dears. Of course you'll make your own plans, only I'm so happy… I shall go to bed early, I think, and have my dinner in my room. I'm tired.'

So presently Judith went downstairs to find Charles in the sitting room waiting for her. She felt a little shy of him for a minute or two, but he greeted her with a casual friendliness, which dispelled that almost at once, enquired after his mother and went on to tell her that he intended seeing the doctor on the following morning.

'I must go back in a couple of days,' he told her, 'and it might be as well if you and Mother returned some time next week. Until then we'd better not make too many plans. Would you agree to a quiet wedding, Judith?'

She sat a little to one side of him, watching his face. He was really very good-looking, and distinguished with it—not that that mattered; she loved him with all her heart and she longed to tell him so. When they knew each other better, she would be able to do that, but not just yet; she had a feeling that he was holding her at arms length. She didn't know why, and it puzzled her a bit. He had been so anxious for her to say she would marry him, and now that she had, he seemed to have lost all interest.

'I'd rather be married quietly,' she told him.

And there the matter ended, what should have been a romantic tête-à-tête turning into a most disappointing evening, with the Professor describing mediaeval churches over dinner and going on to mediaeval bridges with sharp cutwaters. Judith, not having a clue as to what they were, looked intelligent and hoped she sounded as though she knew what he was talking about. The moment she got back to England, she would have to read up all she could about the twelfth and thirteenth centuries, because they were obviously of more importance to Charles than the present one; but she loved him so much that she was prepared to get interested in everything to do with his work. She reflected a little sadly that probably married life wouldn't be quite what she had imagined it to be. Charles would forget birthdays and anniversaries and invitations to dinner; he most likely wouldn't utter a word during breakfast and the children would have to be hushed whenever he was bogged down in a particularly sticky bit of research. But none of that mattered as long as he loved her.

She said goodnight presently, and he kissed the top of her head and hoped that she would sleep well—then suddenly swept her close and kissed her fiercely, sweeping away all her doubts.

The next morning, with Lady Cresswell settled on the patio and Charles in Silves with the doctor, Judith telephoned her mother, to be instantly engulfed in that lady's delighted exclamations. 'And when is the wedding to be?' asked her mother. 'Here, of course, darling, such a lovely church…what's your ring like?'

'I haven't got one yet—we're coming back to England in a week or ten days, I expect I'll get it then.' She added: 'It's all been rather sudden.'

'We'll see you soon?'

'I'll let you know, Mother—I'm not sure what's going to happen. I expect we'll discuss it today; Charles isn't going back until tomorrow.'

Lady Cresswell went to rest after lunch and Judith and Charles went into the garden and stretched out on the grass. It was hot, but in the shade of the trees the air was cooler. Judith lay back, her sunglasses perched on her pretty nose, her hat perched on the top of her head, shading her face. Arthur panted beside her, and Mrs Smith and the kittens lolled in their box. It was very quiet except for the crickets, and she felt a little sleepy, but she came awake at once when Charles rolled over and spoke.

'I've had a talk with Dr Sebastiao, he seems quite satisfied with Mother, but of course she's due for a check-up in a couple of weeks, isn't she? I've chartered a plane for Thursday week—that's ten days more or less. I'll come over the evening before that and drive us all to Faro—I'll arrange quarantine for the animals when I get back the day after tomorrow. We'd all better go straight to London and stay at Mother's flat until she's had her tests. We'll decide what to do next while we're there.'

She waited for him to say something about them getting married, but he had rolled over again and closed his eyes. She said meekly: 'Very well, Charles,' because of course he couldn't make plans yet, he would have to wait until he knew more about his mother. All the same, she stifled hurt feelings.

It was the following afternoon as she was coming downstairs after seeing Lady Cresswell settled for her nap when she heard the telephone in the sitting room ringing and crossed the hall to answer it. But Charles had come in from the patio and was already there; she heard his voice clearly saying, 'Hullo, Eileen,' and despite all her better instincts, she paused to listen—but only for a moment; eavesdroppers were on a par with other people's letter readers, and she would have no part in that. But she had taken no more than two steps when she stopped again. Charles's voice, rather pedantic and decisive, was only too easy to listen to.

'Oh, yes,' he was saying, 'I've arranged everything, although we can't make final arrangements until we're back in England. But it couldn't be more convenient. She'll be there to look after my mother, day and night, and of course mother is very fond of her. She took some persuading, but after all, she'll get a home and security for the future.' He glanced up and saw Judith standing in the open doorway and added very deliberately: 'I'll see you when I get back tomorrow.'

He put the receiver down and sauntered towards her, his hands in his pockets.

'You were talking about me,' said Judith. Her heart was hammering in her chest and she felt a bit sick.

'And…?' He was staring down at her, his face bland.

'Is that why you're marrying me?' she whispered from a dry throat. 'Though I think I knew that already—you see, you forgot to say that you loved me, and I wondered… But I thought that perhaps—well, being a historian and—very engrossed in your work, you'd got out of the habit of saying things like that.'

She thought in a detached way that he looked exactly as he had looked on the very first time they had met—furiously angry. But when he spoke there was nothing to indicate rage in his voice. Indeed he spoke very softly. 'You really believe I would use you in such a fashion?'

She wasn't thinking straight any more. 'Yes, I do—you see, it's such a sensible arrangement. Later on, when you—Lady Cresswell—doesn't need me any more, we can go our own separate ways.'

He said silkily: 'And why should I go to all this trouble?'

'Because of Lady Cresswell, of course. We both know that she's going to die soon—you want her to be happy at all costs, don't you?'

Charles looked away from her, staring into the bright sunshine through the open door. He said at length very evenly: 'I don't think there's much point in talking any more at present.' He gave her a bleak look that wrung her heart. 'Or in the future, for that matter. Marriage to someone you don't trust is about the worst mistake one can make in life, don't you agree?'

She nodded dumbly, to speak seemed an impossibility, but presently she managed it in a voice she tried to keep steady. 'You mean you don't want to marry me now?'

His face was impassive. 'Let me put it another way; we made a mistake and most fortunately discovered it in time. But there is one thing, Judith—my mother mustn't know, not yet, and it shouldn't be too difficult to let her go on dreaming. I leave tomorrow, and when I come again in ten days to fetch you both, there'll be too much to do for her to notice anything. Once we're in England and her tests are satisfactory, she might go back to her flat. Would you go with her, Judith? We shan't need to meet.'

'Yes, of course.' She raised troubled eyes to his. 'Are you very angry, Charles?'

He didn't answer her, his eyes were hard and cold and turned her to ice and she wanted to turn tail and run away, but it was he who walked away without another word.

Lady Cresswell elected to stay up for dinner that evening and Judith spent the worst two hours of her life, laughing and talking and listening to Lady Cresswell's description of her own wedding gown and discussing the probable dress she might choose for herself, and even worse was having to listen to Charles calling her his dear and speculating as to the best place for a honeymoon. There was no need, she thought fiercely, to have brought the subject up. He was a heartless monster, and far from loving him, he was the last man she wanted to see again ever. And if he thought to upset her by such conduct, then he could think again!

This buoyed her up for the remainder of the evening and gave her a heightened colour and a glitter in her eyes which made her quite breathtakingly beautiful. If she could have brought herself to do more than glance at Charles she would have seen the look in his eyes and might even have accepted his terse invitation to walk in the garden after dinner. But she didn't look, instead she went up with Lady Cresswell presently and didn't go downstairs again, and in the morning when she went down to breakfast, Charles had already left for the airport.

Chapter 9

Judith had slept all night, something she hadn't expected to do, but memory came flooding back the moment she opened her eyes; she had sat up in bed, remembering the coldness of Charles's eyes and the awful travesty of a convivial evening, and in a way it was a relief to find that Charles had gone. She wondered what Lady Cresswell would say when she was told, but she need not have worried. He had gone to bid his mother goodbye in the early hours of the morning, seeing her bedside light on from his window. 'I expect he said goodbye to you too, dear,' observed Lady Cresswell happily, 'but it will only be for a few days, so you mustn't look so downcast.'

Judith schooled her features into cheerfulness, assured her that the days would fly and that yes, Charles had said goodbye to her, although naturally enough she

supplied no details but entered whole-heartedly into a
lively discussion as to whether a quiet wedding meant
bridesmaids or not. It wasn't difficult, she found; all
she had to do was to pretend that they were discussing
someone else's wedding. The difficult part was ban-
ishing Charles's loved face from her head.

She had time to sit quietly and consider what she
was going to do once Lady Cresswell had gone to take
her afternoon nap. She had said that she would stay
until she was no longer needed, but of one thing she
was certain, she didn't want to see Charles again—not
once they were both back in England. She couldn't
for the moment see how this was to be done. After
all, Lady Cresswell supposed them to be engaged and
intending to marry as soon as possible. They would
have to find a good reason for putting off the wedding, and somehow her unhappy head was unable
to cope with that. The whole thing really depended
on Lady Cresswell's prognosis after her check-up, so
there was no point in wearing herself to rags trying to
think up something now. She lay back on the grass and
closed her eyes and found herself thinking of Charles
again. He would have to make other plans now, and
be delighted to do so because he was free; he had told
her that he had never wanted to marry Eileen, but he
couldn't have said anything else when she had asked
him, could he? She began to wonder why he had gone
to the trouble of asking her to marry him when she
could have looked after his mother just as well in her
own home.

She frowned. Of course it would be much more convenient to have her at Hawkshead; he would be free

to travel around, knowing that she was there with his mother and he would be near at hand if, and when, she took a turn for the worse; he would be able to get on with his wretched writing in peace. And see Eileen Hunt, added a small voice at the back of her head. She remembered too with enormous relief that she hadn't told Charles that she loved him, and that was something to be thankful for. She longed to have a good howl, but Lady Cresswell had sharp eyes and nothing must give her the least suspicion… If she lay there much longer feeling sorry for herself she would be in floods of tears; she got up and went along to the swimming pool, where she took off her sundress and dived in. Arthur jumped in too, probably he wasn't hygienic, but he made a pleasant companion paddling up and down beside her. Since they had been out in the storm together, he had become even more attached to her. They would have to be parted for six months' quarantine, but after that he could stay with her for always, and Mrs Smith and the kittens too. Lady Cresswell would have to make room for them in her London flat, and afterwards she would find a job where they would be welcome. After all there was no need to get married, she could earn a tolerable living, she had loving parents and Uncle Tom. She drew an unhappy breath and began to tear up and down the pool, leaving a bewildered Arthur paddling round trying to catch up.

They all went to Paraia da Rocha the next day and spent it as they had done before, only this time nothing could stop Lady Cresswell from buying a vast amount of embroidered table linen for Judith. 'Because you'll want pretty things,' she declared. 'I know that Charles has a very well run household, but men do tend to leave such things to their wives—besides, he'll probably set up a second home once you're married.'

She chatted on happily, never once mentioning her own future but throwing herself enthusiastically into plans for theirs, and Judith encouraged her; she hadn't seen the little lady so happy for days.

The outing was such a success that they went to Lagos the following day. Augusto parked the car in one of the small cobbled squares and promised to remain there, and they set out on a gentle stroll round the shops. The height of the season was over now, but the town was still quite full of tourists and there were a number of shops to attract their attention.

Lady Cresswell bought porcelain, crystal glasses and still more embroidery before consenting to stop for coffee at an open-air café in the centre of the town, and then, because she was beginning to tire, Judith suggested that they should drive out on along the coast and find somewhere for lunch before going back to Silves. 'If only Charles were here,' declared Lady Cresswell, 'he would know which restaurant we should go to— they don't look anything from the outside, you know, but the food is delicious, but it's rather warm and I think it would be nicer if we could find somewhere out of town.'

Judith glanced at her with careful casualness. Her companion was indeed tired; her face was quite drawn and her colour was bad. She said with the same casual air: 'Why do we need to go any farther? We've had a lovely morning and you know Teresa always gives us a delightful lunch. We could have it on the patio and have a lazy afternoon.'

It worried her a little that Lady Cresswell agreed so readily. But after a rest and a cup of tea, the drawn look had gone and she declared that she had never felt better, although Judith wasn't entirely happy about her pallor. Indeed, she had every intention of telephoning the doctor as soon as she could do so without Lady Cresswell knowing, but to be on the safe side she suggested supper in bed and an early night, only to be frustrated by her companion's resolve to remain up until Charles should telephone. 'He said he would,' she declared, 'and he must have told you too, Judith. I couldn't possibly go to bed until he has.'

He rang half an hour later and Lady Cresswell talked happily enough for some time. Only when she said: 'Of course you're longing to talk to Judith, she's on the patio...' did he interrupt her to state that he would have to ring off because someone had called and would she give Judith all the usual messages. Before she could answer he had hung up.

It took Judith quite a few minutes to assure Lady Cresswell that she wasn't too upset and certainly didn't blame her for spending so much time talking to her son. He would certainly ring again, probably later that evening, she declared mendaciously, and she was quite happy to stay out of her bed until he did. Privately she admired him for the clever way he had avoided speaking to her, something which she had been dreading ever since she had rather belatedly realised that sooner or later that would be inevitable. She decided that she would have to invent a call from him so that his mother would be satisfied. She didn't like deceiving her, but after all, weren't she and Charles already doing that on a grand scale?

She slept soundly that night, rather to her surprise, and gave Lady Cresswell such a convincing account of the telephone conversation she had had with Charles that she almost believed it herself. But she couldn't have done otherwise, looking at Lady Cresswell's still pale face lighting up so happily as she listened. She had taken the precaution of ringing Dr Sebastiao before Lady Cresswell was awake, and he had promised to call that morning. 'If you could just make it a casual visit?' Judith had suggested, and been delighted that he had understood her immediately. 'I shall not alarm the lady,' he had said.

And he didn't, strolling in casually just as they were drinking their coffee in the garden, spending half an hour talking trivialities, listening to Lady Cresswell's happy chatter about the wedding. Judith walked down the drive to where he had left his car and was reassured by his opinion that her patient was as well as could be expected. 'Although a relapse can be sudden and unexpected,' he pointed out. 'Should you have any further worries you will let me know immediately and I will come. There is blood stored at the hospital and should it be necessary a transfusion can be set up at once.'

'Here?'

'If it must. It might be possible to get Lady Cresswell to hospital, but if her condition were severe, then it would have to be done here. But we are being pessimistic, I think.' He smiled at her as they shook hands. 'I am delighted for you that you are to marry Professor Cresswell, such a distinguished man and so very clever.'

Judith thanked him quietly and wished she could have confided in him. Possibly she would never confide in anybody: it was something best buried and forgotten. She had no doubt that Charles, once his disorganised plans had been adjusted to his wishes, would forget.

They spent the rest of the day in the garden and the following morning there was a letter for Lady Cresswell from Charles. Judith, coming back from a brief walk with Arthur, found her on the patio, reading it. 'And there's one for you,' she told Judith. 'It's on the table, dear.' She glanced up as Judith hesitated. 'Why not take it into the garden to read?' she asked kindly.

And a good thing she had done just that, thought Judith a few minutes later. She had opened the envelope with a mixture of feelings; perhaps Charles wanted to marry her after all, perhaps he was going to explain his telephone conversation. It was neither of these things. The single sheet of notepaper contained only the words, 'In the normal course of events I should be writing to you.' It was signed simply with his initials. She folded it carefully and put it back in the envelope. There was no point in thinking about it, and if she did she would weep. After a minute or two she went back to the patio.

'Isn't it nice to get letters?' she observed. 'I think I like them better than phone calls.'

'You're probably right, dear, and isn't it delightful to think that in a week's time we shall be going back to England? I've loved my stay here, but now I'm anxious to get back, there's so much to look forward to.'

Judith agreed cheerfully, feeling desperate. Unlike her companion she could see nothing to look forward to.

There were other letters as well as the English papers sent up from Silves. The morning passed pleasantly enough, as did the afternoon, because it was cooler now, so that Judith was able to stroll round the garden, cutting flowers, while Lady Cresswell sat in her usual corner. They dined earlier than usual, then Lady Cresswell went to her room immediately afterwards and Judith went with her to potter round the room, hand out her pills and take her temperature. It was up a little, and so was her pulse. Judith settled her in bed with her books and papers, and promised to come in later and turn off the bedside lamp. There was nothing really wrong, but she wasn't happy about the increased temperature. She stayed up later than usual and when she paid her final visit to Lady Cresswell's room, it was to find her asleep with the book open in her hand. Judith switched off the light and went along to her own room and when she was ready for bed, opened the communicating door between them before she got between the sheets.

She was still awake when she heard the faintest of sounds from the other room. She was out of bed in a flash and switching on Lady Cresswell's light within seconds, to find her sitting up in bed, holding a handkerchief to her nose.

Judith fetched a towel, talking soothingly the while, tossing the fruit from the bowl because there was no chance to get to the kitchen and find another one, fetching more towels, propping Lady Cresswell against more pillows. She worked fast with a reassuring calm, even

when she turned back the bedclothes and saw the purpura patches her voice remained even and cheerful.
'I must get some ice,' she said cheerfully. 'I'll only
be two ticks, just keep the towel under your nose and
stay sitting up.'

She knew the doctor's number, she had memorised
it when they had first arrived. He answered at once,
listened to what she had to say, told her he would be
with her as soon as possible and rang off.

When she got back with the ice she could see that
Lady Cresswell was on the verge of collapse. 'The
doctor is coming,' she told her calmly. 'Try not to be
frightened—it looks awful, I know, but it happens occasionally and stops of its own accord.'

Lady Cresswell smiled faintly. 'I have every intention of getting over this,' she said weakly. 'You see, I've
made up my mind to see my first grandchild at least.'

'I'll see if we can manage twins,' Judith told her,
and was glad she had, for a few minutes later Lady
Cresswell lapsed into unconsciousness.

Dr Sebastiao arrived almost immediately after that
and started to set up a transfusion. 'She is too ill to
move, but I think we may save her.'

Judith nodded. 'Oh, we must,' she begged him,
handing him what he needed, making sure that he
could manage without her for a minute or two. 'I must
let Charles know,' she said urgently, then flew downstairs to the telephone. It was barely eleven o'clock, he
would still be up—or out. She dialled feverishly and a
moment later heard his voice.

'Judith here...'

'Yes?' There was ice in his voice now but she didn't heed it.

'Charles—your mother has collapsed. Dr Sebastiao is with her, giving her a transfusion—she can't be moved yet.'

The silence at the other end seemed endless. 'I'll be with you as soon as possible,' he said at length, and hung up.

She flew upstairs again, thankful that Charles hadn't wasted time with a lot of questions. There was plenty to do. She said merely to Dr Sebastiao: 'He's coming,' and rolled up the sleeves of her dressing gown.

The Professor arrived very quietly just before six o'clock in the morning, and by then Lady Cresswell was conscious and holding her own nicely. He came soft-footed into the bedroom and said, 'Hullo, Mother,' in a perfectly ordinary voice, disregarding the bottles and tubes and paraphernalia littering the place. He might have come at speed, but he didn't look as though he had; he was freshly shaved and his clothes looked as though he had just put them on—in direct contrast to Dr Sebastiao, whose chin was as blue as ink and his rather long hair quite wild. Judith looked worse, though; she had had no time to fasten her cotton gown but had wrapped it around her and tied it tight with the sash, all bunched up, and her hair was a golden tangle. There were purple shadows beneath her blue eyes and at some time during the long night she had taken her feet out of her slippers and forgotten to put them back in.

But she was unconscious of the fact. She thanked God silently that Charles had arrived and that his mother was able to greet him and then got on with what she was doing; Lady Cresswell was making a splendid recovery, but there was much to be done and a good deal of careful nursing involved. Judith hadn't stopped all night, but neither had the doctor. He was talking to Charles now, who was standing by the bed holding his mother's hand. They were speaking Portuguese, and that softly, so that she had no idea what they were saying, but presently Dr Sebastiao came over to her.

'I am going to my home now, to prepare for the day and have breakfast, but I will return in two hours. I think Lady Cresswell is safely through her relapse, but the transfusion must continue for the rest of the day and I will do a blood count when I come back. I have the two we have already taken and they will be checked at the hospital. I no longer fear for her life, but she will need constant care. Shall I send a nurse to help you?'

'If I can get a couple of hours' sleep now I shall be quite all right for the rest of the day, but perhaps you'd better ask Professor Cresswell.'

Certainly there must be a second nurse she heard Charles say, perhaps the doctor would be so good as to bring her with him when he came again?

He didn't look at Judith when he spoke, indeed, he hadn't done more than glance at her since he had arrived, but she had been too busy to think about that. She listened quietly to Dr Sebastiao's instructions and finished what she was doing before departing to the kitchen, where Teresa was making tea, to fetch a refreshing drink for her patient.

When she got back, the doctor had gone and Charles took the tray from her. 'Eat something,' he ordered in a no-nonsense voice, 'go to bed for an hour and then come back here. Tell me what I have to do, and if I'm worried I'll fetch you.'

She shook off her tiredness. 'I'm perfectly all right, thank you—a cup of tea…'

He interrupted her ruthlessly. 'You hardly inspire confidence looking as you do now. Do as I say!'

Judith brushed past him, took Lady Cresswell's pulse, saw that she had fallen into a light sleep, and went away without a word. If she had started to speak, she wouldn't have stopped, she would probably have shouted at him, thrown a vase at his arrogant head… How dared he? She looked down at her rumpled person; what had he expected? Starched uniform and smooth hair under a cap and never mind the patient's condition worsening with every minute? She flew downstairs. 'I hate him!' she told herself. 'He's a monster, I hope he marries Eileen and lives miserably ever after!'

She drank hot tea in the kitchen, answering the anxious Teresa as best she could while she gobbled rolls and butter. And back in her room she set her alarm clock for an hour's sleep, had a shower and tumbled into bed. It seemed that no sooner had she closed her eyes than she was opening them again, but once she was up and dressed she felt better for her short rest. She dressed in a sleeveless cotton dress, thrust her feet into sandals, tied back her hair and went into Lady Cresswell's room.

Lady Cresswell was still asleep and the Professor was sitting by the bed watching her. He looked tired now and remote. He got up when he saw Judith, said:

'I'll go and have something to eat, she hasn't stirred,' and had gone before she could say a word.

Judith thought it was a good thing in a way, for if she had given him sympathy, he might have thought she was holding out the olive branch. That was the last thing she wanted, she told herself firmly, and the last thing he wanted too.

Lady Cresswell stirred and woke before long, so that she was able to bathe her face and hands and tidy her hair. Lady Cresswell frowned at the drip above her head. 'How long do I have to have that revolting thing?' she demanded in a weak voice, 'and where's Charles?' and before Judith had a chance to answer her: 'You've been up all night, my dear, you must be worn out.'

'It'll come down later today if Dr Sebastiao is satisfied with you. Charles is downstairs having breakfast, and I'm not in the least tired. Don't talk too much, Lady Cresswell, you're doing fine, but you've some lost ground to make up.'

'Bless you, child!' Her eyes went to the door and she smiled. 'Charles—you got here so quickly. Have you had any sleep?'

He assured her that he had, although Judith very much doubted that. 'And don't tire yourself with talking, Mother,' he begged her.

'I feel better,' she smiled faintly at him. 'And I'm going to get better—I told Judith, I want to see my first grandchild—she's promised to make it twins.' She closed her eyes and dozed and Judith, her head bent over the pad she was using for keeping her records, went scarlet. After a moment she lifted her head defiantly and looked him in the eye.

'Well, it made her happy,' she said softly.

He didn't answer her; she hadn't expected him to, and since Dr Sebastiao arrived just then, the awkward moment passed.

He had brought a nurse with him, a tall dark, serious girl with just enough English to get by. Judith lost no time in convincing the doctor that it would be better for her to do night duty; during the day the Professor would be there to smooth any small difficulties, and at night, if Lady Cresswell couldn't sleep she would be able to read to her. 'Six o'clock until six o'clock?' she asked briskly and since the nurse agreed, the matter was settled at once, much to her relief; she would only have to meet Charles for the briefest of periods morning and evening, for in the morning she could eat her breakfast and have a quick swim when she got off duty, and be in bed long before he was up.

She listened to all that the doctor had to say, made sure that the nurse knew where everything she might need could be found, arranged with Teresa that the simple diet the doctor had ordered should be ready at the times he had suggested, and lastly telephoned to London to Lady Cresswell's own doctor. It was the Professor who took the phone from her. As she turned away, he said: 'I'm greatly in your debt, Judith.'

She mumbled something and hurried upstairs. Five minutes later she was in the swimming pool and very shortly after that sitting at the kitchen table eating her breakfast while Teresa clucked in a motherly way round her.

She was very tired and slept right through the day until Teresa came in with a cup of tea and pointed to the clock. Judith sat up and yawned, then jumped out of bed, and less than an hour later she went along to Lady Cresswell's room, bathed, neatly dressed, her hair just so, and a good meal inside her, feeling ready to tackle any emergency that might arise during the night.

Lady Cresswell had had a good day, Lucia, the nurse, told her. Dr Sebastiao had been and would come again in an hour's time. The patient was dozing again, taking the nourishment she was offered and was quite reconciled to the transfusion remaining up until the present bottle was finished. From the manner in which this was said, Judith guessed that Lady Cresswell had been a bit difficult about that. She wished Lucia a good night, urged her to go straight to the kitchen where Teresa was waiting with her supper tray, and set herself to putting the room in order for the night.

It was still a lovely day, with the early evening sun nicely tempered with a cool breeze. Judith drew back the shutters gently so that Lady Cresswell would see the garden when she woke up and lingered a minute at the windows. Of Charles there was no sign, but she hadn't expected to see him; he would keep out of her way as much as possible, she was sure of that.

Dr Sebastiao came an hour later, looked over the record Judith had written of pulse, temperature, and blood pressure, and pronounced himself satisfied. Certainly the blood pressure was rising nicely and there was almost no fever. He beamed at Judith, and patted her on the shoulder.

'We have been lucky this time, Judith.' She glanced at the sleeping figure in bed. He went on, 'I have been in consultation with her own doctor in London and he thinks that as soon as she is able, she should return to hospital in London for a thorough check-up, with care, she could live a year, perhaps two, who can say?' He put his stethoscope back in his bag. 'I shall not wake her—will you check carefully and let me know if there is anything not as it should be. I will go and speak with the Professor.'

He wished her a quiet goodnight and went downstairs. So Charles was in the house, keeping out of her way. Her heartache was so real that she could only stand still and let it wash over her.

'Judith!' Lady Cresswell's thin voice switched a smile on to her face as she turned towards the bed.

'Hullo,' she said cheerfully. 'Dr Sebastiao's just gone; he's very pleased with you.'

'You looked so sad—is something the matter.'

'Heavens, no—everything's just fine. I'm to take the drip down as soon as it's finished, you'll be glad of that, won't you? It may wake you up while I'm doing it, but I'll be as quiet about it as I can'

'Yes, dear. Where's Charles—you've had no time to be together.'

Lady Cresswell sounded fretful and Judith said at once: 'Oh, yes, we manage—besides, we've got all the time in the world, haven't we? He's downstairs with the doctor. Now I'm going to give you a drink and do one or two chores, and you're going back to sleep.'

'I'm glad you're here at night, Judith. It's not so bad during the day, but at night I get afraid…'

Judith perched carefully on the side of the bed and took a frail hand in hers. 'Well, don't—there's no need, it all boils down to the simple fact that you've had a severe nosebleed and the quickest way to get over it was to keep you quiet in bed and give you a spot more blood. You're going to be as right as rain in no time at all; you'll have your check-up when we get back to England and you'll be none the worse.'

It was almost midnight and Lady Cresswell had been sleeping peacefully for some time when the Professor came quietly into the room. He looked bone weary, and Judith had to suppress a strong desire to go to him and throw her arms round his neck and comfort him; instead she said nothing at all.

He looked at his mother and then at her, his eyebrows raised in query.

'Yes, she's sleeping soundly. I'm going to take the drip down in a very short time.' Judith kept her voice pleasantly professional.

'In that case, will you come on to the balcony for a moment?'

It was dark there and she was thankful that he couldn't see her face; he most likely had something nasty to say to her.

'I have to thank you for all you're doing for Mother,' he told her, his voice nicely schooled to politeness. 'It's awkward that I should have to return so soon, I must ask you to continue the pretence of our engagement for the time being.'

His face was in the shadow, but the cool indifference of his voice turned her cold. 'Yes, of course.'

She could think of nothing else to say, and as he remained silent she went back into the bedroom and checked the drip, thankful that she would be kept busy for a few minutes, taking it down. It was annoying

that he didn't go away, but sat down in a chair a little
way from the bed and picked up a book. Really; the
man had no feelings at all! she thought crossly as she
started to dismantle the drip. Lady Cresswell woke for
a moment as she took out the cannula and whispered:
'Where's Charles?'

'Sitting in the chair in the corner,' said Judith
promptly, and she went to sleep again, satisfied.

Judith tidied away the mess, checked her patient
and went to sit down on the high-backed chair near
the bed. She had letters to write and she might as well
go on with them, but she had scarcely started when
the Professor said from his corner: 'You'll find your
supper on a tray in the kitchen—go and eat it, I'll stay
here until you return.'

She started to say: 'But I can eat my supper here...'
when he interrupted her.

'Do as you're told, Judith.' Just for a second there
was a gleam of amusement in his eyes. 'We don't want
to disturb Mother, do we?'

She got up without a word and he opened the door
for her. As she passed him their hands brushed against
each other; it was like an electric shock to her and she
fled down the stairs as though running for her life.

In the kitchen she pulled herself together and sat
down at the table to eat the meal Teresa had prepared.
She was all kinds of a fool and thank heaven she
wouldn't have to see much of him. He would surely
go to bed soon and she would be in her own bed long
before anyone else was up in the morning. She made
tea and drank the pot dry, and thus fortified went back
upstairs.

The Professor was sitting in his chair, reading. He got up as soon as Judith went in and said goodnight, then went away; which left her the rest of the night to think about him and wonder if she had been too hasty. Perhaps he hadn't meant quite all he said when Eileen had telephoned, perhaps she should have given him the chance to explain, but if she had been mistaken, why had he been so quick to break off everything between them? Her head ached with the muddle of her thoughts and she was glad when Lady Cresswell woke up soon after five o'clock and she could get busy with early morning chores. They were enjoying a cup of tea together when Lucia joined them. Judith waited only long enough to give her report and wish Lady Cresswell a good day, before leaving them together. She was beset by the fear that Charles would turn up before she could escape.

She was tired, and hot and hungry and she decided to shower, get into her nightie and dressing gown, have a quick breakfast and go straight to bed, but down in the kitchen the faithful Arthur got out of his basket, inviting her to go outside, so she drank some orange juice from the fridge, picked up a roll from the table and opened the back door.

The morning was enchanting, the light still pearly and the early sun shedding a gentle warmth. Judith sat down on the grass, well away from the house, and kicked off her slippers. Arthur flopped down beside her and in a few minutes they were joined by Mrs Smith and the kittens, anxious for company and on the lookout for breakfast. Judith shared her roll and sat chewing at the bit which remained, but presently she gave

up and sat, the bread still in her hand and her knees
under her chin, staring ahead of her, not seeing the
garden round her, only a bleak future of years without Charles. Until that moment she had managed not
to cry, but now her feelings got the better of her and
tears poured down her cheeks in an absolute torrent.

She sniffed and sobbed for a few minutes, then
caught her breath at Arthur's welcoming whine and
the busy swish of his tail. He didn't do that for Augusto
or Teresa; he was still a little wary of them and he ignored the doctor when he came to the house; he whined
like that for herself, Lady Cresswell and Charles. So
it had to be Charles. Judith turned round slowly, quite
forgetful of her wet blotchy face, and saw him standing there within a few paces of her. He didn't look as
though he had slept a wink, although he was shaved
and immaculate. Indeed, he looked every day of his
years but nonetheless strikingly handsome in a haggard kind of way.

She could suddenly bear it no longer. She cried: 'Oh,
Charles you mustn't worry so much, Lady Cresswell
is going to be all right and once she's over this she'll
probably be well for months, even years.'

He came towards her. 'I know that, and I'm not
worried.' He sounded harsh and angry and she leaned
away from him, clutching her roll. He bent down and
took it from her and handed it to Arthur, then hauled
her to her feet. 'I've been awake all night,' he told her
testily, 'making up speeches, and now I'm here I find
that none of them is suitable. There are no words…' he
caught her close, crushing her ribs most painfully, and

began to kiss her. It was, she decided, quite useless to stop him, and anyway, she didn't want to.

'I'm too old for you,' he stated severely, 'I have an infernal temper and I like my way…'

'None of these matter,' said Judith, 'because I love you more than enough to put up with all of them, only you haven't yet said you love me, you know.' She gave him a severe look. 'Nor did you choose to explain…'

'Oh, my darling, of course I love you—I fell in love with you the moment I set eyes on you in my kitchen, but nothing went right, did it? You shied away from me like a startled fawn.'

Judith chuckled. 'I'm a bit big for a fawn,' she pointed out.

'You're exactly right, every inch of you.' He kissed her again. 'And it wasn't you I was talking about but an indigent second cousin who's only too eager to live with Mother and look after her.'

'Oh!' Judith glowed with happiness, 'but she should be near us, so that we can see her as often as possible.'

'Well, she will be. There's a charming house in Hawkshead—your Uncle Tom is dealing with the buying of it for me, so you can see her every day if you want to.' He added wickedly: 'The twins will love visiting Granny.'

'The twins… Oh, that was to make her happy.'

'Well, it will make me happy too, my love.'

She had the horrid feeling that she was going to cry again, only this time it was because she was so happy. 'I've been very silly,' she said in a small voice.

'Indeed you have.' Though it didn't sound as though

he minded that. 'But it was my fault—you see, I wasn't sure that you loved me enough.'

'More than enough, dearest Charles,' Judith assured him, and lifted her face for his kiss. Presently she asked: 'But why did Eileen telephone here?'

'Good God, darling, must we keep on talking about the girl? Remember my cousin—you met him at my house—he and Eileen see a lot of each other. It was he who remembered the indigent cousin's address and gave it to me, and he asked Eileen to phone me to see if everything had been settled.'

'You could have explained…'

'My dearest Miss Golightly, could we not forget the whole unfortunate matter?'

'All right, I'll never say another word, only if you annoy me I daresay I'll mention it just once in a while, you know!'

'As long as it's not too often,' observed Charles, and fell to kissing her once more.

* * * * *

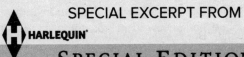
After the walk on the beach, she'd become overly polite
and distant. Knowing he wasn't going to sleep, Noah sat
up and tossed back the sheets. He found a pair of shorts
and slipped them on. Barefoot, he unlocked the screen
door and walked out into the night. He saw something
out of the corner of his eye and spied someone sitting on
the beach. A full moon lit up the night, and as he made
his way down to the water, he couldn't stop smiling.

She glanced up at him and smiled. "It looks as if I'm
not the only one who couldn't sleep."

Noah sank down next to her on the damp sand. Even in
the eerie light, he could discern that the sun had darkened
her skin to a deep mahogany. "I was never much of an
insomniac before meeting you."

Viviana pulled her legs up to her chest and wrapped her arms around her knees. "I'm not going to accept blame for that."

"Can you accept that I'm falling in love with you?"

Her head turned toward him slowly, and she looked as if she was going to jump up and run away. "Please don't say that, Noah."

"And why shouldn't I say it, Viviana?"

"Because you don't know what you're saying. You don't know me, and I certainly don't know you."

Don't miss
Dealmaker, Heartbreaker *by Rochelle Alers,*
available May 2019 wherever
Harlequin® Special Edition books and ebooks are sold.

www.Harlequin.com

HSEEXP0419R

Looking for more satisfying love stories
with community and family at their core?

Check out **Harlequin® Special Edition**
and **Love Inspired®** books!

 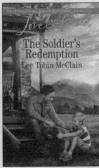

New books available every month!

CONNECT WITH US AT:

Facebook.com/groups/HarlequinConnection

 Facebook.com/HarlequinBooks

 Twitter.com/HarlequinBooks

 Instagram.com/HarlequinBooks

 Pinterest.com/HarlequinBooks

ReaderService.com

**ROMANCE WHEN
YOU NEED IT**

HFGENRE2018

Need an adrenaline rush from nail-biting tales
(and irresistible males)?

Check out **Harlequin Intrigue®**
and **Harlequin® Romantic Suspense** books!

New books available every month!

CONNECT WITH US AT:

Facebook.com/groups/HarlequinConnection

 Facebook.com/HarlequinBooks

 Twitter.com/HarlequinBooks

 Instagram.com/HarlequinBooks

 Pinterest.com/HarlequinBooks

ReaderService.com

**ROMANCE WHEN
YOU NEED IT**

Looking for inspiration in tales
of hope, faith and heartfelt romance?

Check out **Love Inspired**® and
Love Inspired® **Suspense** books!

New books available every month!

Love Harlequin romance?

DISCOVER.

Be the first to find out about promotions,
news and exclusive content!

Facebook.com/HarlequinBooks

Twitter.com/HarlequinBooks

Instagram.com/HarlequinBooks

Pinterest.com/HarlequinBooks

ReaderService.com

EXPLORE.

Sign up for the Harlequin e-newsletter and
download a free book from any series at
TryHarlequin.com.

CONNECT.

Join our Harlequin community to share
your thoughts and connect with other
romance readers!
Facebook.com/groups/HarlequinConnection

HARLEQUIN®

**ROMANCE WHEN
YOU NEED IT**